PRAISE FOR NATIONAL BESTSELLING AUTHOR
SUZANNE FORSTER

HUSBAND, LOVER, STRANGER

"WITHOUT A DOUBT, *HUSBAND, LOVER, STRANGER* IS MS. FORSTER'S MOST AMAZING BOOK TO DATE. THIS COMPLICATED, UNPREDICTABLE AND SIZZLING THRILLER IS TRULY A PHENOMENAL STORY WHOSE END-ING WILL LEAVE READERS GASPING WITH SURPRISE. DON'T MISS THIS BOOK!"

—JILL SMITH, *ROMANTIC TIMES*

INNOCENCE

"THIS ONE HAS BESTSELLER STAMPED ALL OVER IT IN BIG, GLOWING NEON LETTERS."

—JAYNE ANN KRENTZ

"SUZANNE FORSTER TANTALIZES THE READER."

—*AFFAIRE DE COEUR*

"DANGEROUS, THRILLING, AND SENSUAL."

—*ROMANTIC TIMES*

COME MIDNIGHT

"STEAMY, SUSPENSEFUL, EROTIC."

—*PUBLISHERS WEEKLY*

BLUSH

"ABSOLUTELY DELICIOUS."—*PHILADELPHIA INQUIRER*

Berkley Books by Suzanne Forster

BLUSH
COME MIDNIGHT
HUSBAND, LOVER, STRANGER
INNOCENCE
SHAMELESS

HUSBAND, LOVER, STRANGER

SUZANNE FORSTER

BERKLEY BOOKS, NEW YORK

HUSBAND, LOVER, STRANGER

A Berkley Book / published by arrangement with
the author

PRINTING HISTORY
Berkley edition / February 1998

All rights reserved.
Copyright © 1998 by Suzanne Forster.
This book may not be reproduced in whole or in part,
by mimeograph or any other means, without permission.
For information address: The Berkley Publishing Group,
a member of Penguin Putnam Inc.,
200 Madison Avenue, New York, New York 10016.

The Putnam Berkley World Wide Web site address is
http://www.berkley.com

ISBN: 0-425-16185-4

BERKLEY®
Berkley Books are published by The Berkley Publishing Group,
a member of Penguin Putnam Inc.,
200 Madison Avenue, New York, New York 10016.
BERKLEY and the "B" design
are trademarks belonging to Berkley Publishing Corporation.

PRINTED IN THE UNITED STATES OF AMERICA

10 9 8 7 6 5 4 3 2 1

PROLOGUE

He comes awake remembering nothing, nothing but the image of a woman with her arms outstretched, crying sweetly, a woman who will die if he doesn't get to her. She reaches out to him in helpless supplication, this siren of his mind. She has taken possession of his entire being, every cell, every spinning atom.

He comes off the bed, calling her name.

If she dies, he dies.

But when he opens his eyes to a gray cell of a room, she isn't there. She's never been there. Everything except the breathless urgency is gone, even her name. It's vanished like writing on the sand when a wave washes up.

The gleaming chrome equipment tells him he's in a hospital room. The stinging pain he feels is a Hep-Locke he's nearly ripped out of his arm. He turns in a circle. If this is a hospital, he must be ill. Only he doesn't look ill. His reflection comes back at him from everywhere, mirrored in the stainless steel. Hair like black roses. A lean, squared-off face, harshly tanned and somehow savage, though that isn't the right word, savage. Feral is closer, which also describes the corded muscularity of his neck and shoulders.

The effect is pleasing at first glance, unsettling if you linger. But that isn't why he scrutinizes his own image so closely. He's staring at a stranger. There isn't one feature of the face he recognizes, not even the disturbing sharpness of his gaze. Like the prongs of Satan's pitchfork, his eyes. Stabbing blue.

Who is he?

Where is he?

Who is she?

He can't answer any of those questions. His brain feels as if it's been emptied of all vital information. He can only sense things, rely on his intuition, and that tells him he has to escape this place. It isn't a hospital. It's a prison, and he's in grave danger. With the instincts of a near-death survivor, he also understands that whoever he once was, he's no longer that man. And the dream woman—the seductress who brought him back to life—is his only link to reality.

1

"Did you know that men who have pierced ears are better prepared for marriage," Muffin Babcock declared as she spun her bangle bracelet around so that the impressive diamonds showed. "They've experienced pain *and* bought jewelry."

A wry tilt graced Sophie Babcock's wide, sensual mouth as she strung colorful loops of macaroni together to make noodle necklaces for her day-care brood, ten rambunctious toddlers who had no idea they were "underprivileged" and didn't care whether their jewelry was made of macaroni or eighteen-carat gold.

Muffin seemed perfectly serious, however, and her sister-in-law did have a five-year age advantage on Sophie, who was just turning thirty, plus an undisputed knowledge of fine jewelry. No noodles for Muffin, unless they were in handmade *garganelli* with quail sauce, her favorite pasta dish.

"Colby didn't have pierced ears," Sophie pointed out.

Perched on a breakfast bar stool, Muffin peered at Sophie through lashes cosmetically dyed to match the taupe tones in her ash-blond hair. "We're not talking about my late husband, Sophia pet. We're talking about Claude, the apocalyptic mistake you are about to make."

Muffin might as well have called her Chia Pet.

"How's his name spelled again?" Muffin inquired in a droll tone. "Is that Clod with an *O*?"

"Women named Muffin shouldn't throw stones," Sophie reminded her. Drolly, she hoped, though by now she should have known better than to banter with the master. Sophie had recently agreed to marry Claude Laurent, a much older psychiatrist. None of the Babcocks approved, even though he was a friend of the family, and the therapist they themselves recommended when Sophie had desperately needed help. Muffin in particular objected, but her reasons were aesthetic rather than personal.

"I know Claude doesn't meet your standards." Sophie held up a red, yellow, and green noodle necklace for her sister-in-law's approval. "He isn't nearly rich, dashing, or dastardly enough." Not like Jay, Sophie admitted to herself, though she knew it was dangerous to make comparisons to her larger-than-life late husband.

Muffin's reaction was a delicate shudder. "Dastardly? Hon, the word is disaster. I can only imagine Claude naked. He'd make Ichabod Crane look like a stud. What *are* you thinking, Sophie?"

This time Sophie did manage droll. "When did you see Ichabod Crane naked?" she asked, laughing. "I'm thinking Claude is a kind, caring, stable man—and what more could a woman want?" Especially stable, which was exactly what Jay had *not* been.

Still, Sophie had to wonder if Muffin might be right. When Muffin had mentioned Claude's name just now, Sophie had felt a hesitation within, as if there were something incomplete, an emotional door left closed. Her heart and mind were poised on tiptoe, anticipating feelings that didn't come.

It had nothing to do with Claude's looks, however, which had never mattered to her one way or the other. As with everything else with Claude, the decision to marry him had seemed the right thing to do at the time, the next "natural step in the progression of their relationship," as he himself put it. And Sophie had never allowed herself to dwell on the possibility that she might be "settling" because of loneliness, as the Babcocks suggested, or even because she needed moral support for the child-care program she was struggling to get properly funded. She'd been alone for five years and it was time to move on with her life. If there was any ulterior motive on her part, it was probably to escape her formidable in-laws, who included Muffin.

Both Muffin and Sophie were Babcocks by marriage, and both had lost their husbands unexpectedly and tragically. Sophie's Jay had disappeared on an ice-climbing trip in Nepal five years ago, and his older brother, Colby, had died just last year of a stroke, which left the family pharmaceuticals empire in chaos.

The scramble for power and control wasn't over yet, and oddly it was turning out to be a battle between the women of the Babcock Inner Circle—Sophie herself, who had no experience with or interest in running a business empire, and Muffin, who definitely did. The other contender was Wallis Cady Babcock, the ailing matriarch of the clan, who might have been the perfect choice if the board of trustees hadn't decided she was incapable of handling the stress. Meanwhile, Babcock Pharmaceuticals, the billion-dollar industrial giant, was being run by a team of attorneys, and faring badly.

A loud sniff told Sophie what Muffin thought of the macaroni garland Sophie was endeavoring to tie around her own neck.

"Not me?" Sophie pretended to be crushed.

"It *is* you, ducks, that's the problem. If anyone could use a whole new look."

Sophie had heard that refrain before. Muffin had been pressuring her to be "reborn" at some posh Beverly Hills salon with a revolutionary new cosmetics line. A heavy investor in the salon, Muffin wanted Babcock's backing, and she seemed obsessed with the idea that a makeover miracle on Sophie's part could help.

"Soapy! Soapy—"

Saved from the wolf by a lambkin, Sophie thought. The toddler who trudged into the kitchen from the backyard playground was dirt-streaked and bleary-eyed with tears. He promptly sank to the floor, flopped to his back like a dying fish, and stared at the ceiling, stricken.

"Are you hurt, Albert?"

"No, I'm bery sick."

Sophie's noodle necklace went flying.

She couldn't detect any fever as she knelt over the distraught four-year-old and pressed her palm to his forehead. He seemed cool to the touch, maybe a little clammy. This was another reason she wanted a proper facility for the children, with consulting physicians on the advisory board and a staff trained in toddler CPR as well as first aid. Her teaching credentials were for special-needs kids, but the poverty-level families she worked with couldn't pay her, and she couldn't afford help beyond college students looking for part-time jobs.

"Lucy pooped on me!" Albert croaked.

Muffin made a low sound of displeasure. "This is exactly why I never had children, not even to produce a Babcock heir."

"Lucy's a baby gerbil," Sophie explained patiently as she used the material of her cargo overalls to spit-clean a speck of green from Albert's sneakers. "She's one of the animals the children are raising. I want them to have the experience of being responsible for something besides themselves. It's good for them, teaches them caring and compassion."

Hint, hint, she thought.

"How very progressive of you, Sophie. But it simply confirms my theory that where there are children, there's poop."

Muffin eased off the bar stool, shook out her black silk Moschino jumpsuit, and slipped on the delicate silver mesh sandals she had kicked off the moment she arrived.

Sophie adored Muffin's wry wit, but she'd privately decided that her sister-in-law was kid phobic and should probably never have children. When Sophie had confided the news about her engagement to Claude, she'd also revealed that she was pulling out of the family competition to run the empire. Delighted, Muffin had confessed a shocker. She'd taken the precaution of having some of her late husband's sperm frozen, should all else fail in her bid for power.

"Please let it be born toilet-trained," she'd intoned.

Muffin was also Sophie's only source of news about Wallis Babcock these days, who had withdrawn in hurt silence at Sophie's decision to marry Claude. As for Muffin herself, she lived in grand style in the family mansion and openly coveted her mother-in-law's domain. But Muffin also had Darwinian survival instincts. Wallis Babcock was a commanding personality, despite her physical frailty, and there was no love lost between her and Muffin.

"You getting married?" Albert asked the question of Sophie, his voice quavering.

She smoothed the child's coal-black hair from his forehead and placed a kiss on his flushed cheek. His eyes, exotically almond in shape, were wide and dark. "Darling, what's wrong? Does that upset you?"

He nodded, but wouldn't look at her now.

"Can you tell me why?" she coaxed.

"Cuz . . ." At her encouraging expression, he mumbled, "Cuz *I* wanted to get married with you, that's why."

"Albert, how sweet."

"How oedipal," Muffin muttered on her way out the door. "I'll see you later, *Mrs. Robinson.*"

"Later?" Sophie looked up in confusion.

"Your engagement party, ducks. It's tonight—" Muffin consulted her jewel-encrusted Bulgari watch and gave Sophie a sharp glance. "In less than an hour. I have major repairs ahead of me—and from the look of things, so do you."

As Muffin breezed out the door Sophie lifted Albert into her arms and walked to the glass door of the double oven. She studied what she could see of her reflection while rocking the child, and realized with a start that perhaps she'd been doing exactly this for some time now—hiding behind her kids, neglecting her needs for theirs.

Albert was an adorable little shield, but he couldn't conceal the fact that her skin had become pallid and shiny and there were purplish circles of fatigue under the misty eyes that had always been her best feature. Meadow green, Jay had once called the color of her irises.

It seemed impossible that running after small children and animals all day hadn't kept her toned, but she was looking at the evidence. Maybe it was the baggy T-shirt and tights, but she had an uneasy feeling that the lumpy, bag-of-apples look had more to do with her body than her clothing. How long had it been since she actually looked at herself in a mirror? Much as she hated to admit it, Muffin was right. Only a makeover wasn't enough. She needed a body double. It was a wonder Claude or Albert or *anyone* wanted to marry her.

Albert had begun to squirm in her hold. "Do am-am-aminals cry tears?" he asked, his voice muffled by her T-shirt.

It's true, she thought, smiling. Every child's worst fear is true. Adults *could* read their minds. "Did you do something bad to Lucy?"

He nodded against her shoulder. "I called her a dumb doody and a poopmeister," he admitted in a small voice.

"Whoa!" She ruffled his hair, her throat aching pleasurably. Lord, how she loved this child. "That calls for an apology, partner."

A moment later, as Albert trudged outside to make amends, Sophie turned back to the mirror, and to the reality of her situation. Her struggle to work through the loss of her husband was complicated by the fact that Jay's body had never been recovered. She didn't know how to say good-bye to someone who'd vanished into thin air.

He was the one who had died five years ago, but Sophie had not been able to bury him, so she'd buried herself. In this tiny little house. In the staggering demands of her work. But at some point she'd had to accept the fact that her husband wasn't coming back or she would never have recovered from the shock and grief. Only after accepting his death had she begun to live, but it had taken months of intensive therapy.

The strangest part was the relief. She didn't completely understand it. There was the inevitable release that came with letting go of a loved one, but she'd also experienced an odd sense of security at the prospect of life without Jay. She'd never really known him, except that he had ripped through her young world like a cyclone and made everything exciting and dangerous. He'd fulfilled all her romantic fantasies and even a couple of the forbidden ones. And sometimes he'd terrified her.

Sophie had come to live with the Babcocks as their ward at the age of fourteen, but she hadn't met Jay until a year later. He'd been sent away, first to a youth program in the Sierras designed to teach self-control and military discipline, and then to college. But nothing could break Jay's proud, independent spirit. He was an elemental force of nature, a thunderstorm, and when they met, he'd been attracted immediately to the shy, misty ray of sunshine that was Sophie Weston.

For the longest time Sophie resisted Jay's raffish charm out of sheer terror of the man. She would freeze like a stone when he approached, or worse, squeak out a sound and rush away. Mostly he would watch her reactions with a typical male mix of confusion and amusement. But one day he followed her into the greenhouse, where she often took refuge, and he kissed her amid a wild profusion of climbing roses and wisteria.

One innocent kiss, but Sophie had lost her heart and her mind and everything that wasn't physically attached that day. Soon after, Jay was sent away again, to the prestigious pharmaceutical school his forebears had founded, probably as much to discourage the relationship as for an education. But pharmacology was too tame a pursuit for Jay. Eventually he dropped out of school, and the attraction between him and Sophie raged out of control the moment he returned home. She was a few years older, considerably less terrified, and more than ready to surrender the one thing she hadn't already lost to him—her virtue.

Jay had spoken of precautions, but Sophie was a romantic soul—and far too much in love. When she missed her period, she and Jay both assumed she was pregnant and they were secretly married. The family was thunderstruck, but eventually gave the union their blessing, and Wallis, in particular, had great hopes that Jay would finally settle down.

Jay joined the family business, but when Sophie turned out not to be pregnant, and worse, unable to conceive, it put a strain on the relationship. She wanted children and the tests indicated she could bear them. It was Jay who was infertile. The news seemed to increase his discontent with the daily grind of a nine-to-five job, and by this time his wanderlust was so great that Sophie encouraged him to leave Babcock Pharmaceuticals and quench his thirst for adventure.

Her early childhood had been one of abandonment, insecurity, and fear until she came to live with the Babcocks, so it was ironic that a woman with a deep longing for stability would marry a man who thrived on risk. Ironic and tragic. Jay's star took him to the far reaches of the globe, and though Sophie longed to travel with him, the stress of his lifestyle overwhelmed her.

Perhaps she sensed that their relationship was endangered from the first, but she could never have imagined how it would end. She lost Jay in an ice-climbing accident—lost him forever—and though it nearly destroyed her, it saved her, too. Along with her heart, she had sacrificed her identity to her powerful husband, and life on her own gave her the chance to discover who Sophie, the girl with the meadow-green eyes, really was.

Part of that discovery was her relationship with Claude, and the question that had to be answered now, as the clock ticked away the minutes to her engagement party, was whether she wanted this marriage. Was it possible she was settling? The answer to both questions was yes, she realized. Claude would never be Jay. In fact, he was perhaps the exact opposite of Jay—calm and stoical, the voice of reason in a world gone mad.

Claude was the man she turned to when Jay disappeared. He was her therapist through the worst of it and the reason she was here. Not only did he walk beside her in the wilderness and help her salvage her sanity, but he loved her now, today, and she deserved some happiness in life as well as a helpmate.

Yes, some things just felt right.

This was one of them.

Everyone knew engagement parties were lit fuses in search of dynamite. Writ large in the lore were hair-raising tales of ex-lovers making surprise appearances, panicked guzzling of the ceremonial champagne by the betrothed, and even the occasional flight to freedom through a bathroom window.

A fatalist in these matters, Sophie expected the worst. "If we're lucky, it will be a catastrophe of *minor* proportions," she told the party consultant. She'd even prepped Claude on the odds of a disaster, which was why both of them were delighted when their small celebration was still pitfall-free at the halfway point. Sophie would have leaped on it as a sign she'd made the right decision, except for her nagging sense of something left undone. She'd checked her dress buttons and Claude's zipper before dismissing the feeling as jitters and reminding herself that things were going perfectly.

They'd rented Sfuzzi, a charming trattoria where the food, music, and romantic ambience were ideal for the occasion. Even Muffin, the only Babcock there, had managed to be cordial and upbeat so far, although it was early, Sophie reminded herself.

"Did I tell you how dapper you look tonight?" she whispered to Claude, tweaking his sleeve to let him know that the time for their big announcement was nearing. In fact, she had told him many times that evening, and praised him for his courage. The dark suit and wide-striped silk tie were an act of heroism for a man like Claude, who lived in threadbare gray flannel slacks and Mr. Rogers sweaters.

Tonight he was wearing Armani, and Sophie's pale rose wraparound silk dress brought out the meadow in her eyes and softly enhanced his tailored elegance. They'd been receiving compliments all night, which told Sophie what she already knew, that they made a lovely couple, despite what Muffin thought.

She was recklessly prepared to call the evening a rousing success when it came time to share their happiness with the others. Champagne corks popped like rifle fire, and the room was full of noise and laughter as the two of them walked to the front of the room.

Sophie had mentally practiced her part of the announcement all evening, but everything flew right out of her head when she turned to the crowd with a breathless smile. It wasn't nerves that rendered her speechless, it was the unexpected guest at the back of the room. Sophie stared in mute shock, unaware that a hush had fallen over the entire assembly.

Wallis Babcock, matriarch of the Babcock clan and venerable wife of Noah, hesitated in the arched entry of the banquet hall, her voice breaking emotionally as she struggled to speak.

"They've found Jay," she said. "He's alive. He's coming home."

Sophie's hand was cradled in Claude's. She tried to free herself, and felt his grip tighten painfully. There was a frantic quality to his hushed tone, but Sophie couldn't hear what he was saying. She couldn't do anything but continue to gape at the fragile figure in the doorway. Wallis's luminous features were as suffused with awe as if she'd seen a vision.

Jay was alive?

2

Sophie Weston could count on one hand the times in their five-year marriage that she had felt woman enough for Jay Babcock. The most memorable was when she discovered he was ticklish and reduced him to a drooling, jibbering idiot before he could get at her to stop her.

Their ancient Jeep Cherokee had been parked on the front lawn, and Jay had been lying beneath it, fiddling intimately with the suspension system. The only visible part of him was his bare feet, and when Sophie spotted his toes, all pink and perky and naked, some crazy notion had overtaken her. It wasn't like her at all. Jay had always been the crazy one, but for one heedless second she had acted on impulse.

She'd lifted the skirt of her cotton jersey jumper, plunked herself down on his ankles, fanny-first, and begun to tickle his feet. She hadn't even stopped when he'd screamed "Uncle!" and promised to quit hanging sweaty jockstraps on the car antenna to dry.

Risky business, tormenting Jay Babcock. He'd handily escaped her fiendish clutches, thrown her over his shoulder, and threatened to paddle her right there on the front lawn. Her shrieks had held him off, but when he got her inside the house, he'd taken his revenge in terrible, shocking ways that had made her writhe and giggle and plead for mercy. He'd used his superior strength against her shamelessly, ignoring all cries of foul play.

Jay was good at that kind of retribution. Very good. Thrilling. But Sophie didn't dare let herself dwell on his wicked gifts. She could already feel a sensation in the pit of her stomach that was dismayingly familiar. Recently she'd taken her Irish setter for obedience training and learned the way to get a distracted dog's attention was with a firm yank of the leash. The sweet little tug in her belly felt exactly like that— and it definitely had her attention.

"Look out below, Sophie," she warned in the soft sing-song she would have used with her kids. Obedience training was the least of her problems at the moment. She was stranded on the dirt access road that led to the Big House, as Muffin referred to the Babcocks' grand-portico Georgian mansion, and late for the small gathering of friends and family her mother-in-law had arranged to celebrate Jay's return.

Finances had forced her to keep the old Jeep Cherokee, and just moments ago she'd hit a rut and snapped something crucial enough to immobilize the car. Probably an axle, she thought in despair, not entirely certain what an axle was other than that it played some vital role in the operation of the car and was connected to the driveshaft, which she knew even less about.

"This can't be happening," she whispered. "Not today."

She clutched the steering wheel and bowed her head, embracing it like a drowning woman would a life preserver. She'd been waiting—with breath held, it seemed—the entire week since Wallis had broken the news that Jay was coming home. Her mother-in-law had been oddly secretive about the details of his return, but she'd continually assured Sophie that Jay would want to see her as soon as it could be arranged. "He's been through a terrible ordeal," she'd said. "He'll need some time, Sophie. You understand."

When Wallis finally called this morning, Sophie had been heading out the door on a field trip. She couldn't have canceled without disappointing ten kids, and her college-student assistants weren't qualified to take over.

"This afternoon, then," Wallis had urged. "Come early so you and Jay can have some time alone before the rest of them get here. Oh, didn't I tell you? Some family and friends may be dropping by, too. Nothing elaborate, a little 'reentry' party for Jay."

Party? No, Wallis hadn't told her, and it was not the way a wife expected to be reunited with her husband. Sophie couldn't dismiss the feeling that she had been held at bay all week, and that this first meeting had been carefully orchestrated so that her time with Jay would be limited. She hadn't known what to make of that, but she'd been all nerves and unable to concentrate on anything more complicated than the fact that her husband had returned.

It was him. Jay. He was back, and she had spent the entire morning preparing herself. The cargo overalls she lived in were in the hamper and she'd worn the most sophisticated outfit she owned, a long floral print skirt and matching tearose-pink cardigan. Something in black might have been better—sleek and sensual and mysterious against her fair skin and red-gold hair. But this was as mysterious as Sophie Weston got these days, and the color was good. Misty. Soft. Touchable. Like her, she hoped.

She released the wheel with a sigh. "Pretty? Is that too much to ask?" More than anything, she had wanted to arrive at the mansion looking calm, composed, and . . . yes, pretty. That would be nice for a change.

He used to call her that. Pretty baby. And although it was hard for her to admit to such adolescent yearnings now, there was a time when that was all she wanted to be. Nothing more. Just *his* pretty baby.

She wrenched open the car door, drew up the slim length of her skirt, and dropped to the ground with a dainty thud. Dust rose in puffs from the impact, coating her brand-new sandals. They were a pale imitation of Muffin's delicate footwear, but Sophie had so few pretty things, and she loved the way the straps crisscrossed like lacework. Now they were going to be ruined.

Brilliant sunlight forced a painful squint as Sophie peered up the road ahead, trying to make out the regal columns of the Big House through an orchard of apple trees that looked about to burst into bloom. The original Babcocks had subsidized their corner drugstore by raising fruit, so orchards were plentiful on the estate grounds. Sophie had hoped that this was the one bordering the mansion, but she could see no sign of the many-winged house with its impressive courtyard fountain and stately facade.

Moments later, walking at full march down the dusty road in the scorching afternoon sun, she slipped a finger inside the V neckline of her sweater and lifted the material to encourage some air circulation. The natural scent of her soap, rose water and glycerine, haloed her flushed skin, roused by the heat and the movement, she supposed. It was the only fragrance she'd ever worn when she and Jay were together, the only one he'd liked.

A breeze lifted her hair, but it was too warm to be refreshing. Fortunately, she'd drawn the crown waves up and fastened them with a mother-of-pearl clip in the back, lifting some of the weight off her neck. But the loose ringlets and wisps around her face stuck to her moist temples and forehead. Even worse, her feet were covered in powdery dust to her ankles.

Gleaming luxury cars and limos parked in the courtyard driveway brought her to a stop as the mansion came into view. The thought of being the last one to arrive made her want to turn and leave, especially since the sandal straps she so loved had rubbed fiery blisters on both her little toes. She could hardly walk without limping.

As she considered the edifice before her, with its soaringly graceful lines and perfectly sculptured topiary trees, a feeling of despair overtook her. This wasn't just déjà vu, it was the story of her life. No matter how hard she tried, she could never quite seem to get it right, regardless of what "it" was.

Today it was the reentry party for Jay, but there had always been a sense of inadequacy where the family was concerned. She didn't look or dress or talk like a Babcock. She wasn't one of them and never would be, a fact that must be painfully obvious to everyone concerned. They probably secretly pitied her efforts to fit in, and good Lord, why not? She was a mess, a damp, smelly mess, a limping disaster. Everything in her life was a disaster. She couldn't make anything work—

Where'd you get to? Sophie Sue! You hiding again? Those welfare people better show up today. They promised to take you off my hands. If they don't, you're out on the street. Hear me? The damn street!

Sophie could hear her aunt's shrill threat as if she were shrieking it at this very minute. Run-for-your-life words. They'd plunged a cold steel shaft through a child's heart and sent her scurrying for cover. Sophie had cringed behind the water heater in the garage while her aunt searched and shouted. Other times she'd squeezed herself in a moldy chest in the attic or crawled on her belly under the house to hide in the dirt with the bugs and the snakes.

Fear had opened an icy pit in her belly. It had honed her heart and mind to one purpose. Survive. The welfare people had never shown up. Perhaps that was one of her aunt's idle threats and she hadn't even called them, but Sophie had believed with every cymbal crash of her heart that someone was coming to take her away, believed every condemning word.

Gold motes spun before her eyes as she shook off the memory and tried to compose herself. Childhood had taught her how to hide. She was a master at it. Until Jay. He was the one who'd brought her out of hiding. She'd dared to love him, and it had opened her up like a locket that held precious things. But when the marriage had begun to go bad, she'd retreated in confusion, and then suddenly he was gone.

Grief and shock had sent her into a harrowing downward spiral, and eventually she'd begun to blame herself for the tragedy. If she'd been more exciting, vivacious, and sexy, he might have stayed home instead of trekking off into the wilderness in search of thrills. If she'd been more of a wife, more of a woman, more of anything.

Claude had challenged those notions violently. By the time Sophie got to him, she'd been nearly crushed by loss and guilt, but he'd made her see what she was doing to herself, and he hadn't allowed her to wallow in self-blame. He'd reasoned with her until she'd begun to acknowledge that perhaps it wasn't she who was inadequate, perhaps Jay's wanderlust had sprung from an inability to commit.

She hadn't seen Claude since the engagement party. Understandably he'd wanted to wait until she met with Jay and came to some decision about the future, and he was generously giving her time to do that. But now more than ever she understood that he'd been her anchor, her talisman against the fear. She missed him terribly, and hated to think she might be hurting him, all of which added to her confusion.

She bent and slapped some of the dust from her shoes, then gave her wilted skirt and sweater a little flounce, coaxing some life back into them. She was going in. She knew that much. To run and hide now would be to undo everything she'd done, forfeit all the ground. Even Claude wouldn't want that. But as she made her way gingerly to the marbled steps of the mansion, she still felt as if something was about to squash the breath out of her. The house? The family? Life itself?

But it wasn't the structure that cowed her. She'd become reasonably comfortable here in the last couple of years and quite friendly with her mother-in-law, Wallis, until Sophie's intention to marry Claude had become known. It wasn't even life that was about to squash her, she realized. It was him, Jay, the mythic lover, the great white hunter, the man himself. He was larger than life in any condition, even in death.

It began to dawn on her as she climbed the steps that the field trip hadn't kept her from getting here early. Or the Jeep. She'd sabotaged herself, perhaps unconsciously, but she had. She didn't want to be alone with him, didn't know if she was ready or would ever be ready. And what bewildered her more was her sense of utter disbelief. She had never been able to believe him dead, and now she couldn't believe him alive.

Sophie *was* the last one to arrive and her immediate impression as she entered the reception hall where the party was being held was of royalty and a receiving line. Nothing elaborate? It looked as if everyone Wallis had ever known had been invited, including far-flung family members, the company brass, and several of the directors from the board. Jay was obscured by the cluster around him, but it all had the feel of a command performance to Sophie, especially as she watched immediate family and household staff file by to greet him.

"Sophie, darling, there you are!" Wallis appeared from somewhere and clutched both of Sophie's hands. "Where have you been? I was about to send out a search party."

Sophie felt herself being drawn close to her mother-in-law with a forcefulness that startled her. The frail Wallis seemed to have been reborn by her son's return. There were roses in her cheeks and a sparkle in her Babcock-blue eyes. Sophie had never seen her look better. Life was flowing through her veins again, and the joy in her voice put a stone squarely in the middle of Sophie's throat.

We all love him, don't we, she thought. Wallis and I, all of us, helplessly. That was the curse and the blessing of Jay Babcock. He stole your heart away like a sneak thief in the night with his dashing ways and his dangerous passions. He made you want to follow him blindly wherever he went, even if it meant abandoning everything you knew.

A pleasurable sinking warmth filled the hollow pit of Sophie's belly. She knew this feeling. She had lived for it once, her drug of choice. Now her shoulders flared back and her breathing reached deeper. Now she fought it.

"He's been asking for you, darling," Wallis burbled. "He's hardly spoken of anything else. Doesn't he look wonderful?"

"I'm sure he does," Sophie agreed, girding herself with another breath. She still couldn't see him well, except for glimpses of his dark head through the crowd engulfing him. She could see Muffin, though, standing apart from it all by the yellow alabaster fireplace, and looking chic and perfectly put together in a black knit sheath.

Sophie gave her own dusty ankles a despairing glance and discreetly tapped her toe against the carpet, dislodging dust in small puffs. One day she would have the quintessential black ensemble, a sleek Armani suit or St. John knit with gold epaulets at the shoulders and matching geegaws on the cuffs. And the supreme self-assurance to go with it, naturally. One day. One fine day.

Meanwhile, Muffin gave her a sympathetic nod, apparently because Sophie had been taken prisoner by Wallis. Muffin also pointed toward the mysterious dark head in the midst of the admiring crowd and then patted her chest with a fluttery hand, as if to say, Be still my heart.

Sophie smiled. Not only was Muffin a crack-up, she'd just made it unanimous. They were all in it together, victims of the Jay Babcock curse.

For the first time since her husband's reappearance, Sophie could feel her confidence returning. No one had clapped a hand over their mouth yet, trying to hide their hilarity at her dishevelment, so perhaps she didn't look too awful. And Wallis had said that Jay was asking about her. *He's hardly spoken of anything else.*

Could that be true? Sophie wondered.

"Come with me," Wallis said firmly, linking her arm with Sophie's. "I'll scare those scavengers away so you and Jay can say hello to each other at least. He scolded me soundly for not arranging a meeting the moment he got back. Or did I already tell you that?"

No, you didn't, Sophie thought. And God, I wish you had. Suddenly the room felt close and stuffy, almost as hot as the sun blazing outdoors. "It's all right," she assured the older woman. "Let's not drag him away from his well-wishers just yet. I need a moment to catch my breath anyway."

"Are you sure?" Wallis searched Sophie's features anxiously, perhaps looking for signs of a potential problem. It was very clear she wanted everything to go well. For Jay. This didn't surprise Sophie. Neither Wallis nor Noah had hidden their preference for the younger and more charismatic of their two boys. Noah had considered Jay a visionary after Jay advised him to start advertising Babcock's prescription drugs directly to the public. Jay's rationale had been to help consumers make informed choices about their health care rather than to rely entirely on their doctors' advice. But the move had also added greatly to Babcock's coffers, and Noah had tried his best to talk Jay into taking the top spot that ultimately went to Colby.

Sophie eased free of her mother-in-law's grip and smiled reassuringly, squeezing the hand that still clung to her arm. "Can you keep a secret, Wallis? The Jeep broke down and I had to walk most of the way here. I'm parched. If I could have something to drink. Anything—"

"Oh, of course, dear. I'll have Mildred bring you some champagne. Will that do?"

"Water, instead?" Sophie was too dehydrated for champagne, and probably too light-headed. Wallis hurried off to alert Mildred, who'd been with the Babcocks since Sophie could remember and was as fiercely loyal as she was efficient. Before Sophie could stamp more dust from her sandals, the housekeeper had appeared with a Waterford goblet, brimming with ice water and afloat with a thin slice of lemon done up to look like a butterfly.

Elegant, Sophie thought as she thanked the housekeeper. Everything was so elegant here. The hall was decorated with huge sprays of fresh-cut flowers, and the room's abundant natural light made it a perfect gallery for the family's art collection, most of which were Wallis's own oils and watercolors. She'd done countless family portraits and landscapes of the estate over the years, but, sadly, had stopped painting after Noah was stricken with Alzheimer's and her two sons were taken.

Sophie took several sips of the water, savoring the icy crispness as she sought a less conspicuous place to stand. She still wanted to get a good look at Jay before he saw her. She needed that much psychological advantage.

When Wallis had called that morning, she'd issued another vague warning about her son's "ordeal," promising to give Sophie the details when they could talk privately. Unable to wait, Sophie had called Muffin and been shocked to learn that Jay hadn't vanished in the Himalayas as the family was told. He'd been taken hostage by guards at the Nepal/People's Republic of China border on trumped-up drug charges. He'd been imprisoned.

Muffin had "eavesdropped" on a phone conversation between Wallis and one of the doctors who evaluated Jay, a psychiatrist who specialized in post-traumatic stress disorder. He'd cautioned Wallis that Jay would require ongoing treatment, and even though he appeared perfectly normal, there would be times when he seemed remote and withdrawn. He'd advised that if Jay were to make a successful adjustment, he would need to start reclaiming his life and all that entailed— social contact, career goals, the familiarity of home and family, and especially the love and support of his wife.

According to Muffin, Wallis had assured the doctor that Sophie was totally supportive and would be moving back to the Big House in order to be with him. That possibility was almost beyond Sophie's comprehension, but it had less to do with Jay than it did with her independence and how hard she had fought to win it.

The family had urged her to come live with them when Jay disappeared, but she'd insisted on staying where she was, *and* on paying rent, even though the tiny matchbox train of a rambler she lived in was on Babcock land. It was the first of many attempts to escape the vortex that seemed to have swallowed her whole.

Hoping to avoid Muffin or anyone else who might strike up a conversation, Sophie found a spot off the beaten path near the magnificent black Steinway, her favorite of Wallis's many valuable antiques. Directly opposite Jay now, she could see him more clearly, though it was only a profile. He was speaking to a distant cousin on his father's side, an older woman who sat on the board of the company, as Sophie recalled.

Wallis hadn't exaggerated. Wonderful was putting it mildly. Sophie held the goblet with both hands to steady them. Jay had always exuded a magnetic attraction that drew the eye like fire drew moths. He still did. She could feel it from where she stood.

Wallis had also said he would seem perfectly normal, and that was true, too. His experience hadn't diminished him in any visible way. If anything, he seemed taller than she remembered and more ruggedly put together. There was a gauntness in his facial features and a weariness about his expression that spoke of the hardships he must have endured. No dramatic changes, she thought. But then she caught her breath.

Sophie saw the eye patch the moment he turned her way. She hadn't noticed the strap hidden in his plentiful dark hair, but the black triangle had such a striking impact that her heart hesitated. It made him look positively frightening.

She thought he'd spotted her as he swung around, and perhaps he had, because even though he wasn't looking at her, even though he was already deep in conversation with someone else, he suddenly went quiet and lifted his head as though he'd sensed something.

She felt the rising panic of the fifteen-year-old who used to run away from him. Thank God she'd put the Waterford goblet down. Her hands were shaking so hard she couldn't even clasp them. The years of therapy, the shoring up of her defenses, collapsed like a sand castle. Staring at him helplessly, she wondered if the ticking in her ears was a clock or some explosive on a timer, and all the while he continued to turn until he was looking straight at her.

The recognition was instant on her part, as physical as the yank of a leash, and perhaps he felt it, too. He raised a hand as if to quiet the crowd, and by his expression alone, those gathered around him seemed to understand that she had finally arrived. His wife.

They cleared a path, and Sophie could barely draw breath as he walked toward her. She used to dream about his return, lucid dreams so piercingly real, she woke up with his name on her lips. Tears of joy would turn to fire as she searched the emptiness, scalding her all the more hotly because she had dared to hope. She'd felt as if she were going crazy. Images of him haunted her, even during waking hours. It was like being stalked by a ghost, and nothing, not even her sessions with Claude, could banish the eerie sensations. It wasn't until she forced herself to accept Jay's death that they began to fade.

She felt as if she were dreaming now.

"Sophie?" A faint smile touched his mouth, a "Jay" smile, she used to call it. Only then was she able to breathe normally. Maybe this was real. Maybe it *was* him.

She found it difficult to speak or do anything but stare at him greedily and fight back welling emotion. Aware that the entire room was watching, she took swift, private inventory of the Jay she remembered: the split in his eyebrow suffered during a nasty fall from his prized Harley motorcycle. The dark freckle or mole, she could never decide which—he'd facetiously called it a beauty mark—near the side of his mouth. Each characteristic, no matter how small, was a marker on the horizon, telling her that this was familiar territory. She was revisiting a place she knew and had dwelled before. She was home. So was he.

"Would you look at that," someone whispered.

"I think it's sweet," came the instant verdict.

Murmurs rose around them, low voices mixing with the clink of fine crystal and the rustle of silk clothing. A champagne cork popped. Sophie could hear it all, but she was also aware that the sounds of the party were receding in the distance.

Only the ticking prevailed. Louder now, more insistent. It was like some great metronome, keeping count, beating out the cadence to which everything moved, to which she moved. But it was taking her somewhere she'd never been before.

Sophie could feel herself resisting. Her hands were

drenched with perspiration, only this wasn't the familiar panic she associated with him. Caught in the razor-sharp acuity of his exposed eye, she experienced a sense of disorientation. For a split second she had no idea who this man was. She only knew he *wasn't* Jay Babcock. The realization struck with the certainty of a thunderclap and was gone before she could make sense of it. On some level she knew it was an aberration, like her dreams. It must have been.

She hadn't even realized they'd moved, though she was absently aware that he'd taken her arm and led her to the other side of the piano. It was a quieter spot, bathed in warmth from the windows.

"You've changed," he said, studying her in the light.

It was such a deliberate statement she hardly knew what to say. "I have? How?"

"You're all grown up, for one thing. Sophie Weston, girl with the pensive smile, is a person apart now. She stands alone. Even in this room, here by this Steinway." He hesitated, smiled. "You do, Sophie."

Thank God he couldn't see it, but her throat stung as sweetly as when she'd hugged Albert the other day. With three words, he'd acknowledged everything she'd fought so hard for. You stand alone.

"Thank you," she said, feeling silly to be so overcome.

Perhaps he understood, because he began, very deliberately, to examine the tassels of the silk brocade runner that draped the piano. After a moment he picked up the sheet music that sat on the ebony stand.

" 'Ghost of a Chance'? Interesting title."

His faint, quizzical smile reappeared when she looked up. "Are you all right?" he asked.

"Yes . . . why?"

"I could have sworn you'd thrown up a force field. A step in your direction, and I'd collide with it."

She laughed suddenly, aware how deep the conversation had gone in just moments. He'd always had an uncanny ability to tune in. It had reminded her of telepathy, except that he'd lacked the patience and the focus. Some siren was always whispering in his ear. Now he had both, and Sophie strongly sensed that he was going to use them. Maybe it was female intuition, but something told her he was fascinated by this new barrier she'd erected, and if there was any way to get through it, he was the man who'd find it. She could see it in the set of his jaw and the curious male heat of his gaze. He wanted to know her every naked thought, whatever it took. He wanted to be privy to her innermost secrets, even the ones she hid from herself.

"Of course I'm all right," she insisted. "The question is, are you? I thought you'd look like a POW, starved and hollowed-eyed, but you seem strong and fit."

"Rehab, it can work miracles. The first thing they did when they sprung me was ship me to a spa in the Swiss Alps and put me back together again."

"They? Who found you?"

"I'm not sure myself who they were—Interpol, the CIA, maybe." He smiled mysteriously. "Whoever it is that gets clumsy Westerners out of foreign prisons. They didn't introduce themselves, just turned me over to the American embassy."

She was holding herself, stroking the inside of her wrist with her thumb, but wasn't aware of it until she noticed him watching her. The curiosity in his expression was very male. Suddenly she couldn't move her fingers right. They were stiff and unmanageable.

"I'm glad you're back," she said softly.

It was such a ridiculous understatement, her welcome, but he seemed to understand. His smile was odd, sweetly sad.

"How do we start this, Sophie? Or do we start it?"

Again she was caught without an answer. He gazed at her searchingly, as if he didn't want to wait another minute for whatever was to be started. She didn't either.

"Tomorrow?" he asked.

Tomorrow was Saturday, her first day off since Jay's return, and she'd promised herself she would spend at least part of it with Claude. She understood that Claude might want some distance to sort out his own feelings, but she was sure she could convince him to talk with her. There were so many things that still had to be said.

"What about Sunday?" she asked.

"What time?" He didn't give her a chance to answer and his impatience thrilled her. "Crack of dawn?"

"That early?"

"I've been waiting five years. You aren't going to keep me waiting any longer, are you?"

Sophie very nearly couldn't catch her breath again. This man was lethal, even more dangerous than the Jay she remembered. The pressure of his dark restless gaze was a physical thing. It prowled all over the place.

"No," she managed to assure him. "I won't keep you waiting." She didn't expect to have any trouble getting up since she probably wouldn't sleep from now until then. It almost felt like they were kids again, planning their first date, and her heart was going to explode with excitement. "Oh, wait! Where are we going?"

He wagged his head warningly. "That's a secret."

Yes, it did feel like a first date, exactly that.

3

Wallis Babcock had not indulged in champagne in any number of years, but today, in the course of the last hour, she'd drunk nearly two glasses of a lovely, bone-dry Schramsberg brut and was feeling quite giddy.

She was in the mood to do something extravagant, like strike up the band, call the gathering to attention, and propose a toast. Only there was no band and a toast would interrupt the marvelous progress that Sophie and Jay seemed to be making at getting reacquainted.

Destine, she thought. Some things were meant to be, and this reunion was one of them, even if Sophie didn't yet realize it. It was an event conceived in the heavens, and she, Wallis, was merely the catalyst. Or one of them. Laughter sparked a little blaze in her too slight frame, but she didn't dare allow it expression. Two glasses of champagne were bold enough. Soon everyone would be watching the mother instead of the son, and that would never do.

Careful not to spill what was left of her drink, she fingered the charm bracelet hanging like golden lace from her wrist.

Each charm had symbolic meaning, and though her scientist husband had called it mumbo jumbo, Wallis had always believed the figures connected her in some way to the things they represented.

The one she'd clasped between her fingers just now was a circle with an arrow pointing outward, symbolizing Mars, the planet that ruled Scorpio. It was Jay's charm, and her youngest son had effortlessly lived up to the water sign's reputation for energy and sensuality. Wallis had bought it the same year he was born. And the impression she got now as she touched it was heat.

Muffin would have scoffed, too, Wallis knew. Her daughter-in-law thought astrology and the like were for the weak of nerve. But Wallis wouldn't allow such negativity to dampen her mood. She was pleased, more than pleased, jubilant at what the stars and their emissaries had wrought. Jay was back, and it was all going to be different now that there was another Babcock in the picture. The family would resume its rightful role in the company again and everything would fall into place. Finally it seemed the wheel of fortune was rolling her way.

She left her drink on a tray with several other empties that were waiting for Mildred to spirit them away. Normally she would have been concerned about the appearance of so much soiled crystal, but today all she could see was the beauty of her splendid home.

The reception hall was wreathed in enormous bouquets of fresh-cut flowers and shimmering with soft pink light from the Palladian windows. She was also personally delighted with every one of the guests she'd invited, even the ones she secretly detested. Especially them, she thought ironically, considering the occasion.

Hope was what she felt today. The future looked bright in a way it hadn't since her husband was diagnosed with Alzheimer's and relegated by Colby to a private-care nursing home. That was when the tragedies began, as she remembered, though the exact sequence of events was a little fuzzy now. She'd been in a haze from the shock and the grief, as well as from the medication Claude Laurent had prescribed to help her get through it. But even powerful drugs couldn't have blocked the horror of having her entire family struck down. In the course of a few years one Babcock male after another had been felled, until there were none, and she was alone.

She brought her steepled fingers to her mouth, and then impulsively, the charm to her lips. It's over now, she reminded herself, the reign of terror is over.

Well, perhaps not completely over yet, she amended, spotting one of the undesirables hovering at her prized Italian Renaissance console, which was laden with catered delicacies. Portly and balding at forty-two, Babcock's acting CEO had a fistful of baguette bread and was scooping a great mound of hot crab curry from a chafing dish.

Wallis moved a little closer so she could be heard without alerting the rest of the guests. "Jerry?" she called to him, hoping no one could see the glint in her eye. It must be positively demonic. "Champagne?" she asked with wide-eyed concern. "You'll need it for the toast I'm about to propose to Jay."

A mouth stuffed full of spiced crab rendered Jerry White speechless. He shook his head. Rather ungraciously, Wallis thought. But she caught Mildred's attention and signaled her to refill his glass anyway. Keep him guessing, she reasoned, trying not to seem too pleased with herself. In point of fact, nothing would have pleased her more than to have her nemesis lose his cool and make a perfect ass of himself in public.

Jerry was the most senior partner in White, Wexler and Dreyfus, and one of two attorneys who oversaw the Babcock trust accounts. He and his associate, Phil Wexler, were also the team who currently ran the company. Appointed by the board to head Babcock while the control of Colby's and Noah's shares were in dispute, they'd taken a strong and united stand against Wallis's succession, citing drug dependency and emotional instability.

"Philistines." Bitterness dripped from Wallis's tone.

She had made a surprise appearance at a board meeting

once to argue against their master plan for cutting Babcock's research to the bone, and they'd been defaming her ever since. She'd already dismissed White as having an oral fixation and probably a mother complex as well. He'd never been married, and she'd caught him sucking on the arm of his reading glasses more than once. Might as well have been his thumb.

"Wallis."

Her name was spoken so softly it took her a moment to realize that someone had come up behind her and was offering champagne.

"El—" She tried to control the emotion in her voice as she turned to the undisguised warmth of Ellis Martin's smile. He'd been away, presiding over some conference for scientific types, and she was afraid he might not make the celebration. But trust El to come through. He knew how important this was to her, as well as the crucial role he played. Dr. Ellis Martin was an eminent, Nobel Prize–winning neurobiologist, who ran Babcock's fabled research arm and was responsible for developing Ordin-B and Clormax, the company's blockbuster asthma and anti-inflammatory drugs. His public support of Jay's bid to assume control was vital.

"I can't, El," she said, demurring on the champagne. "I'm half in the bag already."

"That's your problem, love. Never do anything halfway." He persisted until she laughed and took the drink.

Boldly, Wallis continued to hold his gaze as she brought the flute to her lips and drank. Bubbles foamed over the rim and her bracelet jingled merrily, a sound as quick and restless as her heart. It gave her both terrible pleasure and terrible guilt thinking about how close she and El had become the last couple of years. But truthfully, she didn't know what she would have done without him.

Other than Sophie, he was her only solace and support through the losses she'd suffered. He'd been a friend for so many years she'd lost count, but she thought they'd all met in college—she and Noah and El and Dotty. At any rate, they'd double-dated, become inseparable, and would have pulled off a double wedding if the illustrious Babcocks hadn't objected to the "circus atmosphere."

Now there were only the two of them, she and El. Noah was in a nursing home, and when Dotty had succumbed to cancer two years ago, El had turned to Wallis for comfort. Sometimes Wallis mourned the warmth and fun they'd all shared, but more often it felt like it should always have been this way. She and El.

"Looks like a love connection," he said, lifting his own glass and returning her gaze.

Wallis blushed like a girl, and was mortified at the thought of anyone noticing. Lately El had been pressing for just that between the two of them, a love connection. "I'm going to bed you, wench," he'd informed her the other night while they were having a light dinner on the terrace. "Make no mistake about that."

Wallis hadn't been the only one flustered by his audacity. Mildred had overheard and dropped her teakettle. Fortunately, no one else had been home.

Reckless man, she thought now as he mouthed the words again.

"Not here, El. Someone will hear you."

"Don't be so presumptuous," he teased. "I meant Jay and Sophie."

He pointed to the couple, who looked even more breathlessly caught up with each other than they had before.

"You dog," Wallis said. "I'll think about forgiving you, but only if you do the honors and make a toast to Jay's return."

It didn't take much arm twisting. In a jovial mood as he was tonight, El rather fancied himself a bon vivant and host among men. And as he walked to the center of the hall and raised his flute, Wallis allowed herself to admire him in the privacy of her thoughts.

He was so unlike her stern, officious Noah that she'd often wondered what had made the two of them such fast friends, other than their obvious interest in pharmacology. El was tall and rangy, his body the perfect hanger for a tailored suit, whereas Noah's stocky, barrel-chested frame crumpled everything he wore. El was handsome, too. And romantic, she was discovering. But Noah had always been the more aggressive of the two, going after what he wanted with a vengeance, which included her, and letting nothing stand in the way. Noah was the empire builder, a giant among men.

Was, though. *Was.* That was how she thought of Noah now, in the past tense. If only she could bury all of it in the past, every ghastly thing that happened five years ago, bury it so deeply there was no chance of it ever resurfacing.

"My good friends," El called out. "If I could have your attention for a moment. We have someone with us who deserves welcoming back with open arms."

As Mildred hurried around filling glasses El talked about Babcock Parmaceuticals as a leader and innovator in the field of research and about Jay as the perfect man to carry on that proud tradition. Bursting with pride herself, Wallis couldn't resist a peek at Jerry White. The attorney seemed to have lost his appetite. At least he had a full glass of champagne, she thought wryly.

She didn't feel a second's remorse about stealing back the company from Jerry White. He hadn't done a thing to deserve it, other than being the beneficiary of Colby's untimely death. Her oldest son's ego was such that he must have believed himself invulnerable, because his will had *not* been in order when he died. No one disputed the money or the property that would go to Muffin. It was the huge block of Babcock voting stock Colby had controlled that had everyone circling like scavengers. In addition to his own shares, Colby had also voted Noah's and held power of attorney over his father's other interests.

White and Wexler now controlled all that. They were kings of the mountain and they wanted to stay that way. They were going to keep the family out of it if they could, and failing that, they could be expected to throw their support behind Muffin, whose commercial vision for the company was much closer to their own mercenary goals.

But Wallis was having the last laugh, literally. Now that Jay had returned, all of the attorneys' arguments were moot. Of course they would demand proof, and perhaps even that he really was Jay Babcock, that he was emotionally and mentally sound, but Wallis didn't anticipate any problems with either.

Babcock had a wonder drug in clinical trials that looked like it might be the answer to post-traumatic stress disorder. Jay had insisted upon being part of the trials in the sense that he would personally undergo the treatment to demonstrate his faith in the company and to answer any concerns about the state of his health, mental and physical. And since El was personally supervising Jay's treatment, Wallis felt a certain measure of confidence in the outcome.

"Here, here!" the guests chorused when El finished his tribute. Glasses were thrust in the air, and Jay was surrounded with well-wishers. Another round of toasting began, and El slipped away to return to Wallis's side.

"Are you sure?" he whispered to her as Jay stepped into the circle to make a toast of his own. "Are you sure about this? About him?"

"Oh, yes," Wallis said, nodding. She didn't have to think about her answer, not for a moment. "Very sure." The timing couldn't have been more perfect for everyone concerned, even Sophie. She'd been rescued from that dreadful wedding, she had her husband again, and Wallis had her son, the son she'd always wanted. If Wallis regretted anything at that moment, it was her slavish concern with propriety. If she'd been more like Muffin, who loved to be at the center of things, she might have held a press conference.

"Jay Babcock is back," she would have told the world. "My son is back. And so am I."

At the moment Muffin was quite content not to be at the center of things. The spectator always had a better vantage point than the participant, and there was a fascinating little drama playing out right before her eyes. She wanted to be front row and center, just in case someone decided to challenge the long-lost Jay Babcock and his claim on the kingdom.

Interesting that no one had, she thought. Yet.

Also interesting that not five minutes ago, Sophie, his adoring wife, had been gaping at him like she'd never seen him before. She'd looked like a frightened animal about to bolt. Well, hell, who wouldn't, Muffin allowed in a moment of honesty. He was tall, dark, and devastating, to be totally sophomoric about it, and that eye patch was killer. Her own insides had turned to vichyssoise when she'd seen him, and she'd been across the room.

Muffin had watched silently, as fascinated as everyone else as he began to walk toward Sophie. They were staring at each other with an intensity that could have been picked up by the space shuttle. It came off them in waves, especially him. But Sophie had still looked for all the world like a small, trapped animal captivated by the Big Bad Wolf, and Muffin had half expected to see her break and run if he yawned.

Bad move, Muffin decided. Running would have been a mistake, because this Jay—or whoever he was—looked like he would take that very personally. Yes, he would be hot on her tail, pursuing her until she dropped.

No matter how hard she tried, Muffin couldn't tear her eyes away from them, and yet it made her acutely uncomfortable to watch. She would rather have been in the bedroom, videotaping their honeymoon night, than this. At least the naked body parts would have been a distraction.

Gooseflesh rippled up the back of her arms, and she couldn't seem to complete a breath. The air was bumping up against something in her chest. Even her legs felt suspiciously unsteady, which was the last straw. Muffin Babcock was not weak-kneed.

She reminded herself why she was there, and it was not to welcome back the heir apparent. She wanted to know what kind of adversary he was shaping up to be, and whether he might pose a threat to her future plans. And she was deeply curious about Sophie's reaction to her erstwhile husband. She'd looked utterly bewildered for a moment, as if he were a total stranger to her. And if Sophie Babcock didn't recognize her own husband . . . well, wouldn't that be interesting.

Taking a deep breath, she began the ritual of rearranging the gold accessories she wore, most of them twenty-two carat. A very calming color—real gold. Her Nancy & David chain belt gleamed like fine jewelry against the sinuous lines of her black knit sheath. And the diamond salamander on her lapel matched the earrings that decorated the lobes of her ears.

Better. Much better, she thought as her breathing began to flow more naturally. With practiced ease, she brought up the inside of her wrist and sniffed the potent fragrance there. Tarty Tangerine was one of a collection of natural plant oils that Muffin's new partner was developing. Delilah, a cosmetician to the stars, who went by her first name only, had laced the fruit oil with an exotic herbal appetite suppressant that worked through the sense of smell, and Muffin had decided to test it today to see if the extravagant claims Delilah made for the product were true.

It also gave Muffin a chance to discreetly check out her mother-in-law, who looked high enough to be back on drugs again. Too bad that wasn't the reason for the old bat's tittering glee, Muffin thought spitefully. This heartwarming mother-and-son-reunion stuff was making her want to eat the flowers.

Frustration made Muffin hungry, and she did seem to be thwarted at every turn lately, which was exactly why she'd tried the fruit oil. The fragrance was a bit much—sharp orangy notes, ghosted by hints of honeysuckle, but the potency was supposed to saturate the olfactory glands and "confuse" the appetite. Muffin had hoped it would keep her from devouring the shrimp taquitos, as well as the Limoges plate they sat on.

She had some bad news for Delilah.

Wallis glanced Muffin's way and smiled, apparently delighted to have caught her spying. Muffin did not smile back. The selfish old biddy was rich enough to be retired in Palm Beach with all those other rotting heiresses. Wallis could have gone anywhere in the world she wanted, but did she? No, not the venerable matriarch of the Newport Beach Babcocks. She had to have her fingerprints all over everything. Now, apparently, she was trying to wrest back control through the return of her youngest son.

"Champagne?"

Mildred again, making the rounds. The woman must have the metabolism of a lab rat, Muffin thought, hating her for her bone-thin, quaking frame, even though it wasn't a bit attractive. The aesthetics hardly mattered to Muffin anymore, given her desperate struggle to stay fashionably thin. She had to watch every calorie, every fat gram, while nervous little Millie was skinny as canapé toothpicks and always scurrying around.

"No thank you, Mildred," she said pointedly, then changed her mind and snatched a flute from the tray as the housekeeper backed away, apologizing. Muffin had nothing whatsoever to celebrate and didn't need the calories, but champagne was safer than an entire plate of shrimp taquitos.

The champagne was dry, almost acrid on her tongue. Muffin much preferred the sweeter, cheaper variety, though she wouldn't have admitted it to a soul, certainly not to anyone in her immediate circle of tony friends. No one except the Babcocks knew that Muffin didn't have the pedigree she pretended, and her secret was safe with them. Wallis would have thrown herself from a freeway overpass before she'd let it be known that Colby had met his widow in the proverbial back room of a massage parlor. Perhaps that was why Muffin was vaguely suspicious of the party's guest of honor. It took an impostor to spot one. And Muffin was one of the best.

There were many things she freely admitted to, however, mostly for the entertainment of those same tony friends. No one seemed to mind at all when you shared the secrets of your psychic pain. In certain circles it never went out of style to be neurotic, and Muffin was as neurotic as hell. Phobic, bulemic, and most damning of all, a Mensa member. She'd spent tens of thousands at a Newport Beach specialty dentist, getting rid of her TMJ, and the damn jaw still popped when she flossed her teeth.

Just for fun, she searched the room for some poor demented soul who would make her look healthy by comparison. But there was nowhere to look besides the Babcock lovebirds. They were like a black hole, sucking up all the energy in the room.

Her heart twisted painfully as she remembered how in love they'd been once, a long time ago. Maybe it should have made her happy that they were being given a second chance, but it didn't. She was miserable, envious, and yes, ravenous. The emptiness in her chest was so pronounced it was difficult to swallow. She wouldn't even be able to turn this into a luncheon story with a nasty little twist at the end for the girls. It hurt too much.

She gulped down the champagne, not caring that it tasted like monkey piss, and by the time she'd drained the glass and set it on the alabaster mantel with a clink, the sharpest of the pain had passed. A twirl of her bangle bracelet brought the diamonds into sight and restored her spirits considerably.

She smiled darkly at the irony of her thoughts. One mess deserved another, didn't it? Maybe she ought to make an appointment with Sophie's Claude. He was a free man now.

Sophie caught glimpses of him as he walked to the end of the half-mile jetty, his tall, bent body nearly obscured by the thickening morning fog. A mythical giant afoot in the mists, he was as forlorn a figure as she'd ever seen.

All around him the choppy slate-gray water was fringed with blue-and-white foam. The sea of sorrows, she thought. That's what they should call this place instead of Newport Bay. Seagulls perched on the rocks, waiting for the sun to clear the horizon and warm their damp, chilly feathers.

A foghorn called repeatedly.

Claude. Dear Claude. What was she going to do? How was she going to tell him? Of course, he already knew, but it still had to be said. She hurriedly picked her way through the exposed rocks, stumbling and scraping her ankles as she went. He seemed about to vanish in the fog, though she knew he would soon reach the end of the jetty.

She'd gone to his home first, a lovely old wood-shake cottage with add-ons that sent it sprawling across the beach. The place had always reminded her of him, long and ungainly, full of unexpected treasures. One of the additions was the office where he saw patients—a small, charming suite with its own entrance.

Sophie had peeked in the door's sidelight windows when he didn't answer, and burned with sadness at the messy splendor of his existence. His bookshelves and cabinets were cluttered with the things he loved best, antique glass, nautical curios . . . and framed snapshots of her. He hadn't put them away, she realized, resting her forehead against the windowpane.

She closed her eyes and sighed. Why hadn't he done that?

She barely had to think about the answer. Claude was just like her. He stockpiled happiness, too. The first time she'd seen his office she'd recognized a kindred spirit. Sophie had started hoarding keepsakes as a child because they were the only stability she had. Her aunt had put far more effort into pawning Sophie off on someone than she ever had into caring for her niece. Sophie had staved off emotional starvation by hanging on to every rare, precious moment. She hid away her "collection of trash," as her aunt called it, until the lights were out and the house was quiet. Then, closeted away, she would pore over the contents of her shoe box—a paper clip touched by a special boy at school, an encouraging mark from a teacher—and relive each experience until she dropped off to sleep, exhausted. Her talismans, those trinkets.

It was Claude who taught her to trust again, with her whole heart. And not just *how* to trust, but who. Jay had been too reckless, Wallis too unstable, and Muffin could be trusted to be self-serving. Claude she had trusted implicitly, but the crucial step in her growth was learning to believe and trust in herself.

"Claude, wait!"

He turned when she got close enough to be heard. As she

neared him she could see the sorrowing weight to his head, the stricken smile that shaped his mouth. It hid nothing. And for the first time Sophie faltered. He was working through this in his own way, and perhaps she ought to have left him alone.

"Claude . . . I was hoping we could—"

"Talk?" His shoulders rose and fell. "I'd rather not, Sophie. What is there to say? You're going back to Jay. We both know that."

She hesitated, aware that she hadn't made that decision. "I don't know—"

He touched the strap of her cargo overalls with solemn fondness, the same strap he used to tug to get her attention. "Well, regardless," he said softly. "We know you're not coming back to me."

The anguish in her expression must have told him that he was right, because the light went out of his eyes.

"Oh, Claude, please—" Please don't hurt, she thought. I can't bear for you to hurt. Grief welled up in her, and made more urgent all the things that still had to be said. With a heavy heart, Sophie forced herself to acknowledge that it was true. She wasn't coming back. He had already accepted that it was over between them, but surely he would let her tell him what he meant to her. He had given her back her life, her hope. She would always carry that with her, him with her.

A flock of gulls took flight, beating their wings fiercely against the raw morning chill. Sophie bundled her car coat around her and tried to talk over the noise, but their cries drowned her out. And finally she gave up. She wasn't doing it for him anyway, she realized, all this talk of gratefulness. It wasn't what he wanted to hear. It was what she needed to say.

When the flock had receded into the distance, he finally spoke. "People grow up," he said. "Sometimes it doesn't happen until we're well into adulthood. But when it does, we often have to leave what we know in order to discover who we are. We have to find our way. Our own way." His smile was steadier now. It was his way of letting her go.

One more thing to be grateful to him about, she thought. He understood.

"I suppose you'll stop the divorce proceedings now," he said as they were walking back to the beach.

"I suppose." Claude had recommended she put off filing until Jay's estate was settled, but then more recently he'd urged her to initiate proceedings. It had been his idea to hold a party and announce their engagement, and of course, he'd wanted it to be official. Sophie hadn't understood the rush, but it had seemed important to him, so she'd agreed. It only made sense that she would stop the process now, or at least postpone it, if that could be done.

"Don't forget to pinch yourself," he told her gently. "Don't forget that, Sophie."

Sophie's throat stung unbearably as she looked up and saw his eyes sparkling with what might have been tears. Her very first session in therapy she'd described her dreams of Jay to him, and he'd given her some commonsense advice. "When you can't tell if you're awake or dreaming, pinch yourself. The pain is real. It will bring you back."

By the next session her wrist was black-and-blue, but the dreams had begun to recede. It was something a child could have told her, but Sophie hadn't thought of it.

"I won't forget," she said. "I promise."

She took his hand one last time, but there was no pressure in his grip, and that simply broke her heart. Impulsively she threw herself at him and gave him a hug. "I'm so sorry," she whispered. "You're the last person in the world I would ever want to hurt."

He hugged her back, suddenly, fiercely. "Just be all right," he told her.

"I will," she said. How could she not be? She had everything he'd given her. But over the call of the foghorns and the crash of the breakers, she heard his muted fear.

"I hope so, Sophie. God, I hope so."

4

Sophie could feel a scream building in her throat as they rounded a curve on the Harley and headed for the freeway exit. She hugged Jay hard and forcibly choked off the sound before it could escape, knowing that her reaction might be exactly what he secretly wanted. Whether she was on the back of a motorcycle or beneath him in bed, Jay Babcock had always loved to make her scream.

The burning bite of the wind blurred her vision and spiked her sense of disbelief. She could hardly fathom that she was on the back of a massive chopper, tearing down the southbound 405 at ninety-plus miles an hour and clinging to the man she had believed dead and gone from her life forever. Not even two weeks ago she was announcing her engagement and planning a future as if he no longer existed, except in the reaches of her memory. And now here he was, carrying her off on the back of his motorcycle, the same motorcycle he'd raised hell on as a kid.

Memories were whipping at her like the wind, and they almost terrified her. The speed did terrify her. He was going so fast the claw clip had been torn from her hair and golden tendrils flew wildly in the breeze, snapping against her flushed and tender skin. It stung a little, just as everything about him seemed to, but it was more exciting than painful.

The exit fell away like the vertical drop of a roller coaster, and she fought back another scream as they rocketed onto the street. She'd never liked carnival rides, which made her wonder why she'd agreed to this one.

He'd shown up at the rambler that morning with the bellowing beast they were riding on. They were going to revisit their past, he'd told her. That was the surprise, and he wanted to do it right, so he'd spent all morning making sure the bike would still run. Well, it ran. It certainly did.

"Everything okay back there?" he called out as they pulled up to an intersection.

"Fine," she lied. *You don't hear me screaming, do you?* "How much farther?" There was only one right answer to that question. If he didn't say they were almost there, she was calling a taxi. She had no idea where they were going, but walking was out of the question. She still had blisters from his reentry party.

He laughed and pressed his hand over hers, the one that was about to rip a new pocket in his denim shirt.

"Girls who are fine don't have white knuckles," he observed wryly. Lifting those same pale joints to his mouth, he kissed each one, and then returned her hand to its death grip on his clothing.

Sophie's stomach dipped and pitched as if they'd hit another exit.

"It's not far," he assured her. "Just another couple of miles down the road." The smile he flashed over his shoulder was as sexy as it was familiar. "Nothing can hurt you when you're with me, remember? We've got special dispensation."

Pain jostled her heart. It felt as if someone had carelessly bumped her in a crowd and moved on, but she couldn't stop the feeling. Even a sigh wouldn't release it. He'd always said that when they were off on one of their jaunts to the hinterlands, pursuing one crazy dream of his or another.

He'd claimed they were protected by the gods who watch over childhood sweethearts, and nothing could ever happen to them as long as they were in love and as long as they were together. It was his stock line when he wanted her to try something that frightened her, like riding donkeys up the side of a mountain instead of taking the tram like everyone else, or hang-gliding across the Grand Canyon, which she had done, to her utter astonishment, and found it close to a spiritual experience.

No, the Grand Canyon hadn't hurt her or the donkeys or any of the other adventures they'd had. It was Jay who'd proved dangerous to her well-being. It was her own husband who'd almost killed her with his unslaked wanderlust and his quest for the ultimate challenge.

As the years went by it became more and more apparent to Sophie that their relationship would never totally satisfy or fulfill him, and that had left her with a sense of inadequacy she didn't know how to resolve. Perhaps she shouldn't have taken it personally, but Jay was the center of her life and her love for him went so deep it defied description.

But so did the hurt go deep. He had told her they would be protected as long as they were together, and then he had gone away. *Lord, how that had hurt.*

In her heart she'd feared she wasn't enough for him and would never be enough, and that's what had nearly killed her—the pain of not having her feelings reciprocated. She had lost herself in Jay Babcock, ceased to exist. She couldn't let that happen again. She wouldn't let it happen.

Dirty Dan McCoy's was a South Orange County landmark with enough no-excuses panache to earn it a place of pride in Elmer Dill's *Meals Under Ten Bucks* restaurant guidebook. Open round the clock, the crumbling stucco tavern catered to the bad-ass biker crowd and anyone else with an acquired taste for greasy-spoon food, brew so ice-cold the 'tenders boasted it was flash-frozen, and a backroom pool hall, thick with blue haze.

Jay throttled down the rumbling Harley and pulled it into

a row of chrome and steel that glittered like a hall of mirrors. Sophie could see that he was going to fit right in as he cut the engine and swung off the shuddering machine.

Yup. Oh yes, he looked like a biker—born to raise hell— with his eye patch, the white T-shirt, already baptized with an oil smudge, and the snug stovepipe jeans that hugged his long rangy legs.

He also looked like a man who could do as much damage to a woman's heart as an F5 twister. And he could. She was the expert on that kind of storm. She'd even had a name for it once. She'd called it the "Jay Vortex" for the way it could suck you up like flotsam and fling you into beautiful, mindless oblivion.

"You okay?" It was a casual question, but the way he perused her features wasn't. His eyebrow slanted like a rifle sight, and the single indigo-blue iris crackled with a curiosity that subtly demanded satisfaction.

Apparently she couldn't even nod convincingly, because her attempt brought a skeptical smile to his lips. He didn't bother with the limp wrist she held out. Instead, he took matters into his own hands. Literally.

Sophie had already figured out what he was going to do. His body language gave her plenty of clues. And if she didn't say anything, it was simply because she couldn't believe it as he bent and scooped her up like a baby. His baby. His pretty baby. Hooked an arm under her knees and swept her right into his arms.

"What's this?" He hitched her closer, powerful biceps flexing against her thighs and shoulders, and gazed directly into her eyes. "Are you shaking? Or am I?"

"Maybe it's an earthquake." She laughed, but her throat was dry and it came out croaky. "Or you."

The humor faded from his expression, replaced by questions as he studied her. "Hey . . . you were really frightened, weren't you? Why didn't you tell me?"

He seemed sincere, which was probably the last response she expected. The old Jay would have tried to tease her out of her fears, a ploy that had never worked and only served to make her hide them away. This man appeared genuinely concerned, and though she was reserving judgment for now, it promised to be a welcome change.

This man?

Startled, she realized that she still didn't think of him as Jay. She was looking at Jay. She was in his arms. But *this man* wasn't her husband. She tried to shake the feeling off and make it vanish as it had yesterday, but it wouldn't go. It hung on and filled her with fear and awe. If he really wasn't Jay, then who in God's name—

He was right about her trembling. That was the only thing she knew for certain. An eruption shuddered from somewhere beyond her control, but she hadn't thought it noticeable, except for the unsteadiness in her hands.

"Easy now," he said, shifting so that she could rest her head in the hollow of his shoulder. "I've got you, and I'm on solid ground. Nobody's going anywhere until you're ready."

His voice was low, yet soothingly strong. She could feel the resonance in his chest, and it made her want to stay right where she was for a moment, warm and safe in his arms. Yet in many ways that seemed the most dangerous place she could possibly be.

Look out below! was the term she used to warn her kids of danger. She wished someone would shout that at her about now. It felt like she should be running for cover, but her fight-or-flight response didn't seem to be paying attention. As resolved as she was to protect herself in the clinches, some vulnerable part of her wanted to ignore all warnings and melt against him. Maybe because he felt as solid as the ground he stood on, and in every way a guy . . . and because it had been so long.

"We don't have to stay," he told her. "If this place frightens you, I can take you back."

"It isn't the place," she admitted. It wasn't even the bike ride, and he knew it.

It's you. It's always been you.

Their gazes collided in the ringing silence, and there was

a moment when it seemed as if that old cliché were true, that words really weren't necessary. With very little effort, their thoughts could have touched like fingertips. That was how it felt to Sophie, and before the image had passed, she had divined that he wanted to kiss her. She also knew that he wouldn't. That would have been too much. Even a casual brush of their lips might unlock everything, doors that were still bolted, shutters that weren't ready to be opened.

She could feel the bunch of his muscles as he settled her on her feet, but resisted a look to see if they were as unyielding as they felt. "You're sure you want to stay?"

"Of course," she said, and meant it. She bent and snapped down the legs of her tights, which she'd worn with a matching Malibu Gym tunic in a pale egg-wash yellow. She'd been told the color made her eyes even more strikingly green, but her real concern had been figure flaws. She wasn't ready to spring the well-rounded Sophie on him yet.

Aware that he was watching as she came back up, she smiled. "Nothing can hurt me while I'm with you, right?"

"That's my girl."

Sophie actually preened a little. It was an offhand remark, and she wouldn't have wanted him to know it, but she rather liked the hint of possessive pride in his voice. And when he dropped his hand to the small of her back and led her toward the tavern, her heart tilted with a silly smile. It was too late to let down her guard, she realized despairingly. He'd already sneaked around it.

One foot inside Dirty Dan's and Sophie knew she had lied about not being afraid of the place. The small bar's clientele was nearly all male and most of them bore a frightening resemblance to the flyers that hung on post-office walls.

"Bad idea," Jay said as heads began to turn and they became the object of intense scrutiny. "This place is worse than it used to be. I didn't think that was possible."

Sophie stepped away from him and was hauled back abruptly. He tucked her firmly in the curve of his arm, a gesture as casual as it was proprietary. The woman is mine, he was telling them. *Touch her, and I'll kill you with my bare hands.*

The conversation in the bar dropped to murmurs as the bikers continued to check them out. Clanking pans and the hot crackle of frying bacon could be heard coming from the kitchen. Other delicious smells wafted in, too—onions and ground chuck, pungent, peppery chili powder.

Sophie breathed in, remembering. That was why they'd come here years ago, after a movie or a ride on the bike— for the rich and spicy chili omelettes, smothered in melting drifts of sharp cheddar and sweet red Vidalias, chopped as fine as silver filigree.

"Mmmmm, smell that," she said.

Jay was still staring down the crowd. "There must be somewhere else we can get a chili omelette. Let's get out of here."

"No, let's stay."

"What?"

"I want to stay."

She ignored the pressure of his hand and wondered what he'd do if she actually resisted him. Pick her up and carry her out? That idea struck some sparks, but she really did want to stay. This place literally reeked of their past. There were so many touchstones, and she wanted to reexperience them with him. It might help her sort out some of her feelings.

"We used to play pool over there, remember?"

There was an actual beaded curtain separating the back room from the restaurant and bar, and through its glimmery strands, men could be seen, clustered around pool tables, drinking beer from tall, gleaming cans and sizing up their shots.

"I remember trying to teach you," he said. "You nearly changed my gender with the cue."

"Oh, that. That was an accident." *I meant to aim for your heart.* "I wonder if they still have the old nickelodeon." She grinned at him and searched the room again, ignoring the slitty stares of the bystanders. "I don't see it."

He pointed toward an alcove by the back door, and she let

out a little gasp of delight as she spotted the huge, boxy thing. What a kick if it still worked. Glowing red and decorated with rusting metal grace notes and octave signs on either side, it looked like the same gawdy machine they'd danced to for the very first time—and got themselves so hot and bothered they had to go out back in the alley and cool off.

It was the first time Sophie had ever let a boy get past first base, a milestone fraught with embarrassment because her knees had buckled and she'd nearly fallen when he slipped his hand inside her bra. She caught her lip between her teeth, thinking that it was impossible to be as flustered as she was that day. But this was close. The last thing she wanted now was to regress to adolescent swooning, but her heart took a funny turn, and when she looked at Jay again, her face was flushed with the memories.

His gaze darkened at the sight of her. "Yeah, let's stay," he said. "I'll fight every bastard in the place if I have to. You and I are staying."

Sophie silently thrilled to the raw force in his voice. It was a vestige of the old Jay, the man who was so quick to respond he could become aroused simply by brushing up against her. There was something utterly primitive in the declaration, too, but at the same time it was gallant and old-fashioned. And if that was corny, she hardly cared at the moment. She loved it.

The scrutiny continued as Jay led her to a booth on a far side of the room. If a man wanted a woman to cling to him, this was the place to bring her, Sophie thought. She was afraid to move from his side as he claimed an empty table right next to the alcove with the nickelodeon. If she could have, she would have been in his lap.

Fortunately, by the time a waitress appeared and they'd ordered their omelettes, the intense interest in them had waned, and most of the regulars had gone back to whatever they had been doing. Sophie was sitting with her back to the room. Jay had wanted it that way, apparently so that he could keep an eye on things. And as she watched him scoping out the place and possibly planning a counterattack should things get rough, she found herself shaking her head.

He'd raked a hand through his hair when they sat down, as if to tame the wildness and make himself presentable. But it was still a wind-tossed tumult, just the way she remembered. And his eyes. Blue black as a rainy night, with a ring of fire around the iris. Who had eyes like that but Jay?

His scent was different, though. Before, he'd always smelled of the outdoors, of pine trees and burning wood, a wild smell. Now he smelled of street sophistication, a cologne as cool and sharp as a barber's straight razor, expensive stuff that pricked the nostrils just a little, forcing you to draw it in deeper.

But this was Jay, and suddenly she knew it. Her Jay, even down to the mole near the corner of his lip. The shock of recognition made her slide back in the booth.

"What is it?" he asked.

"You look so much like him, I guess you must *be* him, right?"

A slight frown covered what must have been surprise. "You're still not sure, are you?"

"Sometimes I'm not. Sometimes I don't have any idea who you are."

He settled back to consider that, his coffee cup cradled in his palms and a quiet, brooding kind of energy pouring off him in waves. She didn't know what to call the energy but masculinity. He was the most effortlessly masculine man she'd ever encountered, and she would not necessarily have said that of the old Jay. Maybe it was an illusion caused by the eye patch, but she didn't think so. The old Jay was brash, impulsive, and passionate. This man was none of those things. Or if he was, he kept them well hidden.

She felt it the moment he looked up. Intensity. That sense that he wanted to know everything about her, unmask her, when they both knew it was *his* identity that was in question.

"Do you want me to be him?" he asked.

She hardly had to think about her answer, and that made her mouth go dry with apprehension. She wanted predictability, didn't she? She longed for a man she could count on, one who would make her feel safe and loved. How many years had she been the woman Jay Babcock came home to, nothing more than his port in a storm?

Her fingers rubbed across some figures scratched into the tabletop. They drew her attention, and she began to trace their spiny edges like braille. It was letters—writing—but she couldn't make out what they said.

"Do you?" he pressed.

He wasn't going to let her hide.

"I think so, yes," she said softly. But once she'd made the admission, she found it almost impossible to look up at him. And when she did, finally, because she had to, he raised his coffee cup in a mock toast.

"I'll see what I can do." Irony brought out the huskiness in his voice.

She didn't know what to say to that. Or how to be the object of such intensity. She never had been before, not like this, and it was so . . . confusing. There was a rush of reaction in her chest, of something skittering like rain against a tile roof. Her pulse?

The carved letters were still there, under her fingers. They felt graceful suddenly, the only thing that did. She began to trace them again.

" 'String me—' " she said, trying to read them. " 'String me along.' What does that mean?"

He stared at her for a long time, not answering, not interested in her silly words. The pupil of his visible eye had shrunk to a dot that was nearly indistinguishable from the iris, and the effect was startling. It was ringed in icy white, like an eclipse of the moon.

"Wallis said you were engaged." He set the coffee cup down and brought his hands up, clasping them in a way that shielded the lower half of his face. "Claude, is that his name?" At her nod, he asked, "Do you love him?"

"Not the kind of love you're thinking about."

"What kind of love am I thinking about?"

Something about the tone of his voice and the force of his stare made her uneasy. Frightening would not have been too strong a word. Her palms were damp against the tabletop. This was the subject in which he obviously had a consuming personal interest. She wasn't sure it was safe to answer the question.

"The friendly kind," she said. "It had more to do with companionship than . . ."

"Sex?"

He wanted to know if his sweet little Sophie had made love with another man. That was what this interrogation was about, she realized, one male wondering if another had encroached on his "territory." And by the expression on his face, he brought to his question the darkest of male suspicions.

The waitress appeared out of nowhere, plunked their omelettes in front of them, and rushed off, leaving an awkward silence in her wake.

"Never mind," Jay said, ignoring the food in favor of his coffee. He had the mug in both hands again and was rubbing the handle with his thumb. "It's none of my business."

Sophie considered her coffee and decided her nerves didn't need any more stimulation.

"Claude and I were very close," she said finally. "It was an intimate relationship in every way . . . but that one."

"I see."

A faint smile appeared, and Sophie couldn't help herself. She smiled, too, then rolled her eyes. Men. That was all he needed to know apparently.

His mood wasn't the only thing improved. Watching him dive into his omelette with animal hunger, Sophie knew she'd been wrong in thinking he wasn't passionate. He ate like a man who'd been starved, reminding her that she still didn't know the details of his prison ordeal. She wanted to know all of it, especially what had happened to his eye, but she wasn't going to press for that information now. Maybe if things worked out between them, he would tell her. Or perhaps Wallis would share what she knew.

The rich, meaty steam that rose off her chili made Sophie's mouth water, but she was too absorbed in watching him to eat. In her fascination with his appetite, she'd completely missed a more subtle difference, the way he held his silverware.

"Jay, you're a lefty, aren't you?" When he looked up, she said, "Left-handed?"

She watched him stop and stare at the hand that held the fork, his right hand, and alarm stirred within her. He was reacting like a man who'd been caught. Jay Babcock *was* left-handed. There was no doubt in her mind about that. She'd known him since she was fifteen, and in some ways probably better than he knew himself.

He switched the fork to the other hand and stabbed a wedge of eggs. As he popped the food into his mouth and began to chew, he gave her a shrug. "Looks like I'm ambidextrous," he said softly.

She could hardly hear him over the chaos in her head. "Since when?"

"As long as I can remember. I'm surprised *you* don't remember, Sophie. I was forced to use my right hand when I fractured my arm in the car accident." He nodded at her plate. "Your omelette's getting cold."

She collected her silverware and dutifully ate several bites, but her stomach wouldn't allow any more than that. He was talking about an accident they'd had while they were dating, one that had totaled his prized Mustang convertible. It made sense that he would have had to use his right hand while he was recovering, but she couldn't remember seeing him favor it after that, certainly not to eat.

"I guess I'm done," she said, hesitating as if she were waiting for him to concur. "I *am* done."

He didn't seem to have heard her. Something across the room had caught his attention, and suddenly he was standing.

"Jay? Is something wrong?"

"No," he assured her. "Everything's fine, but wait here for me, would you, Sophie? I'll be right back."

He headed in the direction of the entrance, and Sophie assumed that he was either going to use the rest room or pay the bill. With a quick glance around to make sure she wasn't noticed, she slipped from the booth and casually wandered over to the nickelodeon. She was curious if the old music box still had any of the songs they'd danced to that night.

Someone came up behind her as she was reading through the selections. The edgy scent of his cologne told her it was Jay, yet he said nothing, and the longer they stood in silence, the more she expected some sort of contact. She couldn't imagine what he was waiting for, except that she might turn. But that possibility had too much seductive appeal.

He moved in closer and reached around her, a quarter in his hand. She watched him slip the coin in the slot and punch a button on the selection menu. The song he selected had been a huge hit when they were dating, and one they'd both loved. As the ballad started to play Sophie smiled and swayed her shoulders.

"If you were to turn around," he said, "we could dance."

He was crowding her now, giving her the fleeting contact she'd been waiting for, and more. Something hot and hard came up against the curve of her hip, and her stomach fluttered sharply. His body had answered her question. *He could become aroused just by brushing up against her.*

Every inch, she thought. He was every inch as effortlessly virile as she remembered. The gush of dampness in her underwear startled and embarrassed her. She had always responded to him this way, with a swift rush of longing that matched his own. Her body knew he was Jay. It was her mind that couldn't decide.

"If I were to turn around," she informed him, "we could make tracks and leave."

"Why don't you turn around . . . and we'll see what happens."

"I really think we should go." She wheeled and faced him, quite serious about that. Men so loved having the upper hand that he was probably enjoying the fact that she was off balance.

"What's the rush?" he wanted to know.

"Well . . . it's the breakfast hour, if you'll notice. No one else is dancing, and this is a biker bar. We'd probably start a riot.''

She had other reasons, too, plenty of them, but when he brought his hand out from behind his back and she saw what he was holding, all she could do was stare at him, blink at him.

It was a black baseball cap with a Dirty Dan's insignia.

''A man's entitled to forget everything when he's with Sophie Weston, the girl with the pensive smile,'' he told her. ''Even whether he's right- or left-handed. That's a law of nature.''

God, he was good. She wanted to close her eyes and sigh with dismay he was so good.

He smoothed her hair back in preparation for the crowning, but finally despaired of catching the golden scatter around her face. When he had the cap settled on her head, he scooped her long tresses through the opening in the back and then snugged everything down tight.

''You wanted one of these the last time we came here,'' he explained. ''You said it would keep the wind from whipping your hair, but I didn't have any money. I'd just bought the bike and blown every cent I had on it.''

She'd wanted the silly thing desperately, even pouted when he wouldn't buy it for her.

His voice went hushed, husky. ''Sorry it took so long.''

He tilted her chin up, and Sophie couldn't help herself. Her heart was as tight and full as a balloon about to pop. She knew her teary smile must look quite ridiculous. ''We can't dance now,'' she said inanely. ''You'll mess up my hat.''

''I wasn't thinking about dancing.''

In the shadows of the alcove, his gaze was even darker than before, and the silvery corona created an eerie hypnotic quality. The odd little tug in the pit of her stomach was awe. Her mind was caught up in the puzzle of his identity, but her body was caught up in a very different kind of mystery. It burned with the memory of how he'd felt when he brushed against her. Burned to know what he would feel like inside her—

The sensation in her belly flared sharply. It was a leash tugging at her vitals, bringing her to a halt.

Her mind flooded with questions, but her body only wanted to know one thing. What would it be like if they made love? What would he be like? She had no doubt of this man's seductive power. But would he be so meltingly tender she couldn't breathe? Would he thrill her to her soul and leave her in a heap?

Would he be like Jay?

Dangerous thoughts, she realized, staring up at him and wondering if she would forever be fifteen with this man. She was an adult woman now. She'd outgrown these feelings, exorcized them like demons, and in doing so, had empowered herself. She wanted to meet him on level ground, but nothing about this meeting felt level, especially the ground.

"You weren't thinking about dancing?" she managed.

"No, but if you're worried about losing your hat, we'd better not do what I had in mind either."

She flushed and he smiled. Impossible. This was impossible. God, she felt silly. God, she felt wonderful.

"Well?" He meant the hat. "Do you like it?"

She made a face. "Nah."

"Then what *would* you like?" he asked, pretending to be crestfallen.

The lump that filled her throat kept her from answering. And she wouldn't have dared tell him what was going through her mind anyway. Dangerous. Too dangerous. *Much.*

I want you to be him, she thought. I want that so much. If there are gods who watch over childhood sweethearts, if they really exist, then they'll grant me this one wish. They must. It's the only thing I'll ever ask for. Please be Jay Babcock.

5

Jay lunged up and kick-started the engine, bringing the Harley alive with a ferocious burst. Sophie gingerly settled herself on the hot seat behind him, aware of the vibrations that throbbed deep in the heart of its leather contours. The irony of "Soapy, the day-care lady" as a biker's mama did not escape her as she placed her feet on the chrome footrests and dropped back against the sissy bar.

"Grab hold," Jay cautioned, revving the engine.

Wouldn't I love to, she thought, eyeing the back pockets of his shrunk-to-fit jeans and wondering how in the world a person was supposed to get her hands in there. Sophie stayed where she was, mulling over that intriguing possibility as the bike rumbled and jerked forward.

"You ready?" he asked, glancing over his shoulder.

She tapped the brim of her hat. *Ready for anything*.

His fleeting smile confirmed that it was the right answer.

Gravel churned and spat as he pulled the chopper out of the lot and onto the highway. The power that shook the bike surged through her, too, energizing her. She could see why men liked these big machines. It brought them into intimate contact with the energy source. The bike roared out its primacy over the highway, and they silently roared, too. Man and beast were one.

"Hang on!" he called back.

"I am." She was hanging on to her hat.

Suddenly the world careened in a dizzying spin. Roadside trees tilted at crazy angles and the ground rolled up in waves, a concrete ocean. Sophie let out a little yelp and hooked her fingers in Jay's waistband as he wheeled the bike around and headed back the way they came, toward the tavern.

"Did we forget something?" she shouted.

His answer was a nod. But he didn't pull into the parking lot when they reached Dirty Dan's. Instead, he drove around the back of the tavern and barreled down the alley. The narrow corridor magnified the deafening noise of the engine and rocked it back and forth like thunder in a canyon. Sophie feared they were going to shake the old building down to its foundation.

Finally the bike shuddered and went silent.

"What are we doing here?" she asked.

"I wanted to see if it was still there." He pointed to a sign they had defaced in their wild and reckless youth.

Actually, Sophie herself had done it with a nail file, which probably surprised Jay as much as it had her. She'd told him it was all his fault, that she'd been driven to desperate measures by his "unseemly behavior." But he'd just snarled softly under his breath and silenced her with a kiss.

The sign had originally said NO LOITERING ALLOWED, but to keep Jay from getting amorous, she'd hastily changed the four middle letters to a *V*.

"No loving allowed," she'd informed him primly, adding that she was a good girl who *always* followed the rules.

He'd swiped her file and scratched out the first word. "Let's see you follow those rules."

She'd kissed him back that night, slipped her tongue in his mouth, and let him do much worse to her. She could vividly remember his hand in the heat of her panties and his palm curved to the red-gold thatch between her legs. He'd cupped her firmly, rubbed her until she moaned for mercy, and then attempted to delve deeper, eliciting the sweet little scream that had seemed to bewitch him ever since.

It was the sound of a young woman in sexual flower—urgent and throaty and fever-pitched, yet soft as an unbreathed sigh. There had been something wild going on inside Sophie that night, and she hadn't been able to stop it . . . or him.

"You dared me," she said now, as if that could explain her behavior.

He swung his leg over the bike and shifted around, sidesaddle. "And you took the dare." He glanced at her, his voice a grainy reminder of their passion.

"Defacing public property is a criminal act."

Her knee was pressed up against the outside of his thigh, and he seemed to be studying the possibilities of that connection. After a moment he began to trace the inseam of her jeans with his forefinger.

So like Jay, she thought. Whenever he'd paid visits to what he referred to as his "favorite places," he'd seemed totally absorbed by the terrain, whether it was her wrist, her collarbone, or the curves that graced her cheeks and her brow.

Sophie found his touch wildly arousing, especially since he'd never hurried or turned it into a prelude to sex. That wasn't the point. Touching her was all he wanted at those times. He seemed to derive a satisfaction from it that was unusual for a man, yet wholly masculine.

"Not kissing you would have been a criminal act," he said.

"A young girl's downfall," she murmured, remembering the darkness of the alley and the way the moon had sheened his hair and made the fire dance in his eyes.

"Who . . . me?"

"Most definitely you, Jay Babcock."

"I thought it was the other way around, that you were leading me astray with those sexy noises you make."

His hand dropped away, and she felt the loss of contact

instantly. Her belly tightened with yearning. Don't stop, she thought. Don't take it away, this little taste of heaven you give me.

"Do you regret what we did?" he asked.

She shook her head, but it was mostly for show. "I think I fell in love with you that night," she admitted.

"Then I must have done something right."

His thumb began its hypnotic dance again, stroking rhythmically, back and forth in a short arc against the inside of her knee. The path it burned along her inseam shot straight to her loins and made her wonder what she would have been allotted if moral character were handed out like goods in a supermarket. A box of cornmeal mush? How was it that he could set her thoughts ablaze by doing next to nothing?

She was still waiting for a response. To admit love, even when you were referring to the past, was to leave yourself wide open to rejection. Jay had gone quiet. Worse, he'd turned away and was staring down the alley with the air of a man whose mind was somewhere else. Typical of Jay Babcock, she thought. There for dinner, gone for the dishes.

"We should go," she said sharply. "We're blocking the alley. What if there's an emergency?"

He angled her a look that said, What's the problem, little girl? Apparently he wasn't fond of being dictated to in that tone, which was just fine with her. He hadn't heard anything yet.

"Spoken just like a good girl? One who always follows the rules?"

Now he was making fun of her. Air jetted from Sophie's nostrils. "Don't be too sure about that."

She couldn't tell if it was passion or more of his egotistical male need to have the upper hand, but he caught hold of her T-shirt and pulled her toward him. She was sorely tempted to give him a fight. Oh, yes, she was. He seemed to value only what had to be conquered and won, and she had surrendered without a whimper all those years ago.

"So . . . what is it? Good girl or bad?" Gathering a wad

of her shirt into his fists, he pulled the material tight against her spine.

She would have loved to give him the answer he deserved, but contented herself with a dismissive sniff. There was something dangerously predatory in the way he was holding her, even in the way he looked at her. Maybe this wasn't the time to put her head in the lion's mouth. She was angry, but that didn't mean she had to be reckless.

And yet, she *was* angry.

"I'm waiting," he said softly.

"Waiting's good for you. Builds character."

His lip curled at the corner, soft and sultry, but more snarl than smile. The low rattle in his throat sent a weird thrill rocketing through Sophie. He sounded as if he were going to eat her alive. She ought to be holding him off. That much was clear, but some part of her couldn't quite believe any of this was happening. It felt like one of her dreams of him. One of her *sexier* dreams.

"Good . . . or bad?"

"You figure it out—"

A sharp tug silenced her. His mouth came down on hers with breathtaking force, jumbling the words in her head. It was a hard, sweet, drowning kiss. A ship would have sunk beneath its weight. Sophie moaned softly, mostly from shock. Her eyelids fluttered and drooped. But even as she spiraled downward some stunned part of her mind struggled to detach.

This wasn't happening.

He moved over her, pressing down, and she felt as if she were a swimmer being held under water and suffocated in some sublime way. No, this could not be real. She must be dreaming.

"Good," she gasped weakly, the second he let her up for air. "I'm a good—" Her head was swimming, and she hardly knew what she was saying. But he knew.

"And whose good girl are you?" He ground the words out against her teeth. "Whose, Sophie?"

Yours. Only yours.

She hadn't thought she'd said the words, but he emitted a

harsh, triumphant sound. "Finally, the right fucking answer."

He tilted her head back, stroking her mouth with his.

Sophie's sigh was as full of despair as it was surrender. She had no idea what was real and what wasn't. Who was real. Some instinct told her it was hopeless to try to decipher fact from fantasy. It all felt delusional, but what frightened her, dream or not, was the awareness that she hadn't been able to hold him off. She hadn't even tried. He was too overwhelming. He shocked her into wanting his rough kisses and his tender hands. He made her want to be swept like a clinging leaf into the vortex.

He lifted her to him and his hands began to work her clothing, drawing up the T-shirt, sliding against her skin. A groan broke low in his throat. Sophie could hear it, feel it. *That was real.* He wanted her. He might have undressed her right there in the alley if the creak and thump of a door hadn't stopped him. It slammed shut behind them, and Jay was instantly alert.

He turned, shielding her with his body.

His arms went out protectively, but Sophie craned around him and saw the tall, barrel-chested man who'd just come out of Dirty Dan's the back way. His long, kinky black hair was gray at the temples and flowed down his back in a ponytail that looked like it might reach the small of his back. He had tattoos everywhere, even his neck. Snakes and flowers. He looked like the Garden of Eden.

Sophie's first thought was that he was a bouncer who was going to tell them to get out of the alley. But the way he stared at Jay made her wonder.

He propped his massive hands on his hips, his head cocked. "Don't I know you from somewhere, buddy?"

"I'm not your buddy. And no, you don't know me from anywhere."

The veiled menace in Jay's voice startled Sophie. She knew instinctively that there was some threat, but she didn't understand what it was. All the other man had done was ask a question. He didn't seem to be looking for a fight.

"Jay?" she said softly.

"Quiet," he bit out.

Sophie froze as Jay swung his leg back over the bike, grounded himself, then hit the kickstand hard with his heel. As it flew up he brought his foot down with violent force.

The engine caromed angrily.

"Hey, wait a minute," the biker called over the noise. "I do know you. You're—"

Jay cranked the accelerator, and the Harley raised a deafening clatter, drowning the man out.

"Jay!" Sophie cried.

"Hang on and don't let go!" he shouted at her.

This time she knew better than to ignore him. Something was terribly wrong. She grabbed his shirt and the bike bucked and quivered. The engine screamed like a banshee.

"Hold on a fucking minute—" Glowering, the other man flung out an arm as if to block their passage.

A glint of steel flashed in the sun, but Sophie couldn't make out what it was. A cry locked in her throat as the Harley shot forward, barreling straight at the biker.

"Jay, no! Jay, you're going to hit him!"

She shrank down and buried herself in Jay's shirt, anticipating the impact. At such short range, there was no way to miss him, and her senses were already shrieking. She could hear the crunch of bones, the screams of pain. She could see crushed limbs, bodies. What in God's name was he doing? Had he gone insane or was she caught in some kind of nightmare?

She was still huddled and moaning softly, horrified, as they rocketed down the alley. Back entrances and trash cans flew by, but it was a moment before she realized they hadn't hit anything. There had been no collision. She glanced behind them and saw the biker standing in the middle of the alley, waving his fist.

The relief she felt barely registered before shock and disbelief engulfed her. She'd been told that Jay would need ongoing therapy, but no one had said anything about violence. She wouldn't have believed him capable of this. He *wasn't* capable. Her husband—the man she'd loved and lived with—

could never have run down a defenseless man.

As they reached the end of the alley he hit the brakes and skidded into a turn. The bike wheeled and banked sharply, leaving smoking strips on the pavement. Burned rubber sent up an acrid stench, and the force of the wind whipped her cap off. Sophie choked back a sob.

"Something is wrong, Wallis. He's not acting like Jay. There are times when I don't even know who he is."

"Darling!" Her mother-in-law reached across the table and clasped Sophie's hand firmly. "Don't be silly," she chided. "Have some tea now. It will do wonders, I promise, and once you've composed yourself, I'll tell you all about your Jay and set your fears to rest . . . all right?"

Sophie reached for the bone-china teapot, but Wallis got there first. With steadiness worthy of a safecracker, she dangled the sterling tea strainer over Sophie's cup and poured the fragrant brew through it.

"Rosy Posy, dear. It's marvelous. Have you tried it?"

Sophie hadn't, and she couldn't imagine how tea floating with stems, bark, and rose petals was going to settle her nerves. But she'd urgently needed to talk with her mother-in-law, and she hadn't wanted to do it at the Big House, where Jay might overhear. Wallis, who rarely went out, had chosen this place, the McCharles House, for their meeting, and Sophie doubted the quaint Victorian tea parlor served anything much stronger than hot rose petals.

"One usually pours the milk in first," Wallis remarked as Sophie doctored her drink with a splash of tepid milk and the rainbow sugar crystals that were traditionally served at this establishment.

Sophie didn't realize she was angry until she had the cup halfway to her mouth, and it was all she could do not to slam it to the table. Had everyone gone mad? Her alleged husband—and Wallis's son—had nearly run down a man that very morning. He'd risked both their lives with his reckless driving, and now Wallis was acting like Sophie was the one deranged?

"Tea, dear. Drink."

Sophie held the delicate cup with both hands and drank deeply, well aware that that wasn't how one did it. She'd swilled down nearly half the Rosy Posy, or whatever it was called, before she realized that the rich, darkish concoction was actually delicious, lightly and sweetly perfumed with flower petals, and every bit as soothing as Wallis had promised.

"Better now?" Wallis asked as Sophie settled back in the chair. "I was right, wasn't I? And isn't this place lovely?"

Wallis gestured grandly, and Sophie dutifully glanced around the patio, where they were sitting. Yes, the place was lovely. And so were the patrons, many of them decked out in the hats, gloves, and lacy finery of another era. Even the latticework fences bordering the patio were dressed in their best—pink climbing roses and magenta bougainvillea, nature's finery.

Wallis had worn a white silk slacks outfit with silver trim that brought out the dramatic gray streaks in her dark hair. And she'd never looked better. Sophie felt quite plain in her navy cotton jumpsuit, but that wasn't the immediate problem. It had become painfully obvious that her mother-in-law was trying to distract her.

"Wallis," she said abruptly, "Jay is left-handed, isn't he?"

Wallis carefully settled her cup in the saucer. "They serve champagne here, Sophie. Did I mention that? Would you like some?"

"No, thank you. *Is* he left-handed?"

"What an odd question. Why do you ask?"

Sophie briefly explained what had happened that morning at Dirty Dan's, including the incident at breakfast. "When I saw the fork in his right hand, I knew something was wrong."

Wallis gazed off, thinking. Her index finger tapped the table. "As I remember, he used both hands for his rock climbing. Yes, I think he did. What do they call that? Ambidextrous?"

"Wallis, I was married to him for five years. Jay was left-handed."

"Darling, I gave birth to him and raised him from the cradle." She laughed and jingled her bracelet, singling out Jay's charm. "I had this one made after he was born, but then you know that. I do go on about him, don't I?"

Sophie felt a familiar twinge. At times it was difficult hearing Wallis talk about her boys because it reminded Sophie that she'd been the illegitimate child no one wanted. All she knew of her humble beginnings was that her mother, a fourteen-year-old runaway, had been found dead in a gas-station rest room with Sophie in her arms. The girl had hemorrhaged after giving birth, and Sophie had been reluctantly taken in by her aunt, who wasn't much older than the dead sister. Sophie had been forced to raise herself. She'd had no real family at all until she came to live with the Babcocks at fourteen. But even that had happened under such unusual circumstances no one ever spoke of it.

"Yes, I do think Jay is ambidextrous," Wallis said, breaking into Sophie's thoughts. "Don't you remember how he used to throw the Frisbee with his dog, first one hand and then the other?"

Even if the waitress hadn't arrived with their tea sandwiches at that moment, Sophie would have conceded the argument. It was possible Jay had some latent ability for either handedness that she'd never noticed—or didn't remember. At any rate it hardly mattered right now.

"Oh, my, try the chocolate sandwich," Wallis gurgled, holding up a small triangle that appeared to be filled with chocolate chips and preserves. She'd already taken a delicate bite. "You'll love the bread. It's cinnamon raisin."

Sophie looked over the finger sandwiches and knew she ought to be hungry. She hadn't eaten that morning either, but the thought of a *chocolate* sandwich made her nearly ill. Her stomach was churning, and Wallis's bright banter was only making it worse.

"Do you know what Jay said when he left me off at the house?" She leaned into the table, hoping to get through to her mother-in-law. "He said he was sorry if he'd frightened me, that he thought the man was going for a knife. Just that— 'I'm sorry if I frightened you, Sophie.' I asked him who the man was and Jay swore he'd never seen him before."

Sophie pushed her plate away untouched. "It doesn't make sense, Wallis. Very little of what happened this morning makes sense. It felt like a bad dream."

Suddenly her mother-in-law was serious. She was leaning into the table as well, speaking in a hush, and her blue eyes had sharpened until they were piercing. Sophie was reminded of Jay, although he'd never had the Babcock-blue eyes. His were much darker.

"Exactly, Sophie," Wallis insisted. "It was like a bad dream, and you're not thinking clearly yet. Jay only did what any man would do if he believed the woman he loved was in danger. If he went to extremes, it was to protect you. For heaven's sakes, Sophie, that man in the alley had a weapon."

"I didn't see a weapon." Sophie had seen a flash of silver that she'd thought was steel, but it could have been a watchband.

"Your husband has been through a terrible ordeal," Wallis went on, "and we all need to make some allowances for that. There are things he'll never be able to tell us because he can't bring himself to talk about them."

Sophie felt as if she were being scolded, and perhaps she was. "Yes, of course," she started, but got no further. Wallis was determined to make her point, and Sophie hadn't seen her this adamant in years. This was the old Wallis, the powerhouse. There was no sign of the crippling emotional fragility.

"Of course there will be problems," Wallis acknowledged. "The doctors admitted that. 'Adjustment problems,' I think they called them, and acting out aggression is one of the symptoms of delayed stress. But he would never hurt you, Sophie. You do realize that, don't you? Jay adores you."

Her tone had changed subtly, Sophie realized. Now it was coaxing and cajoling.

"This new drug sounds as if it's going to do wonders,"

she went on. "Wonders, Sophie, for Jay and for the company. But Jay will need support through this, from all of us, and especially from you. Please try, darling. He has a big job ahead of him."

Sophie wished she could be supportive. She didn't want to let any of them down, but there was so much she still didn't understand. "If you mean running Babcock," she said, "how do you know Jay wants the job? He's never had any interest in that. Noah begged him to start preparing himself to take the reins years ago, and he refused."

Flower petals floated down from the trees that shaded them, and a waitress hovered nearby, waiting to heat up their tea. Wallis waved her away impatiently.

"Jay is not the same man, Sophie. He's endured a lot, and it's matured him. Once he's gone through this period of adjustment, I think you'll see very clearly that he's capable of a full and wonderful relationship."

"Wallis . . ." She didn't know how to ask the question, but it had to be done. She couldn't rest otherwise. "You said he was a different man. Isn't it possible that this man who came back isn't Jay? That he's trying to pass for Jay."

A sharp shake of Wallis's head said that was nonsense. "I know my son," she insisted. "There's no doubt in my mind. And if there's any in yours, the tests will lay it to rest. Jay will be going through the full battery—blood and DNA typing, fingerprinting. No expense will be spared to verify his identity."

"Tests? Is that necessary?"

"I'm afraid so. If Jerry White doesn't insist on it, the board will. Fortunes are at stake here, Sophie. Careers. Futures. There are people who don't want to see Jay take over, a fair number, unfortunately. They'll try to prove him incompetent and they'll question his stability, anything to prevent his succession."

Jay was being tested, and Wallis seemed supremely confident of the outcome. That should have reassured Sophie, except that she was dealing with an intuitive feeling that no test could address, and the feeling persisted that something was wrong. Only she was beginning to wonder if it was with her, not Jay.

Wallis might be certain he was her son, but the man who'd come back still felt like a stranger to Sophie. There had been moments when she so desperately wanted to believe he was Jay that she would have done anything, forced her doubts away and lived in denial in order to realize her dreams of happiness with him. But something held her back, and maybe it was her own fear of being hurt again. Maybe she really didn't want him to be Jay so she wouldn't have to love him.

"Sometimes he frightens me, Wallis," she admitted after a moment. "He's different than before, so intense and focused. Haven't you noticed that? The way he looks at you, as if he were a burning glass and you a flimsy scrap of paper, about to ignite."

"I suspect that's the eye patch, don't you? I find it attractive."

Sophie did, too, very attractive, but there were times when she felt as if he were spying on her inner life. "It sounds crazy, but he seems to know more about me than he could possibly know, even if he were Jay, thoughts and feelings, things I'm barely in touch with myself. He's more like the Jay who came to me in the dreams than the one who vanished."

She dropped back in the chair, embarrassed. "You must think I'm going off the deep end again."

"No, darling, not at all. He *has* changed. No one would dispute that. But what you're describing doesn't sound so bad. Most wives would love their husbands to be so involved and attentive."

She reached over as if to take Sophie's hand and then smiled instead. Her napkin was crumpled alongside her plate, and she began to fold it, smoothing the wrinkles out of it.

"Be careful," she whispered suddenly.

Sophie sat forward, wondering if she'd heard her mother-in-law correctly, but Wallis had turned to get the waitress's attention and she was waving the napkin at her. There was little point in asking what she'd meant, Sophie suspected. Wallis would not tell her the truth.

Her mother-in-law had withdrawn into her own world of silence and whispers after she lost Noah and Jay. She'd closed out everyone, including Sophie. Only El was allowed admittance to that world, and their relationship had grown symbiotically close. Sophie had been hurt at first, especially when Wallis asked her to stop visiting Noah at the rest home. Sophie had always loved the stern old man who was so instrumental in her having a home with the Babcocks, and though his deterioration was profound and painful to see, she'd looked forward to the visits.

But Wallis had insisted they were upsetting to Noah, and Sophie would never have gone against her mother-in-law's wishes. But it had made her wonder why Wallis was so mysteriously guarded. Even years afterward, she'd refused to talk about the tragedies.

We are all hoarders, Sophie thought. We clutch close the thing that allows us to feel special and fulfilled. For her it was keepsakes. For Claude it was his nautical treasures. Sophie wasn't sure what Jay hoarded now, but once it had been adrenaline rushes. Muffin hoarded love in the form of food. And then there was Wallis. Her mother-in-law hoarded secrets.

Everywhere Claude Laurent looked there was a hulking skeleton of a man looking back at him. The glass bookcases, the windows of his office, even the shiny plaques on his walls bounced his reflection. He couldn't get away from himself or the glaring physical evidence of who he was. It was everywhere, freakish.

In grade school the little girls had darted around him like fireflies, calling him names and scampering away. They'd laughed and shrieked when he chased them, a sad game that had made him feel like some kind of monster. But he had never felt more like a monster than he had these last two weeks.

Men with his academic credentials didn't believe that love

could miraculously and swiftly transform people. That was the stuff of novels. Therapy was a slow process, taking months, and in some cases, years. And yet her love had transformed him. Absurd as that sounded, it was somehow true. She had kissed a frog and created a prince.

What was he now that she was gone?

Prince? Frog? Or monster?

"Ahh—" A bubble of blood appeared on the tip of his forefinger. Startled, he let the syringe he'd been trying to fill clatter into the steel sink. He'd pricked himself with the needle.

"Dr. L-Laurent?"

"I'll be right there, Mary."

The fear and hesitation in his patient's voice brought Claude back sharply. She was a new intake and severely agitated. Based on the history she'd given him and her responses to his questions, he'd already begun to suspect that he was dealing with a multiple-personality disorder. He'd persuaded her to let him conduct a sodium-amytal interview, but he'd neglected to tell her that the barbiturate was the popular "truth serum" of television dramas. In fact, the interview was as likely to reveal fantasy as truth, but at least it would give him a glimpse of the workings of her subconscious.

"Comfortable?" he asked. He reassured her with a fatherly smile as he tossed the contaminated syringe away and got a sterile one from the cabinet. A slender schoolteacher in her late twenties, she was lying on the recliner that he used for much of the work he did, which included hypnosis as well as the interview he was about to conduct.

She gave him a stiff nod that screamed what she couldn't say. She was frightened of him and whatever he might be about to do, but she was more afraid of herself and the way her mind and body were running away with her. She felt crazy and hopeless, a lost cause, which was why she was allowing herself to be drugged and subjected to what some considered the equivalent of psychic rape. It was the lesser of two evils.

Claude knew this because he had worked with so many

like her. He was known for taking on cases no one else could
help, and his success rate was high because he went far beyond the limits of conventional therapy. Nothing unethical,
of course, just hands-on, involved, round-the-clock care when
that was necessary.

Most of his small client load had been abused as children
and virtually all had been deprived of the nurturing required
to thrive. They needed reparenting in the form of uncondi-
tional love and acceptance, and they needed it more fre-
quently and consistently than fifty-two minutes a week, the
"psychiatric hour."

Claude's ritual at the end was to give his patients a Saint
Jude's medal, Saint Jude being the patron saint of lost causes.
Regardless of the patient's religion, they all understood the
symbolism of the gift.

Sophie had understood it. Now that she was well, she was
moving on, leaving him as they all did eventually. That was
the ultimate goal of therapy, and though he always felt pangs
when the birds flew the nest, his sense of pride and accom-
plishment far outweighed any feelings of loss. Except with
her. With her it was wrenching. He was struggling to let her
go just as she'd had to let Jay go, and sadly, there was an
even darker irony involved. He had saved her from Jay Babcock only to give her back to him.

Fighting to control the unsteadiness in his hands, he dou-
ble-checked the syringe's scale to make sure the dosage was
correct. He'd had no choice but to bow out of Sophie's life
immediately and wish her well. It was the only thing he could
have done, given who he was. But the gesture had cost him
more than anyone could possibly know. Or would ever know.

Thank God he had people who needed him, people like
Mary.

His new patient managed a smile when he joined her, but
her hand was icy cold in the warmth of his. "Mary, do I
frighten you?" he asked. "Because it's important that you
feel safe with me, that you trust me, as we go through this."

He saw her release a breath and knew that she had just let

go of the safety rail. He would be her support now, her guide, and her bridge to a new life. She would cling to him like a drowning woman, and he would have to be strong enough to keep them both afloat. But maybe he needed that as much as she did.

"Good," he said, "good, Mary. Think of me as a lifeguard. I can save you, but only if you let me."

She flinched when he injected her. He still couldn't manage his hands, and he'd inadvertently hurt her. But the drug would take away all the pain. For a time it would miraculously free her from agitation and give her the peace of mind she longed for. It would also flush out the secrets her psyche was hiding, even from her.

Claude's beeper signal went off as he was about to begin the interview. He thought about ignoring it, but many of his patients suffered depression, and twilight was the time when they were at their lowest. He'd saved lives by being responsive.

The remote was in his sweater pocket. He fished it out and brought up the caller's number on the digital display. He recognized it immediately, and his first impression was shock. His suffix had only been one digit different when he worked at Babcock's research facility in La Jolla. The mystery was why El Martin would be calling him now.

As he stared at the blinking numbers and listened to the soft bleat of the signal, he knew. Instantly he understood. It made perfect sense, but that didn't stop the icy rage that gripped his heart and twisted shock into bitter certainty. He could think of only one reason Babcock's research chief would be contacting him now. Jay Babcock.

6

Blue-white fire spit obscenely from the tip of the acetylene torch, searching for its next clean cut. Welding had always struck Jay as a strangely sensual craft, but today the low hiss of the torch set his teeth on edge. At six thousand degrees Fahrenheit, the flame rivaled the surface of the sun, and like the sun it could fuse elements. The sound was hungry, hot, destructive.

Like the flame burning inside him.

Jay pulled off his welder's mask and tossed it aside, absently aware of the clatter as it landed on the wooden worktable a few feet away. A twist of the torch's valves killed the flame. It should always be this simple, he thought. With a mechanical device, the flame never burned higher or hotter than you wanted it to. The safety valves allowed it to salvage what it would otherwise have destroyed. Could be that was the problem with human nature, he thought. No valves.

Sophie's Jeep was up on the blocks, waiting to be made whole again. He'd had the car towed to the garage here at the Big House, and his first thought when he saw the mangled axle was that Sophie looked like such a harmless little thing to have racked up a rugged off-road vehicle. But then looks could deceive. He knew that better than most.

With a hitch of his shoulders, he let the heavy black apron drop to the floor with the mask. There was a picture of her in the back pocket of his jeans. He'd discovered it in his wallet when he woke up in the Swiss clinic, and although he recognized Sophie, he didn't remember the snapshot. The tattered edges and yellowing folds told him he must have had it with him for years, even through prison. But according to El and the clinical team who were treating him now, he'd blocked most of the prison experience from his mind. Christ, he would have shut it off completely if he could have found the valve.

He fished the snapshot out and leaned up against the table. She had changed. The girl in the photo couldn't have been much more than a teenager. Tilting and shy, she was a swan in training, waiting for some prince to appear and see beyond the awkwardness to her inner beauty. A blind man could have seen it, he thought. She would glow in the dark.

Irony put an edge on his thoughts as he compared this image with another one, fresher in his mind. The woman standing by the Steinway grand looked as if she had given up on princes. She was determined to be the soul of self-possession and dignity, dirty feet or not. In her unassuming way, she was resolute. If the teenager was still there, she was locked in her room.

Jay couldn't decide who was more appealing—the wistful girl, or the woman trying desperately not to be.

Who are you, Sophie Weston? A faint smile appeared as he realized she must be thinking exactly that about him.

He folded his arms, the picture tucked between his fingers. Who was Jay Babcock? He had all the man's memories, a lifetime's cache of them. But that's all he had. There was nothing else, no color, no context. No emotions attached. It was like watching videotape without the sound.

The Swiss doctors had told him his memory might be impaired. It was one of the myriad symptoms of delayed stress, but he'd assumed they meant blank spaces and amnesialike episodes, not this strange fugue state he was in. The man in his memories—the man he was supposed to be—obviously cared about his wife. He was protective and loving, if not particularly attentive. But none of that explained the impulses Jay felt now. There was no evidence that he had ever been darkly obsessed with Sophie Weston. Nothing to account for the powerful way his mind and body responded, even to this, her picture.

Lying in wait. That was the hunting impulse that seemed to fuel his every thought. Circling, watching from a distance, resisting the urge to cut her from the others like a fleeing gazelle and drive her into a canyon blind. The impetus within him was to possess Sophie Weston, but not quickly or brutally. There was no gratification in that. For a hunter, the challenge came in cornering his prey before she realized she was trapped, and gradually invading her space until everything she had was his, everything she was.

These were the things that preoccupied him. Watching her, stalking her. And if he was struggling to understand the source of the drive and its darker implications, that didn't make it any less compelling. It had been with him from the moment he'd seen her picture.

He had come back for her. The rest of it was bullshit.

He scooped up the mask and brought it down over his head, then fired up the torch. The searing sound ignited whatever was burning inside him. Sparks flew as he spiked the flame and went after the broken axle again. It gave him great satisfaction to watch the metal melt and meld, to see it go molten red as the elements fused.

With surgical focus, he burned in a bead and studied the result. It was a clean cut. The trick with compressed gases was controlling the working pressure to produce a perfect blue-and-white inner cone. Too much pressure and the vapors could back up and combine in an explosive mixture. Obviously that was the trick with her, too. Control. His escape valve was the company, the campaign to retake Babcock.

That would bleed off just enough energy to keep the mix from blowing.

He was looking forward to tomorrow's meeting with El Martin, if only for that reason, the distraction. El would introduce him to key board members and trustees and brief him on the changes of the last five years, including where Babcock stood in relation to the other pharmaceutical giants like Eli Lilly and Johnson & Johnson.

Jay already knew from Wallis that the rift at Babcock was between the research and marketing arms. Science versus commerce, in this case. The young turks, Jerry White and his partner, wanted to minimize research and maximize proceeds. Their goals were to push more Babcock drugs to over-the-counter status, reap a higher profit margin, and possibly expand into cosmetics. El and Wallis, the old guard, wanted to go back to the research-intensive mode and develop important new drugs in the tradition of the family-run company.

They were anxious about the takeover. Too anxious from Jay's point of view. He had his own reasons for taking the company back. Private and deeply personal reasons, and no one was going to stop him. But the way he saw it, the empire was easy. It had no soul. All it took to win a proxy fight was muscle, gut, and nerve, a willingness to do what the next man wouldn't and no one else could. There were others with the nerve and the desire, but Jay had something none of them possessed. He had nothing to lose.

"Is this gunk edible?" Muffin asked, nicking a bit of the Hungarian moor mud from her facial mask and peering at it. She touched her tongue to it and nodded as if it had possibilities. "Beats the egg pie at Lola's."

A snort of amusement came from Muffin's business partner, Delilah of the first name only. Prison-camp thin, the disgustingly beautiful redhead was stretched out on a chaise next to the bubbling vat of mud where Muffin was all but submerged in greenish goo.

"You bingeing again?" Delilah looked up from the legal pad where she was making notes.

This meeting wasn't just about Muffin's beauty rituals. They'd planned to pitch Jerry White on the fruit-oil fragrances Delilah was developing as part of her cosmetics line. But Muffin was having trouble getting an appointment with the acting head of Babcock, which infuriated her. He wouldn't have dared put her off like this if Colby had been alive.

"Bite your tongue," Muffin grumbled, then laughed. "I had a toasted jalapeña bagel, slathered with lite cream cheese this morning, so I can't eat for at least four days."

Delilah pretended shock. "Not even blue-green algae, the ocean's answer to Prozac *and* hormone-replacement therapy?"

"Drink plenty of wheat-grass water," the spa attendant advised cheerfully as she perched on the side of the vat and slopped handfuls of mud on Muffin's breasts. She squished the goo up toward her neck. "It neutralizes free radicals, reduces bloating, and keeps you regular."

Another snort.

Muffin thought it an indelicate sound coming from so streamlined and sophisticated a creature as Delilah, and not for the first time she wondered about her new partner's sexual preference. There'd been other telltale quirks, and frankly, Muffin was curious on her own behalf. She'd thought she detected an interest that went beyond business in her partner's glances and offhand comments, and that possibility had her more than a little curious. Was Delilah toying with her?

"I've got a personal trainer who does all that," Delilah bragged. "The boy's better'n fiber. Calls himself Roto."

"No! As in Rooter?" Muffin was appalled.

Snort number three.

The woman's problem was sinuses, Muffin decided, not sexual preference. Still, the cosmetician was intriguing on many levels, which was what had attracted Muffin to their business arrangement. In addition to some of the more unique products she was developing, she owned and operated the salon that had been expanded into this full-service spa.

The facility offered massages and exfoliations, herbal

wraps, cellulite treatments, and workout rooms, as well as hairstyling and manicures. By catering to celebrity clients and providing trendy little extras like an oxygen bar with masks and fruit-flavored O_2, Delilah had turned it into one of the hot spots of the Southland. Rumor had it that even Hillary had stopped in once, for a comb-out while she was book touring.

"Are there calories in fruit-flavored oxygen?" Muffin wondered aloud. "I could sniff to my heart's content?"

"Two words," Delilah cautioned. "Michael Jackson."

"Maybe I'll get a herbal wrap." Muffin rose from the primordial ooze like a female Swamp Thing and climbed out of the vat. Delilah didn't even give her a glance as she sashayed naked and trailing green muck to the showers.

But the spa girl did. Muffin smiled back.

"Snob appeal!" Muffin shouted over the racket of the shower a moment later. Delilah was making a list of her products' sales points, and she kept harping on the quality ingredients that went into the various products.

Essence of tulip, orange zest, and bee pollen were terrific, but they wouldn't make the difference, Muffin had just realized. "Snob appeal," she repeated to herself, delighted that she'd thought of it. "Like the mustard."

Excited, she zipped through the shower, padded to a rack of terry robes, and grabbed one of the fluffy, lilac-scented wraparounds that hung about the place for the use of the spa guests. Delilah had done miracles with the expansion, she thought, looking around. She'd turned a cute, bustling little Santa Monica clip joint into a luxurious hideaway for the rich and anxious, like Muffin.

Luscious smells wafted from a room down the hall where they were doing aromatherapy with Delilah's concoctions. Muffin adored yummy smells above all other things, except for the food making those smells. Oh, to be an anorexic, she thought recklessly. An aversion to eating had to be better than wanting to gobble everything in your path. So oral.

She looped the terry belt around her waist and pulled it tight with a sense of ambivalence about her size-two body.

No one would ever suspect her secret shame, but was that a blessing or a curse? Such a great whammo package outside. Such a mess inside. If it were the other way around, she might be forced to do something about it.

"What do you mean, snob appeal?" Delilah asked as Muffin came to sit at the foot of her chaise. There were plenty of other places to sit, but it was cozier this way, Muffin had decided. More like girl talk.

"You know what they did with Grey Poupon, don't you?" she explained. "It costs no more to make than regular mustard, but they came up with the idea to give it cachet by putting it in a tiny bottle and advertising it as a gourmand's delight."

Muffin was terribly pleased with herself. "People were thrilled to pay twice as much for it, because suddenly mustard had social status. And they'll pay twice as much for your products if we 'snob' them up a little bit. The natural ingredients are fine, but we need something else, don't you think?"

Delilah pursed her lush, unpainted lips thoughtfully. "Like the spores of some magical tropical fungi or wild yam cream with natural progesterone?"

"Exactly."

She sighed heavily, as if a great burden had been dropped from the heavens. "All right, I'll come up with something. But meanwhile, tell me about the mystery man, your brother-in-law. I've been waiting all morning for this. Is he gorgeous?"

Impulsively, Delilah flipped from the chair in a balletlike vault over the arm and ended up on the floor at Muffin's feet. "Is he?"

Muffin actually felt a little flutter as she thought about the mole next to Jay's lip. What would that taste like? Better than dark chocolate? "You could say gorgeous, yes."

"Spill, girl!"

"Well, a D-word comes to mind," she said conspiratorily. Now they were dishing about guys, which felt like familiar territory.

"Dangerous? Devastating? Demented?"

"Dastardly. He could be the reincarnation of Errol Flynn, except that he looks more like the diet Coke guy, only darker and more sensual than Lucky. There's a menacing quality that neither of them have."

Delilah had begun to take an interest in Muffin's bare feet and Muffin was ticklish. "Lucky Vanous from hell," Muffin managed.

"Whose side is he on?" Delilah asked.

"A better question—who the hell is he?"

Delilah looked up from her travels, intrigued. "Say what?" The delicate white-gold ring that pierced her nostril gleamed in the recessed light.

Apparently women with piercings weren't too cool to get excited over truly juicy gossip, Muffin thought, pleased she had something this exotic creature coveted, besides feet.

"I have my doubts about whether or not he's really Jay Babcock—and so does his wife." Muffin hadn't realized her mouth was so dry, and she wasn't quite sure how it got that way. She would have blamed it on Jay except for her business partner's cavalier interest in her naked soles.

Delilah drew her fingernail lightly up the middle of Muffin's instep and winked. This is toying with, Muffin thought. I'm being toyed with.

"Teri," Muffin croaked to the assistant, who was stuffing soiled towels in a hamper, "some mineral water, please. Evian with lemon, thanks."

Muffin's robe had gaped open, offering a generous peek at one of her smallish, but voluptuously rounded breasts. Delilah, who was now openly helping herself to the view, looked up at her and smiled.

Muffin's mouth turned to chalk dust. "I don't know whose side he's on," she admitted raspily. "But Jay or not, there's a good chance he's going to be running things soon, so I plan to find out."

Delilah nodded, but she was clearly more absorbed in what was inside Muffin's robe than anything else. And meanwhile she was drawing dirty pictures on her sole.

Muffin eased her foot back.

"Are we ticklish?" Delilah inquired.

"We have a crick." Casually Muffin shifted her weight, pretending to stretch out her spine, and the collar fell back, covering her, to her great relief. Perhaps she wasn't as open to life's possibilities as she'd thought.

"Don't worry," she assured the other woman. "I'll deal with Jay."

"I'm certain you will. Poor baby, I'll bet he'll never be the same."

Chicken, Delilah's expression seemed to say as she slithered into a cross-legged pose and languorously stretched out her own spine. "Teri!" she called to the attendant. "Get our friend some water quickly, before she expires."

7

Just because Sophie couldn't imagine herself in the sleek, plum-black, nearly backless mini didn't mean she couldn't stare at it longingly. It was a ritual with her now. When she came to Laguna Beach to pick up arts-and-crafts supplies for her day-care projects, she also stopped by Vavoom and window-shopped.

The tiny boutique specialized in dramatic fashion statements, whatever was hot, whatever was next. This week it was plum-black retro "glam-trash." Nothing Sophie could wear in a million years of Fen-Phen or being stretched on a health-spa rack. But she'd come to think of it as visualization therapy. If she stared long enough, she might be able to catch a glimpse of Sophie Weston backless, and that image would go a long way to balancing the one of a woman in baggy cargo overhauls and a ponytail, lugging a sackful of Day-Glo fingerpaints.

Her focus wavered for a moment, and she thought she saw another reflection in the glass. Her head snapped up, and her heart nearly stopped. There was a man standing behind her, and she had the feeling he'd been there the entire time, watching her. His shadowy features were breathtakingly familiar, and the black triangle made her breathe his name.

"Jay?" She touched the pane to ground herself. She was looking directly at him, but something had frozen the image in her mind and it was a moment before she realized it was gone. He was no longer there.

There was a man striding up the hill away from her, his hair gleaming like polished onyx in the afternoon sun. Sophie turned just as he rounded the corner at the end of the block and disappeared. She wanted to follow him, but her legs were shaking. The lower half of her body had turned to ether, and she couldn't imagine what was holding her up.

She said his name again, knowing it could not have been him. Jay had been undergoing treatment the last couple of days at the La Jolla research facility where Babcock often ran its clinical trials.

Pinch yourself, Sophie. Quickly. Wake up.

Anyone else would have brushed off the reflection as one of those tricks the eyes play. But Sophie couldn't. She'd dreamed about him too many nights, come awake with his name on her lips too many dawns. His ghost had haunted her for years, elusive and tormenting, and for a moment it felt as if she were sinking into that world of shadows and pain again.

She glanced down at the blue veins of her wrist and saw the red streaks left by her fingernails. She wasn't dreaming. There was no need to dream anymore, she told the eerie emptiness that pervaded her chest. Jay had come home.

8

"Wheeeeeeeeeeee!" the chubby toddler squealed gleefully as she skated across the huge canvas tarpaulin. The ruffles on her hot pink swimsuit danced merrily, and her fluorescent-green feet left great smears of vibrant color on the canvas, which was already heavily crisscrossed with glowing streaks.

Right behind the little girl, several more pint-sized artists were lined up at pots of orange, yellow, and blue, waiting to dip their toes and do some freestyle foot painting. Brian, one of Sophie's student interns from the local college, was on hand, too, sitting in the swing of the playground set and supervising the melee from a distance.

Sophie had stationed herself near the patio door with the garden hose. Dressed in a yellow slicker and rain hat, she was primed and ready for the moment when her charges had exhausted their artistic zeal and were ready to be hosed down, which she hoped would be anytime now.

"G'won, twerp! Move it!"

"Git goin', doofus!"

"Sophieeeeeeeeee! Katy won't *move!*"

There was some kind of a logjam at the paint pots. The kids were jumping up and down and generally writhing with impatience, and from what Sophie could tell, it was the little girl at the head of the line who was holding things up.

"Come on, Katy-did," Sophie called to the round-eyed cherub, who looked a bit overwhelmed by it all. "You don't have to skate, sweetheart. Just dip your tootsies in the paint and walk on over here to Soapy, 'kay?"

Sophie signaled Brian to rescue the stranded child, but Katy squawked the instant the tall, gangly college student tried to take her hand. The little "cherub" was going to do it herself. Without bothering to dip her tootsies, Katy trundled determinedly across the canvas toward Sophie, but she wasn't halfway there before she'd become enamored of the gooey stuff squishing between her toes and stopped to investigate.

When she flopped down in the mess with a happy splat, the other kids began to howl. "Git her out of there or'll feed her to the gerbils!" came a strangled threat. The outraged voice sounded suspiciously like Albert's.

Sophie waved Brian back and went in for the rescue herself.

Fortunately, Katy gurgled happily as Sophie scooped her up and rushed her out of harm's way.

"I just saved your bacon," she told the toddler, who was cooing with pleasure and swacking Sophie's cheek with a tiny, fluorescent-orange hand. "And this is the thanks I get?"

The other kids went back to their skating with squeals of delight, leaving Sophie to deal with the task of cleanup.

"Lucky you get to be my first customer," she informed Katy, who merely grinned as Sophie cranked on the hose. A moment later the little girl was enveloped in a rainbow cloud of Day-Glo bubbles.

"What the hell?"

Sophie jerked around, startled by the deep male voice. "Oh, sorry!" she cried, aghast to see that the hose was still gushing.

Jay Babcock was standing in her patio doorway in a dark,

single-breasted suit that must have been quite elegant once, before she soaked him to the skin with the hose. Water was spewing full blast and her speechless visitor was virtually dripping wet. But Sophie couldn't think what to do at that moment besides apologize.

"I'm sorry. I'm so sorry!"

"Are you going to turn that thing the other way?" Jay asked.

"No," she told him, rushing to the spigot. "I'll turn it *off*. I'm turning it off, see?"

She threw the hose to the ground as the gushing ceased and then forced herself to look at the mess she'd made. Of him. Which took some courage.

"I really am sorry," she said. "Are you all right?"

"I'm doing fine compared to her." He was looking past Sophie. "Why is that kid foaming at the mouth?"

Sophie whirled in confusion and saw that Katy had turned into a tiny Technicolor Alka-Seltzer. She was buried in mounds of bubbles up to her neck, and the billowing froth was about to engulf the child. Her gurgling noises made it look like the iridescent suds were coming from her mouth and nose. But far from unhappy, the little tyke grinned rapturously and flapped her arms, sending great crayon-colored clouds aloft.

"Mr. Bubble," Sophie explained to Jay. "I put it in the fingerpaint. The kids get a big charge out of the way it lathers when I hose them down."

"I'll bet."

Sophie was desperate enough to put a lot of stock in the hint of dryness in his tone. If he thought this was even the least bit amusing, then he probably wasn't going to string her up by her toes, which was good. She didn't want her children to have to witness adult male behavior that might scar them for life.

"I guess you came to see me?" She posed the question as she went to get the hose and finish with Katy, who was now bobbing around in circles like a human fright wig in miniature.

He began gingerly to unbutton his soggy jacket. "That was the plan."

"Nice of you to dress up," she said softly.

He gave her a quelling look as he peeled the jacket from his body. "If I'd known, I wouldn't have bothered with a shower. Actually, I have a meeting with El Martin later. I was hoping you and I could talk, but this doesn't seem to be a good time—"

"No, it's fine. Brian—" She waved at her helper. "Could you finish with Katy? And be sure you get some dry clothes on her, okay? I'll help you with the rest of the kids when they're done skating."

Sophie's foul-weather gear got deposited on the patio steps, and once she and Jay were in the house, she pointed him toward the bedroom they'd shared when they were married. The rambler had been their first home.

"Take off your wet stuff," she told him. "I'll blow-dry and steam-press it for you." It was the least she could do after trying to drown him.

When he emerged from the bedroom, it was in a man's hooded robe that she immediately recognized as his. He'd brought it back from Morocco and a climbing expedition in the Atlas Mountains. Astonished, she asked him where he'd found it. She thought she'd packed everything away. It had been part of the process of letting go and an essential step in her therapy.

"The cedar chest," he said, wrinkling his nose. "It smells like dead moths, but the only other choice was that lacy white thing you wore on our wedding night. It was in there, too."

Something inside Sophie went deathly still. He must mean the peignoir set she'd insisted upon when they ran off to get married. They couldn't have a traditional wedding, but she'd been determined to have the traditional lingerie for their marriage bed. They'd picked it up on the fly at one of those discount stores that sold everything from toilet paper to patio furniture. Sophie hadn't cared. The ruffles and lace had made her feel like a princess. And so had he.

But no young girl should ever do what Sophie Weston had

done that night. She had blindly grasped for what she wanted, denying everything else. He had married her, so he must love her. She told herself that and longed to believe it. One day he would love her the way she did him. Chasing that hopeless dream, she had given him her body, knowing he would cherish it. And she had given him her heart, knowing he would break it.

A movement brought her out of her thoughts. He was coming toward her.

"I'll take your suit," she said abruptly.

"It's all right." He had the clothing draped over his arm, and he'd seemed to sense the change in her. "I can dry them. Just get me something, a blow-dryer."

She thrust out a hand. "I got them wet. I'll dry them."

"Sophie—"

"Give them to me!" She nearly shouted the words, and it startled both of them.

"Sure," he said quietly, handing over the clothing.

She wadded the suit in her hands, barely aware she was doing it. For a short time that night she had been happier than she'd thought possible. Everything she'd ever wanted had been hers. And all she had ever wanted was him, this man, her husband. He'd loved her body with such sweet, primitive lust, she'd allowed herself to believe he loved her soul.

Drunk on dreams, she'd asked him the question no woman should ever ask a rogue. Would you have married me if I wasn't pregnant? Do you love me that much, Jay Babcock? Do you love this child? His silence had crushed her into dust. The answer was no, he wouldn't have, and they both knew it. He was a nomad, an adventurer, with strings only to his star.

Now he stood back silently, watching her as she crushed his clothing into dust while she dug through the broom closet in search of spare hangers. Oblivious to the noise she was making, she hastily hung the jacket and pants, then hooked the hangers on kitchen-cabinet knobs.

I'm glad I wasn't pregnant, she thought, wishing she could tell him and devastate him as carelessly as he had her. Her bitterness wouldn't allow her to think about how badly it must have hurt this virile man to learn he couldn't have children. That was his punishment. He would have made a lousy father anyway.

We're not the evil creatures pain twists and shapes us into. Pain makes us cruel. Claude's words. Sophie felt them twisting inside her now, the words, the pain, the cruelty, but she couldn't stop any of it. It was an old wound, but the hurt was fresh.

"Out of the way," she said, brushing past him as she headed to the bathroom for the dryer.

When she returned to the kitchen, he'd taken a chair at the kitchen table, but he wasn't slouched with his feet kicked up the way the Jay she remembered would have been. He was quietly alert, one arm at rest on the table, the fingers of his hand splayed like a man prepared to move. And he was watching her with that same banked flame. Endlessly watching her, as if that was why he'd been sent here.

The blow-dryer was old and noisy, but it felt good in Sophie's hand. Like a gun would have felt, she imagined. Metal rasped against metal as she pulled the hanger claw free and turned it around so the back of the jacket was facing her. The dark material billowed and whipped under the force of the hot air. Some emotion flared through Sophie's heart as she realized what she was doing. It was anger, hot and pure. She didn't want to dry his suit. She wanted to set fire to the wretched thing.

Suddenly the jacket was on the floor in a heap. She had no idea how it got there, but it had fallen on her feet, and the impulse that stirred was unthinkable. She wanted to kick it across the room. With a moan of despair, she jerked her foot back and was horrified that it clung to her shoe. The hair dryer wailed in her hand.

Jay came up behind her and gripped her arm. "What's wrong?"

She couldn't answer him. He took the appliance away from

her and shut it off. He even gave her a shake to get her attention, but she just stood there, stunned.

"Goddammit, Sophie, what's going on?"

"Don't talk like that," she blurted weakly, refusing to look at him. "There are children here. That's what I do in case you hadn't noticed. I care for *children*—"

He whipped her around and saw the tears in her eyes. His jaw tightened and his mouth formed a pained grimace.

"Jesus, Sophie, what is it? Is this about the other day? If it is, let's talk about it."

"No, it's nothing. I'm working too many hours. I'm tired."

"I don't believe you." His voice was rough with concern. "Does this have anything to do with Dirty Dan's? I thought the guy was armed, and I lost it. But I didn't do it to frighten you. I was trying to protect you."

She still wouldn't look at him. She could hardly speak. "It's all right, really—"

"It's not. I want you to understand. I need you to—"

"I don't care what you need, Jay. When is it ever going to be about what *I* need?"

If she'd startled him, he didn't show it. "Now," he said on an indrawn breath. "It's about you right now. It always has been. I just didn't know it."

It was exactly what she'd always wanted to hear, but Sophie was afraid to let herself trust it. There'd been a split-second hesitation before he spoke. No one else would have noticed it, but she had. She was a lightning rod for that devastating space of silence that meant a man wasn't speaking from his heart.

"Sophie, please, let me make it up to you," he said. "Whatever I did wrong, let me make it all right."

She shook her head, shook all over.

His voice had dropped to a whisper, nothing but a whisper, and yet it rustled with the magical force that could sweep her blindly into the vortex. It tapped into her deepest yearnings for a good man, a strong man, one who would love her to distraction. Everything that Jay Babcock wasn't.

"Why won't you look at me?" he asked. "What are you afraid of?"

His tone was soft and challenging, and despite her need to withdraw, something in her rose to the bait. She couldn't let him win anymore, even if what he wanted was to engage her in a battle. He'd won more than his share of those.

When she lifted her head, she saw the flickering pain in his gaze, and it surprised her. She could feel herself responding, yet she knew how dangerous that was. She seemed to lose something vital, a little part of herself whenever she was with him. But if she lost everything else, she had to remember that he was the one who'd lured her heart out of hiding. He was the thief.

She moved free of him and bent for his jacket. Expensive, she thought as she plucked it from the floor. Hand-tailored, fully lined. Not like Jay at all.

"You came over here to talk about something, so talk." She had the jacket on the hanger and had rehooked it on the knob before she repeated the last word. *"Talk."*

He stood quietly, watching her as she came around. At last he spoke. "When did you turn into such a bitch?"

Her hand flew to her mouth. God, how she ached to slap him. But something made her fingers close into a fist, something made her stare at him and shake her head. Tears filled her eyes. That was all she could seem to do lately. Shake her head and cry.

She backed to the counter and leaned against it, exhausted. There was no fight left. "Whatever it was you wanted to tell me, go ahead. I'll listen," she said. But he had already gone to the patio doors, and he was staring out, watching the skaters, who showed no signs of letting up. Little Katy was dressed now and sitting in Brian's lap on the swing.

"Nothing momentous," he said. "I thought I ought to explain about the other day. And I wanted to bring this by."

He pulled a dark object from one of the robe's pockets and turned it around in his hands. It was the hat she'd lost when he'd sped down the alley, the one he'd waited five years to buy her.

He looked over his shoulder at her and dropped the hat on the table. His voice was tight with some emotion. "I'm sorry about what happened, Sophie. I'd cut out my heart before I'd hurt you. You know that, don't you?"

She didn't know what to say and her lack of response turned him back to the window. There was a bowl of carrots and celery on the countertop that she'd cleaned and chopped up earlier to make vegetable friends for the kids' afternoon snack. She grabbed one of the carrots and began snapping it into pieces.

He'd brought back her hat?

The music of children's laughter filtered from outside. They sounded giddy, happy. Sophie wondered if it was possible to be that happy again, or if she'd ever been.

"Cute kids," he said after a while. "Wallis told me about the grant you applied for. She said the children are from destitute families, and you're doing all this for free. She also said you've been getting by on the allowance from my trust fund, that you won't take any money from the family. It's admirable that you insist on doing it yourself, but—"

"I don't know if it's admirable or not," she cut in. She didn't want to be defensive, but her mother-in-law had put her on the spot so many times. "It's just the way I have to do things."

"Why not let someone help you? If not Wallis, then me. I'd like to help."

"I don't want charity—"

"Charity?" He seemed genuinely surprised. "That's not what this is about. Not for me, anyway. Maybe I'm missing something, but I thought what you wanted was to give these kids the best possible care. Accepting an offer of help takes nothing away from what you've already done. Look at you, Sophie. You're independent. You're incredible. Whatever it was you set out to prove, you've proved it."

His praise startled her. A quick rush of gratitude made her fight a smile. No one knew she'd been up nights, slaving away on grant proposals, trying to get funding for her program. Not even him, but it felt good to have all the back-breaking work acknowledged in some way. But hadn't he also told her that she was letting her pride get in the way of providing the best care for her kids? That stung.

She snapped the carrot into smaller and smaller pieces. "I'll think about it."

"Any chance those clothes are dry yet?"

He wasn't pleased. She could hear it in his voice. He wanted her to accept his offer. Or maybe he just wanted her to stop being so rigid and defensive. "The jacket maybe, I don't know."

"Give them to me anyway. I'll get by."

She fumbled with the hangers. "Here," she said.

He took the clothes and was halfway across the room with them before he halted with an angry toss of his head. On a deep breath, he turned around. His voice was edgy and sad.

"There are so many things I want to do now that I'm home, and I want to do them all with you, Sophie. You're the reason I'm here. You know that, don't you? I came back for you."

Came back for her? It was insane how badly she wanted to know what that meant. So badly she couldn't bring herself to ask. Maybe she was being bitchy. All he'd offered was help.

The carrot was in a million pieces. Contrite as one of her kids, she deposited the mess on the counter. "Sorry," she murmured.

"If you're feeling remorseful, there is a way you can make it up to me. Or even if you're not."

"How's that?"

"Come back there with me."

Something raw had crept into his voice, and she was already shaking her head no as she looked up. "Come back where?"

"Pilson's Creek."

"I—but why?" She knew why. Pilson's Creek was where they'd met each other in secret, hiding from a world that didn't want them to be together. It was where they'd made love for the first time. She couldn't go to Pilson's Creek. It would rip away every bit of the fragile scaffolding that she'd

built. She'd sworn on everything that was holy she would
never go there again.

A low wolf whistle zinged past Wallis Babcock's naked ears.
It startled her so badly, she nearly burned herself with the
curling iron she'd was laboring to twist into her wiry dark
hair. Smoke rose from the tight corkscrew she released.

"Don't you get fresh with me, young man. I've got a
weapon!" She brandished the appliance at El Martin, who
stood in her bathroom doorway with his arms folded across
his chest and a cocky grin decorating his lean, handsome face.

"What are you doing with that thing?" he asked. The
khaki slacks, jacket, and crisp white shirt were the casual
professional style he preferred, despite his stature as Babcock's senior VP and research director. He liked to brag that
he'd only worn a tie once in his life, and he wouldn't confess
the occasion.

Wallis knew it wasn't his wedding or the Nobel ceremony.
She'd been to both. "Shhhh," she hissed. "I 'borrowed' it
from Muffin, not that she'll ever miss it in that Macy's cosmetics counter she calls a bathroom."

"Borrowed it? May I ask why?"

"A new look, of course."

"Is there something wrong with the old look?"

"Exactly that, it's *old*." Wallis often wondered what God
could have been thinking about when He made men so dense.
What more evidence did they need that the creator was male?
A woman would have given the poor souls a couple of clues
about the workings of the female mind. Wincing, she made
another valiant attempt to capture a section of hair and roll
it up.

A Schumann piano concerto played softly in the enormous
Italian marble bathroom suite, its dulcet tones coming from
an old-fashioned long-playing record. Art and music were
Wallis's passions, but century-old mansions didn't come with
sound systems, and Noah Babcock wouldn't hear of installing
one. Fifth-generation Babcock and a staunch traditionalist,
he'd been his own preservation and historical society in his
years as patriarch.

Wallis had yielded to her husband's wishes in their long marriage because it had been easier all around. She continued now out of guilt more than anything else. But wickedly, she had made a few changes since Noah went to the rest home. The miniature Tivoli-type fountain gurgling in the center of the dressing room was original to the manse, but it wasn't the only indoor waterworks to be found in the Big House these days. She'd had an immense marble spa installed with Jacuzzi jets and gilded waterfall faucets. Deliciously indulgent it was, too.

Noah would have disapproved.

"Ouch! The damn thing bit me!" Wallis set the curling iron down and heaved a sigh. "It's hair suicide, El. Call a hot line."

El observed her crisis with a fondness that warmed his tolerant smile. Guilty as charged, his expression said. He was one of those "men" she often complained about, and he didn't have a clue what her problem was, but he obviously loved her enough that he was willing to puzzle it out.

Brave soul, she thought. Courage makes up for acumen.

She peered at herself in the mirror, scrutinizing the crow's-feet and loosening jowls, the pinch of her frown. "The ship has sailed, El. It's time to call in the boatbuilder."

"Did we just change the subject?"

Wallis's prominent cheekbones became even more prominent as she lifted skin that was still lovely and fine-pored, if slightly slack, and turned her head this way and that. "Men," she murmured.

"That I can help you with. Boatbuilding's a little out of my line."

"You're incorrigible. How can you joke when I'm contemplating a major life change?" She locked her hands over her forehead and drew up both eyebrows, creating a look of mild surprise. "So . . . what do you think, El? Seriously. Should I do something with my 'look'?"

"Like?"

"I don't know. A lift? A nip, a snip? Something?"

At that, he came to stand behind her and gaze deeply into

the mirror at her frowning reflection. "How about a screw?" he asked, cupping her bottom with his palms. "I can do that and it won't cost you anything."

"You *are* incorrigible." Now she had another dilemma. If she were to remove her hands and go after his, everything would drop, and she rather liked the "refreshed" look. Vanity is all, she thought. She held the fort and pressed backward, giving herself to his plundering hands. "I have to do something."

"By all means, do something . . . with me." He nuzzled her neck and coaxed a sigh out of her.

"You're taking advantage," she informed him, still unwilling to let go of her forehead.

"What a good idea." His wolfish grin flashed in the mirror, and he gave her fanny a gentle squeeze as he turned her around.

"No!" she cried, helpless to protect her breasts and her other precious parts as he eyed them evilly.

"I think you should go through life this way," he said, balling the silk of her kimono in his hands and laughing at her squirming horror. He gripped her by the waist and hoisted her onto the countertop.

"What's gotten into you?" she gasped as he nudged open her legs and moved between them. "We need to talk about Jay. You haven't told me about your meeting with him."

"I can talk and screw, Wallis. Just watch me."

"Have you lost your mind?" She jerked back and peered at him suspiciously. "You've got a new sex drug in development, don't you? You're on something."

"I want to be on you—"

"El!" Wallis really was astonished. She'd thought they were bantering, a flirtation. They'd done that before with only the briefest kind of bodily contact—an accidental brush of their shoulders, a lingering touch of their hands. But he wasn't playing today. It wasn't like him to be this aggressive, and he had certainly never talked "dirty" before. No one had ever done that with Wallis Babcock.

Admittedly, her heart was pounding, which clearly meant

she found it stimulating on some level, but what he'd suggested was out of the question. She couldn't—

"Kiss me." It was a demand, not a request. He might as well have said dammit.

Wallis's hands fluttered and dropped helplessly as he bent toward her. His mouth came down on hers in a hot rush of desire, and he pulled her swiftly into his arms. She could feel the hard wedge of male flesh through his slacks and was breathlessly shocked.

She twisted away, breaking the kiss as his hands sought her breasts. "El," she pleaded, serious now, "what are you thinking about? We can't do this. I'm still married. Noah is still alive."

"Noah isn't here," he said, breathing hard. "I'm here."

He was gentler than she would have expected as he rearranged her on the counter in front of him like a wayward child. His mouth was taut with desire, but he seemed to be holding back, and his hesitation told Wallis that he was struggling, too. Noah was his friend and colleague.

She wanted to start over, back at flirtatious. "Don't force me to use this," she warned, grabbing the curling iron. "Now stop this nonsense immediately and tell me about Jay."

He held up his hands, pretending defeat. But as he backed away she could see what their brief passion had done to his body, and it disturbed her deeply. Her pulse was a hot white spot in her throat. It throbbed sharply. She suspected he could see the way it pierced her.

The sensations were more painful than pleasant, but Wallis knew she would always remember them in some odd, pleasurable way. Something had happened between her and El today, and as much as she might have secretly wanted to respond, she feared their relationship would not be the same because of it.

"The information or your life," she said.

Her smile was quick, awkward. She wanted him to go along with this game of hers because so much depended on their being able to work together now that Jay was back. It frightened Wallis when she thought about what was actually at stake. It was Babcock. It was everything. The future of the pharmaceuticals empire hung in the balance.

The soft crash of the fountain water stirred vacant yearnings within her. Hope. She had been resurrected for this. There were times when she truly believed that. Her five years of wandering among the emotional dead were over. Like Lazarus, she'd been brought back to life, but it was for one purpose only: to bring the company back to the family.

Noah would want that. Even Colby would have wanted it. Her body might tell her that she needed the fiery pleasure El could give her. Her heart might cry for it, but it wasn't to be hers.

"Jay's met everyone he needs to meet for now," El was saying. "And a few he didn't need to, simply because he insisted. He impressed the hell out of them, I'm happy to say. But your 'son' has a mind of his own, Wallis."

"Is that a problem?"

"It wouldn't be if I knew what his agenda was. He seems to be on our side, but I have the feeling he has a surprise in store."

"Surely not for us?"

"For someone," El said.

Wallis didn't like the sound of that. The plan had been for Jay to meet key board members and trustees in an attempt to win their support. Technically, once he assumed control of Colby and Noah's voting shares, he would be majority stockholder. But a leader still needed a show of support. In that respect it was like a political campaign. There could be no surprises.

"Has he asked about Noah yet?"

El's whispered question made Wallis shake her head.

"What are you going to say when he does?"

"That it's better for him to remember his father the way he was, especially now while Jay is still recovering. It would be too much of a shock."

El was watching her thoughtfully. "You're not going to tell him that Noah goes into a rage every time he hears Jay's name? Or that he blames Jay for everything that happened?"

"God, no, El. Why would I? What Jay doesn't know won't hurt him—or us."

"He'll hear about the trial, Wallis. It may have been years ago, but it was in all the papers, national news."

"Of course, but he'll never know what really happened. No one will, El. No one can." She searched his face, wondering how he could even pose such frightening questions. If anyone understood the precariousness of their situation, El should. He was in this as deeply as she was. Maybe deeper, considering everything.

"And what about Sophie?" he asked.

"She could be a problem," Wallis admitted. "Jay frightened her on the bike the other day. I think I convinced her it was delayed stress. I begged her to give him more time to adjust. But she's starting to question his identity, El. Frankly, I'm worried."

He muttered an obscenity under his breath. "If she goes against us, we're lost. You do understand that. Jay Babcock's wife doesn't believe he's Jay Babcock? Christ, it's all over."

Wallis was silent, struggling with the implications. The soft gurgle and splash of the indoor fountain normally soothed her. Now it seemed to echo her agitation.

"Do you want me to do something?" he asked.

She wasn't sure what he meant by "something" and didn't intend to pursue it. They'd already done too much as far as she was concerned. In her experience, scientists were oddly comfortable with the extremes of life and death. They routinely played God in the laboratory, and to some of them, the planet was just a bigger lab. But she couldn't go through that hell again. She was only just beginning to see a way out of the maze of pain and confusion she'd been lost in for years.

"Let me handle Sophie," she said, forcing a reassuring tone into her voice. "She seems to trust me. She's coming to me with her concerns, and I think she can be guided through this. Let's hope."

9

Liar, he thought. A muscle in his jaw tightened pleasurably, echoing another deeper, darker sensation. Irresistible little liar.

From his vantage point atop the bluff, Jay watched her steal through the apple orchard below, her gauzy dress fluttering on the breezes like the snowy white blossoms. She was on her way to the meadow, and she had no idea that she'd been caught.

A broken branch, heavy with flowers, lay on the ground. She knelt to pick it up and created a flurry of petals as she brought it close, drinking in its heavy perfume. She usually wore her hair drawn back in a single braid or a ponytail, but today it was loose, and with her head bent to the flowers, the reddish-gold wealth was free to fall at random. She looked like a princess in one of those illustrated children's books.

No one but she would have recognized the slight curving of his lips as a smile, and perhaps it wasn't in any true sense, but she would have known what it was about.

It was about her, sweet liar that she was. She'd been putting him off, insisting that she wasn't ready to revisit their meadow hideaway, and here she was, slipping back like a ghost.

Maybe this was better, he thought as an impulse stirred deep within him. Now that she'd been caught, she would have to pay for her crime. And that could prove to be interesting.

He had free-soloed the bluffs today, using no equipment but his rock boots and chalk bag. White grit coated his hands and fingers. He wiped the dust on his jeans, careful not to break loose any shale and alert her of his presence. He'd taught himself to climb on these bluffs when he was a kid, but that wasn't why he'd come back today. He was here because of an image that had invaded his thoughts. It had been haunting him since his return.

He could see a bloodstained hand slipping into a dark vaultlike interior, and he could hear the *ching* of something metal. At times it felt as if he were watching someone, but then suddenly it was his hand, and there was something cool and heavy in his grasp, like steel, like a gun—only not a gun. Whatever was in the vault was crucial in some way, but he didn't know why, or even how he knew that it was.

It's too late for Noah, a voice kept chanting, which made no sense either because it was Noah's voice. *He slipped through the cracks. Don't look back.* His father was talking to someone, perhaps to him, and there was the distant roar of wind or water, which told Jay it was outside. The bluffs were riddled with dark nooks and crannies, and he'd explored them all as a kid. It was the first place he'd thought of to investigate, and he'd come out early this morning. But he hadn't found anything yet . . . except her.

Sophie, the surprise package.

He tracked her progress with a focus that had become near telescopic since he lost the sight in his right eye. Maybe he should have known she would get here before him. It was easy to take her for granted, she was so everyday normal in most ways. But she could be unpredictable. And now, if she chose to, dangerous, especially to him.

She came to a halt when she got to the meadow. Looking

out at the small stream that zigzagged through the rich green grass, she drew the branch of flowers to her cheek and absently caressed herself. She was standing with her back to him, but he saw her head sway and imagined that her eyes were closed—and that she was remembering.

Was it the same thing he remembered? One meeting stood out like diamonds in his mind—their first rendezvous with young, unbridled passion. Most of the images that scrolled through his head were blunted and emotionless. But that time at the creek was as vivid as if his nervous system had supplied the missing feelings.

She'd been waiting for him by the water, quaking with apprehension as he approached her. But despite her fears, he'd sensed that she was eager for wherever the next step in their relationship might take them. He'd known exactly where he meant to take her that day, but he hadn't been prepared for where she might take him.

Perhaps she'd had it planned all along.

She'd surprised him with her daring, over and over again. The first time was her kiss. He'd sensed a difference the moment he saw her standing by the stream. Instead of waiting for him, she'd breezed over and pressed her hands to his chest, then bobbed up to kiss his mouth.

He'd hardened immediately, ached with startled pleasure. There'd been something breathless about her. Reckless. This was a Sophie he didn't know. And though his brain might have been a little slow to catch on, his body responded like lightning.

The next surprise came when she whispered to him that she had nothing on beneath her dress but a pair of silk panties. She couldn't have known what that did to him, how crazy with lust the thought made him, or she wouldn't have dared to tell him. The urgent ache in his loins made him want to take her that very moment.

"I love you, Jay," she had whispered, softening beneath him, her lips parted and yielding. Her body had seemed to melt under his hands.

I love you, Jay.

With a tight heart, he remembered the sweetness in her voice. But the real shock had come when he'd stepped back to slide the straps of the sundress off her shoulders and had seen that her panties were down around her ankles. He hadn't touched them, which meant that somehow she'd slipped them off herself.

Nothing could have stopped him after that, not even her throaty cries. The sight had aroused him to the point of splitting hardness. He'd thought he was coming out of his skin. It aroused him now, and his thoughts went immediately to the billowy dress she was wearing—and what she might or might not have on underneath. The play of sun and breezes told him it might be nothing more than creamy white skin.

Sophie had often told her kids not to go out the back gate without someone big to hold their hand. They might wander off and get lost in the woods, she'd warned them. She should have taken her own advice. Her plan to take a walk through the orchard had ended up here at Pilson's Creek, and everything about the place was conspiring to make her remember how young and foolish she'd been in the days when she used to meet Jay here.

The silvery splash of the brook babbling next to her. The intoxicating perfume of fruit trees in full, lush bloom. They were like latches, unlocking a dusty old chest. It felt as if someone had taken a lever to her heart and pried open the seals. Everything she'd been avoiding for years was here, immediate and sharp. She could hear the ragged sighs, feel the touches, see the young girl with her head bowed in awe.

Sophie could have wept, the memories were so sweet. It was painful, yes, but her romantic nature was dangerously close to running away with her again, just as it had then. She'd been fifteen and nearly stuporous with messy adolescent urges, all of them directed at him. She felt about twelve now. Growing up had made it worse.

"Hey," she said with a chagrined sigh, "I defy anyone not to go mush-brained in a place like this. It's Eden."

With a shake of her skirt, she sent the apple-blossom petals flying and rose to her feet. If only she could shake off the feelings that easily. But the floodgates were opening, and it was futile trying to hold them back. She didn't have the strength.

The stream struck at her eyes with its brilliant facets.

As she walked toward the glittering water a fleet shadow dropped across her recollections, and she looked up to brightness that revealed only a soaring black silhouette. It might have been a bird swooping in the skies or a tree branch bowing in the breezes. She would never know. It was already gone, but that shadow had seemed to be telling her something.

With a sense of foreboding, she stood at the water's edge. There was some threat here, and it wasn't just from haunted memories. It crawled across her skin like a feverish chill. She told the kids that fear was their friend, that it could alert and protect them, but the hollow sensation in her stomach didn't feel very friendly.

She sensed movement behind her and turned to another silhouette, larger and vaguely menacing. A man stood in the clearing, not twenty feet from her, but the sun was so bright at his back all she could make out was a small black diamond.

"Jay?" She blinked to clear her vision. It must have been the covering over his eye she'd seen, but she couldn't make out any details now, nothing but a dark, frightening form. How had he gotten so close without her hearing or seeing him? And why did it always feel like she was dreaming when she dealt with him?

"What are you doing out here?" he asked. His voice brought the chill back to her skin. It was pronged like a fork.

"Nothing . . . taking a walk." Maybe it was fear, but she felt guilty all of a sudden, as if she had to defend herself. She couldn't take a walk? It was a big meadow. "And you?"

"I saw you in the orchard."

"And you followed me here?"

A butterfly flitted through the space that separated them, pure and white against his black form.

"Did I misunderstand?" he asked. "I thought you said you weren't ready for this."

"I wasn't." Hesitantly she looped a skein of hair behind her ear and glanced around at the water. "I'm not. I shouldn't have come."

"But you did . . . why, Sophie?"

It was a question she ought to have been asking herself. There was a reason she hadn't set foot in this place since he disappeared. She'd known what coming here would do to her. It would shake her fragile support system. Worse, it would remind her how much she had loved him and what *he* could do to her. She'd known. She had known. But she'd come anyway.

A little shudder moved her shoulders. "The apple blossoms," she said. "I wanted to see the trees in bloom."

"Liar," he murmured.

"What?" She couldn't have heard him right. His voice was so soft it might have been the brook whispering. Or the wind.

She strained to see him, and to her relief, the light was shifting away from his back. Details were still muted, but as his form began to take on color and definition, Sophie's sense of relief turned to surprise. He was wearing denim jeans and a white T-shirt, and except for the eye-patch, he could have been the childhood sweetheart she'd lost her virginity to right here in this meadow.

For a second the past was as vivid as the present.

It was then. And him. *Jay.*

Petals fluttered as if a wind had blown up. Sophie would never forget that day as long as she lived. This was where the two of them had hidden from prying eyes and a disapproving family. She had shared everything that she was with him here, her secret dreams, her secret heart. It was the place where he'd brought her starved young body to such a pitch of aching passion that she had learned what it meant to need someone with every fiber of your being.

He'd told her she was beautiful that day, and the grip in his voice had made her feel beautiful. But the way he stared at her now made her throat tighten with apprehension. She felt as if she were being taken apart like a child's toy, pried open and examined.

"You look ready enough to me," he said.

Jay had never looked at her like this. He'd never spoken to her like this, as if he were intent upon her, and only her, to the exclusion of everything else on the planet. Now she understood the sharpness in his voice. He was angry that she'd come here without him. He wanted those hours back, perhaps even to relive them. But, God, she couldn't. She could barely deal with remembering.

He seemed to be reacquainting himself with every detail as he stared at her. And even more unnerving was the direction his gaze had taken. She could feel its heat on her breasts. The scoop neck of her dress had dropped, and if she let out the breath she was holding, it would slide lower still. More embarrassing, she wasn't wearing a bra and the sheer fabric revealed the slightest hint of physical arousal.

She brought her hand to her chest protectively. Warmth rose from the awkwardness of the moment, and she prayed he wouldn't notice the way it mottled her skin.

"Leave it," he said as she adjusted herself. "It reminds me of the sundresses you used to wear."

The husky force in his voice caused a second's hesitation. She wasn't sure what to do, and he didn't give her a chance to decide. She still had her hands poised in the air as he came up to her, slipped his thumbs inside the neckline, and with a gentle tug, dropped the dress back down where it was.

"It was made to be worn this way," he said.

"No," she protested. "It wasn't."

"Then it should have been."

His hands slid down her arms. Warm palms grasped the sides of her breasts, and he drank her in like she was something delicious, nectar so sweet it made his throat ache. "Your skin reminds me of the flower petals."

"But I'm all blotchy and—"

"*Soft* as the petals," he said, ignoring her.

"Well, I doubt it's that sof—"

"And this," he whispered, bringing her to her tiptoes with a possessive jolt, "reminds me of the way you kissed me—and a few other things you did."

Sophie caught back her surprise. The pressure on the sides of her breasts was thrillingly firm and unflinching.

"Now it's my turn," he said, lifting her higher, to his mouth this time. He crowded her breasts so possessively she could feel her flesh jiggling nearly out of her dress.

He didn't kiss her, but his mouth hovered above hers until she could taste the pleasure of it deep in the curve of her throat. It was wonderful, *wonderful*. His lips came down with a whispering sigh—or at least she could imagine them doing that. He had given her another reminder of how suddenly he could turn male and powerful, a man in need and heaven help her, she longed for the rest of it.

Her stomach clutched with fluttering swiftness. It was achingly hollow. She was achingly hollow, so taut inside she could have cried. The very sharpness of her longing told her how risky this was. He could have swept her up and laid her down in the fragrant grass of the meadow just the way he had that day, and she would have surrendered with nothing more than a sigh. How could that be? How could she respond to him this way after fighting so hard to regain control of her feelings? God, the pain she'd suffered because of this man. But none of that seemed to matter now. She was racked with desire and despair.

She couldn't even end the torture by stealing the kiss he promised. He held her too tightly, and her head was bent back too sharply.

"What are you wearing under this dress?" he asked. "Is it as soft as petals?"

"Softer."

He cupped her with a slow, ardent growl of pleasure. She could feel his thumbs sliding over her nipples, but lightly, so lightly it could have been a breeze skimming the water. The only thing that could have aroused her more would have been his skin on hers, his hands *inside* her dress.

"Touch me," was all she could manage.

His chest rose with a deep, sustained breath. The hot mist of his respiration bathed her senses as he slipped her dress off one shoulder and freed her breast. Its fullness dropped sweetly into his hand, a perfect fit, and the sound he emitted was savage in its satisfaction.

The power of it ran through Sophie like current. It rocked her, shocked her. He lifted her flesh to his mouth and let his tongue slide over and around her, then drew on the glistening pebble with his lips, bringing it to an unbearable state of tension. Her spine arched sharply, and she caught hold of his shoulders with but one thought, to escape the sweet torment of his hands and mouth.

"Jay, I can't—" It was too much.

"Can't?" He rose to his full height and pulled her close. She could feel how aroused he was. "Why?"

Because you haven't even kissed me yet.

He was vibrant against her leg, as stony hard as the bluffs he climbed. "I'm sorry," she tried to explain, "but we need to slow down. I'm not sure I can do this."

"Liar." He took her face in his hands, held it like he might have a child's, and slowly searched her anguished features. The patch he wore had the effect of drawing her focus there first—to the eye that was hidden, then to the one that was visible.

"Jay, please."

"We're married, Sophie, husband and wife. We took vows, and we still want each other." His voice was rough. It shook. "At least I want you."

"Yes, we're married, but we're strangers, Jay. We barely know each other, and we should have enough respect for those vows and for each other to take the time we need, whatever that is."

It was the right reason. Even he could see that.

He looked away briefly, then released her with a nod that spoke of powerful wheels grinding into place—an act of will beyond her experience. The steely flex of his jaw was meant to bring every last quiver under control.

"There is only one thing you need to know about me,"

he told her, stroking honeyed wisps away from her temples.

He caressed her mouth, and Sophie thought that at last he was going to kiss her. Instead he lifted her into his arms and carried her toward the stream. Astonished, she realized what he was going to do.

"Jay, no!"

He set her in the water up to her ankles, and the stream's aching chill pierced her to the bone.

"Don't fight it," he said. "Let yourself feel it. Breathe."

She grasped his hands. It was so cold she couldn't move, *couldn't* breathe. The frigid bath assaulted her senses and ripped the breath from her. Needles stung her tender soles, and fiery pain rocketed up the backs of her legs. Even her teeth ached unbearably.

"What are you doing?" she cried softly. "The water's freezing."

"I know." He tilted her chin, giving her no choice but to look at him, yet there was something gentle in his touch. "That's the point."

"What do you mean?"

"Feel the ice? Feel the fire?"

She did feel it, blazing heat and cold. "Yes."

"But *how* does it feel?"

"It hurts."

"That's me," he said, his voice dropping to a whisper. "I hurt, Sophie. Down low in my gut. I burn like a torch."

He brought her knuckles to his lips and kissed them, and though the gesture made her start with surprise, all she could think about was what he'd said. He hurt. Was that possible? He hurt for her?

"Help me, please." A soft bleat of pain whistled through her lips.

"Come on," he said harshly. "Let's get you out of there. It was a bad idea."

It was difficult to navigate, even with his assistance. She could hardly manage her legs. They felt paralyzed and clumsy, and finally, he had to curve an arm under her knees and pick her up that way. If this was an object lesson, she thought, it was a good one. What he said would be seared indelibly in her memory. She would never be able to free herself of the images, the fiery pain or the words.

Her own thoughts were on fire now, burning. Strange as it seemed, she was terribly aroused. If he were to make love to her, it would be a fierce and abandoned thing, explosive in a way she'd never made love before. Part of her wanted that, part of her was afraid. But it wasn't to be.

He must have thought her shaking hands and the sharp little moan she made came from pain. Instead of bringing her fantasy to life, he helped her to a seat on a large flat rock by the bank, yanked his shirt over his head, and began to massage her frozen feet with the cotton warmed by his body heat.

Even that, she found, was stimulating. She wouldn't have called him bodybuilder brawny, but the muscles of his shoulders and arms were beautifully corded and defined. His pecs were hard, high curves graced with ebony hair. They bunched with tension as he gallantly rubbed warmth back into her limbs. Ironic that he was giving his all to keep her from lapsing into hypothermia, when she was getting warmer by the moment.

He was on his haunches, bent over her feet, but when he drew back, she saw the rest of him. She could almost count his abdominal muscles. His entire body seemed leaner and more sinewy, yet larger, too. She was puzzling over how that could be when she saw the scar. A jagged diagonal slash that spanned the inside of his wrist and forearm.

"The car accident," she said. "It happened when you rolled the Mustang."

His expression was blank when he looked up at her. "*What* happened?"

"How you got that scar, the one on your right arm."

It was actually his left side, she realized. Because she was looking at him, she had confused his right with hers. But he reached for the exact spot, and his fingers traced the old injury.

He glanced down at it, then back at her, obviously not

understanding what she was talking about. "I got this scar in prison. A guard came at me with a—"

She could almost see him flinch. Certainly this was something he wanted to put behind him, but she couldn't believe what she'd just heard.

"Machete," he finished.

The horror of what he was saying—what he hadn't said—struck at her heart. She knew why he might not want to talk about such a ghoulish experience. But she couldn't let him go on thinking that was how it happened. The guard and the knife could even have been a dream or a delusion, created by the ordeal he'd gone through.

"It was a car accident," she persisted. "Your old Mustang convertible, the one you loved, remember? The car flipped and you cut yourself on a broken window when you pulled me out of the passenger side."

As he stared at her, recognition slowly seemed to dawn. "I remember the wreck, but you've got the wrong scar." He pointed to his other arm, where a whitened ridge snaked up toward his elbow. "This must be the one you mean."

Sophie went silent, confused. She had not meant that scar. She knew everything about the injury he'd suffered in the car accident, even the amount of blood he'd lost and the number of stitches he'd had. They hadn't realized he'd fractured his arm until an X ray revealed it later. She knew all of that because she had always felt responsible for it.

They'd had an argument, which he'd won resoundingly, as always. Gifted with charisma and a passionate nature, he'd won when they argued about most anything. But Sophie had had her fill of it this particular time, and she had been trying to even the score. She knew of only one way to level the playing field with her unassailable husband, and that was to tickle him. She was ashamed to say now that she'd gone about it fiendishly. The result had totaled his prize Mustang, but neither of them had been seriously hurt. The only injury had been to his arm, his left arm.

He sat back on his haunches and pulled his T-shirt over his head in a way that said the subject was closed. She wasn't going to push it, just as she hadn't pushed the issue of his left-handedness, but something was wrong. She could feel it now more than ever. That empty, icy feeling she'd had the day he'd walked up to her at the party in the Big House, and she'd known with a certainty that terrified her that he wasn't Jay Babcock. That feeling had vanished almost immediately, but it wasn't going anywhere today.

Sophie, she thought, this man that you have been flinging yourself at like a crazy woman, the one you almost had sex in the grass with today? He's not your husband, Sophie. He's not.

10

"Life is pain, Sophie," Wallis said, studying the canvas she was dappling with a bloody mixture of red and umber acrylic paint. "If you ask people what their vision of perfect happiness is, they have no idea. But if you ask them their greatest regret, they can tell you immediately. Isn't that interesting? And sad?"

Wallis didn't seem to need any confirmation for her theory, but Sophie found herself nodding anyway. It *was* an interesting premise. There had been times when Sophie's life felt like nothing but pain, and if she were to name her greatest regret, it would probably be her blind, unreasoning love for Wallis's son. And yet without that pain, she wouldn't have been who she was—or where she was. It had forced her to grow up, to become her own woman. Swiftly.

"What do you think?" Wallis asked, stepping back from the canvas so that Sophie could see it.

Sophie studied the oddly disturbing representation of a bird in flight, not sure what to say. It had been years since her mother-in-law had taken up her palette. Wallis Babcock had been a celebrated local artist once. Her medium had been watercolors and pastels, her subject nature. But after Noah fell sick and Jay vanished, she locked and bolted her studio. Just this week, she'd opened the loft and set up shop again. And now, with sunlight pouring through the soaring skylights and Wallis poised at her easel, Sophie felt a compelling need to be supportive, even if the painting was a bit gruesome.

"It's . . . well, not what you usually do."

Wallis laughed. "You're wondering what the blue blazes it is, aren't you, darling? You can be honest."

Sophie lifted her shoulders apologetically. She had come to talk about Jay, about her burgeoning fears, but Wallis's situation had seemed more pressing. Why was that always the way? she wondered. No matter how badly you hurt, someone else hurt more. There was never the right time, or the right reason, to insist that it be about you.

A wide-mouth mason jar of water sat next to Wallis's paint box on a crowded, spattered table. She dropped her brush into it and picked a painting knife from a tin pitcher.

"To be perfectly honest," she admitted, dipping and dabbing among the blues and greens on her palette, "I'm as perplexed as you are. I woke up knowing I had to do birds today, and the shrike is such a fierce little warrior, don't you think? Just look at the way it impales its prey on thorn trees. Dead or alive, for God's sake."

She used the knife as a pointer to indicate a graceful black-and-white bird in flight. The image might have been lovely, except for the dead mouse dangling from its hooked beak. In the near distance a spiny tree was adorned with its victims—more small rodents, insects, and even a few reptiles—all of them hung like ghoulish Christmas ornaments.

Sophie couldn't look at the thing. It made her almost ill. Wallis's "fierce little warrior" would have been her "Jeffrey Dahmer of birds."

"Sacrificial offerings," Wallis said, cutting more trees into the foreground with the knife. "That's what I think they are. But not even ornithologists agree on why the shrike does it. They say there must be some evolutionary gain. All scientists, even El, seem to think that nothing in life is done without a self-serving motive . . . but I disagree.''

Sophie's knapsack lay heavily between her shoulder blades, loaded with the produce she'd just picked up at the Farmer's Market. She slipped it off one shoulder, but stopped short of removing it. She'd called to ask if she could drop by when she finished her errands this morning, and Wallis had been delighted, even hinting at a surprise. She must have meant this creepy work-in-progress.

However macabre, the bird's behavior was instinctive. Wallis's reasons for painting it were more perplexing, and Sophie doubted they were simple. Still, it was good to have the studio opened up again. She'd always loved the wooden loft with its celestial glow and its smells of primed canvas and cleaning solvent.

A sparkle of gold caught Sophie's eye. Her mother-in-law's bracelet glittered in the sunlight as she worked. Sophie felt a pang and wondered if it was envy at Wallis's new zest for life. Jay's return seemed to have released Wallis from her self-imposed bondage, whereas it had created some kind of bondage for Sophie. Fear, maybe. Fear could tie you up tight.

''Is everything all right, dear? You seem so quiet today.'' Wallis came around as if she'd picked up on Sophie's thought waves. Wallis had made the mistake once, during a dinner party, of claiming to have psychic powers, and Jerry White and his partner, who'd been among her guests, had later used the statement against her. They'd suggested to the board that Wallis was emotionally unstable and not fully recovered from her dependence on prescription drugs.

Sophie herself had never been able to decide if Wallis was truly fragile or simply the California version of a steel magnolia. Anyone who could intimidate Muffin had to have some kind of mojo going on. And lately, Wallis radiated strength. Sophie could feel it now from where she stood across the room.

Both the Babcock boys had inherited their father's height and imposing physical presence, but Jay got his charisma

from Wallis. He seemed to have picked up some of her intuitive abilities, too.

"Maybe I'll take a break and we'll have some tea?" Wallis
suggested. "Would you like that, Sophie? I brought some
Rosy Posy home from that lovely patio restaurant where we
had lunch the other day."

Sophie hugged the strap of her knapsack with the intention
of leaving. Her denim sundress, a sturdy Laura Ashley, was
concealing and cluttered with pockets for carrying "stuff,"
including the list of things she still had to do. Denim armor,
the dress was so much more Sophie than the sheer thing she'd
worn to the meadow yesterday.

"Don't you dare stop," she warned Wallis with mock
sternness. "I'm fine, probably just a little tired. Those kids
run me ragged."

"And how about my son?" A conspiratorial warmth invaded Wallis's voice. "Is he running you ragged, too, I
hope?"

Sophie wasn't sure how to take that. It was far too blatant
a sexual innuendo for Wallis to actually have meant it that
way. And anyway, Sophie had already decided to do the un-
selfish thing and keep her newest batch of fears to herself.
Telling Wallis would only upset her, and instead of giving
Sophie's concerns a fair hearing, Wallis would insist that she
was overreacting and not allowing Jay time to adjust.

And maybe she'd be right, Sophie thought. Considering
what Jay had been through, it was understandable that he
might be confused about the events of his past, especially the
traumatic ones. It had also occurred to Sophie that her suspicions of him might be about her more than him. If she
hadn't been giving him a chance, it was probably because
she was afraid of letting herself become involved with him
again. Doubting his identity was good protection. She
couldn't very well make love with the man if he wasn't her
husband. It kept everything in limbo.

"You aren't going, are you?" Wallis dropped the knife in
the Mason jar along with the brushes and slipped out of her
flowered smock. The tights and sweater she wore were as

vibrantly blue as her eyes. "I was hoping we could talk."

"Of course. What about?"

"The results of Jay's tests came in this morning. I thought you might like to know what they were."

Sophie could do little but stare at her. *Might like to know?* As understatements went, this was a doozy.

"Come over here," Wallis said, beckoning Sophie to join her on a ladder-back bench by the window. As they both settled into the chintz cushions Wallis heaved a sigh that sounded as if she were about to burst. But something made Sophie pull back as Wallis reached for her hands.

"Sophie, whatever is the matter with you these days?" Wallis cried softly. "You must try to relax. I have the best possible news for you. Whatever fears you may have had about Jay, you can put them to rest."

Something roared like a thunder squall in Sophie's chest. That couldn't be her heart. She was almost nauseated with the rush of blood through her body. If she needed proof that this was about some conflict within her, her dizzying reaction was it. But was she afraid to believe that he was really Jay? Or unwilling?

"He passed the tests?" she asked. "All of them? Even the DNA?"

Wallis was almost childlike in her delight. "Passed isn't quite the right term, but yes, they do confirm his identity."

"But there's always some margin for error, isn't there? Even with DNA testing? No procedure is foolproof."

Now Wallis did grab her hands, and hold them firmly. "Darling, his fingerprints are Jay's. There are no two sets of fingerprints alike in the entire world. He *is* Jay. You have to believe that and stop doubting him now. You do love him, don't you?"

Sophie was spinning with some emotion she didn't understand. Love him? She couldn't have answered that question if the lives of her day-care brood had been at stake, and yet the words spilling out of her mouth were, "Yes, I do love him."

"Then what's the problem? I don't understand."

Sophie freed her hands and rose from the couch. The room was so full of light and space, she could have been outdoors, yet she was suffocating. I don't understand either, she thought. But there is a problem.

She made a hesitant path toward the door, hugging her knapsack to her body and aware that Wallis was still speaking to her. She wanted to run. She wanted to run and keep on running. Something was wrong, terribly wrong, and it wasn't just her own fear of intimacy. This was too violent a reaction. It was him, too. Jay Babcock had emerged from the shadows. He was a mystery. Why was she the only one who thought so?

"Jay started his treatment regimen this week," Wallis was telling her. "It's going to be miraculous, Sophie. The success of the Phase One trials has everyone abuzz. They're talking about our Neuropro as the wonder drug of the decade, so I don't want you to worry. Jay will sail through this. El and the clinical staff at La Jolla will make sure of that."

She hesitated, as if choosing her words. "Jay will be carefully monitored, of course, and he'll see a therapist as part of the protocol. But I was wondering if you might want to talk with someone, too. This is as big an adjustment for you as it is for him."

Sophie's fingernails dug into the canvas material of her bag. She'd known it was coming. Poor Sophie. First she's so desperate to have Jay back she sees ghosts everywhere, ghosts she believes are him. Now he's here in the flesh, and she refuses to believe it, even in the face of conclusive evidence. Poor *crazy* Sophie.

"I'm all right, Wallis." She forced a smile and turned back to her mother-in-law. Wallis meant well, and there was little point in upsetting her, too. "Or I will be," she promised. "I just need some time to get to know him again."

"Of course you do. That's it exactly. Some time and the right environment." She rose from the couch, excited now, all her dreams within reach. "Have you thought any more about coming back here to live? The Hyacinth Cottage is so lovely. I'll open it up again, and you can have it all to yourself. Noah and I were delirious there, before the children were born.''

The Hyacinth Cottage was actually a little-used wing of the Big House, totally self-contained and with a separate entrance that made it more private. Wallis and Noah had made it their living quarters until Colby was born, and then they'd moved into the main house to be closer to him.

The cottage was a love nest, but Sophie wasn't ready for marital bliss, whether Jay Babcock was the real thing or not. However, she couldn't tell Wallis that. Her mother-in-law had come to life again. She was so intent upon her grand plans and dreams that Sophie couldn't be the one to burst her bubble.

As Wallis rushed over to hug her Sophie simply nodded and hoped that she wasn't going to be ill. That thunder squall was still roaring somewhere. She could feel it in her temples, hear it in her ears.

''I can't,'' she said. ''My kids, I have to be at the house for them.''

Wallis gave her one last squeeze and drew back. ''Do you really want to continue with the day-care project, Sophie? Do you feel you must?''

''Oh, yes, I have to. I won't give up my work.''

Wallis beamed indulgently. ''Of course then, of course. If it's that important, we'll work out the details. Don't worry about any of that now. Just think what this is going to mean and know that you're doing the right thing, Sophie. You really are.''

''What it's going to mean?''

But Wallis had already wandered off. She hesitated at the window where they'd been sitting and gazed out at the foothills in the distance. Her voice was soft and reverent. She seemed to be remembering better days, sweeter times.

''What it means for the family,'' she said. ''For the company. You two are the new beginning. Babcock has a tradition of pioneering research and innovation that dates back a century, and it nearly kills me to think of a world leader in research being turned into an over-the-counter 'whore,' as

Noah would have called it, by these interlopers, these attorneys. Jay won't let that happen. Under his leadership, the company will flourish the way it once did.''

She spun toward Sophie with a frantic expression. ''He can't do that without you, Sophie. He needs your support. Oh, I can see it so clearly in my mind. I can see the two of you, working together to pass this fine, proud legacy on to the next generation of Babcocks.''

The next generation? There wouldn't be any next generation of Babcocks. Jay was infertile. Either Wallis had forgotten that, which didn't seem possible, or she was as irrational as the attorneys claimed.

Confused and suddenly exhausted, Sophie made her excuses, profusely, knowing Wallis wouldn't be satisfied with anything less. She promised to consider Wallis's offer of the cottage as she left, but out of the corner of her eye, she caught sight of something that made her whirl in the direction of the painting. A black triangle.

The image stood out in her mind like a warning sign. She associated it so strongly with Jay, she found herself casting about to see if he was there. But it was the painting that had caught her eye. She hadn't realized that the markings on the shrikes were triangles. Stark, beautiful black-and-white birds. Fierce little warriors, Wallis had called them, involved in some kind of blood ritual. The unbidden thought that flashed through Sophie's mind was about whether she was going to be one of those sacrificial offerings.

Fear set off a recording in her mind. It was Wallis's voice, admonishing Sophie as she blindly left the studio.

He is Jay. You have to believe that. . . .

11

A cautious woman needed a few rules of thumb to guide her through life. Sophie had several. To the undiscerning ear they might have sounded like clichés. To Sophie they were self-evident truths. She even shared them with her kids for motivational value. Their favorite was "when life gives you lemons, pucker up," which mostly motivated them to giggle.

But Sophie would not be sharing her newest rule with the kids. "Never give your heart to strangers," she advised the black felt wad she'd mangled in her hands. It was the hat he'd bought her at Dirty Dan's. Her plan had been to toss it in the trash can and symbolically free herself, but as usual, Sophie was experiencing separation anxiety.

Face it. She was an emotional pack rat.

It had taken her years to get rid of the other mementos of her life with Jay. Everything he'd touched had become a precious keepsake, even the dark hairs in his boar-bristle brush. Letting go of his things had meant letting go of him, a wrenching process that had left her emptied, bereft. Perhaps that was why her other keepsakes had taken on even more meaning.

Her dresser top was a treasure trove of gifts and souvenirs. There was a milk-chocolate Santa with tiny teeth marks in his belly, a Looney Tunes yo-yo Albert had thought she would love as much as he did, and in her closet, an enormous pair of hippo slippers. The troops had pooled their pennies to buy her those because they knew how much she loved animals.

Most people would have called it junk, just as her aunt had, but Sophie couldn't bear to part with any of it. It wasn't the object she cared about, it was the feelings she associated with it. She hoarded feelings. Good ones.

"And this thing doesn't qualify." Soiled and misshapen, the hat seemed to embody all of her turmoil and conflict about Jay Babcock. Worse, it screamed of unrequited love.

She sent it sailing across the room, only to throw up her hands when it snagged on the bedpost instead of dropping into the wastebasket. "I probably would have gone and dug it out of the trash anyway . . . knowing me."

The scroungy headgear did look right hanging there. It went with the room's decor, which she liked to think of as "Toddler Gothic." Sophie preferred comfortable old-fashioned things, and so the bedspread was a patchwork quilt she'd picked up at a garage sale and the curtains were ruffled sheers. She had chenille rugs and the white wicker bedroom set she'd brought from the Big House.

The canopy bed was her sanctuary and perhaps the most special object in the room. It was the first one she'd felt safe enough to sleep in. Anywhere else she still woke up in a cold sweat, looking for a place to hide.

Now she lifted the hat from its perch and swacked it against the wicker post to straighten the brim. The same forces that had intervened when she tried to get rid of it before made her slap the pup on her head.

The wardrobe mirrors opposite the bed made it impossible to avoid the scruffy chick in the cargo overalls with the baseball cap squashing her ponytail. She spun it around, bill to

the back, and her hair disappeared altogether. Still, the cha-
peau worked, she had to admit. So why was she trying to get
rid of it? And him?

*The man was imprisoned for years, Sophie. What do you
want? Ghandi? Spiritual perfection? You're going crazy because his memory's patchy and he experienced a moment of
unjustifed rage, which wasn't in fact unjustified if he was
trying to protect you. Maybe it's your memory that's patchy.*

She breathed out a groan. They were right, all of them.
She was going nuts. And she was paranoid, too. There was
no reason in the world for her not to give this reunion with
Jay a try. What more evidence did she need that he was her
husband? He remembered details about their relationship that
no one could possibly have told him. He not only knew about
the hat, he knew about the back alley where they rewrote a
sign with their own self-evident truths. LOVING ALLOWED.

She ought to be welcoming him back with open arms, into
her bed as well as her life. Lord knew she found him attractive enough. Her body felt more liquid than solid when he
was around. But this wasn't about chemistry. And it had nothing to do with Wallis or Babcock Pharmaceuticals or any of
that rally-round-the-family stuff. This was about a man and
woman who'd been friends as well as lovers. It was about
rediscovering each other and seeing if what was lost could
be found. It was about second chances, she realized.

Jay had complimented her on her independence, and yes,
it was true. She was self-sufficient. But she had never come
out of hiding. With her aunt it had been under beds or in
closets, but now it was her chosen profession. Her day-care
efforts took all her time. There wasn't a moment left over,
and the man she'd chosen was her own therapist. How much
safer could she be?

She had made herself into a self-sufficient fortress. But Jay
Babcock was bringing her heart out of hiding. Again.

''Blaze! Here!'' Sophie had just transferred the last of a
brand-new litter of baby gerbils to the egg incubator when
she heard the Irish setter barking ferociously out front. The

newborns were premature, and she was trying to ensure their
survival, but something had the dog in an uproar. Rushing to
get the tiny, squirming things arranged at their mother's belly,
she listened for the sound of the bell. Maybe it was some
brave soul at the front door.

Sophie's mad dash into the living room told her immediately what had the setter agitated. It was the same thing that
had her agitated. Jay. She could see him through the room's
bay window. He was standing at the curb, near a sedan he
must have borrowed from Wallis, but to her horror, it looked
as if Blaze was about to attack him.

The setter growled and snapped menacingly. Sophie had
never known him to behave this way. He was an excellent
watchdog, but he'd never had a vicious streak, not even with
strangers.

"Blaze, no!" she cried as the dog suddenly tore at Jay.
She rushed to the window, expecting Jay to make a break for
his car. Instead, he crouched and faced the dog.

Astonished, she watched Jay throw out his arms as the
setter came hurtling at him, full bore. The dog looked like a
snarling demon, and Sophie pounded on the window frantically. But the screams died in her throat as she saw the bright
blue disk in one of Jay's hand. A Frisbee.

"Oh, my God," she whispered. She knew instantly what
was happening. Jay wasn't under attack. It was quite the opposite. A sacred ritual was taking place before her eyes. They
were playing Frisbee, as if five years and a lifetime of hell
hadn't intervened.

Kai-yaiiing like a maniac, Blaze sent Jay sprawling to the
ground and began to bathe him in big, wet, doggy kisses.
Sophie watched the two of them with a bittersweet shake of
her head. Clearly Blaze had no qualms about welcoming Jay
back. Even the eye patch hadn't fazed him, but then dogs
identified by smell. And who was she to question animal
instinct?

"What are you doing to my dog?" she hollered at Jay,
pretending to be aghast as she opened the front door.

"You got that wrong, lady," Jay managed between swipes

of Blaze's marauding tongue. "What's your dog doing to me? His tongue qualifies as a lethal weapon."

"Need some help?" She walked over to where they were roughhousing. Not much besides Jay's long legs and arms could be seen beneath the dog's wagging torso.

"Maybe the National Guard?"

"Sorry, only I know how to call off the beast, so treat me right," she warned.

"What do you want? You got it. Money? A kidney?"

"Blaze! Heel!" she commanded. The dog quivered, hesitated, then backed off with a yelp.

Jay mopped his face with the sleeve of his parka as he sat up. "You tame lions, too?" He was wearing a white crewneck sweater beneath the black jacket, and his blue jeans were ripped out at the knee. Most men couldn't have carried off the dirt and grass stains, she conceded, but with him, they added to the rugged, outdoorsy look. The outfit personified the Jay she remembered.

"I had Blaze obedience-trained." She knelt to reward the setter with a hug and some power scratching under his chin. "Had to with so many kids around."

Jay reached over to rub the dog's ears and Blaze gave out an ecstatic sigh. "It's been a long time, buddy," Jay said, his voice husky with emotion. "Too long."

Blaze couldn't seem to decide which of them he was supposed to heap his affections on, so Sophie graciously backed away. This time Jay subjected himself to the bath willingly, and with touching eagerness, the setter began to lick his long-lost master's face.

The sharp, breathless keening that issued from Blaze's throat made Sophie's heart hurt. Suffused with longing, the sound tapped into her own unfulfilled needs. She knew all about that kind of helpless puppy love.

Moments later the three of them were in the rambler's kitchen, Jay at the sink, cleaning up, and Blaze sitting at his master's feet, red tail switching, seeming perfectly happy to watch Jay extinguish all trace of doggy essence with hot water and bar soap.

"Coffee?" Sophie asked, aware of the way she clipped the word off. Now that she'd made a conscious decision to move forward with their relationship, she was nervous. Of course, he didn't know what was on her mind, and she didn't have to tell him until she could do it calmly and with conviction.

"I'm fine, thanks," Jay said, shaking his wet hands.

He turned unexpectedly, and Sophie took a quick sip from her mug. "Good decision," she said. "It's lousy."

He was wiping his hands on the towel and she couldn't help but notice how effortlessly masculine even that gesture seemed when he was doing it. As soon as he'd entered the kitchen, he'd draped his jacket over a chair and pushed up the sleeves of his ribbed knit sweater, revealing forearms that were etched with blue cords and luxuriously cross-grained with dark hair. She could see the scar that was under dispute, the one she remembered him suffering in the car accident. The smaller nicks must have been from his bouts with the elements.

Sophie had always been reluctantly intrigued with his shoulders and arms, even as a girl, perhaps because of the power they symbolized. A woman instinctively knew what a man's arms could do, how they could hold and surround, either to shelter or to subdue. Somewhere in her woman's mind she understood all that force could be used for or against her, even with a man she implicitly trusted. And so a part of her was always vigilant, and yet somehow already surrendered to the strength. It depended on the man.

Sophie had seen Jay climb rocks, bare-handed. Watching him had transfixed her as a young, impressionable girl, especially the way his fingers stroked and caressed the granite, magically seeking out invisible nicks and crevices. The sensitivity of his fingertips was heightened to the acuity of a psychic. He climbed with his eyes closed, reading the face with his hands, "brailleing" its hidden places, tenderly coaxing it to confess every secret to him . . . every trembling lie.

Lie? *Liar?* How had he known?

She shivered somewhere in her depths, and was glad that his voice brought her out of it.

"I could go for a beer if you've got one."

She didn't. Claude drank only Pernod, and somehow she couldn't imagine Jay sharing her former fiancé's tastes. They were as different as two men could be.

He dropped the towel and surprised her by spiriting the mug of coffee away from her. "Let's share," he suggested, gazing at her over the rim as he took a sip.

He couldn't have been drinking where her lips had been, but that didn't stop her from thinking about it.

"Not bad," he allowed.

"You're being kind," she responded, almost bitterly. How could she risk intimacy with a man who constantly had her off balance? A woman needed to feel safe before she could give herself over to the primal passions of sexuality, and she did not feel safe with this man.

"I'm never kind." He had the cup cradled in both hands as he offered it to her. "Not when it comes to coffee. Now you."

It would have taken quite an entanglement of hands and fingers to get that cup back, she realized. Her hesitation made him smile.

"That's a great hat you've got," he observed.

Was she still wearing the Dirty Dan cap from that morning? "Oh, my God!" She grabbed it off. "It's so mangled I was thinking about tossing it, and somehow it leaped onto my head."

"Really? Right onto your head? Clever hat." He'd commandeered the coffee and was leaning against the counter, watching her. She seemed to remember him doing that before. Blaze was lying contentedly in front of the fridge, luxuriating in the warm air that billowed out from underneath the door, and the entire kitchen was redolent with the yeasty smells of rising dough that wafted from a huge bowl sitting atop that same appliance.

Sophie had been planning to bake bread. Cinnamon rolls maybe. She found the whole process deeply calming and centering, though more than likely it accounted for the weight she'd put on since he'd been gone.

"Have you thought any more about my offer?" he asked.

She nodded, silent. They both knew he meant the financial help he'd offered, and she had been considering it. His arguments were sound, as well as sobering. She didn't want her kids deprived because of her pride and need for independence. That was not only selfish, it was self-defeating.

"It doesn't have to be a loan from me, if you're uncomfortable with that. Babcock gets involved in all sorts of charitable ventures. We can work out the details later. Just think of me as the Money Fairy."

She fought a smile. He used to tease her about her belief in a cosmic elf with a slush fund, ready to handle emergency cash-flow problems. But after so many years of laboriously submitting grant applications without any success, she had no illusions. "I'll think about it. I will."

"I'd like to be involved, Sophie," he said, serious now. "In some small way. It wouldn't be taking anything away from what you've done."

She turned to the oven and caught a glimpse of herself in the glass door. She was grateful she'd changed from cargo overalls to a T-shirt and shorts. The good news about putting on a few pounds was that it had filled her out. She wasn't voluptuous by any means, but her breasts did sort of "strain" against the stretchy material. Even she could see it.

"Anybody in there we know?"

Jay's reflection appeared behind her, and Sophie felt as if she'd been caught. He couldn't have known that she was mentally taking her measurements, but still it embarrassed her to be so absorbed in the mystery of her own allure. If she had any. Allure. What was this uncanny ability of his to penetrate her defenses and expose her most vulnerable thoughts and feelings? She could almost hate him for that. Certainly it was the reason she had so much trouble believing he was Jay. Her young adventurer of a husband had never had the ability to unmask her this way. Or the interest, she had to admit.

That was it, of course. That was how he kept her off balance, and she had little doubt but that he knew it. She felt like a speck under a microscope the way he studied her. Her chest was tight, her breathing shallow. Her body was testimony to the fact that he could reduce her to rubble with a look. But she didn't want to be reduced. She didn't want anyone having that kind of power over her, especially now that she was contemplating intimacy with him. Sex should not be about rubble.

"Why did you come here?" she asked him. It sounded like an accusation. Maybe it was.

"Where else would I be? This is where you are."

Her throat closed to an aching knot. It always started there, she realized, in her throat, and then it plummeted.

"What do you want with me?" Such a stupid question, but she had to ask.

He took a moment. "A chance."

"For what?"

"To prove who I am. To make you believe."

Never give your heart to strangers. *Sex shouldn't be about rubble.* Her two new rules of thumb.

"You have to give me that, Sophie. You owe me that much. You owe *us* that much."

"What do you mean by 'chance'?" she asked.

"I want time with you, alone. I want to create some private space for the two of us where we can find out exactly who we are, and what we mean to each other."

She shouldn't have been surprised. What he wanted made perfect sense. Reconciliation was about the things he mentioned—being alone together, spending time, rediscovering each other. She caught hold of her shoulder and rubbed. It felt as if she'd strained the muscle.

"No strings," he said, "at least not the kind you're thinking of. I just want us to be together, get to know each other."

"Are you talking about dating?"

"Yes, exactly. I want to pick you up at your door and take you out on a date. Will you go?"

She had no rules of thumb handy for dating, but maybe there wouldn't have to be rubble involved. "What would we do?"

"Let's call it a mystery date."

Her reflection in the glass looked startled. His was there, too, intent, expectant.

"What does that mean," she wanted to know, "a mystery date?"

"If I told you, it wouldn't be a mystery. I can say this much, though—it's something your heart has always longed for."

Something her heart had always longed for. Only Jay Babcock could have come up with that line. Only Jay. The mystery was why he was doing this now, telling her everything she'd ever wanted to hear. It almost seemed cruel. There was a time when *he* was what her heart had always longed for, but he couldn't possibly mean that.

12

The engines of the chopper had already been fired up and rotary blades whipped powerfully overhead, but inside the bubble cabin, occupying one of the two passenger seats, Muffin was the picture of poise as she waited for her hostage to arrive.

Her Mensa compatriots would probably have dismissed her little gem of an idea as showboating. Envy would have kept them from admitting the brilliance of what she was about to do, but Muffin harbored no such false modesty. Her plan to take Jerry White captive was nothing short of genius. She needed the attorney's undivided attention for at least an hour, and one sure way to get it was to hijack his helicopter.

Her new Chanel suit had been exactly the right choice for such a bold move. It was Nassau pink with black silk braid on the pockets and collar, and the skirt was this year's answer to the mini. But what pleased her most was her first-strike strategy. There were no weapons involved except the one she always found most effective. Money. She'd bought off Jerry's pilot and hired one of her own.

When she glanced up from arranging her bangle bracelet, a slightly rotund form was loping across the helipad toward them. That would be the hostage, she thought, noting that if anyone needed the immediate services of a health spa, he did. If he had any sense, he'd be thanking her for the opportunity she was about to provide him.

Jerry's briefcase came sailing into the cabin ahead of him and crash-landed at Muffin's feet, where she let it lie while she watched him attempt to heave himself inside with the help of a ground attendant. He wasn't even aware of Muffin until he'd settled heavily in the other seat and the copter was lifting off the ground.

He fished a crumpled handkerchief from inside his coat and massaged his dripping brow without so much as a glance her way. Muffin supposed he wasn't able to give her his full attention until he'd finished the mopping-up process, but she wasn't fond of being ignored, and she didn't intend to let it become a habit. She hitched up her skirt, crossed her legs, and smoothed her nylons, right under his nose.

"What are you doing here?" Flushed and rosy, still panting for breath, Jerry peered at her over the handkerchief. "This is the company helicopter."

"Really?" she said sweetly. "I thought it was your magic carpet and that I was your genie. Guess not?"

His blank stare told her there was no point in wasting her breath on cleverness. It was hard to imagine how such a dolt ever came into a position of power, but perhaps his slowness could be used to her advantage, she decided. Meanwhile, subtlety was getting her nowhere.

"I'm kidnapping you, Jerry. You're my hostage for the afternoon, and it will be one you'll always remember. I guarantee it."

Certain realities were finally beginning to dawn on Babcock's acting CEO. She could see the panic rising in his close-set, weasel eyes as he gaped at her. He looked around the cabin and down at the ground in bewilderment.

"It's too far to jump," she told him gently. "So why don't you just relax and enjoy this, hmmm?"

"What are you talking about? I'm on my way to Century City for a one o'clock luncheon."

"Not anymore. I called and canceled for you."

He sprang out of the seat like a jack-in-the-box, thumping his head on the Plexiglas ceiling. "You did what! That's impossible. It's the American Association of Pharmaceutical Scientists. I'm their luncheon speaker."

The helicopter dipped sharply and veered sideways. The pilot craned around and shouted something Muffin couldn't hear, but she got the gist of it.

"Jerry, sit down!" she yelled, hating him for being such a clumsy fool. The man was making a perfect ass out of himself. Where was his dignity? "You're endangering all of us!"

All of the pleasure of her cool calculation and planning was lost, squandered on this blundering Neanderthal. Didn't he realize he was in the presence of genius, a Mensa member? Was he too obtuse to see a perfectly executed scheme when one was staring him in his Mr. Potato Head face?

Seething with frustration, Muffin grabbed his arm and wrestled him back to the seat. The helicopter rocked like a boat about to capsize, but she was too annoyed to care. She had imagined this playing out like a scene from a James Bond movie, and he was turning it into the Three Stooges. But he was not going to rob her of her cherished fantasy. No way. He was going to sit down and behave like a VIP who'd been kidnapped by a beautiful, incredibly clever woman.

The attorney slumped back, seemingly in defeat. Muffin assumed possession of his soggy handkerchief and daintily dabbed at his temples.

"That's more like it," she said soothingly. "Here, let me make you more comfortable." She reached to loosen his tie, but he caught her hand and nearly crushed it in his.

Muffin sucked in a gasp. Pain hissed in her throat, but Jerry didn't let go. His weaselly eyes bored into hers and his voice shook with rage.

"Where the hell are you taking me?" he demanded.

"To a health-and-beauty spa—"

"What?"

"Let go, please. I'll explain—ahhh!" She cradled her throbbing hand as he released it, aware that she had made the grievous mistake of underestimating him. The roly-poly, clownish facade masked an adversary capable of swift and brutal retaliation.

However, as Muffin massaged her hand and composed herself she realized more clearly than ever that she was a fox in a rabbit warren. Most people would have been frightened by the attack, but she was relieved. Jerry White had just given her reason to believe that he might be worth the time and effort to win him over. She was faced with the challenge of turning an adversary into an ally, but perhaps her mistake wasn't fatal.

"Either you order the pilot to land this rattletrap on the roof of the Sun America building," he warned, "or I'll do it for you. And you may not like my methods."

There was nowhere to discard his nasty handkerchief, so she dangled it distastefully. "Hear me out first? It could be the most important ten minutes of your life."

"Talk fast." He glanced at his Jaeger Le Coutre tank, a watch much too elegant for his heavy wrist. "That luncheon starts in exactly ten minutes, and they're serving New York pastrami on Russian rye. It's the only goddamn reason I agreed to go."

Arrogant bully, she thought. He wouldn't dare be so cavalier if she had the voting shares that should have come to her when Colby died. But as long as those shares were in dispute, Jerry White controlled them.

"I may carry the Babcock name, but that isn't where my loyalties lie," she assured him, hoping he believed her. It happened to be true. "I'm in complete sympathy with your vision for the company. That's why I'm here. I have an idea for expansion that could be worth a fortune in profits—millions, tens of millions."

"A health spa?" He shuddered. "Do I look like a man who frequents health spas? I loathe the things."

"It's not the spa I want you to see," she hastened to explain. "It's the owner's line of products—cosmetics, toiletries, herbals. They're revolutionary. Deceptively simple formulations, but with results that can be profound. They can even alter your appetite."

"For food?"

"For virtually anything."

She touched the back of his hand, pressed her fingers there lightly but passionately. "You must see this, Jerry. You really must. It is revolutionary. You've heard of Delilah, of course. She developed the products herself from natural herbs and extracts. The idea came to her when she was in Ecuador, visiting the rain forest."

"Delilah?"

"She'll give you a full demonstration. There's even an oxygen bar."

His stomach rumbled so loudly it could be heard over the sound of the engines. "What do they serve for food at this spa?" he grumbled. "Not pastrami, I'll bet."

Muffin felt her sense of confidence returning. She was beginning to understand Jerry White and what made him tick. He might have control over everything else in his life, but food controlled him. He was an addict. She knew what that felt like, and she knew what the gift of control was worth—to him. To millions.

She began to stroke the sleeve of his suit with her forefinger, aware that she finally knew how to speak Jerry White's language. "I can't promise a pastrami lunch, but what if I could promise you this—that for the space of two hours you will forget that pastrami ever existed."

He looked her up and down, clearly intrigued by the possibilities. "We're not talking about sex, right?"

She shrugged as if to say sorry.

"Pastrami's better anyway."

"Yeah, it is," she agreed, "any day of the week. A tripledecker hot pastrami on Russian, slathered in mustard, pickles on the side. All that rich, moist, spicy meat, steaming with mouthwatering flavor. Makes your jaws ache to think about it, doesn't it?"

His stomach rumbled again. "Mmmmmm," he murmured. "I can make you forget it."

"That's impossible."

She laughed, delighted. She had him now. He was hers. "Stick with me, Jerry. I'll prove it."

They called it the Raptor because of its stratospheric heights and death spiral dives. These were the feats of a ravening bird of prey, and if modern theme park lore could be believed, two people had already died in the Raptor's talons before the ride had been open a year. Both were gone before park attendants could get them unbarred from their seats, one of cardiac arrest and the other of no known cause except fear. Park officials staunchly denied the rumors, but however undeserved its killer reputation, the Raptor was still the hairiest, scariest ride in all of Six Flags Magic Mountain. And, of course, exactly the one Jay had in mind.

The long trip up the short ramp felt like walking the plank to Sophie, but she was honor bound to go through with it. Jay had finally convinced her to accept his mystery date offer, and he'd also extracted a promise from her. He'd asked her to open her heart and mind, to entrust herself to him and the things he had planned. A leap of faith, he'd called it, reminding her that the two of them had special dispensation.

"Do you know what you're asking?" she'd come back.

"Yes," he'd said, but a huskiness had wrecked his beautifully grave tone, "and I have no right."

By that time it was probably a foregone conclusion that she would have said yes no matter what his conditions, but she'd done it for the wrong reason. She hadn't known how else to quiet the stab of longing she felt. She was going to take the leap of faith, and for no other reason than that he had asked her to. She hoped he would be there to catch her this time. God, she did.

All too soon the Raptor line drew close enough for Sophie to see riders being safety-barred into gleaming black cars, linked in a snakelike chain. Their nervous chatter told her they were more excited than frightened, and confirmed what she'd long suspected. She was living in a society of adrenaline junkies, who thrived on near-death experiences. Even more disturbing were the gasping victims staggering off the ride, hysterical with glee that they'd survived. Some were clearly in need of assistance, but all were drunk with conquest.

"Why are we doing this?" she asked the rusty metal ramp beneath her feet.

"Because it's fun?"

Surprised that Jay had heard her, she gave him a look. "And this is what you thought I'd been waiting for my entire life? Fun? Cheap thrills?"

She detected a suspicious alertness glimmering in the sapphire facets of his eye. Was he smiling in there somewhere?

"Okay," he said, taking the reasonable approach, "cheap thrills may not be precisely what your heart has always longed for. But as long as we're here, what could it hurt?"

"It could hurt plenty." She eyed a chalk-white teenage girl making her way down the exit ramp. "When do we get to the part where my heart—you know."

"Sometimes the things we've always wanted take a little longer," he said soothingly. "Trust me, it will be worth the wait."

Sophie came to a halt, and so did the line behind her. "Worth the wait? What does that mean?" His silence only piqued her suspicions. "This is our mystery date, isn't it? That's why I'm here, right?"

He cupped her elbow and brought her along with him, reminding her that she was holding up the most popular ride in the park. "I never said the mystery date was limited to one night."

She stopped again, oblivious to the pileup she was creating.

"Laaaaady," someone whined.

"What's her problem?" another muttered.

Sophie would have shushed them, but she couldn't take her eyes off Jay. Now she understood what he was up to. This was a blatant attempt to lure her into several more dates.

And he was using the ultimate enticement—her heart's desire.

"Blackmail," she said. "That's what this is."

He flashed her a wicked grin, the one that had been lying in wait all evening. "I like the term *incentive* better than blackmail. Admit it, Sophie, you'd be home cutting up carrots for vegetable friends if you weren't here with me. You're so busy taking care of kids, you never get a chance to be one."

That had the ring of truth to it. Still, her idea of fun would have been a repertory theater play or a quaint little Italian restaurant.

He tugged on the sleeve of her cropped cardigan sweater, coaxing her up the ramp and seducing her deprived child's soul with his reverberant male tones. "Be a kid again, Sophie. If you can't do it for yourself, then do it for me. Just this once. I want to hear you laugh."

"And scream?"

Her skeptical expression coaxed a laugh out of him. "Oh, yeah, that, too."

Sophie had screamed that night. To Jay's delight, she'd clung to him for dear life and all but swooned. When the ride was over, she'd had to peel herself off him like a wrapper off taffy, only to scream and cling again on the next ride. But he'd been right. It had been fun, maybe the most fun of her life.

This morning, however, she wanted to scream for an entirely different reason. Last weekend was Mystery Date, Part One. This weekend was the second installment, and Jay would be arriving any minute. But Sophie couldn't decide what to wear. It was partly his fault. He wouldn't tell her where they were going, so she'd been forced to come up with the perfect all-occasion ensemble from a closet full of baggy sweats and cargo overalls. Even Cindy Crawford would have been challenged.

She rifled through the pile of clothing on her bed, picked out the simple lime-green linen shift that had been her first choice, and held it up to herself, trying to imagine his reaction. The dress wasn't designed to shake a man's nerves and rattle his brain, which was too bad, because Sophie wouldn't have minded a reaction along those lines. In fact, she was hoping for one.

Jay had dropped by the house unexpectedly a few times since their Raptor date, and Sophie had surprised herself with the thoughts she'd been thinking and the things she said. She'd teasingly suggested she might keep his bathrobe for herself, since he'd always slept nude, and when he admitted that he still did, she'd actually blushed. His jokes brought breathy laughter, whether they were funny or not, and she had to fight to keep her eyes from darting to certain forbidden parts of his body. She told herself it was nothing. They'd agreed to date, and that's what they were doing. But when she found herself reduced to hair twirling and eyelash fluttering, there was no more denying it. She was flirting.

If that startled her, his reaction startled her even more. He'd behaved like a perfect gentleman. Sure, he'd flirted back, but that was it. She hadn't expected him to clear the table with a sweep of his arm and take her on top of it—although the idea did interesting things to her pulse. But he could have done more than look hot and bothered, couldn't he? He could have touched her. In the privacy of her thoughts, she'd consoled herself with the fantasy that he was sweetly obsessed with her and driven nearly mad by the mere idea of just that, touching her.

By his second visit, she'd begun to imagine what he might do—steamy little reveries of him coming up behind her and brushing his lips over her nape, whispering her name, and spinning her into his arms. But as her imagination heated up she became even more baffled by his ability to resist her. How could he not know that she was ready for more than sexy conversation, that she was dying for him to revisit some of his favorite places? Nothing too terribly intimate. Just a couple of lazy circles around her wristbone would have been heaven.

By his third visit, Sophie had convinced herself that he didn't find her attractive. No surprise there. He'd seen her without the denim armor once too often and decided the built-to-last woman wasn't his thing. Either that or he was superhuman.

"Decide, Sophie," she cautioned, "or greet him in your bra and panties."

At least the dress still fit, she thought as she slipped the sheath on, pleased with the way it slimmed her and complemented her fair complexion and grass-green eyes. She also liked the coppery tones it brought out in her hair. Some real effort had gone into re-creating the long honeycombed braid he used to love when they were young. He'd even done the honors for her once, weaving the soft, rich tresses into a glowing golden skein.

She was putting on her lipstick when the doorbell rang.

"How'd you get so beautiful?" Those were the first words out of his mouth when he walked into the rambler and saw her standing by the couch. She hadn't gone to the door when he knocked. She'd called to him to enter instead, hoping to give him the full impact, and it had worked. He had her step into the light and turn to let him get a better look.

"I like it," he said, traces of what might have been nostalgia in his voice as he swayed back, hands on his hips, and drank in the sight of her. "Your hair looks great that way. Turn for me again."

Sophie stepped around self-consciously, but the giddy adolescent inside her could have turned and turned and never stopped. She could have whirled like a kid, spinning for the pure joy of getting dizzy. She was crazy for this man. Still. Unthinkable as that seemed, she was, and part of the craziness came from allowing herself to admit it.

For the seconds that she had her back to him, she closed her eyes and floated in that awareness, stealing just enough time to let her heart finish its soaring. When she came around to face him, she was breathing normally again. But he wasn't.

He had the look of a man with an appetite for lime sherbet and she was very much on the menu. His steamy expression was a variation on the intensity that had always unnerved her—the burning-glass focus—but now she welcomed it,

breathed it in. She wanted his eyes on her that way, possessively, heatedly.

"How *did* you get so beautiful?" His voice dropped to a
whisper as he rephrased the question.

The irony of it made her want to smile. Okay, so maybe
it was fair to assume that her attractiveness wasn't in question. That left only one other option and even Achilles had
his heel. Jay Babcock couldn't be superhuman. He just
looked that way.

"You're pretty sexy yourself," she said appreciatively.

The tilt of his head registered mild surprise, and Sophie
couldn't believe she'd said it either. It was so *not* her. Muffin
maybe, but not Soapy, the day-care lady.

"Are you blushing?" he asked softly.

"Who . . . me?" Her face probably rivaled a brake light
for brightness. The purse and sweater she'd left on the coffee
table were momentary distractions, but he was still studying
her intently when she ran out of ways to drape her sweater
over her arm.

"You aren't going to let me get out of this gracefully, are
you?" she acknowledged with a sigh. "Would you believe
allergies? I always get blotchy this time of year. You know,
the spring?"

"I would believe that you're adorable."

She ducked her head in despair, but it was the secret
delight she didn't want him to see. If they kept this up, she
would be a brake light.

He did the noble thing and grabbed her hand. "Your
mountain awaits," he said, whisking her out the door and
into the brand-new Jeep Grand Cherokee he'd apparently just
bought.

"Mountain?" she asked when they were rolling down the
street.

"Didn't I tell you? We're going to a monastery in the
Sierras. We'll be 'high as heaven and deep as hell.' "

Sophie was understandably curious, but she quelled her
other questions. A monastery was so not Jay she didn't know

what to make of it. But that was all he was going to tell her by his cryptic expression.

It was an interesting experience riding in a car with him again. They hadn't gone a block before Sophie saw that he drove differently, too. The old Jay had believed that yellow lights were starter's pistols. No matter how far he was from the intersection, whether in a car or on the bike, he floored it. Freeways were drag strips, put there expressly for Jay Babcock's entertainment.

The man opposite her drove aggressively, but he wasn't reckless. His feel for the road seemed intuitive, and when he hit the gas it was to pass a slower car, not for the thrill of an adrenaline rush. His command was impressive, yet so was his responsiveness. Smooth leather slid through the loose curl of his fingers as his hands glided and caught the spinning wheel, glided and caught, sensitive to every nuance.

He handled the car like it was a woman, she thought.

She didn't have to ask if he would make love differently. She knew. The other Jay had been breathtaking, if a bit frightening. Every encounter had felt like a game of seduction, every scream of pleasure extracted like a confession. She'd rarely thought about whether she was unhappy in those days. He'd kept her too dizzy, even when he was gone. It wasn't until he disappeared that she realized how few of her emotional needs he'd actually met.

This man was shadow where Jay was light. The mystery that surrounded him told her he would go about seducing a woman in an entirely different way. Not that it wouldn't be breathtaking. It would. Completely. But he would not play games. He would play for keeps.

She tried to clear her throat, and the scratchiness rasped like laughter.

"Private joke?" he asked, glancing her way.

"Would you believe allergies?"

"I'd believe you're a smart-ass."

"What happened to adorable?"

''That's easy. Tell me I'm sexy, then sigh and blush.''

She dropped back in the seat and laughed. She liked this new, improved Jay Babcock. So far she liked most everything about him.

13

The monastery wasn't just *in* the mountains, it was *part of* the mountains. Looming like a great medieval fortress, its rock walls thrust themselves at the delft-blue sky like a natural outcropping of the imperious cliffs they were built into.

Eternal, Sophie thought. That was the word that came to her mind when she spotted the cloister suspended above the clouds. The sight had inspired a great many emotions, but the one she was left with was awe. Mountains were eternal things, ancient symbols of power and mystery, and the monastery, with its religious associations, was powerful, too, mysterious. Its reach went beyond the physical and encompassed the spirit, and the rocks that cradled it seemed to be on a sovereign quest to reach the sky.

Sophie was surprised she'd never heard of this place.

"Mount Hope was a Benedictine order until the seventies," Jay explained as they wound up the narrow access road toward their destination. "That's when the monks started reporting UFO sightings and doing things that were a little too weird for the orthodoxy. They split off from the church, but continued to practice their faith.''

Sophie smoothed the plaits of the thick chestnut braid that lay over her shoulder. ''Sounds a little like the Church of Intergalactic Light and Life in Azuza. I saw one of their services on the news, and it involved medical experimentation, Jay, the exchange of bodily fluids with two-fingered aliens.''

''Better than one-fingered, I guess.'' Jay was philosophical as he pulled into the grove that served as the monastery's parking lot. ''If you're expecting little green men, this could be a disappointment. I've heard there's a waterfall that glows in the dark and is rumored to cure almost everything—but no invaders from the planet Mongo.''

But would it answer the question that no one else could? Sophie wondered as he got out of the Jeep and came around for her. Would it reveal the truth about the man she was with?

''Rumor has it that some of the monks have a special ability.'' He helped her down and then cupped her elbow, apparently in preparation for the steep flight of wooden steps that awaited them. ''They can sense imbalances hidden in the body, undiagnosed. It's supposed to have something to do with cell mitosis and the odors it gives off.

''If they detect something they invite you to drink from the waterfall. Their cure rate is supposed to be phenomenal.''

''Babcock should buy the water rights and bottle it.''

''Don't think that hasn't occurred to me.''

Their laughter echoed like thunder as Jay opened the massive wooden doors. The cavernlike interior was lit only by flaming torches, held by wall sconces, but as they entered the murky anteroom, the torches flared and blew. The sound of their mirth died out almost immediately, as if something had smothered it.

Guess laughter isn't allowed, Sophie thought, looking around. They were in a dark, roughly octagonal chamber that brought the hub of a wheel to mind. Spoked hallways branched out from it that looked more like tunnels than corridors. But far more compelling than the chamber was the hush. The silence was so oppressive it made her eardrums ache.

A shuffling noise announced the presence of a slight man in a hooded brown robe who fit Sophie's image of monkdom exactly. He emerged from the central spoke, and she was actually quite relieved to see that he looked reassuringly human and had all his fingers. Her concerns about the place eased some as he welcomed them with a deferential nod of his head.

He introduced himself as Brother Lary, and after a few polite questions about the nature of their visit, he beckoned them to return with him the way he'd come.

"If either of you need to use the *domus necessarium*," he cautioned, "I would ask that you do so now, before we begin."

"*Domus—*" Sophie whispered, trying to speak as softly he had.

"The facilities," he explained.

"Oh . . ." Sophie didn't have the need, but she was tempted anyway, if only to see what a *domus necessarium* looked like.

"This may not be what you expected," Brother Lary told them as he began their tour of the monastery.

A wild understatement, Sophie realized mere moments into the curious journey. The monk referred to the serpentine tunnels he led them through as catacombs, and just as Sophie was sure they would be lost forever in the bewildering maze, a natural rock formation materialized in a stairway that took them out of the subterranean depths to a sunlit world of peaceful gardens, rambling ambulatories, and vaulted arcades.

The refectory and most of the other buildings were above-ground, and Sophie was charmed by the ancient simplicity of their design. Her favorite place was the *columbarium,* a dove house where dozens of the graceful creatures flocked and nested, free to come and go at will. Brother Lary had taken care to explain that although the birds were reared as a delicacy for guests in medieval Europe, at Mount Hope they symbolized the peaceful coexistence that had all but disappeared from modern society.

"Our goal is to keep physical needs to a minimum,"

Brother Lary explained. "We seek the essence of existence rather than the deadweight of possessions. Our guiding principle is the presence of absence."

"Less is more?" Jay ventured.

The monk's smile was grave. "The rule of subtraction, yes."

Sophie sensed that Jay was as affected by the serene beauty of the monastery as she was, but by the time they returned to the anteroom, he'd drawn inward, growing quiet and remote. She'd seen him retreat to brooding silence before, but this was different. He seemed preoccupied with the dark passages they'd just left, with the recesses and hidden fissures. She'd never intruded on his moods before, but this time she might have if they'd been alone.

A disturbing realization hit her. She was starting to care in the way that women do when they're getting involved with a man and suddenly his inner life is of vital interest to them. She wanted to know what he was thinking and whether it had anything to do with her. With them. She almost hoped it did, even if it was bad. At least then their relationship held some promise of compromise and resolution. Maybe her fear was that it might be something else, some dark place that she couldn't reach. Or that he couldn't let her into.

"And now, if you're ready to visit the subterranean springs," Brother Lary said, beckoning again. Always beckoning. He floated toward the tunnels like a ghost returning to his crypt.

"The rule of silence must be observed in the catacombs," he reminded them as he melted into the darkness.

The narrow spoke he led them down plunged deep underground. Sophie thought they really were descending into the depths of hell, but then the passageway widened to a wonderland of caves and a misty grotto. The waterfall Jay had spoken of was a natural spring that bubbled from the stones and splashed into an iridescent pool.

The water was alive with shimmering blues and greens and shocking pinks. It glowed with the depth of an enormous fire opal. There were no torches here, Sophie realized with a sense of disbelief. It was all quite magical and otherworldly. The mists that rose and hung in the air were bright enough to illuminate the area.

Caught up in the light show, Sophie hadn't noticed that Brother Lary was motioning for her to join him at the pool's edge. He knelt and simulated the act of drinking with his cupped hands, indicating that she should do the same.

She felt Jay's palm pressing into the small of her back, but the encouragement made her realize how reluctant she was. Only the infirm were allowed to drink from the pool, which meant the monk must have sensed something wrong with her. She was sworn to silence and couldn't ask what it was or how glowing water was supposed to help. But those questions must have been in her eyes when she looked at Jay.

His nod was reassuring and implicitly concerned for her well-being. You're safe, he seemed to be saying. Don't you know that yet? Nothing can harm you when you're with me.

The wistful pang Sophie felt told her how much she wanted that to be true. It was one of life's ironies that as fiercely as the mind tried to teach it, the heart never learned. It always wanted to hope and believe. Always wanted to love, even bearing the scars of what love had done. She was undoubtedly the queen of wishful thinking, but here, now, in this place called Mount Hope, what else could she do?

The silvered water ran like moonlight through her curled fingers. It tasted oddly sweet, but there was a strange bitterness that lingered and made her think of sea minerals like iron and copper.

When she was done, Brother Lary beckoned Jay over and signaled him to kneel, too. Jay did so with a searching glance at Sophie, then drank without hesitation. When he finished, the priest had them rise and face the waterfall. Within moments they were drenched by a luminous mist. It cloaked them like a rain cloud, yet the glittery droplets seemed to evaporate on contact.

Sophie shivered as the vapor dissipated, but it wasn't from cold or damp. She wasn't chilled, just shivery with sensation. It felt as if the mist had penetrated to her center and was glittering there. Prickling like tiny prongs of light.

A faint echo caught Sophie's attention. It sounded as if it had come from some distance, like a sprinkle of tiny rocks in one of the tunnels. She caught hold of Jay's hand, and they turned to the vaultlike emptiness of the grotto. Brother Lary appeared to have gone. They were alone in this maze.

"Do you know how to get out of here?" she whispered to Jay.

He shushed her and pointed to a passageway that looked vaguely familiar, although she couldn't imagine how he knew which one it was. The cave could have been Swiss cheese, there were so many tunnels.

Still bedazzled, she glanced back at the pool. "Does this mean we're both unhealthy?"

Another sprinkling of shale announced a muted male voice from somewhere nearby. "Not unhealthy," the voice said. "But there was something incomplete."

It could have been Brother Lary speaking, though Sophie wasn't sure. She scanned the craggy limestone walls and pillars for any sign of him, but the pool's luminosity had faded and there were too many shadows. All she could make out was a darkened form in the mouth of one of the tunnels. Perhaps the monk had retreated to give them some privacy.

"And we're complete now?" she asked him.

"You are . . . and always were. Go the way you came. Go in peace."

"But wait, what does that mean?" She searched the shadowed walls, but the light was fast dying, his voice receding.

"It is not for me to tell you that. Only you know what it means to be complete."

"But, Brother—"

"Come on," Jay said quietly, urging her with him.

Fortunately he had picked the right passage, and their trek back was a quick, if exhausting, climb out of the bowels. Sophie kept her questions to herself, even though her brain was spinning. But once they were safely outside, she fell against the heavy monastery doors with a gasp that was part laughter, part disbelief.

"What was that all about?" she asked.

"I guess we'll know when we know."

"Complete," she whispered, savoring the word and the strange quickening that stirred inside her when she said it. "Complete."

She met his gaze and wondered if he was spinning, too. His self-control was phenomenal. She'd almost given up hope that anything could shake it, but there were a few signs that he was as deeply affected as she was. His visible eye was inky black, dilated despite the bright sunlight, and his focus was darkly intent on her. His breathing was slow, deep.

She was becoming aware of the implications of what they'd done in the grotto, and perhaps he was, too. Surreal as it was, it had been some kind of ceremony, a union. They were complete. The word was a magnet to her nerve endings. She wanted to say it again, and she had the feeling he wanted to hear it, but she wouldn't let herself. It would be too intimate.

He drew her braid over her shoulder and tested its softness with his fingers. "Sophie—" His hand seemed not quite steady, and Sophie felt her heart lurch.

"Why does the water glow?" she asked swiftly.

He took his time answering. Clearly he wasn't happy about being diverted. "Some believe it's plankton. Others say it's divine energy. Who knows, maybe it's divine plankton."

Her laughter became an inner shudder. He'd given her his jacket to wear while they were making their way back through the tunnels, and she hugged it around her now.

"I think we should go," he said. "It's a long trip back, and you're cold."

"No, I'm not cold, not at all. Just confused." She sensed that he was closing off again, but there was too much she didn't understand.

"Was this it?" she asked. "Was this the something my heart has always longed for?"

"Has your heart always longed to be complete?"

"Yes, absolutely."

"Then this must be it." He'd already stepped back and

folded his arms. The green roll-neck sweater he wore accentuated the corded strength of his neck and shoulders and gave him the appearance of innate physical strength. He looked aloof and powerful, and now he was studying her again, with that infuriating control seemingly intact.

"Can we go now?" he asked.

"No, we can't, no, Jay— Why did you bring me here?" she insisted on knowing. "Why specifically this place? Why specifically the amusement park, for that matter? I don't believe either was a coincidence. I just don't."

He took in her stubborn stance and absently wet his lips, but she doubted it was lime sherbet on his mind. "I told you what the park was about," he said with a matter-of-fact shrug. "It was about fun. It was about hearing you laugh out loud . . . and knowing I had something to do with it."

The grainy hesitation in his voice caused her to scrutinize him more closely. She wanted—needed—to believe he wasn't as self-contained as he appeared, that maybe there was something going on inside him, too. His shoulders rose and fell, a signal that she was right. His deep exhalation welled like music.

A soft cooing rose on the breezes, its own kind of music, made by the doves and the rustle of wind through the trees.

His smile was faintly sad. And so was hers, she realized. She felt dangerously close to saying something silly, like imploring him to tell her how he felt, if he cared, if he ever hurt like she did. Such gentle questions, and yet it felt as if they could break everything apart. His iron control. All the careful pearl stitching that seamed her world together.

"And this place?" she asked.

"This place is like your self-evident truths. It reduces the mind to its essence. In so many words, Brother Lary was saying that we don't have to find something to be complete. We have to lose it."

Some statements were difficult to get your thoughts around logically, but made intuitive sense. This was one of them, Sophie realized. She couldn't have explained it, but she knew what he meant.

''If you're wondering what you lost today, I can't answer that. Fear, maybe. Doubt. Like the man said, 'Only you know what it means to be complete.' ''

Doubt? That was an interesting possibility. She would never deny that she felt different, though she couldn't have said why. Probably it would come to her while she was baking bread. That's when most of her self-evident truths emerged.

He slipped his hand into the sleeve of the jacket he'd loaned her and sought out hers. Giving it a warm squeeze, he said, ''Ready to go?''

As they began to descend the steps to the car, Sophie experienced a compelling urge to turn and go back. She didn't want to leave this quiet sanctuary with its ''presence of absence,'' whatever that was, and its serene beauty. She wanted to reside here in peace the rest of her days, and what was more, she wanted the rest of those days to be with him. *She did.* She had never felt so connected to anyone as she did to this man walking next to her. But as transcendent as that feeling was, it made her heart pound very fast. No, it wasn't fear she'd lost here today.

When they reached the Jeep, he opened the passenger door and tugged her into his arms for a moment before lifting her to the seat. His tone was warm and teasing. ''Amusement parks. Monasteries. All that's left is the thing your heart has always longed for.''

''Really? But I thought I had that, that we were complete.''

''You are. *We* are. Only you don't believe that yet. Your head may have accepted it, but I have a hunch your heart's holding out, or you wouldn't have said 'I thought.' It's going to take a little something extra to make you a believer.''

''And you're not going to tell me what that is.''

''Oh, but I am,'' he said with the Jayest of smiles. ''On your birthday.''

Sophie'd been so distracted she'd almost forgotten that she would be thirty in a few days. The kids were going to make her a no-bake cake out of peanut-butter Play-Doh, but she doubted he had anything that benign in mind. Whatever it was would probably shake her until her teeth rattled, if she knew Jay Babcock. While he calmly watched it happen. Call her suspicious, but she couldn't help but wonder if he'd known what would happen today as well.

Or was that more wishful thinking on her part?

Jay peeled off his swimming suit as he entered his bedroom and hung the dripping trunks on the French doors. He'd just come across the terrace from the pool, but he was reasonably sure no one was up and around to be offended by his nudity. It was late and everyone else in the mansion had gone to bed hours ago, even Muffin, who'd inquired archly at dinner about the progress of his "courtship" of Sophie.

"We haven't killed each other," he'd quipped.

"Give it time," she'd retorted.

Don't you wish, he thought now as he went to the dresser where he'd left his eye patch. He slipped the shield on without looking in the mirror. He didn't need to see the congealed mass of scar tissue that had once been his eye. He knew how grotesque it was, and how it affected others. He'd watched them recoil in disgust, even doctors.

In fact, he had wanted to be alone tonight to swim and think and prolong the impact of his day in the mountains with Sophie, though he doubted Muffin would understand that concept. He'd been waiting for some kind of sign that Sophie had begun to trust him, but today was more of a breakthrough than he'd believed possible. He'd seen the longing in her eyes, known what she wanted, what she needed.

There was a grappling hook caught in the reaches of his gut and the pain had told him how much he wanted to fulfill that need. How badly he needed it, too. But today would have been too soon. Whatever was happening between them had to build to gale force, a tsunami that could catch them up and not let go until they were dropped from the clouds.

Today had been a flurry, but the real storm was coming. Its forces had been gathering inside him for days, weeks. Maybe even years. There was no way to stop it. The best he could do now was hold it off until she was ready . . . ready to be taken by storm.

He abandoned the idea of a hot shower and stretched out on the bed instead. This mood he was in was too rare to waste. It felt as if he were still submerged, still stroking in the pool, and the quiet of the deep water was speaking to him. But what he actually thought he heard as he lay there on his back, staring at the ceiling, was not the peaceful voice of enveloping currents, but something vastly different. Vastly disturbing.

A guttural cry pierced his ocean of calm.

Jay's spine bowed like a gymnast's. His hands clenched at his sides. His body reacted as if to a physical threat, but his mind went cold and still as the deep. Filmed in icy sweat, he saw a graphic image superimpose itself on the ceiling.

The rational part of his brain fought to anchor him in reality, to tell his stampeding nervous system that this was only a hallucination, but the flooding of impressions was too great. Something, maybe even the air vent on the ceiling, had triggered a flashback. A black hole in his past had opened without warning and sucked him into a noxious, stinking pit.

He could see a man imprisoned in a dank concrete hole, dug into the frozen earth like a vertical grave. The only light that had reached the prisoner in his subterranean tomb filtered through a metal grate high above him. They'd taken his clothes, taken everything. He'd been left in the pit with nothing but a concrete slab to sleep on while the guards stomped on the grate above and hurled insults at him.

"Pig! Filthy fucking pig!"

Suddenly someone ripped the grate off his tomb, and the light that flooded in was even more painful than the bucket of frigid water that doused him. His body had been battered, his spirit brutalized. Now it was his masculinity they vowed to destroy, the only defiant urge left in him. When he'd come awake this way—splitting hard, dreaming of pleasure with a woman, the only pleasure his shattered soul could still imagine—the guards had spotted him through the grillwork.

"Rutting animal!" they'd bellowed.

One of them had dropped into the pit and come at him with a machete. The prisoner'd had nothing but a concrete wedge, broken from the slab. It was a vicious fight, but somehow he'd knocked the guard unconscious, then blacked out himself. When he'd come to, a heap of flesh and bone on the floor, the guard was gone. The prisoner was still alive, but his hand had been nearly severed at the wrist. And his eye had been cut from his head.

"Christ," Jay whispered, soaked in sweat. He wrenched himself free of the grisly scene and scanned the room, expecting the bedroom door to blow open and guards to pour in. He had lived that scene. He was that prisoner.

Bent forward over his knees, he fought to control the shaking. It was several moments before his heart stopped roaring and he could begin to take in the aura of quiet that surrounded him. The signs of normalcy were everywhere. He stared at them, studied them, one by one. His bathing suit was hanging on the doorknob, still dripping from his swim. Babcock's annual report to the shareholders lay on the writing desk where he'd dropped it, intending to read through the night. *He wasn't under attack. No one was going to break down the door. It was nearly midnight and the rest of the household was asleep. The only raging violence was in his head.*

He began to breathe more normally, to think more normally.

Several things made sense now—why he'd been excruciatingly light sensitive when he regained consciousness in the Swiss clinic, why he'd stashed weapons everywhere, and why just today, deep in the catacombs, he'd been haunted by flashes of violence and incoherent shouts. The monastery's tunnels had reminded him of being buried alive, and tonight, the icy chill of his nakedness had done the rest, brought it all hurtling back.

He was still naked now, still sheened with sweat.

When he moved to get up, a pain jagged like lightning through his sightless eye. He clamped his hand to the patch, aware that it was cool and wet, perhaps from the dampness of his skin. He'd told them at the clinic that he was having episodes of severe pain. They'd been diagnosed as cluster headaches and El had assured him it was part of the symptom matrix for delayed stress. Neuropro, Babcock Pharmaceuticals' new post-traumatic-stress-disorder drug, could take up to a month to work, he'd explained, urging Jay to be patient.

But Jay had begun to question whether he was actually getting Neuropro, and even whether he was receiving the same treatment regimen that was used during the formal clinical trials for the drug. Either El had become careless or he'd forgotten that Jay had studied pharmacology and was familiar with the administration of antidepressants like the wonder drug they were testing.

Pulsing pain brought him forward again in a deep tuck.

"Fuck." The obscenity escaped as he rolled to his stomach and rested his forehead on the edge of the bed. There was no way to stop the throbbing except to let it run its course, so he let the headache rage. It was better than the pain he was lying on, better than the eternal ache in his loins.

He'd learned to control every impulse down to the twitching nerves in his eyelids, but he couldn't control his subconscious. She was the woman he'd been dreaming of in that cell. She was the dark obsession that none of their brutality could touch.

The flashback had triggered more than a memory of living death. It had triggered the sledgehammer of male need. Splitting need. Even now the urge to roll over and relieve the tension was powerful. He wanted to give in, wanted that badly. But he couldn't risk it. In his present state, to give in to one urge was to give in to them all.

At last the headache subsided and he could move without feeling as if his skull were coming apart. Now he needed that shower, but there was something he had to do first. Heaving himself up, he wedged his fist under the bed mattress. The knife he pulled out glowed like the sterling-silver heirloom it was. The years in solitary explained why he might have hidden away the most lethal object on the breakfast tray Mildred had brought by that morning. But there were too many things it didn't explain.

The cutlery felt solid and heavy in his palm, just like the cool metal object that kept playing through his thoughts, the dark vault. And his father's accusation. *Blood on your hands.*

Jay told himself to put the weapon on the writing desk, where Mildred could collect it when she made her rounds tomorrow. That was what any reasonable, rational man would do. But the instinct for self-preservation was too ingrained. Muttering another curse—cursing himself for his animal craziness—he forced it back under the mattress.

Moments later, as he stood under the burning shower spray, free of the hammer in his skull, he thought about the pain that never went away. The pain of wanting, of needing. A woman. Her. *Yes.* That was the agony that felt like pleasure now, would soon *be* pleasure. It had to be or he would die of it.

14

"Happy Birthday, baby . . ."

Standing in her living room, with the hot sun flooding through the bay window behind him, Jay was a breathtaking reminder of why Sophie was losing the battle with her sanity. He didn't look real. Pitted against the dazzling light, he could have been her faceless dream monster come to life, both beautiful and evil. He was so darkly silhouetted, she couldn't discern the triangle that concealed his eye. But she could see that he had his hands behind his back. He was hiding something.

"Thanks," she said with a couple of advance steps into the room. "Guess I'll soon be a thirtysomething." She wanted to get close enough to see if she was right, but not close enough that he could grab her, in case he actually turned out to be a faceless dream monster. He did bring out the child in her.

"Ready for the final installment?" he asked.

"Yep, sure . . . ready for anything."

"Brave girl." His tone was wry and faintly quizzical. "I

know you're dying to get started, but I brought you a little something. It's not a cake with candles, or diamonds and furs, or any of those things that are supposed to be a girl's best friend. But it came through today, and I thought you'd rather not wait.''

"Came through?'' She had no idea what he was talking about. But when his hands appeared, he was holding a manila envelope with an HEW seal. "The grant?''

"It's official.'' He barely got the words out before she whisked the envelope away and tore it open.

Jay had dropped by one evening while they were "dating'' and found Sophie working on a grant proposal, laboriously filling out forms, calculating a budget, outlining her goals and objectives and composing a "statement of purpose'' that explained why her modest day-care program deserved to be funded. When Jay had suggested he might be able to help, she'd given him the proposal to take home and read, thinking he meant help with the wording.

Now she skimmed the envelope's contents breathlessly. "Look at this! I'm listed as the executive director. Me!''

He laughed at her piglet squeal of triumph. "I give it a year,'' he said. "By then you'll be so sick of the forms and bureaucracy, you'll be begging me to set up a Babcock charitable foundation. Meanwhile, good luck, Ms. Executive Director.''

"Oh, my God—'' She brought her hand to her mouth, not wanting him to see what was happening to her chin. She couldn't stop it from shaking. Tears welled uncontrollably. She'd been struggling for years to get funding, and help or no help, she was overjoyed. "Thank you,'' she said.

"I didn't do anything except get your proposal read,'' he assured her. "You were ready. They knew it the minute they saw what you've done.''

The paper got a little crumpled when she threw her arms around him and hugged him. Please don't be a dream, she thought, gathering up the soft material of his shirt and hanging on to him with her fists. Please still be there when I wake up. Please be real.

Longing welled up like a wave as he hugged her back.

"It's the best present I've ever had." She managed that much before her voice gave out. She could tell by the emotion that stung her throat that she had to get control, and there was no other way except to disentangle herself and put some distance between them.

"My certificate! It's getting crushed," she croaked.

His arms dropped away, but the paper in her hand looked well and truly mangled. "Maybe if I iron it?" she said, smoothing the wrinkles as best she could. "I wanted to frame it."

"I can get you another one," he promised.

There was a rasp in his voice that tugged at her heart. Was he emotional, too? The thought took hold as she went to put the certificate back in its envelope, but she couldn't bring herself to look, because if he was, what would she do?

"I guess this must be it, right?" she asked when everything was safely stashed away. "The thing my heart has always longed for? In a way the grant was the gift I've always wanted. You know, helping the kids, being able to give them what they need."

He seemed faintly perplexed. "Except that this isn't about giving, Sophie, it's about getting. It's about trusting someone enough to let them help *you*. Isn't that what your heart has always longed for?" He studied her as if he were remembering the shy, tilting teenager. "Haven't you always longed to trust someone?"

Sophie blinked at him. He was right. "You're right."

"And as long as I'm on a roll," he said, "let's assume I'm right about this, too. Isn't there a tradition called a birthday dance?"

"You're going to dance for me?"

"No, smart-ass, with you. Come on."

He clasped her hand and twirled her around. Sophie followed his lead, confused. They weren't dancing. They were walking toward the back of the house. "Where are we going?"

"The kitchen."

"To dance? There's not much room."

He laughed. "I'm not much of a dancer."

He wasn't much of a singer either, but none of that seemed to matter as he took her in his arms and hummed the melody to Springsteen's "Desire" in low husky notes that weren't precisely on key, which somehow made the gesture irresistibly masculine.

The moment's shyness Sophie had felt was gone as he curved his hand to her back and brought her close. With a sigh, she snuggled up to him, lifting her face into the hollow of his throat and nestling it there. Mmm, he smelled good. What was that cologne? It made her want to inhale deeply, to drink in as much of it as she could.

He nuzzled her hair and said something, perhaps her name. She could feel his arm braced against her back, and the tips of his splayed fingers curling around her side. It was a possessive, intimate thing he did. She could feel it, and she loved it. Surrounded. He had her surrounded.

"What is it?" he asked after a moment.

She swayed back and looked up at him, a smile in her eyes. "The music stopped. Do you need another quarter?"

Her collarbone showed in the boat neckline of her top. She had worn the tee purposely, hoping he would notice. He had. She could see the appreciation in his gaze as it drifted down and found her, touched her there. He glanced up at her mouth, but only for a moment. Her collarbone was where he wanted to be.

"What I need," he said, "is this."

Now he really was touching her, the way he used to, lightly, with the pad of his thumb, as if the slope of her throat was so fascinating he could explore it for hours and never solve the mystery of feminine softness.

Sophie was being tugged and pulled at. Sensations stirred in her depths. They were thrillingly familiar, and at the same time there was this ravishing warmth, this plummeting warmth.

"Isn't there also a tradition about birthday kisses?"

That most innocent of questions had been her own. She'd said it rather matter-of-factly, a woman on the street making an inquiry. But she'd never been more sincere. She really did want to know, despite the fact that she couldn't catch her breath as she looked up at him.

Now he gazed at her mouth. "Should we start one?"

"It might be a good thing. There's so much apathy and alienation in this culture."

"You're the good thing."

Amused, he cupped her face. His shoulders rose, and a sound roughed up his exhalation. She liked what it said about him, that he was having trouble breathing, too. She wasn't the only one struggling with fundamental bodily functions.

"Happy birthday," he whispered, bending toward her.

Sophie closed her eyes. She rose on tiptoe, floating.

Her throat convulsed as she imagined the warmth of his kiss, and when his mouth brushed over hers, she moaned. Dear God, it's love, she thought. It must be. What else could it be? This wild, unruly passion I feel will never die, not until I do.

He kissed the way he touched, feathery glancings that reached into her and pulled up a sweet, gnawing hunger. He gave her a little bit of heaven, but it was only a taste, just enough to make her desperate.

She took hold of his arm and felt him shudder.

"More," she whispered, "more." She was a child asking for ice cream. She would have done anything to keep the sweetness coming, to have it fulfilled.

He drew her closer, deepened the kiss. His hand slid down her back to her buttocks, gathering her in, and as their bodies came together Sophie came apart.

A gasp foamed into her throat. "Jay—"

Dazzling light filled each point of contact. The heat of him turned her insides to chaos and her mind to a laser focus. There was only one thing she wanted, and she wanted it immediately. Birthday sex. If there wasn't such a tradition, there should be.

"Make love to me—"

The words were barely said before she understood the urgency behind them. She was shaking with the physical need to be intimate with him. Shaking. But it was much more than that. Once they'd made love, she would know. The question of who he was would be answered forever. Her body wouldn't lie. If this was Jay, she would know.

"Please," she whispered.

He drew back and searched her expression. His breathing deepened and his hold gentled, but he didn't say anything, not for a long time. And then, at last: "Why?"

"What do you mean?"

"Why are you doing this, Sophie?"

She had no idea how to answer him, and worse, she was embarrassed at the necessity. "I would have thought it was obvious. I . . . I want to be with you. I thought you felt the same way."

Frustration burned through his surprised laughter. "Sophie, please understand me. It feels like I'm splitting in two, I want that so badly."

"Then why did you stop me?"

"Because something's wrong. You're shaking, and it's not from passion. I don't know what's going on, but I don't want us to be together, not the first time, not this way."

She stepped back, then broke from him and walked away, confused. She was too muddled to fight the embarrassment that crept over her, but she felt sure he hadn't meant it that way. She didn't understand what was going on either—why she'd done it, why he stopped her. She'd all but begged him to make love to her and he was refusing. She ought to be the one asking the questions. She didn't understand how he'd summoned the will. She'd been lost from the moment he kissed her.

The kitchen was quiet except for the shuddering of the old refrigerator. And once Sophie's senses had quieted a little, she began to realize how much a predicament it was. Maybe she ought to be thanking him for stopping her instead of feeling mortified, but her thoughts had already locked on another reason why he might have done it. He'd undoubtedly seen through to her ulterior motive. She was still desperate to prove who he was, and he knew it.

• • •

"You're a woman of the world, Muffin." Sophie sucked in a breath, startled to find that she could now button *and* zip the skinny Calvin Kleins she'd bought last year as a dieting incentive. "How long can a man go without sex?"

"You mean the record?" Muffin stood in the doorway of Sophie's bedroom, eyeing the colorful clutter as if to enter might contaminate her. "I don't think Guiness documents sex deprivation. Why do you ask?"

"Just curious." Sophie turned her back to the full-length wardrobe mirrors, inspecting the miracle from that angle.

"Five more pounds and that's a gorgeous butt." Muffin muttered the next word under her breath, "Bitch."

"No kidding?" Coming from Muffin that was the ultimate compliment. Sophie took another look. "I think the jeans are size eight."

Wise in the ways of dieting, Muffin absently adjusted her gold bangle. "Stress and aggravation," she said. "That combo melts the pounds off. Good sex, too. But I guess you're not getting any of that."

"Who says?" Sophie couldn't tear herself away from her butt. It did look good. *She* looked good, actually, better than she had in years. Stress. Nerves. Same thing. She'd been a bundle of loose wires, all sparking at once, since Jay returned. She wasn't eating, sleeping, *or* having sex. But she was sure thinking about it, that last thing.

"You can't tell me that man is having libido problems." Muffin peered down her nose, demanding confirmation. "Not Mr. Nasty. I can't believe it. I won't believe it."

Sophie debated whether to confide in her sister-in-law. She needed to talk to someone, and Muffin had already provided more reassurance than she could possibly know, whether intentional or not. But she'd also been asking some probing questions about Jay lately, and Sophie was beginning to suspect a hidden agenda. She wouldn't have put it past her sister-in-law to contest Jay's claim on the company. Still, Muffin had confided in Sophie about the cosmetics line when it was a deep, dark secret, and she was one of Sophie's few friends now that Claude was no longer in her life, though perhaps that was a sad comment on how isolated Sophie had become.

"I'm sure Jay's libido has all the power of a superb racing car. He's a Grand Prix Ferrari. The problem"—Sophie emitted a tight little sigh—"is getting him to let out the throttle."

"You're shitting me. Tell me you are."

"Wish I were," she said. "He's either trying to drive me around the bend or save me from myself. I can't figure out which. We've been officially dating for two weeks now, but all he's done is kiss me, and that was *my* idea. Do you think it's me?"

"My dear child, I was at the reentry party. I saw the smoke. What was going on between you two should have triggered the mansion's sprinkler system."

Muffin emitted a nostalgic sound. "A man of steel. They are irresistible, aren't they. Colby could get stingy with the 'Big One' when he wanted to. I fooled him, though. I had his sperm frozen in case I ever decided to grace the Babcocks with an 'official' heir."

Sophie had heard the frozen-sperm story and wasn't sure she believed it. Muffin so loved to be outrageous. But she could easily imagine the officious Colby declaring a moratorium on sex. He was that way, a bit of a martinet, while Jay had been exactly the opposite, a hedonist, if anything.

Sophie unbuttoned the jeans with a groan of relief. Five pounds to go, at least. "Maybe I should stick with 'easy fit' for a while," she said, speaking mostly for her own benefit.

Muffin nixed that blasphemous thought with a shake of her head. "Tight is might, pet. You've got the goods. Flaunt them."

Sophie slapped her hands to her backside. "One look at this beauty and the male gender will lose control? Promise?"

"I think one particular male wants *you* to lose control," Muffin explained with a wise nod. "Keep in mind that there is no greater aphrodisiac than anticipation. Maybe Jay is seducing you by not seducing you."

"It's working," Sophie admitted.

"In that case what you need now is a killer top. Something

that makes you look like you're wearing a Wonder Bra.''

Sophie gave up without a fight. With Muffin standing by as the arbiter of bimbo chic, she tried on a pale pink polo shirt that was pronounced ''too butch,'' a cropped cardigan that ''reeked of L.L. Bean,'' and a plaid blouse that prompted an immediate grimace. ''Den mother,'' Muffin whispered. ''Throw it away.''

Given her choices, Sophie decided to ''reek.'' The cropped cardigan could be unbuttoned to sexy effect and it showcased her derriere rather nicely, which seemed to be the point.

Muffin arched a brow. *''The pièce de résistance,''* she said smugly. ''A trip to Delilah's for the works. I swear to you, Sophie, Jay Babcock will be driven to the brink of sexual madness if you do this.''

Sophie was more than a little concerned about coming back looking like Delilah, but she agreed to go, and Muffin swiftly promised to set her up with an appointment. The woman knew how to close a deal.

Muffin had braved the clutter by now and was gingerly sorting through the paraphernalia on Sophie's wicker dresser. She plucked up the chocolate Santa with some interest, spotted the teeth marks, and just as quickly dropped it.

''Sophie . . . do you ever wonder about the way he came back?''

''Jay? What do you mean?''

''The convenient timing? The campaign to move him into power?'' Muffin gave her a glance. ''Have you ever wondered if he *is* Jay?''

Sophie's hesitation must have given her away.

Muffin was suddenly serious. ''Listen, be very careful,'' she said. ''If he wants the empire badly enough, and I think he does, you could become an impediment.''

''What are you saying?''

''That you're in a perfect position to expose him. And if he's figured that out, you're already a threat.''

Sophie had confided all that she dared. This could be the hidden agenda she'd suspected or it could be real concern on Muffin's part. Whichever it was, her sister-in-law had succeeded in alarming her. "The tests proved his identity."

"Tests can be rigged."

"Not these, not fingerprints."

Muffin rubbed her fingers together, the universal gesture that said money bought anything. She glanced in the mirrors, tweaking her crimson blazer into place and apparently unaware of the havoc she'd just wreaked. "Well, it's been fun," she said, "but I have to run—dinner with a Babcock boardie. We budding entrepreneurs have to . . . bud."

Muffin had been gone for some time before Sophie began to wonder how long she'd been sitting cross-legged on the bed, staring at the sweater on her lap. It wasn't the cardigan on her mind. She was germinating with a great deal of paranoia the seeds Muffin had planted.

First she'd suggested that Jay was letting her seduce herself. And if that was true, if it *was* all part of a plan, then he was a diabolically clever man, because it was the perfect way to undo a dreamer like Sophie Weston. Absolutely the perfect way. That possibility alone was enough to trigger paranoid fantasies. But it was Muffin's other comment that had taken possession of her thoughts.

Do you ever wonder about the way he came back?

Sophie's fears had taken her well past that question. For some time now she'd had a feeling she was reluctant to tell anyone about, or even admit to herself, probably because of the delusional thinking she'd suffered during her illness. But as persistently as she'd tried to talk herself out of it, she couldn't shake the sense that she was being watched. It wasn't like being followed, nothing quite that sinister. It was more like being observed, as if something were hovering in the periphery of her life, just outside her sight line.

It had started the day she'd seen Jay's reflection in the window at Vavoom's. She'd dismissed that incident just as she'd dismissed the eerie feelings since then, but the urge to look over her shoulder, to search the shadows, had stayed with her.

She glanced around the room now, feeling foolish because she knew no one was there. Her relationship with Jay was already complex enough without bringing some kind of threat into it. She couldn't imagine why he would have her under surveillance, and her strongest inclination was to push the disturbing notion away, to write it off as the product of an overactive imagination. It had been imperative she do that during her recovery, or she would never have gotten well. Jay's presence had haunted her night and day. She'd seen him everywhere, and it was natural to think she was doing that again, "seeing" things that weren't there.

The sweater's soft cable pattern warmed Sophie's chilly hands. She brought the cardigan to her face, wishing she could hide in its warmth the way she'd hidden as a child—pull a blanket over her head and ward the demons off. How simple that would be. How simple everything would be if there were magic blankets around that you could grab when things got tough.

She gathered the sweater close, seeking whatever comfort it could give her, but the cold sensation in the pit of her stomach told her it wasn't that simple anymore. It would never be that simple again. She might be able to block out her own fears and fantasies, shove them back until she couldn't hear their whispering warnings, but Muffin's prediction was going to be harder to dismiss.

15

"So . . . do you want a pastrami sandwich?"

"Hell, yes, I want a pastrami sandwich. If I were on a heart-lung machine, I'd want a pastrami sandwich. I always want pastrami, just on general principles, and no tutti-frutti perfume is going to change that. Even death probably won't change that."

Muffin failed utterly to hide her disappointment. She knew her face must have fallen a foot. Jerry White was one of the toughest customers she'd ever dealt with. He'd had a lovely time at Delilah's spa, wallowing in the mud baths like a baby elephant, but the Tarty Tangerine fruit oil had bombed.

Delilah had doused him in the appetite suppressant, but he'd insisted he was starving even when all the treatments were over. They'd finally had to order deli takeout to appease him. Thinking on her feet, Muffin had told him the effects were cumulative. They built over time, and she'd given him a vial to take with him.

A week of dogged effort had gone into scheduling this lunch with him today at Newport Beach's premier deli, but apparently she was to have nothing to show for it. Whoever said persistence always paid off did not know Jerry White and his obsession with pastrami.

Muffin sank into the cushions of the creaky wooden booth with a weary sigh. Bernie's Pastrami Palace was a bustling, noisy place with waitresses calling out orders and busboys scooping dishes into clanging wheeled carts. Normally the delectable smells alone would have sustained her. Their pastrami was world famous, and no one else on the coast did New York cheesecake with fresh strawberries like Bernie's. But today Muffin had no appetite, and Tarty Tangerine got none of the credit.

"Just because it didn't work for you," she said, "doesn't mean it won't work for anyone else." Gads, Muffin, could you *be* more petulant?

Jerry rubbed his hands together, an impish smile emerging. He was a powerful man, and a sycophant might have characterized his grinning idiocy as charm. To Muffin he was an oversized munchkin with an eating disorder and a cruel sense of humor.

"I never said it didn't work." His smile turned smug as he wrapped his lips around the straw in his diet Coke.

"Beg pardon?"

Half the soda disappeared with two deep pulls. "You asked me if I wanted pastrami. Of course I want pastrami. But that doesn't mean I'm hungry. I haven't had any appetite at all the last couple of days."

"And you've been wearing the fruit oil?"

"Religiously."

"So . . . ?" Muffin was afraid to think what she was thinking.

"So what's *in* this stuff?"

He fell against the seat with a chuckle. The dark oak booth let out a great groan, and by now Muffin had decided he was completely charming, a captivating man. Delighted, she fell back and joined him, laughing gaily, until finally he began to peer at her. He was waiting for her answer, she realized. And there was that problem of, well—

"We don't know," she admitted.

His smile vanished. "What do you mean? Your partner came up with the formula, didn't she?"

"Absolutely," Muffin assured him. "Delilah alone developed the formulations for all her cosmetics. But some of the ingredients are rather exotic. She picks them up on her trips to Mexico and South America—mostly wild plants and herbs—but she's never had them analyzed for their chemical composition."

That's where you come in, she thought.

He pushed the soda glass away, and Muffin knew she had his attention.

"How does Tarty Tangerine work?" he wanted to know. "Sense of smell? Does it penetrate the skin? Or are we talking power of suggestion?"

Something told Muffin not to bluff. If Jerry White could be allowed to think that he might be getting in on the ground floor of a major new discovery, he was much more likely to commit the resources they needed. He would be part of the team, rather than just the moneyman.

"We don't know that either."

His forehead scrinched several times as he studied her. She hoped it wasn't a side effect of the scent. A hovering waitress approached with an air of impatience, waiting to take their order. Jerry waved her away without so much as a sidelong glance.

"It could be nothing more than suggestion, you realize." He was all business now as he bent forward and rested his forearms on the table. Each booth had brass coat hooks, and he'd hung his jacket there. Muffin had spotted the Andrew Fezza label. His shirt was unmistakably Charvet and his cuff links shimmered with a twenty-four-karat gleam. Muffin knew fashion, and she also knew when Jerry White started eating, there would be mustard stains on those French cuffs.

"You tell me it will suppress my appetite," he went on, "and the placebo effect kicks in. That's enough to make it work, temporarily."

Muffin conceded that yes, he might be right. "Do we care

as long as it does work?'' she sincerely wanted to know. ''Does anyone care?''

The grin returned, but with a new quality of respect. Jerry White had found a soul mate. Or perhaps a partner in crime. At any rate, this was a woman who thought the way he did.

Muffin read all that in his expression and hoped she wasn't being overly optimistic. She had waited too long and worked too hard to have her dreams go begging. Everything she'd done for as long as she could remember, including marrying Colby Babcock over his mother's objections, had been about gaining the upper hand in some way.

She hadn't been certain about the details early on, but she'd aways had the urge to do things, run things, make things happen. She was a natural leader, an empire builder, in fact, but she was perfectly willing to take over an empire someone else had already built.

''I'm ready to order,'' he said. ''How about you?''

Muffin shook her head, suffering the familiar pangs of deprivation.

''Waitress!'' Jerry craned around to peer outside the booth for the woman he'd dismissed. ''Bring me a pastrami on rye, would you? Extra lean, lots of mustard.''

''I thought you weren't hungry,'' Muffin said.

''What's that got to do with eating?'' He was still flagging down the waitress. ''Throw a couple of pickles on that plate, too,'' he called to her, ''and maybe a side of potato salad. Thanks!''

When he came back around, he looked like a man who'd just made an appointment with a hooker for the works. The anticipation of pleasure in his expression was that erotic.

He winked at Muffin and finished off his soda.

A happy man, Muffin thought, grateful all it took to satisfy him was a slab of pastrami. Colby had not been a man of strong sexual appetites either, and that had suited Muffin fine. Her lifelong attitude toward sex had been what's in it for me? Perhaps that was her lifelong attitude toward everything. And it hadn't served her badly.

"You having anything?" the waitress asked Muffin as she approached their table.

Muffin considered the mineral water she hadn't touched and decided to stick with that. "Thanks, no," she said, aware of the hunger rising inside her, a desire so ravenous it frightened her. She wanted desperately to order something oozing with chocolate and carbohydrates. Maybe their Snicker's-bar cheesecake.

Her belly clutched at the thought of it. Her throat went slack, and her mouth began to water like Pavlov's dog. But no food could satisfy her cravings, she knew that. She'd tried gorging on starches and sweets, eating until she became ill or passed out. She'd tried every kind of purge: vomiting, diuretics, and laxatives. Sadly, even enemas. None of it had touched the hunger. And perhaps she knew in some resigned, despairing way that nothing ever would.

A psychiatrist had given her a bunch of that "inner child" crap, told her it was love she craved, not food. Muffin had paid the man his one hundred and fifty dollars and walked out of his office, her flashing derriere telling him what he could do with his theory. So her mother had kept her on starvation diets her whole life because she was a chubby infant, and her father had once shaved her head to reveal the fat rolls at the back of her neck, his purpose to humiliate her for "sneaking." It was pretty heinous, but she doubted she'd been through that much more hell than most other kids. Besides, she was an adult now. What was she supposed to do with a starving inner child?

The waitress clunked a plate down in front of Jerry that had a sandwich stacked four inches high, dripping with mustard and meat juices. Muffin would have killed for the smell alone. And Jerry's eyes gleamed like a hungry hyena's.

He'd hit it right on the nose, she realized. What did hunger have to do with eating? Both of them knew fruit oil wouldn't solve anyone's eating problems, but the public was so "hungry" for help, they wouldn't care. Muffin understood that hunger. They would buy Tarty Tangerine by the truckload and make her a wealthy and powerful woman. She knew that because she would have bought it, too.

Muffin swept up her mineral water and settled back with a mordant smile. Fuck the psychiatrist *and* his inner child. Her problem was that no one had ever seen her potential. Or perhaps they had, and it had scared them. At any rate, they'd always dismissed her. This man would not. There were ways to make sure of that.

The tiny white creature reared up on its hind legs and emitted an earsplitting squeal. A layperson might have called the sound terror, but Ellis Martin, Nobel laureate in neurophysiology, knew better than to anthropomorphize a lab rat's behavior. It would have been sloppy science to attribute human emotion to the reaction. And for that matter, if El had been inclined to label this particular rat's behavior, he would have called it joy. Lucy wasn't frightened. She was ecstatic.

The structure El hovered over was about as big as a medium-size freestanding backyard swimming pool. Lucy had just completed the water-maze task successfully for the first time, and now she was perched on a visible platform, receiving stimulation through electrodes implanted in her brain. The object was to reward her as well as to "burn" the learned route indelibly into her neural pathways.

El liked to think of it as the nearest thing to instant learning known to modern science. The digital remote he held was half the size of a television clicker, but infinitely more versatile. He could control the program and Lucy's stimulation with the touch of a button.

Lucy was raring to go when El ran her a second time. She paddled the learned route eagerly and scrambled onto the platform without a quiver of hesitation. Ears pricked and whiskers danced as she raised her snout in the air. Her sharp little squeal nearly drowned out the sound of the door opening behind El.

"You go, girl." El chuckled and turned to see who'd come in. "Rat kicks ass," he said.

El had been expecting a lab assistant, not the old friend

and colleague he was scheduled to have lunch with today. Dr. Claude Laurent looked on with wry interest, his dark hair in need of some crisis grooming and his slacks and sweater hopelessly rumpled.

Normally El's secretary announced visitors to the research facility. But then the psychiatrist did know his way around the place. He'd worked for Babcock right here in the La Jolla complex several years ago.

"Claude, come in!" El waved him closer, thinking that Laurent had always reminded him of a bear awakened mid-hibernation. He looked tall and shaggy and undernourished enough. But there was also a stricken quality behind the eyes that made one think of unbearable hurts being inflicted upon him at a tender age.

Peculiar notion to have about a psychiatrist, El thought. Claude had dabbled in both animal and human studies during his time with Babcock, but a run-in with Noah over the safety of a blockbuster antidepressant had led to his leaving the company and taking up private practice. El had always been fond of Claude, though, and had recommended him to Wallis when she was having her troubles.

"Taught her everything she knows, did you?" Claude indicated the twitching rodent with a nod of his head.

El preened like a proud father. "If there were a measurement for rat IQs, Lucy would be in Einstein's percentile."

Both men were silent as El prepared the rat for her final task. Claude was already intimately familiar with animal-learning research, and no commentary was necessary. This wasn't the time to discuss the parameters of the test itself or to engage in catch-up small talk. They were as intent as two football fans at the play-offs.

"Watch this," El said when everything was in place. He hit a button on the remote and a quick, bewildered whimper broke from Lucy, who dropped to a crouch on the retractible platform that was the start position for the task. "What the Lord giveth, the Lord taketh away."

When the platform disappeared and the trembling creature was in the water, Lucy didn't seem to know which way to swim, even though there was only one choice. She reached the first T intersection and spun in circles, apparently hopelessly confused. El kept his finger on the button as she floundered and flailed.

"How quickly they forget," he murmured. This was exactly the response he'd hoped for. Lucy was lost, her brilliant feat erased from the circuits as quickly and effectively as it had been burned in. Einstein's place on the scale was safe.

The rat's panicked thrashing had exhausted her, and she was losing the battle to stay afloat. El could see her frantic struggle to keep her snout above water and wondered if she'd retained enough learning to save herself. She had only to paddle back to the holding cage, where there was another platform. Come on, Lucy, he thought.

But the rat was still striking out in circles, hopelessly entrapped in a new response pattern, learned failure. Even her ability to tread water seemed to have been impaired, which was not what El intended. She was supposed to forget where to swim, not how.

Lucy emitted a pathetic little squeak and went under. Her struggles to resurface triggered desperate bursts of activity. She fought hard, but her strength quickly ebbed and her futile efforts weren't enough. Finally, with slow, weighted strokes, she sank to the bottom.

Claude moved to the side of the tank. "She's going to drown," he said with a glance at El.

El signaled the psychiatrist to hold off, his voice sharp. "Give her a chance."

"Fuck you." Claude rolled up his shirtsleeve and dipped his hand in the tank. He had some trouble getting a grip on the animal and ended up soaking himself, but he was clearly determined.

El was tempted to chalk Claude's behavior up to nerves. It had been a long time, and private practice didn't require the scientific detachment of the lab. But another concern took over his thoughts as he watched the other man's efforts. Was El imagining the tremor in Claude's hand? Even his mouth seemed to be oddly twisted.

El moved to help just as Claude plucked up the rat.

Poor Lucy dangled from his fingers, lifeless.

Undaunted, Claude took her to the countertop and laid her out on the white Formica surface. His hand was steady as he kneaded her slack, dripping body until, with a racking shudder, the rat choked up a tiny geyser of tank water. Her lungs freed, Lucy coughed up another gray trickle, and began to breathe again.

"The God complex?" El asked, watching the heroic attempt with ironic resignation. "Or too soft a heart for hard science?"

"God complex?" Claude retorted. "Is the pot calling the kettle black? Maybe I'd rather rescue rats in the name of humanity than sacrifice them in the name of science. And I do come across some rats in my practice."

El managed a nod for Claude's benefit, but his mind was already back on the experiment. "Pretty impressive, yes?" He indicated the remote he'd set on the countertop, all the while making a mental list of what might have gone wrong. "Once the bugs are worked out?"

Claude conceded as much with a shrug.

"There's more," El confided. "We're working with light at different frequencies, using it in conjunction with the neuro-hormone factor to stimulate certain pathways and jam others. No drugs or electrodes. There are no lesions, no permanent damage."

Now Claude nodded. "What's the method of stimulation?"

"I thought you might be interested," El said with a chuckle, "which is exactly why I called, besides wanting to see what my old friend was up to. We've done human safety trials with convicts with promising results. But we're getting some temporary side effects—fugue states, dissociation—the kind of thing you work with."

"And you want my input on the subject?"

"Come on." El headed for the door, motioning for Claude to follow. "I'll buy you lunch and pick your brain, what do you say? We'll get a lab technician to take care of Lucy, the Stouthearted.''

''You never did tell me what the stimulation was,'' Claude reminded him as the two men wandered off down the research wing's ghost-white hallway, once again as intent as football buddies. ''Any other anomalies? Headaches? Auras?''

16

"Sophie? Don't keep me hanging this way. I've been calling all day. The kids are gone by now, aren't they?" A harsh sigh filled the silence. "You're scaring me."

Sophie had the refrigerator door open, but she couldn't for the life of her remember why. She let it swing shut, her gaze fixed on the wall unit. It was Jay on the phone, but she didn't pick it up. She couldn't pick it up. Not yet.

She hadn't seen him since her birthday that weekend. She'd needed some time to get her bearings, and then he'd gone to the clinic for an extended treatment session. Her intention had been to talk with him when he returned and bring her suspicions out in the open instead of letting them fester inside. She'd wanted them to examine the situation in the clear light of day like two adults, bring some reality to it and perhaps put a stop to her growing fears. But the sound of his voice on the phone had stopped her, the mere sound.

Muffin's warning, and Sophie's other concerns, had flown right out of her head when he called. The grainy catch of emotion as he spoke her name with genuine warmth and confessed how much he missed her had triggered flashbacks of birthday dances and kisses—and the embarrassing fiasco of having propositioned him.

A bowl of Jell-O alphabet letters sat on the countertop next to the fridge, its rubbery cargo dissolving around the edges. Obviously that was why she'd opened the door. She was going to put away the Jell-O Jigglers she and the kids had made in their "cooking" class today.

"Genius," she said indignantly. "Jell-O melts when it's left out. It turns to soup."

The ceramic bowl was surprisingly heavy as she hoisted it off the counter, balanced it on her hip, and banged open the refrigerator door. She made room by stacking the coconut balls and the banana treats, tomorrow's snacks. And when she had that done, she slammed the door and fell against it.

Why couldn't she be the way she was before he returned? Sane. She'd just recovered her balance, just learned to breathe again—those elemental things everyone else took for granted. She'd mastered them, but barely, and then he'd come along and turned her to soup.

She was acting like a love-starved idiot. That much was glaringly obvious. But in point of fact it had been a long time and starving might not be too strong a word, she acknowledged. Claude had wanted to wait to "ensure the sacredness of the union," and since it was his first and only marriage, of course she'd respected his wish. So, okay, she was starved, and her behavior was more understandable on that basis. But that didn't mean she had to act like an idiot. Jay must be starved, too. Five years in a third-world prison and look at his control. Phenomenal.

Leaning against the refrigerator, head tilted back, Sophie gradually came to another realization. Where Jay Babcock was concerned, she was her own worst enemy. The man had a power over her that felt like chemical dependency. She would have been more than willing to have sex with him in her kitchen the other day if he hadn't put on the brakes. Ironically his birthday gift to her had been a lesson about trust, and yet that was the very issue that remained unresolved between them. Only now Sophie knew why. It wasn't him she didn't trust, it was herself.

The sense of being watched felt like a separate threat, but it was probably all part of a whole. She'd been overwhelmed by him as a girl, haunted by him as a surviving spouse, and now she was stumbling right back into the vortex again. The siren call was sharp and sweet. It was longing. Wild longing. Lethal stuff for a deprived child's love-starved soul. It figured that she would be an addict. She was ripe. She'd always been ripe. But the truth was she wanted to answer the call or she wouldn't be in this mess.

I came back for you, Sophie.

What did that mean? What did he want?

"For God's sake, girl," she whispered, gripping her elbows and never more serious in her thirty years of searching for a place of safety. "Find out who he is and what he's up to before you get near him again."

She wasn't answering her phone.

Jay had been trying all day, and she hadn't picked up, even though he knew she had to be there. He tossed the cellular in the bucket seat next to him and glanced in the rearview mirror, absently aware of the heavy commuter traffic as he checked out the fast lane. He'd ruled out illness or injury. One of her helpers would have called immediately with that kind of news. This was about what happened on her birthday.

His gentle attempt to put her off must have upset her pretty badly. Maybe he hadn't been as gentle as he thought, but she'd seemed almost reckless, a woman on a suicide mission, and he'd felt compelled to do something. Obviously she'd given in to a forbidden impulse and now she was backing away as fast as she could.

If she'd asked, he could have told her that was the wrong move. It brought out the hunting instinct in a man. When the quarry retreated, the hunter advanced. If she ran, he chased. If she hid, he found her. It was a reflex action, pure animal instinct. Fortunately for her, Jay had learned the hard way how to keep those drives in check.

He spotted a break in the thick stream of cars and cranked the wheel, easing the Jeep into the fast lane. He was on his way back from Babcock's corporate offices in the Newport Center facility, where he'd spent the morning with the marketing people and the afternoon with the bean counters. He had a little surprise in mind for the next board-of-directors meeting and he wanted to know everything there was to know about the company before that time.

His all-night session at the La Jolla clinic had proved interesting, too. The plan had been to monitor his sleep while on Neuropro. That was *their* plan. He'd had one of his own, and he'd wanted to be there when El wasn't. A little vigilance on his part had added to his suspicion that he wasn't being given the wonder drug. He'd faked swallowing the tablet the attendant gave him, which had turned out to be a mild sedative, but he couldn't avoid the injection. He had yet to find out what was in the syringe, but it had knocked him out cold, and he'd done enough sleuthing to know that Neuropro wasn't administered that way.

He didn't have the evidence he needed yet, certainly not enough to confront El, but he would in another session or two. Right now he was headed for the beach house to search it for any sign of the vault and the metal object he kept seeing in his head. It was going to be a busy weekend.

Moments later, as he pulled onto the freeway, he considered the cell phone again. There was little point in calling her, but he couldn't help wondering if she knew the effect her resistance was having. No matter where his thoughts took him, they always veered back to her—to the sudden reckless lust that shook her body when she'd implored him to make love to her, to the soft cry for completion in her throat.

His hand tightened caressingly on the wheel. The seduction of Sophie Weston, he thought, glancing in the rearview mirror. It was her image he saw this time, the tilted, yearning smile, the wishing-well eyes. It might have been her birthday they'd been celebrating, but she was the gift. In a perfect world, she would have been everything a man needed all wrapped up in one woman. He wanted to undo the ribbons again. Sophie, his surprise package. A bundle of soft, lush curves that promised all kinds of sweet secrets.

But this was not a perfect world. And she was increasingly unpredictable these days. He never knew quite what she was going to do next, which way she was going to go, and that made her dangerous.

He hit the gas and glanced into the rearview mirror again, looking for her, of course. But she was gone. The breathless girl by the stream had vanished, and in her place was a man he barely knew, a man who wanted to laugh at the ludicrous thought that was reverberating in his head.

Sophie Weston, dangerous?

"You need a real-live model instead of that dead fruit. How about me? I work cheap."

Ellis Martin stood in the doorway of Wallis's studio and watched her sketch an arrangement of d'Anjou pears and cheese on a marble cutting block. The setting was a Tiffany lamp and a much-ruffled and scalloped occasional table. Not the sort of thing Wallis usually painted, he noted, although the rotting fruit and moldy cheese could revolutionize the term *still life*.

"But do you pose nude?" She made that dry inquiry without taking her eyes off the disappearing pear.

"Sure do." He parted company with his jacket, letting it fall to the floor, and began to unbutton his shirt. "No charge for the erection."

She shot him a warning glance, but more than a hint of intrigue shimmered in her eyes. "Show-off," she said.

He came up behind her, his shirt half-buttoned and his thoughts full of admiration for the way she looked in a smock. Admiration with a bit of lust mixed in, he freely admitted. She wouldn't reveal her age, but El had gone through school with her husband, and she wasn't much younger than Noah. El had just turned sixty-two, so he knew Wallis must be pushing sixty.

She didn't look it, certainly not this morning. She looked like she'd discovered the fountain of youth, and though El wished he were the cause of her rejuvenation, he would have been content to be simply the beneficiary of her new lease on life. All things considered, he would take what he could get.

She was wearing black tights under a black tuniclike top, and the effect was amazingly sexy. If her outfit had been white, she could have been one of his lab assistants, but none of them had ever done for him what she did.

"Want to play truth or dare?" He slid an arm around her waist and drew her back against him, loving the way her bottom melted into the curve of his pelvis and the delicate dip of her spine pressed invitingly against his belly. "What am I thinking about right now? Tell me the truth. I dare you."

"That's not the way you play." She pretended indignation, but he saw her hand fall, the one holding the graphite pencil, and she let herself soften against him with a little sigh.

El's chest squeezed tight. Too tight, he thought ironically. It felt like he was flirting with a coronary.

"You feel so good," she said. "I wish you didn't."

"That's nothing compared to how good I'd feel if you turned around."

"Good to which one of us?"

"Both of us, silly. God, Wallis, I could make you so happy if you'd let me." He rubbed his cheek against the salt-and-pepper silk of her hair, inhaling deeply. She smelled like baby powder today and he liked that far better than the expensive perfumes she sometimes wore.

She let her head drop into the pocket of his shoulder and nodded her agreement. "I want that, too, El. You know I do, everything you want. And someday . . ."

He released her as she turned, but the concern in her eyes told him that today was not going to be that day. The tightness in his chest released, but a dull aching took its place. The feeling was all too familiar. He'd lived with it nearly all his life. Why couldn't he have the one thing he wanted?

"I know, I know." He stepped back, lifted his hands in defeat. "You're married, married to a man who doesn't even know you're alive. Christ, Wallis, Noah doesn't even know *he's* alive.''

He had long ago convinced himself that this ''thing'' he had for Wallis had nothing to do with her husband, Noah, the stern, friendly rival who had reigned over an empire and outdone him at nearly everything except academics—and possibly loving this woman, his wife.

With a half turn, she dropped her pencil into a can of spares, then became preoccupied with rearranging things for the next phase of her work, red pencils here, blue there. ''This isn't about us, El. It's about Jay and Sophie.''

How many times did she intend to reorganize that can? he wondered.

At last she seemed satisfied, or at least finished with it. With an exasperated shake of her head, she walked to the windows, but was silent so long he finally prompted her. ''What? They hate each other?''

He was kidding, of course. But she wasn't.

''She won't see him, won't take his calls, won't even take mine. I suppose I've been pushing too hard. I did so want it to work.''

All the anxiety she'd been fighting seemed to build to a head. ''It has to work, El. It has to.''

He wanted to go to her, to calm her and tell her everything would be fine. He wanted to do that because she was right. It had to work. But there was an unfinished painting propped against the wall by the window, and El couldn't take his eyes off it. It looked like any other bird in flight, except that it was carrying some kind of bloody prey in its beak. In the background, more ''offerings'' were impaled on a spiky, denuded tree. What in God's name? he thought. Could Wallis have painted that? It wasn't like her at all. It was ghoulish.

''Have you discussed this with Jay?'' he asked.

''Jay volunteers very little these days, but he did tell me that Sophie thought things were moving too fast between them and had backed off. I'm only guessing, but I think perhaps they got carried away and it frightened her.''

"Sounds like they're moving faster than we are," he grumbled.

"They're married, El. It's different."

"They may be married, but Jay's been gone for years," he pointed out. And I've been right here, he added silently, hoping, waiting, constantly at your service, my lady. Case in point, he thought, even now she looked so desolate he felt compelled to come up with some kind of solution.

"Where is Jay now?" he asked, already having assumed the role of analytical, problem-solving scientist.

She turned away from the window in surprise. "Newport Center, didn't he tell you? He went to talk to our marketing people. I thought you'd suggested it. He drove up there from the clinic—you *must* have known about that—and said he might stay over at the beach house."

El knew nothing about any of it, but he didn't want to alarm Wallis any further. Jay had a way of resisting being "groomed" for leadership, El had noticed, but one solo flight shouldn't do too much harm. He was rather surprised that Jay would strike out so boldly on his own when he'd seemed reasonably content to accept El's "mentoring" up to now. Obviously El would have to take measures to see that it didn't happen again, especially if Jay was arbitrarily rearranging his treatment schedule. That left El no choice but to intervene.

"And where is Sophie?" he asked.

"Why?" Wallis cocked her head, clearly curious. "Have you got some kind of plan?"

"When have you known me that I didn't have a plan?"

Her interest sharpened, and he could see that she was intrigued. It seemed that people never failed to be attracted by what was withheld from them, the mere hint of a secret. Well, let her be drawn, he thought. He rather enjoyed having the advantage for a moment or two. He wasn't going to reveal anything more, not a word . . . unless she decided to cooperate.

"What are you going to do?" she asked, approaching with exaggerated wariness. She was tiptoeing right into his trap.

"Nothing all that exciting. I think they call it matchmaking."

"Really?" Her eyes blinked so wide that he smiled inwardly. Women, he thought, they couldn't resist matchmaking, couldn't resist meddling in the intimate affairs of others.

"Tell me," she said coaxingly.

"What's the information worth?"

"Let's put it this way." She made a dash for the pencil and snatched it from the can. "Tell me or die."

Foolish woman, she'd wandered close enough that he could reach out and grab her. The pencil went flying as he pulled her forcefully into his arms, squeezing a gasp out of her. God, he loved the sound of it, loved the quick heat of her shock and excitement. "Kiss me or die," he said.

"Kiss me or *I'll* die," she whispered, pressing her mouth to his before he could respond.

The passion welled up in El so swiftly it almost made him dizzy. He'd been expecting her to put up a fight, if only for show, and it was all he could do to catch his balance as she curled her arms around his waist and molded herself to him.

He'd never thought of her as short, even though she was several inches shy of his lanky six feet, but she seemed tiny now, pressing herself to him so avidly. He combed his hands into her silver-streaked hair and locked his fingers together at her nape, holding her fast as he kissed her deeply and with all the passion and lust of a twenty-year-old, which was how she made him feel.

"I want you, Wallis," he told her. "And I'm going to stop at nothing to have you."

His declaration seemed to galvanize her, but when she drew back, her eyes were dark with fear. "El, we have to be careful. No one can know what we've done. No one can ever know about Jay. It would destroy so many people."

"No one ever *will* know." He could promise that with a clear conscience, but he couldn't tell her what else he was thinking. This was his chance. It was all coming together perfectly, and he was going after it. Everything that should have been his.

17

Sophie had been waiting most of the morning to see Raymond Navares, UCI's head geneticist and chief of the Southern California Center for Human Genome Research. Now that she was sitting in the renowned scientist's immaculate office and the sole focus of his cool curiosity, she found it difficult to break through her own inhibitions and appeal to him as one human being to another. For that was surely what she would have to do to secure his help.

A good part of Sophie's difficulty was the man himself. To say that he was lordly and intimidating was to belabor the obvious. Poised against a wall of sunlight-sheened diplomas, awards, and commendations, he looked like God in a designer blazer. A heraldic crest dominated the pocket of his dark gray jacket.

There were pictures of him with several presidents, including Clinton. And a bust of Navares himself sat proudly on a marble pedestal by the window. Undoubtedly sculpted by someone eminent, Sophie imagined.

"Dr. Navares," she persisted, "I understand your position,

but I am the patient's wife. If Babcock's CEO and its board of directors were allowed to see the results of Jay's tests, why shouldn't I be?''

''Mrs. Babcock, it was Jeremy White and the board who ordered the tests. They hired me in the capacity of a private consultant to verify your husband's identity as Jay Babcock, so of course, I made the results known to them.''

Sophie tugged at her slim linen skirt as she crossed her legs. She hadn't worn the boxy navy-blue suit in years, and though the style was coming back into fashion again, she couldn't imagine that anyone would mistake her for a trend-setter.

''Are you saying I need their permission to see the tests?'' she asked.

''I'm saying *I* would need their authorization to open your husband's file.''

He touched the medical folder that lay to one side of the gleaming black Lucite desktop. Sophie could see his reflection in the surface from where she sat, but it wasn't his graying temples and distinguished features that caught her attention. She was wondering how he got any work done, staring at himself that way. It was nearly impossible to avoid your image in this office, she realized. It was one big reflecting surface.

''I can tell you what the results are,'' he offered. ''But I was given to understand that the Babcock family had already been notified of the findings.''

She eluded his probing stare with a nod. ''I was told by my mother-in-law that he passed with flying colors, if that's the terminology.''

A forced smile. ''I don't believe the lab used exactly those words, but they were able to show with a high degree of certainty that he is the biological son of Noah and Wallis Babcock. Then, of course, there was the blood-typing and fingerprinting.''

When she didn't respond, he said, ''Those results seemed to be acceptable to everyone but you, Mrs. Babcock. Does that seem odd to you? It does to me.''

"What do you mean?" She'd been looking at her tightly pressed knees. Now she raised her gaze slowly.

"I mean that even my clients who stand to lose their position of leadership in the company if your husband takes over have accepted these findings as valid. Why can't you accept them?"

He settled back in his chair, studying her. "Is this about the tests, Mrs. Babcock? Or could it be something personal? Maybe you need some help making the transition now that your husband's returned."

Another nudge toward therapy. Soon they would be taking steps to have her committed. She'd be sharing a cell in the sanatorium with Noah. At any rate it was none of Navares's business, and she had no intention of answering. He didn't give her time anyway.

"If you want to see the lab results," he reiterated, "you'll have to speak with my clients."

Sophie didn't want to ask permission of White or the board. Jay would certainly find out if she did. Everyone would find out, and they would be questioning her motives, just as this man was. It was difficult enough dealing with Navares—and risky as well. She expected he would be on the phone to his clients the moment she left.

"Are you prepared to do that, Mrs. Babcock?"

There was anger in the swift negative shake of her head. Perhaps she'd known all along that he wouldn't help her, but the emotion burning in her heart was despair. God, what a nightmare this was turning out to be, all of it. She had thought by coming here, she could prove to herself that he was Jay and put the craziness behind her. She hadn't known what else to do. She had isolated herself so completely that Claude and her day-care brood had become her entire life. Now there was no one she could turn to. No one she could trust. She needed help. Someone on her side. Anyone.

Suddenly, inexplicably, her eyes welled up. The tears threatened to spill over, and in an attempt to hide them, she reached for the purse she'd left by her feet. She had some Kleenex stashed in there somewhere. The sudden anguish that gripped her told her she was close to the emotional edge, and all her fiery blinking was only making the situation worse. Her lashes were soaked. Dear God, she thought, don't lose it, Sophie. Not here, not in front of him.

"Mrs. Babcock . . . are you all right?"

She had the tissues, but couldn't see what she was doing. He called her name again, and she tried to reassure him that she was fine, but her voice broke and she couldn't go on.

"I j-just need a minute," she said, blotting furiously. She desperately needed to blow her nose, and she hated to think what her makeup must look like, mascara all over the place. Sadness burned like a fever. It swelled in her throat. What was wrong with her? What was she going to do?

"Is there anything I can do?" he asked. "Would you like me to call my assistant?"

She heard his chair squeak and was afraid he was getting up. "Oh, no, please!"

Sophie sincerely didn't want anyone else involved. It was humiliating enough losing her composure in front of him. She'd heard the horror in his voice. It was politely veiled, but horror nonetheless. The thought of an emotional scene unnerved him as much as it did her. Perhaps more.

Raymond Navares was a perfectionist who liked things precise and orderly, Sophie realized as she hunched over her bag. He probably had little tolerance for messiness of any kind, especially tears. Sophie wasn't given to displays of emotion either, but desperation had crept into her thinking. And now, some barely understood instinct for self-preservation told her this was no time to fight the tide. If Navares was as flustered as he sounded, she might even have the distinguished doctor at a slight disadvantage.

"Mrs. Babcock, you really are distraught. I—"

She abandoned the Kleenex and forced herself to look up at him. Tears streaked her face, and pain filled her voice. She could hardly talk, but to her surprise, a strange defiance took over, prompting her to reveal things that perhaps even she didn't want to admit.

"It nearly killed me when I lost Jay," she told him. A sob

lodged in her throat, but she kept going. "And now that he's back, I can hardly believe it's him. Do you know what I mean, Dr. Navares? Have you ever wanted something so badly that when you got it, you were afraid to let yourself believe? Afraid it would be snatched away again?"

"I'm sorry, Mrs. Babcock. I really am."

Navares simply stared at her, shaking his head. He seemed stunned, and despite her own turmoil, Sophie understood that this was a man so cut off from his own emotional pain that any hint of it, even another person's, could paralyze him. She also suspected that he had been afraid in the way she'd mentioned, so afraid he'd shut himself off from everything except the image he'd shined to a high gloss.

"I could call Mr. White," he offered, reaching for the phone. "I'm sure he wouldn't object to your looking at the results, under the circumstances."

She shook her head and the tears began to flow. It felt as if they would never stop. She fleetingly wondered if any of this was for his benefit, but she honestly didn't know which part it could have been. She was truly overcome.

"I thought if I could see the tests," she said pleadingly, distressed at how desperate she sounded. "Just see them with my own eyes, then I could stop being so frightened and accept that I have him back. That's all I was hoping for. I don't want to involve Jeremy or the company in this. It would be too embarrassing."

"Oh, I see."

"Never mind, I already feel like such a fool."

"No, wait." He rose with the file and came around the desk.

Sophie dragged another tissue from the purse-size pack she was holding and wiped her eyes, hardly daring to believe what was happening as he set the file on the edge of the desk nearest her, opened it, and invited her to look.

Shaky and uncomfortable, she joined him. "This isn't like me," she said, the tissue wadded in her hand. "I never do this."

"No, of course you don't." His voice was almost soothing,

but he moved quickly through each test, explaining its significance in terms that Sophie was only able to follow because she'd seen such evidence belabored in televised court cases. Navares obviously wanted her gone and his world back to normal as soon as possible.

Sophie really had hoped that with the proof right there in front of her eyes, she might be able to let go of her doubts. She was looking at actual DNA samples, and Navares had pointed out how the various bands of Jay's sample matched those of Noah and Wallis. But something continued to bother her, even as Navares finished.

"Is there any way to be sure that these tests weren't tampered with?" She pointed to results of the blood-typing. "Did you run them here?"

He reached around her and closed the folder with a sigh of exasperation. His compassion was obviously wearing thin.

"Mrs. Babcock, I was asked to coordinate and oversee the effort, knowing exactly what was at stake for everyone concerned. I have complete faith in the experts who conducted the tests and analyzed the results. They are all on the university staff and they are trusted colleagues that I have worked with throughout my tenure here."

"Fine," she said quickly. He'd taken her question personally and she had not meant it that way. She was only trying to silence her doubts, not to question anyone's integrity.

"The evidence couldn't be more conclusive," he went on. "But if you want more, I have that, too."

He returned to his desk, slapped the folder down, opened a cabinet, and pulled out what looked like X-ray files. A moment later he was holding two pictures side by side for her benefit.

"You're looking at a hairline fracture of the radius bone in the forearm," he explained. "I think even you will agree that they're identical in every way. One of them was taken when Jay Babcock was in his twenties, the other was taken the same day as the blood and saliva samples for the tests you're looking at. It's an X ray of your husband's arm."

He laid one X ray over the other. Except for the angle of the arm, they were identical.

Sophie felt an icy shiver in the pit of her stomach. There was no reason why this should have been more compelling evidence to her than the rest of it, except for the fact that she was with Jay when his arm was broken. "How did the fracture happen, do you know?"

"A car accident, I believe. I have copies of his medical history in my files."

"No, that's all right." Her voice had dropped to a whisper. "It *was* a car accident. Thank you," she said, feeling dangerously light-headed. For a second she thought she might be about to faint. It was the car accident she'd caused by her own childish need to get even with him. It had to be Jay. Either that or she really was going crazy and none of this was happening.

"Are we finished, Mrs. Babcock?"

She nodded. They were. This time they were.

"Good, then if you'll excuse me." He waved her toward the office door. "You realize that I overstepped my bounds by showing you what I did."

"Of course. I'd like our meeting kept confidential, too."

"Of course," he echoed, "because if any word of this gets out, I'll deny it and sue you for defamation."

Sophie had no doubt that he would. Navares's image was far more important to him than the accuracy of the tests, and he would probably go to any lengths to protect his reputation. But none of that mattered to her as she left his office, because she didn't doubt the accuracy of the tests herself. Not anymore. It was Jay they were testing. Unless this was some bizarre conspiracy to replace her missing husband, there was no other way to explain the results. And it couldn't be a conspiracy because Jeremy White had everything to lose by Jay's return.

No, Sophie didn't doubt the tests. It was something else she doubted now. Herself. Her own perceptions. Her own sanity.

Sophie dear,

Everything went fine today. The kids loved the new Bumpy Paint, and Albert's "masterpiece" is a portrait of you, he says. I stuck it to the fridge. Personally, I think he's got you confused with Benny Hill.

The critters are all fed and the cages cleaned. That was our afternoon "project." We couldn't round up Blaze, though. He's probably playing in the woods. See you next week.

                                        Ellen

Sophie set the note on the kitchen countertop, relieved that things were working out well with the new full-time assistant she'd hired. Ellen was a fiftyish former teacher with a great sense of humor, who'd become weary of the grind and retired early, but still wanted to work with kids.

"Toddlers don't know about boom boxes, do they?" she'd asked at the interview. Her credentials and references had been sterling, and so far the kids seemed to love her.

Sophie loved her, too. Having Ellen meant she could take off an entire day occasionally, as she had today, and know the kids were in good hands. She hadn't been able to do that since she started the day-care center and Jay took over for her occasionally.

Her stomach rumbled loudly, reminding her she hadn't eaten since that morning. The meeting with Navares had pretty well killed her appetite, and afterward she'd spent the remainder of the afternoon running errands. She'd needed the busy work of one routine task after another, doggedly attacking the list until she had everything done. It had left her tired but with the sense that she still had some control over her life.

She was also pleased that the unnerving feeling of being watched had dissipated. She hadn't felt the weight of someone's eyes on her all day. Hadn't looked over her shoulder yet either.

"Benny Hill?" Sophie arched an eyebrow at the grinning picture attached to the refrigerator door with a magnetized carrot. Ellen was being kind. The moonbeam face and huge smile were vaguely reminiscent of the English comedian, but Sophie would have said Cheeta, the chimp, on a bad-hair day.

Her refrigerator had become a miniature gallery of her daycare experiences. It was cluttered with pictures by the kids and snapshots of them. Feeling organizational, she moved her portrait next to a recent snapshot of Albert and drew an arrow, pointing to him.

"The artist," she murmured as she liberated a magnetized pencil and wrote the words.

It amused her that Albert apparently saw her as a grinning idiot. Given the day Sophie'd had, she could think of worse things—like a blubbering idiot. Actually, she was flattered. She had been on a roller coaster since Jay returned, literally and figuratively. There'd been moments when she'd felt almost joyous for the first time in years. Albert must have picked up on her mood in the perceptive way that only children do. To him, her smile was probably the most dramatic change about her.

She was tempted to have a look at herself in the oven door and see if there was actually any resemblance to Albert's vision, but Ellen's note had said they couldn't find Blaze, and Sophie's first concern was for the dog.

By the time the light had begun to fall that evening, Sophie was frantic. She still couldn't find Blaze anywhere. He hadn't responded to her calls, though she'd searched the meadow several times and ventured into the woods, thinking the worst, that a pack of coyotes had attacked him. But the coyotes rarely came down this far out of the hills, and the ones who had were always more afraid of Blaze than he was of them.

Moments ago she'd phoned the Big House, in case he'd shown up there, but Mildred hadn't seen any sign of him either. Sophie had even driven down the road as far as the next town, fearful that he'd been the victim of a hit-and-run.

By midnight, she'd been out back calling every ten minutes, and she'd placed phone calls to nearby neighbors and anyone else she could think of who might have seen the dog. Grotesque visions of Blaze's fate tormented her, even though she knew they were probably triggered more by her exhaustion than by reality.

Some time later, sprawled across the bed, she fell into a fitful sleep that was burdened with images of animals lying hurt and bleeding on remote highways. Sirens whined in her head, along with a horrible keening cry that could have been Blaze.

Near dawn she struggled awake to the realization that the keening cry wasn't a siren or the dog. It was the phone. In the pitch-black room, the only thing she could see was the luminous dial of the clock radio. Why would someone be calling now? she wondered, and feared the worst. They must have found the dog.

18

"Sophie? Are you there? Sophie!"

Still groggy with sleep, Sophie could hear someone yelling at her as she hung over the side of her bed and struggled to find the telephone in the dark. She'd knocked it off the table, trying to get to the light. Groping with both hands, she gave up and tumbled to the floor with the phone.

"Who is this?" she whispered, hoping it was the mouthpiece she had pressed to her lips. Her sleep shirt was twisted around her waist and she couldn't get it untangled.

"Are you missing something?"

The familiar male voice sent a bolt of adrenaline through Sophie. Blood pounded in her temples, but her thoughts were thick and slow. "Jay?"

"You're missing *me*? I thought you were avoiding me." His quick breath could have been laughter. "I meant Blaze. He's here with me."

"Oh, thank God." She hugged the phone with a great shudder of relief. "Is he all right?" she asked. "Where are you? I called the Big House last night and Mildred hadn't seen him."

"I'm at the beach house for the weekend," he said. "Somehow he found me here. He's fine. Hungry, but fine, and I don't know what the hell I'm going to feed him unless I can find an all-night market."

It was four A.M. by the clock radio, and Sophie was beginning to make some groggy sense of the situation. She should have realized that Blaze might head off to the beach in search of Jay. They used to go there for weekends in the summer when they were first married, and they'd always taken the setter with them. After Jay disappeared, Blaze had made the trek regularly, hunting for his master.

"Is there anything in the fridge?" she asked.

"Some frozen pizza and a six-pack. Why?"

"Blaze loves both. Warm the pizza in the microwave, chill the beer, and he'll be in heaven."

"Are you sure?"

"I have to fight him off when I have pizza. And I always ration him, so this will be a treat." Something had just dawned on her. "What are you doing at the beach house?"

"I was at the Babcock corporate offices in Newport Center all day, talking to suits. And since the beach house is just down the road in Laguna, I decided to hang around for the weekend. Blaze was a nice surprise, although I'm not sure the neighbors appreciated his mournful howling. Just say the word, and I'll bring him back. Right away, if you want."

Sophie did want the dog with her. The way things had been going lately she felt safer with Blaze around. It was Jay she didn't want, especially at dawn. This was the first actual contact they'd had all week.

"Not tonight," she said. "I'll come by and get him tomorrow. I'm going out anyway—to do errands." She'd actually finished all her chores earlier that day, but somehow it gave her a little extra measure of control to be the one making the trip.

"I'll be here," he assured her.

Sophie could hear the soft whine of Blaze's breathing in

the background and knew the setter must be in ecstasy at having found his master. Blissful whimpering over Jay Babcock at four A.M. easily made the top-ten list of things Sophie did not want to hear. But even so, an odd thought struck her. If animals mourned loved ones just as humans did, then Blaze must have been brokenhearted when Jay disappeared. Yet now the dog could pour out all that love, as if the loss had never happened—and without the crippling human fear of it happening again.

Animals lived in a state of grace, she decided. They didn't have to deal with issues of trust and intimacy and emotional safety. No inner conflicts for Blaze. When Jay was there, he was happy. When Jay was gone, he was sad. It was brilliantly simple.

"I'll be over tomorrow, around noon," she said.

"Come earlier."

His sexy, coaxing voice was the only thing Sophie heard as she hung up the phone.

Sophie showed up at the beach house at seven in the morning. Apparently Jay had decided to go back to bed, because she was forced to shower the bedroom window with handfuls of pebbles to get him to answer the bell.

He arrived at the door in shorts that looked as if he'd hastily pulled them on. They were the gray athletic variety he used to live in, with the drawstrings he always left undone. Though she wouldn't have shared her secret with him, she still loved the way the shorts rode his hips, held only by flaring male bones, and a reckless, I'd-rather-be-naked attitude. She'd also loved the feel of the downy soft cotton in her hands—and the feel of him inside them.

Apparently he was still blithely indifferent to the effect of an overexposed male body on the unsuspecting female population. But she wasn't. The tugging sensation in her belly was familiar by now, as insistent as the pull of a leash.

He looked at his wrist, where a watch would have been strapped if he'd been wearing one. "Noon is coming earlier and earlier these days."

"I was concerned about Blaze. I brought dog food." She held up a grocery sack and rattled the cans.

"He'll appreciate that. Anchovy pizza wasn't a heavy favorite."

"Anchovy? Is that what you gave him?"

"It's all I had."

"Oh, poor baby, where is he?"

Jay was a good-size man, and the diagonal stance he'd taken against the door frame very effectively blocked the way. While she waited to see what he was going to do next, she was acutely aware that he was studying her with a certain laconic male fascination, as if he wasn't sure whether he wanted to know what was going on inside that female head of hers or not but couldn't seem to help himself.

Sophie felt the pressure of his deceptively casual gaze, and it was making her fingertips curl. She had never dealt with this particular kind of male attention before, except from this particular man, and she would probably never get used to it.

Claude's involvement had been more deliberate and fatherly. And the old Jay, though intense and passionate, had been too caught up with whatever his next adventure was going to be. He'd always made Sophie feel as if she were a rest stop, maybe an adored one, but a rest stop nonetheless. This man made her feel as if *she* were his next adventure.

He could still singe a hole in paper with the intensity of his gaze. All that energy channeled through one source probably explained the burning-glass effect, but it didn't explain what he found so absorbing about her outfit, if that's what he was looking at.

The denim shorts she'd picked actually flattered her thighs, and her cropped T-shirt in butter yellow was good with her fair coloring. Plus, the wide V-neckline looked like it could drop off her shoulder without too much trouble at all, which created a look of being half-dressed in public. All in all she liked the effect. And so did he, it seemed.

"Are you going to let me in?" she asked.

"I could do that." He hitched himself up and stepped aside with a faintly wolfish smile.

Into the lair, she thought. Nevertheless, she walked straight through the house to the kitchen, careful not to brush against him as she left him standing there on the threshold. She was very glad to have something to do. Poor starving Blaze. She would feed the setter a quick bite and leave.

"Need help finding anything?" Jay asked, entering the kitchen as she was wedging a can of dog food into the metal jaws of the electric can opener.

"No thanks, I remember where everything is."

The kitchen was small but warm and charming, with its warm maple cabinets and flowered curtains. Every spare nook and cranny was crowded with Sophie's collection of salt-and-pepper shakers, which she'd moved here when the kids' stuff overtook the rambler. Blaze was sitting right next to her while she prepared his food, his tail thumping loudly.

"The old Blaze would have knocked you out of the way and been up on the countertop by now," he pointed out. "Eating out of the can."

"Obedience training," she said. "It does wonders."

"Not on all of us."

She wanted to turn, but didn't. If he was talking about himself, he could only mean his imprisonment. She imagined he was standing across the room behind her, probably leaning against the kitchen door frame now. She was trying not to think about what he looked like in that loose-limbed stance. Nobody could lean like Jay.

It actually hurt to breathe for a second as she realized how much she wanted to be here . . . with him. She had no idea if she was setting herself up for some new disaster, or if she was finally coming to accept the reality of who he was. Maybe the heart of her conflict truly was about trying to protect herself. That thought had occurred to her before, but it had never felt more immediate than it did now. If she let herself love him again, he could hurt her again.

She couldn't escape the feeling that she was about to entrust him with something priceless, a fragile bone-china cup he'd already broken once, knowing he would drop it again. *Go ahead, break it, Jay, but don't just crack it in two this*

*time. Shatter it so there's nothing left. Because that's what
will happen if you don't love me back.*

If there was anything more frightening in life than this,
than love, Sophie couldn't imagine it.

"You must be wanting to get dressed," she said, opening
the cupboard for a dish to put the dog food in. It was a
gourmet mix of turkey, giblets, and gravy that smelled like
the real thing. "Don't let me keep you."

"I *am* dressed. This is pretty much what I plan to wear
around here. It *is* a beach house."

He planned to wear nothing more than underwear? Eat fast,
Blaze, she thought as she set the bowl in front of the dog.

But Blaze was in no particular hurry to eat—or to leave.
He finished the delicacy at a leisurely pace, and when he was
done, trotted over to where Jay stood and sat beside him,
bright-eyed, tail wagging, as if to let Sophie know that he
quite liked it at the beach house, and had no intention of
going anywhere else, regardless of her plans.

Sophie shot him a glare. *Traitor.* She had his leash in her
bag, but by the time she'd fished it out a moment later, Blaze
had crawled between Jay's legs and began to emit pathetic
whimpers. *Please, Mom, don't make me go home. Can't I
stay and play some more?*

"Obedience training does wonders?" Jay murmured dryly.
He bent to scratch the dog's ears. "Looks like he isn't leaving, not without me."

"We'll see about that."

Sophie gave it a valiant effort. She cooed, coddled, and
coaxed. And finally barked. "Blaze, come!" But the setter
stubbornly proved Jay right. Sophie couldn't lure him away
from his master, even with the promise of a Frisbee game
when they got home. And Blaze's only response to her obedience commands were little yips and howls. The dog would
not budge.

With a dark look at Jay, Sophie tossed him the leash.
"Okay, you try."

"Sorry." He draped the leather strap around his own neck
and walked to the sink. Blaze leaped to follow. "I'm no good

at obedience training until I've had my coffee. How about some breakfast?''

"I really should go.''

"In that case, good luck with the dog.''

As Jay busied himself brewing the coffee Blaze huddled next to him and eyed Sophie as if she were an operative from Animal Control. The term *man's best friend* took on new meaning as Sophie began to harbor dark suspicions about what was going on. Maybe the strange experience in Dr. Navares's office was still resonating in her mind, but this situation also smacked of conspiracy.

She didn't doubt that Blaze had wandered here on his own, but there was something too convenient about his refusal to come home. And the way he'd attached himself to Jay. They're in it together, she thought. Jay had never meant to let her get out of here alive with the dog, and perhaps he'd even coached Blaze. If the setter hadn't weighed nearly as much as Sophie, she would have picked him up and lugged him out. At any rate, she wasn't leaving without him. She hadn't felt safe alone in the rambler for some time now.

Jay had moved over to the stove, where a skillet was sizzling, and he was now slicing up mushrooms he'd taken from the refrigerator, along with red onions, green peppers, and bite-size chunks of honey-baked ham. Oh, no. Oh, God, she thought. Denver omelettes. They were Jay's specialty, and he had cooked them for her on their honeymoon, right here in this beach house.

How could he? She adored Denver omelettes, and he knew it.

The week she'd spent here with him had probably been the happiest of her twenty years. At the time it hadn't seemed that life could offer anything more magnificent than a future with a thrilling man like Jay Babcock. He was an adventurer at heart, but his position in the family company was also assured. And he could cook! For herself, she'd pursued a teaching credential with the goal of working with special-needs children in some capacity. The horizon had been as bright and full of promise as a summer sunrise.

Irresistible smells wafted her way—diced onions and peppers being brazed in crackling hot butter. Her senses quickened as she watched him whip the eggs with a fork and pour the frothy liquid into the pan. Even her mouth had begun to water in anticipation. This *was* a conspiracy. The poignant memories alone should have killed her appetite, but oddly, she was starting to recall the good times more vividly than the bad, the happiness more than the heartache. And by the time he'd flipped the huge omelette onto a platter and transformed it into a golden puff cloud with a crispy brown fringe, starvation had won out.

"All right, breakfast," she said. "How long could it take to eat some eggs? And maybe Blaze will be ready to go by then."

There was a quaint, sunlit breakfast nook off the kitchen that had always reminded Sophie of a gazebo. Mullioned windows looked out over sand dunes on three sides, and fragrant flowering plants hung about the knotty-pine walls. She'd always felt a close communion with the elements while in that room, the cobalt sea, the chalk-white beach. And now Jay was at the rustic table, setting her omelette on a place mat shaped like a huge sunflower.

"You can tell me if I've lost my touch," he said, drawing back a chair for her.

She slipped into another chair and smiled at him. "With omelettes?"

"What else?" He went back for the rest of it, his half of the eggs and the coffee. When he returned a moment later with a laden tray, he'd also remembered his table manners and put on a shirt. She'd seen the old maroon polo draped over a living-room chair. It was very much like the ones he used to wear when they were married. But something she hadn't noticed made her quell a sound of surprise. A button was ripped off, the top one on the placket, and Sophie could remember the exact moment it happened.

"Everything okay?" he asked. He'd speared a forkful of eggs, but he set it down when he saw her expression.

"Your shirt—" Impulsively, she reached over and touched

the torn placket. The shock of recognition that leaped through her fingertips was strong enough to be live current. She couldn't possibly know that it was the same shirt just by touching it, but her senses were telling her that it was.

"Do you remember how this happened, Jay? Do you?"

She was forced to draw back as he reached for the sugar bowl. It was almost as if he hadn't heard the question. He stirred a heaping teaspoon into his coffee, then added another. *He was using his left hand now.*

She'd decided he wasn't going to answer her when he suddenly put the spoon down. Without a glance at the torn placket, he looked up at her.

His dark gaze bored into hers. "Yes, I remember. We were playing—roughhousing—and your hair got caught in the button. We couldn't find any scissors, so I ripped the button off my shirt."

She nodded, but said nothing. Her lips felt suddenly dry and unmanageable, like they were stuck to her teeth. He'd picked up the spoon again and was slowly tapping it against the table.

"Did I get it right?" he asked.

She wasn't consciously aware that she'd been testing him, but it did feel like that, a test. "Yes, that's how it happened. You swiped my good-luck abalone shell, and I was trying to get it back."

His smile was rueful. "Hey, don't make me the bad guy. I tried to save your 'goldilocks,' but you ended up having to cut a chunk out of them anyway," he admitted. "It was the only way to get the 'devil' button out of there."

The spoon stopped tapping as he realized she was still staring at him. "What is it? You said I got it right."

"You did. It's the coffee."

He glanced at the cup.

"You don't take sugar in your coffee," she said. "You've always hated it that way. You used to say it tasted like molasses."

"Christ." He shook his head, his voice searingly soft.

He seemed almost angry, and she assumed it was because

she'd called him out. She'd had to. Surely he understood that.
She was the one at risk. She had to know what she was
getting into, and who she was getting into it with. She
couldn't be quiet about the questions crowding her heart.
They hurt, these questions. She had to have answers.

She waited, but he made no attempt to explain the situation. And her smile went sad as she gradually began to realize
what she was doing to him, that he had a right to be angry.
Was she going to go on testing him forever? For the rest of
their lives? She had to stop.

She pushed back from the table and walked through the
kitchen, not sure where she was going. The one thing she
knew was that she couldn't eat, even though her stomach was
rumbling so loudly he must be able to hear it, too.

There was another, much smaller, collection at the beach
house, her shells. She hesitated when she got to the cabinet
that held them. The rosewood curio cabinet was in the deepest
corner of the L-shaped living room, and it overflowed with
treasures that they—she, Jay, and Blaze—had picked up on
the beach during the days they'd spent here. Jay's contribu-
tions had probably been his way of humoring her penchant
for collecting things. Blaze was another story. He was as
much a pack rat as Sophie.

"If you're hungry enough, you'll eat anything, Sophie.
Dirt, slime mold, feces . . . insects were a delicacy."

He'd come up behind her. The angle of the sun had thrown
his shadow up against the curio cabinet and the wall behind
it, and it made her feel as if she were standing in darkness.

"Did they starve you in prison?" she asked. This was all
she wanted, for him to explain. She'd seen the tests, and she
was almost there, ready to believe. But it felt as if she were
about to step off a cliff, and she had to know that he would
be there, that he would catch her this time. If only he could
explain away her doubts and convince her that he was really
Jay. She wanted that. God, she did.

Please, she thought, make me believe.

"They fed us twice a week, some kind of gruel, but once
in a while, they gave us sugar packets. I was in a regular

lockup for a while, with cell mates. Eventually they both died, and I didn't tell the guards for days. I hoarded their sugar. It kept me alive."

No wonder he refused to talk about his prison experiences. They were even more ghoulish than she could have imagined. She wondered how many other things had happened that he didn't want to admit—or even remember. "It must have been horrible. I'm sorry."

"At least I got out. There were hundreds who didn't. Prisoners died every day in that cesspool."

He probably felt guilt about them, too, survivor guilt. Considering what he'd been through, perhaps she ought to feel guilty that she didn't believe him, but the questions persisted. It didn't seem possible he could have been through all that and be so healthy. "You must have been skin and bone."

"Nothing but bones, as I remember. In rehab they concentrated on nutrition, physical therapy, and bodybuilding. Counseling, of course, to help me deal with the demons. I assume they were the ones who notified my family."

She was making pleats in her shirt with her fingers.

"You okay?" he asked.

"No." Her throat was tight, and for some reason she felt frustratingly close to tears. Maybe it wasn't about his being there to catch her. Maybe she was incapable of jumping. That's how it was beginning to feel, as if she were the one who was fatally flawed.

"I want to believe all this," she said, turning to him. "You know that, don't you? But you don't seem like Jay. I don't know what it is, but there's something different."

"Of course something's different, Sophie. *I'm* different. If you'd known all along that I was in prison, you wouldn't have expected the same man to come back, would you?"

"No. Perhaps not."

She'd clutched her elbow and nestled her other hand diagonally across her breasts. It was a protective stance, but eventually she realized that something was touching her wrist, the one down by her waist, touching it so lightly she'd felt a sensation of warmth, but nothing else. He was making those circular motions that melted her brain, and his expression was one of rapt concentration. She almost wanted to laugh. She could never have believed that anyone would have found her so fascinating as this man seemed to.

"Maybe you need to give yourself time to get to know me again," he said. "That's all I'm asking for, some time. It wouldn't cost you very much."

It could cost her *everything*. The more time she spent with him the more likely she was to fall in love with him again. And yet, how could she live with herself if she didn't give this a fair chance. She would always wonder—and have regrets.

"We could try again," he suggested, "starting now. I promise, no surprises, no amusement parks, no monasteries. You make the rules. We won't do anything that makes you feel uncomfortable."

She considered his hand, the one that could seduce her mindless with a caress. Already the leash in her belly had pulled disturbingly tight. "No touching," she said.

"Touching?" He hesitated. "Define that for me."

She glanced down and he paused mid-stroke.

"You're not serious. This kind of touching? I can't even hold your hand?"

"You don't *just* hold my hand, Jay. You play with it, you fondle it. You do that whenever you touch me, *wherever* you touch me."

"And you don't like it?"

Her voice grew throaty and soft. Her lids felt heavy as she raised them to look up at him. "I love it. That's the problem."

His gaze darkened as he studied her, darkened into something so mesmerizingly sexy she had to look away again or risk losing what little command of the situation she had.

"If I loved something," he said, "I think I'd probably want to do more of it."

"Yes, but what if it turned your ankles to water, your insides to soup, your brain to slush, and you couldn't think straight?"

"Well now, that could be a problem."

"No kidding."

She heard him sigh.

"How's this?" he asked. Suddenly his arms were folded and his hands had disappeared. "Good enough?"

The good-little-boy grin that tilted one corner of his mouth charmed a smile out of her. Now if she could just forget how hot and possessive and sensual that mouth had felt on hers. If she could only forget the kindling blaze that had flared up when he kissed her.

Hopeless, she thought. It seemed hopeless dealing with him from any kind of normal perspective. She wanted to sigh, too.

A soft series of whines announced Blaze's appearance. The setter wandered into the room as if he'd been searching for them, spotted Jay, and bounded over to him. Sophie felt a tiny twinge of jealousy over the dog's sudden and total devotion to Jay. Blaze was acting like she didn't exist, and she was the one who'd fed and cared for him all these years. Still, she did understand the impulse. Jay could do that to you, make you forget everyone else existed.

"Okay to touch the dog?" he asked.

"Be my guest." She leaned against the cabinet, relieved to have some breathing room as Jay knelt to work his spell on Blaze. Within seconds he had the poor helpless creature moaning and crooning, in total ecstasy as Blaze sank to the floor and rolled over. The setter seemed to go into an hypnotic trance as Jay stroked under his chin. The dog's eyes fluttered shut and his head lolled back.

Sophie watched the goings-on skeptically, fortifying herself with the short list of her reasons not to jump. Muffin's warning ran through her head, as did reminders of the creepy feelings she'd had lately, feelings of being unable to escape this man's eye, even when he wasn't around. She made no attempt to push the concerns away. Quite the opposite, she had decided to entertain them, to make them a meaningful part of her decision about the situation.

But the longer she watched, the less substance any of the

reasons for caution seemed to have. Muffin had her own motives for casting doubt on Jay, and Sophie's other feelings
were too vague to pin down. As the minutes ticked away she
found it increasingly difficult to hang on to her objections,
any of them. Maybe it was the salt air, the melody of the
waves, but something was spiriting her short list off on the
breezes. The only thought that stuck with her as she watched
Jay Babcock work his wiles was her intuition about animals.
They did live in a state of grace. She envied Blaze. She really
did.

19

I t was a luscious night, the kind that flooded your senses with rich fragrances and shimmering sounds and made you want to spoon it up like dessert and eat it. The sunset was the color of rainbow sherbet, raspberry streaked with orange. The salty incoming tide crashed gently, rhythmically, against a soft melon-pink shore. The air smelled of smoldering beach fires, and seabirds swooped as black as licorice against the horizon.

Sophie nibbled on the orange slice she'd fished from her goblet of sangria and wondered at all her concerns about staying on at the beach house. It had been perfect so far. She was nearly stuporous with contentment. She and Jay and Blaze had prowled the shore during the day, looking for shells for her collection. Afterward, they'd napped in the sun and then gone shopping for the groceries Jay would need to fix *albóndiga* soup and chilis relleños, his southwestern specialties.

Now they were sitting out on the deck, relaxing after a meal of his rich, spicy concoctions and sipping the sangria he'd laced with slices of fresh orange, lime, and bright red strawberries. Sophie could hardly keep from whimpering with pleasure.

"Feel like a swim?" he asked.

They were sitting next to each other in deck chairs and Sophie knew he would have reached out and touched her if she hadn't passed a law against it. She was beginning to wish she hadn't. She already missed the warmth.

"I'd sink after all that food. I'm much too full, and besides, I don't have a suit." By the sound of the noise Blaze was making, Sophie was alone in her reluctance. The setter was down on the sand, yipping and leaping in his excitement to go into the water.

"There are plenty of spare suits inside." Jay inclined his head toward the house. "I think one of them's yours."

"What? From years ago?" She hadn't been to the beach house since Jay disappeared, not even to check on her collections, especially not that. They'd all gone on excursions together to find her shells—him, her, and Blaze.

"Out of style?" he asked.

It wasn't the suit, it was her. She hadn't worn one in years. Claude didn't swim, and the kids took so much of her time, and then, of course, there was the other problem. Chicken, she thought, imagining what Jay would say if she tried to explain. She was still looking for places to hide. It was a little late to be ducking under beds, but her kids were a great way to avoid having a life, as was her less-than-perfect body.

"I'd sink," she repeated, but with less conviction. She thought that was the end of it, but to her surprise, he rose from the chair and pulled off his shirt. "Looks like one of us had better hit the surf before Blaze gets us arrested for disturbing the peace."

Blaze had begun to howl pathetically and the sound carried well down the beach. Jay took the short flight of steps and loped toward him with the long, slow grace of an athlete warming up. But when he raced past the dog to the water, calling for Blaze to follow, Blaze didn't budge. Instead, the setter gave Sophie a look that said, What gives? Ignoring

Jay's coaxing, the beast sank to his haunches and stared at her.

"Better go put on that suit," Jay called back to her. "He's not going in unless you do."

Sophie plunked down the drink and sprang from the chair. "Have you got that dog trained?"

Sophie's trajectory as she came out of the water was a straight line to her beach towel. She was dripping wet and shivering cold, but body warmth wasn't nearly as high on her list of priorities as getting the towel wrapped about her waist.

She'd finally gone up and wriggled into the five-year-old suit, congratulating herself on her valor, especially since it was one of those one-piece leotards with absolutely no support that sixteen-year-old Olympian swimmers wore. She looked much better than she'd expected to, but that didn't mean she was ready to expose her dimpled thighs for the amusement of the masses, at least not any more than she already had.

"Brave girl," Jay said, coming up behind her. Sophie wasn't sure what he meant until he bunched up his own towel and used it to rub her shoulders and back. "That water's freezing."

Blaze was still bounding through the waves and ka-yaiing for them to come back in. Sophie laughed at the dog's un-bridled excitement. The thrill of victory was running through her veins, too, spurred as much by conquering the icy Pacific as by conquering her reluctance to come out of hiding. She was feeling quite pleased with herself when suddenly the towel she'd so carefully secured was ripped from her body.

The surf drowned out Sophie's startled cry.

Blaze took off down the beach, the towel flying in his jaws like a banner. Apparently when he failed to get their attention with the barking, he'd raced up and nipped the towel off her. Sophie glanced down at her pale, naked thighs and a stomach that still pooched more than she wanted it to. Well, there it is, she thought. Nowhere to run, girl, nowhere to hide.

Jay picked up on her distress immediately. "Are you all

right?'' he asked. "Cold? I can run up to the house and get you another towel.''

"No, I'm fine.'' Either he was being very gallant about the whole silly mess, or he really didn't know what was bothering her. She hoped it was the latter. Men didn't seem to get it about women's body-image issues, and the human race was probably better off that they didn't. It was bad enough that Sophie had to be afflicted with these embarrassing insecurities in his presence; she certainly didn't want to discuss them. Let him think she was freezing.

"Maybe you better go after the dog,'' she suggested.

"In a minute.'' His glance brushed almost imperceptibly over her body, and then he met her gaze and held it, silent for a moment. "Is it the suit?'' he said with a hesitation that appeared to be completely sincere. "Are you feeling self-conscious about something?''

"No, well . . . maybe.''

"Your legs?''

She gaped at him. "How did you know that?''

"The way you're shielding them with your hands?''

She'd splayed her hands over her thighs without even realizing it. Now she yanked them up and hugged her waist.

He did look at her then, letting his powerful focus climb her body as slowly as a sunrise. "Sophie, your legs are beautiful,'' he assured her, with husky emphasis on the last word. "What are you worried about? Some imperfection here or there.''

"Imperfection? I've got ricotta cheese for thighs!''

"See, now, we haven't got a problem. I love ricotta cheese.''

The breath she caught sounded like a sucked-in gasp. "Are you saying my thighs are *that* bad?''

He laughed despairingly. "That's not what I'm saying at all. I'm saying you make my mouth water, you look so delicious in that bathing suit.''

She didn't believe him for a second, but there was that sexy, raspy quality to his voice, and his gaze had heated considerably as he looked at her. The strange fire that encircled his iris had sparked a slow blaze.

"Well, the suit is five years old, and I've gained some—"

He overrode her explanations with a shake of his head. "If you'd come over here, you wouldn't have to worry about anyone looking at you, if that's what you're concerned about."

The way he opened his arms to her and the engaging tug of his smile made her feel as if she ought to pinch herself. Surely she must be dreaming.

"Come on, shy one," he coaxed. "I'll be your towel."

Sophie awoke in a state of mild confusion to a cozy chamber painted goldenrod with sunshine. The surroundings were seductively familiar. She recognized the master bedroom's sunny charm and shuttered windows, but it took her a moment to figure out where she was, primarily because she couldn't have arrived there under her own power. She'd fallen asleep in front of the fire last night, her head nestled in Jay's lap.

She'd been utterly spent from their day on the beach and their evening of swimming, and yet she could hardly remember anything more freeing. The love-hate relationship she'd been having with her body seemed to have been eased by Jay's calm acceptance of her figure flaws. When he had taken her protectively into his arms, he had embraced all of her.

She lifted up on her elbows to look around for a clock. She could hardly believe she was still here at the beach house, with him. Normally she would have spent the day mucking out the petting zoo and preparing for the next week's activities. Thank goodness for Ellen. She had alerted her assistant about coming in to do the chores for her.

Sophie still hadn't spotted a clock when she tossed off the bedcovers and realized she was wearing his maroon polo shirt. She sprang to her feet, sparked by panic before she could recall exactly what had happened. He hadn't undressed her, although she'd probably wanted him to, given the lustful thoughts that had crept into her weary, defenseless brain once she'd rested it on his muscled thigh. He'd offered her the shirt to lounge in after they'd come in from the swim, and feeling a little reckless, she'd put it on and then shucked her wet suit off right there in front of him.

He'd observed her stunt with a narrow-eyed smile, picked up the suit, and hung it on a lamp shade to dry. Maybe she was a teensy bit disappointed that he hadn't begun to paw the ground and snort, but she was impressed by his will-power, as always. Her laws of touching had been temporarily repealed because of the towel-napping incident, but he'd made a promise not to make her uncomfortable, and apparently he was going to keep it, even if *that* made her uncomfortable.

Gotta love a man of his word.

Still, that was probably why she'd dreamed about him all night long. Haunting dreams of someone trying to get to her, searching for her, a man who watched from the shadows, then disappeared when she turned to him.

At one point she could have sworn he was there in the room with her. She opened her eyes, or thought she did, and saw someone standing alongside the bed, staring down at her. She called him by name, but he didn't answer, and it couldn't have been Jay, because he wasn't wearing the eye patch.

Had her phantom returned? The dream monster whose presence she could feel even when he wasn't around, watching her, stalking her, his reflection peering at her in the glass. He was everywhere. But toward dawn he was nothing more than a voice, calling to her from a distance, imploring her to come to him.

"Sophie, where are you?" he'd called again and again.

She was still trying to shake off the dream's eerie effects as she made her way to the bathroom. A glimpse of herself in an antique wall mirror made her stop in shock. "Have mercy," she whispered.

The scrollwork engraved in the glass lent a wild aura to her reflection, but even without it she would have looked like the Madwoman of Chaillot. Hair was flying out of her braid and her eye makeup was smudged all over her face. Strange that she hadn't given any of that a thought last night.

Moments later, tilting over the bathroom sink toward the mirror, she finished repairing the damage as best she could. Rebraiding had been too great a challenge, so she'd pulled her hair into a ponytail and secured it with one of the velvet scrunchies she carried for such emergencies. This one was white to go with everything, because Sophie was practical about such things. Fortunately he'd left her purse on the nightstand by the bed, and she had the makeup she carried with her. But her cutoffs and top weren't in the room.

The kitchen was empty when she wandered in, and there was no sign of Jay having been up and around, so she put some fresh food and water out for Blaze and set about making coffee. The pot's digital display said it was ten A.M., causing Sophie to shake her head in disbelief. She never slept this late. And where were Jay and Blaze? The door to the spare bedroom where Jay must have slept was closed when she passed it, which meant he was probably still abed, the lazy slug. Apparently they'd all been bitten by a tsetse fly.

There were several vacuum-sealed packets of coffee inside the refrigerator door. She grabbed one marked JAMAICAN BLUE MOUNTAIN and ripped it open. The hiss of air saturated her nostrils with an aroma so potent it made her dizzy. She felt as if she'd already had several cups before the first drop was brewed.

She was measuring out the last bit of coffee when a shadow dropped over the counter. The scoop slipped from her fingers and bounced sharply across the ceramic tile as a pair of hands slipped over her head. They clamped tight as a blindfold, and the lights went out.

''Guess who?'' a familiar voice whispered in her ear.

Sophie's heart wobbled and nearly tipped over as she realized what he was doing. This was a game they used to play when Jay returned from his trips. He would come up behind her in the mornings and cover her eyes, and she would always pretend to be terrified.

''The Nightstalker?'' she would guess. ''The Boston Strangler? John Wayne Gacy?''

''The man who made you scream last night,'' he would whisper.

At some point in the game, he would draw her back against him, and she would discover how aroused he was, how very hard and ready to make her scream all over again. And when she turned, he would scoop her into his clutches and do just that, right there, wherever they were, make her cry out with excitement and heart-rocketing pleasure. Make her quake with need. She had nearly been crushed with the sweetness of her need for him, her love. And she *had* loved him—that Jay—so much.

''Guess,'' he whispered again, more insistently.

''Son of Sam? Grandson of Sam?''

''Last chance. Get it this time or you pay the price.''

''What price?''

''You cook breakfast—''

''I'd do that anyway. You'll love my oatmeal with M & M's. You drop them in just as you serve it, and they don't melt.''

''—wearing only an apron.''

''Hey! Aren't these new rules?''

''*Guess.*''

The command in his voice sent an odd little jolt through Sophie. ''Is this the man who was my towel last night?''

He might have laughed. She wasn't sure, but she could feel his breath, steamy on her neck. ''This is the man who wanted to make you sigh with pleasure last night,'' he said.

''Sigh?'' Now it was her whispering. ''Not scream?''

''That, too.''

His body moved with a hard breath. She was afraid to brush against him, afraid of what was there. *Afraid of how much she wanted what was there.* She closed her eyes beneath the blindfold of his hands and quieted all her other senses, allowing herself to feel the magic. Something irresistible flared between them. It was concentrated in his fingers and the pressure of his cupped hands. But it ran all up and down her spine, too. Light. It seemed to spill out of him and pour into her, a frisson of bright, sparkling light that went straight to her veins.

"Guess, Sophie," he said again. "Guess who's behind you."

Her eyes blinked open to darkness. She'd been drifting in the radiance of their bodies, and everything else had slipped away, even the game. She tried to think of another quip, but there was a quality in his voice that made her realize he was serious. He was asking her to acknowledge him. To believe what she couldn't believe.

"Jay," she said, surprising even herself with her conviction. "It's you. You're Jay."

He let out a shaking breath, and one of his arms fell across her breasts, locking her against him. "Jesus God," he said, his voice hopelessly raspy. "I was beginning to think I'd never hear you say that."

His passionate relief made her want to surrender. She could hear her own heart exhorting her. *Let it be, Sophie, just let it be, at least for a little while. Don't make it go away. Don't make him go away.*

She fell back with a heavy sigh, resting her head in the crook of his neck. "Jay," she whispered, her chest tightening as she realized how good it felt to say his name, to let go and trust that he would be there.

His voice was still rough with emotion. "You win. What do you want for breakfast?"

"Just this," she said, "to be like this . . . with you." There was no blindfold now. He had long since enfolded her with both arms, but she kept her eyes closed anyway, certain that the magic would vanish if she opened them.

"This," he told her softly, "works for me."

Warmth emanated from him. She felt as if she were sinking into a pool of it as he gently reorganized things so that her head was tilted back, and he could stroke her face and throat. His touch was light yet possessive, unless that was more wishful thinking on her part. One of his hands lifted the wisps from her forehead and coaxed them back. His other arm was still locked tight to her waist.

"Mmmmm," she murmured, turning her face to the sweetness, feeling it sprinkle her mouth and flit along her throat like butterfly wings. The sensations were so lovely she wanted more. Her lips parted like a hungry child's, moist with anticipation. Some honeyed, unrecognizable taste in her throat sent a ripple of longing through her.

Her thoughts were suddenly patchy, jumbled, all except one. One thought that rose to the surface like bubbles in a stream.

I love the way he touches me.

A sweet narcotic rush of pleasure filled her as his fingers traced the delicate arc of her eyebrow. The feathery lightness tickled a little, but his strokes were fluid, and the steady rhythm made her feel as if she were being put in a trance. Images of flower petals filled her mind, but they weren't airborne. Languidly floating down the river, they drifted toward the waterfall, drawn by an irresistible force. Each stroke brought them closer to the edge. Did they go willingly into sweet oblivion? Did they have a choice?

Something in her tugged yearningly.

All she'd wanted for days was to be touched, she realized. Wanted it so much she couldn't allow it. This was her heaven. Her drug. He was drenching her with affection, and that should have been enough. But there it was again, a sweet little ache that she couldn't quite release, no matter how deeply she breathed.

"Jay," she murmured. She moved to turn in his arms, but he wouldn't let her.

"I'm not done with you yet," he said, moving to that place just beneath the crest of her brow, the flared bone that makeup artists loved to highlight. For Sophie it was one of those ultrasensitive zones, like her lips, that one caress could awaken.

The clutch of need inside her was suddenly sharp.

She had no idea that she had reached up and touched him until she felt the stone of his jawline. Her eyelids were heavy with pleasure, but there was something she had to see. Him. She needed to see who was making her feel this way. She tilted her head back and gazed up at him. Her fingers sought the mole by his lips, then brushed searchingly toward the eye patch. But he stopped her before she could reach it, snatched her hand right out of the air.

"Can't I see?" she asked pleadingly.

She thought he was going to crush her fingers. Instead he brought them to his mouth. His lips groaned out a kiss that unfurled in the depths of her belly and whispered there like a swing in a summer breeze. Sophie rolled and sighed. She would have drawn up her legs if she'd been lying down.

Such vibrant feelings . . . but he really *wasn't* done.

He stroked her knuckles with his mouth, then turned her hand over and softly brushed the inside of her wrist.

Her fingers curled in ecstasy.

"No more," she whispered as his tongue touched her palm. It swirled in the tender bowl of her flesh, warmly, and so sweetly that she cried out. The next slow, sliding caress made desire rise inside her like a flame. She couldn't wait any longer. Her need was immediate, hurtful. It flared so urgently she whimpered.

Tears stung her eyes, and he saw them. "Sophie?"

He turned her to him then and cupped her face. There was fire in his expression, pain.

"You're crying?"

"Yes."

"Because of me?"

She couldn't answer, but there was no need.

He touched her trembling mouth with his fingers, and his jaw clenched.

It all spun out of control then. Every thought of restraint, every law Sophie had made, any secret plan she might have had to resist the blaze. He bent to her mouth, and she rose to his. The first kiss burned brightly through her body. The second transformed her, some kind of alchemy, and when she said his name this time, her voice shook with belief. "Jay—"

A primal sound burned through him. His lips were at her throat, one of those soft, snarling kisses she used to dream about as a girl. They were on her mouth, an inferno.

When he picked her up in his arms and carried her out of

the kitchen, time took on a strange, unreliable pace. She
didn't know if it was years or seconds later that she was
quaking beneath him on the living-room couch, the polo shirt
drawn up so that one swollen breast was exposed. Her nipple
was tender pink and throbbing sweetly from his questing lips.

She saw him there above her, a dark triangle of mystery
and sensuality. She felt him there, between her thighs, and a
sound of anguish formed. It rose and died in her throat.
Everything was lost as he bent to claim her, lost in the tidal
swell of desire, everything except one last request.

"Be him."

He recoiled from her as if she'd struck him. She didn't
know what to say, but after a moment his breathing slowed
and his hand hesitated on a tendril of gold hair. "And if I'm
not?"

The question left her breathless. She didn't know why he'd
said it. Or perhaps she couldn't let herself know. Her thoughts
hesitated, but her body did the opposite. It shouted at her not
to deny her needs again. Shouted and screamed. He was
pressed up against the most sensitive part of her anatomy,
and her thighs ached to enclose him. Her belly trembled.
Sweet upheaval overtook her.

How did she answer him?

Sophie reached up and touched his mouth. He was not her
husband, this man who could seduce her mindless with a
touch. This man whose body was primed to press into hers
with wild, sweet, violent force, he was not Jay.

Was that what he was telling her?

His face was hidden in shadows, and though the features
were as familiar to her as her own, they weren't the proof
she needed. Only her body could tell her who he was. If her
thighs had ever opened for this man, if her hips had ever
yielded, she would know. And this hardness, this searching
male hardness. If she had ever felt it rock deeply inside her,
she would know that, too.

With an inner shudder, she understood what was happening. The guessing games were over. The man she was about
to give herself to might well be a virtual stranger. That

seemed to be what he was telling her, but even so, there was nothing she could do about it. Some powerful impulse had taken hold of her, and she felt as defenseless against it now as she had at fifteen.

His fingers brushed her lips restlessly. His body moved against hers. "Tell me what you want, Sophie. Should I stop?"

"Stop?" No.

"Even if I'm not him?"

He wouldn't let her hide anything, not even this.

She reached out, and he caught her in his arms, burying his face in her throat. "Am I the one you want?" he whispered. "The man your body cries for?"

Words jumbled in her throat. Confession stirred the wildness inside her. Her hands flew to his neck, his hair, and she arched as he lifted her to him.

With a deep flex of his hips, he impaled her. Sophie clutched at him. He rocked her onto her back and sank deep within her, and her entire body convulsed.

She couldn't manage the words. All she could do was nod her head, but he knew what she meant.

"Then cry for me," he appealed huskily. "Tears of joy."

He moved inside her so beautifully that Sophie was racked with pleasure. She wanted to weep, she did. Her heart was breaking with joy. She clawed at him with yearnings that were almost angry, something she had never done before. The cries enveloping her were choked and primitive. Her cries. Need. Joy. Nakedness. She sounded like a lunatic. God, she felt like one!

He rose up above her on locked arms, and it was like seeing a dream materialize. The wild dark hair and black triangle, the power of his bronzed frame. This was the terrifying presence who haunted her, the vision that had such immense power over her, and suddenly it was imperative that she touch him. Somehow she had to bring him back and make him real. She had to touch skin, bone, hair. His hard brown flesh and deep respiration would reassure herself that he wasn't a vision.

"Sophie, no!"

"I didn't mean it—" This time she truly hadn't. All she wanted was to be close, but her fingers got tangled in the elastic band of his eye patch and she nearly tore it off him before he seized her wrists.

"Yes, you did." He dropped down and enclosed her hands beneath his. "You meant it, Sophie. You meant it all. There isn't anything you've said or done that you didn't mean."

"No."

"You wanted to see who I am, the man who's on top of you, inside you."

"*Yes.*"

He bent to kiss her, but hesitated. His mouth was so close to hers she could feel the shake in his breathing, the tension vibrating in his lips. He was going to tell her the truth.

"No, wait," she whispered suddenly. "I don't care." Shock made her rasp the rest of it. "I don't care who you are or what you've done. I want you anyway."

He shuddered and gathered her up, searching her face. His arms forced an arch in her back so extreme that it thrust her pelvic bones against his. The firebrand between his legs burned its shape into her mind as well as her flesh.

"I can be whatever you want, Sophie. Whatever your heart longs for."

The taste of him made her ache in her throat. Weak with need, she lolled back and took him with her. Her tangled fingers were deep in his hair, and he was deep in her mouth. He'd come down on top of her, and the male weight of him nearly crushed the breath out of her.

"Complete me," she told him. "*Please* . . . that's what I long for."

They kissed and his tongue touched hers. It slid across the surface and stroked the underside. Languidly now, secure in its mastery. She was his, her tears, her sighs.

His teeth stung so sweetly she gasped.

Her mouth went slack with need, and at last he began to move again, plunging with the heat of his tongue, taking her everywhere at once. His body searched within hers, hot flesh seeking solace. The pressure built until it was everywhere, nudging her walls, caressing her nerves, rippling up her spine. It was so beautiful she couldn't find a name for it. He felt like part of her, the perfect part of her.

It was beginning. She could feel it, that glorious surge of sensation, the crashing ride over the waterfall. But she resisted. She hadn't been able to take that ride with Jay toward the end. As their relationship had deteriorated she could no longer let herself go. Sexual fulfillment had begun to feel like emotional surrender, and she didn't trust him enough for that.

Feminine muscles quivered and clung as this man began to move more slowly, and yet somehow, more powerfully. He was doing exactly the opposite of what her body longed for. She wanted sexual frenzy, oblivion. But he was as still as stone. And at last she understood why. She understood everything when he stopped moving altogether, and her hungering, quivering muscles reached for him.

"Come for me, Sophie," he whispered, huge inside her. "Don't hold back. I want to feel your body crying for me. Drown me in tears."

He did very little but that, flex slowly inside her and coax her toward sweet and utter devastation with the husky sensuality of his voice. Her body did the rest. Her body wanted to love him. Every part of her wanted to quiver and cling and feverishly embrace him. And with the grainy urgings of his voice, she felt herself beginning to swell and turn over like a wave.

When the waterfall caught her, she tumbled with it, end over end, out of control and shrieking like a child. Rapids spiraled her downward, sucked her into the beautiful oblivion that was Jay Babcock.

It felt like life and death, as glorious and terrifying as that. And in the wild throes of completion, she knew. Knew it all. Who he was. Who she was. What it all meant. Even why they'd been brought together. And the enormity of it made her eyes fill with tears.

When their bodies were free, she rolled to her side, away

from him, and began to sob. He touched her shoulder, perhaps to let her know he was there, but also to reassure her
that he wouldn't impose. He seemed to understand that this
was something she had to go through, regardless of his own
personal concerns, and he let her cry.

Never give your heart to strangers, Sophie.

She was racked with sobs, yet she was weeping with abject
relief, with sheer wonder and incredulity. The stranger she'd
just given her heart to had proven his identity the only way
he could. His body. Her body. The language of their bodies.
The two of them had sung this song before, danced this
dance, though maybe not as eloquently. This time they had
been *one* song.

Fear had been the dominant force in her life since he came
back. It was easier not to believe because believing meant
she risked losing him all over again, and she couldn't have
survived that. But now she had to face her doubts and find
the courage to deal with them. She had to be fearless, because
this man *was* Jay Babcock. He was her husband.

Her body had told her what the tests and X-rays couldn't,
that he was her childhood sweetheart, the one who had
brought her out of hiding. This was Jay. Her Jay. But he was
also a stranger, an entirely different man whom she would
have to learn to know and love all over again.

Huddled and still damp from the tears, Sophie felt a sensation swirl between her shoulder blades. It was him, but he
wasn't making the lazy circles that were his specialty. He
was writing something, a letter, though she couldn't tell what
it was.

Letters On My Back, she thought. It was a game she'd
often played with the kids, especially to lull them asleep at
nap time. With firm strokes you traced the letter and let them
guess what it was.

"M?" she said. He didn't answer. He was busy writing
another letter, an easy one this time. "I?"

Sophie grew quiet as he traced two more letters on her
back, and then she began to laugh. MINE. He'd written the
word *mine* on her back.

"Are you?" he whispered.

She rolled over and threw her arms out to him, still laughing, jubilant through her tears. "Yes! Oh, God, yes, Jay. I'm yours."

20

Sophie's shriek brought Ellen running from the kitchen. "What is it?" the older woman asked. "Is somebody hurt?"

Sophie gaped at the contents of a package that had just arrived. The box was lying open on the coffee table, and according to the package, it had come from Vavoom's. She'd opened it immediately, certain she hadn't ordered anything.

"The dress," she whispered. "That's the dress."

She'd taken the delicate plum-black confection out of the box and draped it across the gold tissue paper before she'd realized it was the same one she'd been fantasizing about in the boutique's window. The dress she would never in a million years wear.

"Things must be going well with Jay," Ellen observed.

"Better than even *I* knew."

"He's going to love that dress."

"I think he sent that dress." Sophie wagged the card that had come with the package. "But how did he know this was the one I wanted?"

"*He* sent it? Jay? Interesting taste."

"If it wasn't him, I have a secret admirer who's into black and backless."

Ellen's little whistle of surprise made Sophie realize what she'd just done. She'd handed her assistant the card without thinking. Luckily they were alone in the living room. The kids were out back with Brian, "wallpapering" a large refrigerator box with construction paper they'd colored and decorated themselves.

" 'Happy belated birthday,' " Ellen read aloud, her voice dropping to a husky alto. " 'Wear this for me . . . with nothing underneath but you.' Oh, my word!" She touched her throat.

"This is Jay," she declared passionately. "I don't know the man from Adam, but from everything you've told me about him, it has to be him."

Sophie didn't disagree. It was exactly like Jay. They'd been nearly inseparable since their weekend at the beach house, and Sophie had never been happier. Jay could still be very mysterious, still do things like this. He was not a man you could take for granted, but that didn't shake her conviction for one moment about who he was. The time they'd spent together had only strengthened her belief that he really was her husband.

"But how did he know?" she wondered aloud.

Ellen, who had probably worn slips with more material, was poking the garment as if it might spring at her. "Are you actually going to wear it?"

"Only if he's blindfolded." Sophie realized how that sounded and blushed. The dress had to be a coincidence. She'd seen a man's reflection in the store window that day, and although he'd resembled her husband, Jay had been in the clinic, so it couldn't have been him.

Ellen had picked the dress up and was turning it around. Her eyes widened as she held the skimpy thing up to herself and grinned at Sophie. Sophie nodded, banishing the questions from her mind and allowing the excitement to return. For once in her life she wasn't being ruled by her fears and suspicions. Everyone deserved a little happiness, even Sophie Weston. For the first time in years she was content, even joyful. She had everything she'd ever wanted.

Ellen was putting the dress back in the box, arranging it like the lingerie it truly was. Sophie's sigh of nervous despair made her glance up. "You're actually going to do it, aren't you?" Ellen was clearly impressed.

"I suppose."

"Way to go."

Sophie clasped herself at the waist, and they exchanged a look. For a moment, that moment, they were sisters, two women, linked by ancient female mysteries, rituals only partially understood, but deeply felt. Implicit in their gazes was surprise and wonder, sisterhood and support, as they contemplated something that neither of them could ever have imagined herself doing, a role exclusive to the boldest among them. This was Sharon Stone territory. Madonna.

"I don't have the body," Sophie moaned, suddenly afraid.

"Fake it," Ellen insisted.

"In *that*?" Sophie pointed to the dress and let out a little squeak of horrified delight.

Ellen hiccuped mirth and nodded. "You can do it."

"I can, dammit." But when Sophie heard the patio door slide open and the patter of little feet approach, she panicked and rushed to cover the box. "Don't let the children see!"

With malice aforethought, Muffin undid the top buttons of her black satin pajamas and tucked her finger in the opening, tick-tocking the collar apart. She wanted a little breast showing. If Jay had been a leg man, she would have worn her silk charmeuse baby dolls and tempted him with a juicy serving of thigh instead. Two pieces at least, she thought wickedly.

"Dinner's ready," she told the steam heat curling from under his closed bathroom door. "Get it while it's hot."

He was in the shower when she'd entered his room moments ago, so she was expecting the door to open and the Babcock heir to appear soon, possibly naked and dripping wet. Works for me, she thought. But she was even more

curious about his reaction to the "midnight snack" waiting
for him on his bed, especially since it was only six P.M.

By the look of the smoky black suit jacket and slacks hanging on the valet rack, he was going out for the evening . . .
unless she could change his mind.

Rearranging herself on the comforter's paisley swirls, Muffin drew her legs to the side and thrust out a shoulder in her
best imitation of a Victoria's Secret model. When the shower
stopped drumming, she quickly gave her head a shake to
scatter her hair. Her final concession to seduction was a fetch-
ing smile.

Jay emerged with eyes closed in concentration and biceps
bulging as he towel-dried his hair. Muffin felt a pang of disappointment at the bath sheet knotted around his hips. Crass
of her maybe, but she'd been hoping for a full frontal. The
eye patch intrigued her, though. She'd never seen him without it, even now. Surely he didn't wear it in the shower?

She was wondering how long she might get to watch unnoticed when he opened his eyes and her cover was blown.

"One of us seems to be in the wrong room," he said,
drilling her with a quick, hard stare. He didn't seem overly
thrilled to see her. Still, she felt an undeniable flutter of anticipation as he checked her out with male thoroughness,
minesweeping from the tips of her bare toes to the fat blond
ringlets that she and her curling iron had labored over.

"I sleepwalk," she explained sweetly, rolling her shoulder
so that the pajama top slipped off it.

The towel he'd been using on his hair landed on the floor
by the bathroom door. "Need help finding your way back?"
He reached for the dress shirt hanging on the valet rack.

"Maybe . . . eventually." Muffin responded to his shuttered glance with a quick smile, aware that she was uneasy
in his presence and not sure she liked the feeling. She didn't
dare tell him the real reason she'd paid him a visit. Jerry
White had blown her off that afternoon. He'd told her on the
phone that the way things were going it looked virtually impossible to stop Jay's succession, short of drastic action.

"Know any hit men?" he'd asked snidely, then given her some cold, hard advice.

"If you want Babcock behind your cosmetics line, you're going after the wrong cajones," he'd told her. "Tickle the big balls."

Now Muffin eyed the towel, wondering how big they actually were. All they had to be was proportional to the rest of him to fill the bill, she decided. His shoulders were lovely and broad, and the wedge of muscle that fanned from under his pectorals to his groin was an amazing bit of body sculpture. She couldn't see what was under the plush terry, but a feathery shaft of dark hair promised even more in the way of male magnificence.

"Hot date tonight?" she asked.

"Volcanic," was his dry response. "*Krakatoa, East of Java.*"

"Couldn't be with Sophie, then," she mumbled. She hadn't meant him to hear her, but, of course he had.

"Do I detect disapproval?" He glanced her way as he put on the shirt.

"Disappointment, maybe." She was just being honest. Why was he looking at her that way? "Sophie's sweet as can be, Jay, but I figured you for more imagination. She's the Breck Girl, and I'm *not* being catty. It's just true. Don't you need more stimulation?"

"Like what? Electric paddles to get my heart started?"

"Really?" Muffin shimmied off the bed and sidled closer, the pajama top still hanging off her shoulder. "She's that hot? Vampira lurks within Rebecca of Sunnybrook Farm?"

She wrapped an arm around the bedpost and leaned against it, feeling uncomfortably adolescent. Why couldn't he just act interested and put her out of her misery. I'm in my pajamas, Jay!

But no, his shirt hanging open, he was engrossed in the terra incognita of his cuff links at the moment. The man was about as forthcoming as the rocks he liked to climb, which Muffin supposed was the gentlemanly thing to do where the details of his relationship with Sophia-pet were concerned.

As for her, he'd aroused her competitive instincts.

"Actually, I'm here for something specific," she informed him, unwinding herself from the post. This coquettish scene wasn't her, but if shy little Sophie turned him on, what did Muffin have to lose.

She was close enough to touch him now, and before he could stop her, she took charge of the cuff link he was fumbling with. "Let me do this," she insisted.

"You're here to dress me?"

Muffin's laughter had a nervous ring. She had a case of the jitters and couldn't imagine why except that physical contact had been achieved. Of the two Babcock brothers, she'd always preferred Jay for pure sex appeal. Who wouldn't have? But Colby had been the heir, and that was all that had mattered to her then. All that mattered now.

She fought to clear the rasp from her voice. "I'm here to make you a business proposition, but I like your idea better." Now she *was* going to embarrass herself. She couldn't manage the cuff link any better than he could.

She froze as he pulled away from her. For all her bravado, she was cursed with a deep-rooted, paralyzing fear of rejection. Her father had constantly let her know when she wasn't measuring up. He'd even publicly exposed her "defects."

"Thanks, Muffin, but I've been dressing myself for a while now," Jay pointed out. Not unkindly, but the damage was done.

The jewelry fell to the floor, and the clank it made was the sound she loathed above all others. Doors slamming. Backs turning. Rejection. He didn't want her touching him, much less dressing him. Why wasn't she surprised?

"I'll get it," she said sharply, crouching to pick up the gold pieces. Her nostrils stung as if she'd been crying, though she would never have allowed that to happen. Still, she knew her eyes must be red. It would have been easier to crawl out of his room on all fours than have him see her this way.

"Muffin?"

She cringed at the unasked question in his voice. *Is something wrong with you?* Given the circumstances, his concern took on sinister meanings. It dragged up every fear she'd ever harbored that her father might be right about her. No matter how ferociously she tried to be clever and fashionable, she would always believe that she was a fat and ugly child, supremely unlovable, and yes, maybe even better off dead.

"I found it," she said, spotting the jewelry under the valet rack. How was she supposed to stand and face him now? How?

Muffin brutally wrenched her emotions back under control. The best defense was a good offense. She had to distract him, there was no question of that. With the cuff link crushed in her fist, she faked an attempt to stand, and then actually lost her balance. She bumped up against him, grabbing for something to steady herself. What she got was the bath sheet.

The towel came off in her hands.

"Mama," she whispered, and sank to her haunches, gaping at his nakedness. She was wondering how big they were. Now she knew. Lord, revenge was sweet. Plus, there was a totally unexpected bonus. Unless he was endowed like a farm animal, Jay Babcock had an erection under way!

Muffin's pulse throbbed, along with her imagination. It hardly mattered to her that he didn't seem to be humiliated by the situation. He couldn't deny that he found her attractive now. The physical evidence said it for him. Hope took flight, nearly crushing her heart.

"Forgive me," she implored him, giddy, laughing. "I'm such a klutz. I can't believe—"

"Muffin!"

She hated the way he said her name.

He knelt to pick up the towel, speaking to her in low, apologetic tones. "I'll admit to being easily aroused these days," he told her. "But I wouldn't be telling the truth if I let you think that any of this was for—"

"Was for me?" Muffin's swollen heart withered. If she had tried to get up then, she really would have fallen over. She could barely manage the words.

"Hey," he said, searching her features and clearly wanting to spare her any hurt. "Don't take it personally. This is my

towel karma,'' he explained with a ''guy'' grin that was
faintly sheepish. ''Sophie would understand.''

Muffin had no idea what he was talking about, except that
somehow her pathetic attempt to distract him had reminded
him of the Breck Girl, and no matter how reasonable that
might seem to him, it was unthinkable to her. Muffin wasn't
just being ignored and rejected, she was invisible in this
man's mind. She didn't exist.

A brackish taste filled her throat, one she couldn't swallow
away. Somehow she had to salvage the last shreds of her
pride and get out of this room. Was it too late to crawl out
on all fours and never look back? Too late to crawl to the
Godiva counter at Saks? The awful clatter in her chest felt
as if it were a diamond drill that might bore right through
her.

Muffin could feel a kamikaze binge coming on.

''Zip me up?'' Sophie presented her daringly bare back to
Jay and inclined her head a little, waiting for his response.
His reflection filled the dresser mirror, but she purposely did
not make eye contact. The moth was a butterfly tonight. The
flame could come to her.

He took it all in with dark, kindling interest: the hot dress,
the bolder stance, the seductive Sophie. She could feel the
appreciative touch of his gaze as it traveled up her naked
back and then dropped down to the place where her clingy
sheath gaped open. She caught all this as he walked across
the bedroom toward her.

''The dress makes me dizzy,'' he said. ''Is it new?''

She pursed her lips and shrugged a smile, deciding to let
body language be her answer. He *knew* it was.

''You like it?'' she asked.

''Killer. It was made for you.''

Coincidence, that phrasing? Sophie didn't think so. The
zipper tab was at the base of her spine, the place where everything flared into soft fleshy curves. When she felt his hands
there, she shivered.

''You're in a rare mood tonight,'' he observed.

"Maybe." Such fun, she thought. Such fun toying with instead of *being* toyed with.

"What happened to the braid?"

It sounded a little like an accusation, which pleased her even more. Now she did smile at him, directly at him. Chestnut-gold silk fell in a gleaming arc to the hollow of her throat. And on the other side, a graceful golden scythe curved around her ear, à la the cinema sirens of the forties. It was a cool, streamlined look, and she'd done it all with jumbo hot rollers and a tube of Dep gel.

"No braids tonight," she said, returning his burning-glass stare. "Deal with it."

Deal with me, she thought, richly amused. She *was* in a mood, anything but cool and streamlined. Pretty feisty as a matter of fact and not quite herself. It felt good. God, it did.

"Remember this?" Jay asked.

"Hmmm?" Sophie glanced over her shoulder. He was supposed to be doing up her dress. Instead it felt as if he were drawing a line down her bare arm with a pen. But all she could see was a tiny white curve of a stick. "What are you doing?"

"Making a wish."

She'd never heard of making a wish by tracing on someone's arm, but she thought it was a rather sweet idea. "What are you wishing for?"

"World peace." He smiled.

"Z'at all?"

"And a package of Malomars, in no particular order."

"Oh." Her disappointment must have shown. At least he could have wished for something that had to do with her. He'd been giving her "time" for a week now, and she'd had plenty, thank you. Didn't he know she'd worn this dress so he would go crazy and tear it off her?

As he continued to trace lines, wandering down her spine and making a loopy, lazy eight in the small of her back, she shivered lightly, but otherwise didn't respond.

"Feel good?" he asked.

"Mmmm . . ."

"Sure?"

"Mmmm."

"I was hoping for more enthusiasm."

Was he. She moved imperceptibly. It was fleeting contact, but the brush of their hips was electric. The sound that vibrated in his throat was a rich little growl of satisfaction. Under the circumstances, it might have alarmed her. Tonight it incited her to move again.

You want enthusiasm? she thought breathlessly. I'll show you enthusiasm. "I'm not wearing panties," she whispered under her breath, afraid he would hear her, afraid he *wouldn't.*

He whipped her around, the growl of satisfaction locked in his jaw. His smile darkened, bordering on something savage as he held himself in check, eating her alive with his gaze. His hands tightened on her arms as if to subdue her, and Sophie felt a thrill as sharp as it was sweet. She let her head loll back as he began to nuzzle the pale flesh of her throat. He nipped her there lightly, just hard enough to leave tender pink marks, then caught her chin between his teeth and bit down. She was afraid he was going to gobble her up, afraid he *wasn't.*

"You *are* world peace," he told her. "With Malomars thrown in."

This was more like it.

"Mmmmmmmmmmmmm." He looked like he wanted to devour her right then and there. But with what must have taken considerable restraint, he began to mesmerize her with the dainty little stick again. The front of her dress was crisscrossed over her breasts and cut away at the bodice, creating lots of creamy décolletege that begged to be explored. He dipped and stroked, languid in his movements. The pressure was light, yet surprisingly sharp.

He was tickling her. Not that it wasn't his turn.

"What is that thing?" she asked. Tingling flesh had brought her to full attention now, which was obviously what he intended.

He held the stick up and she saw that it was actually the larger half of a wishbone, popped in two.

She couldn't swallow, couldn't breathe. She felt as if the thing were lodged in her throat. "Oh . . . oh, Jay! Is that—"

Filled with disbelief, she watched him nod. It couldn't be the same wishbone they'd broken on their wedding night. How had he managed to keep it with him all these years? She had no idea where her half was, although she'd searched high and low over the years, and even sent Blaze on several hunting expeditions. It broke her up that she had lost hers when he had so obviously treasured this keepsake of theirs. It broke her up.

"Jay," she whispered.

He tapped her trembling lower lip with their memento. "You found this in a bucket of KFC Crispy on the night we ran away and got married," he said. "Remember?"

"How could I forget? You nearly tossed it away before I railed at you about the significance of finding a wishbone on our wedding night."

Always lucky, Jay had snapped off the larger half, and he'd teased and teased her about his wish, but she wouldn't let him tell her what it was. She wouldn't even guess for fear of ruining the chance of it coming true.

"It was in the packet of my things when I left the clinic," he told her. "Someone must have recognized it as a good-luck charm, but it was much more than that. It was my link to the past, to you, and it probably kept me sane."

Perhaps more than anyone, she understood how that could be true. Her childhood treasures had been that important. "You never did tell me what you wished for that night."

"If I tell you it won't come true."

"It's something you still want?"

"You could say that."

Something in his expression made her heart pause and wonder, eluding her understanding. There was obvious sensuality, even physical desire, but this wasn't about sex. Some ancient male instinct was at work. She knew that by the way her body responded. It tightened with another, deeper kind of longing. What *had* he wished for? She wanted desperately to know.

"Don't tell me," she warned. "Maybe it can still come true."

His head lifted. "It has to."

Kindling desire struck a match that ignited the small space between them. Sophie could see it flickering in his gaze, and the brightness fed the wavering flame within her. They were like two sparks, arcing toward each other, ready to touch.

But Sophie didn't want things to flare out of control. Not tonight. She was the siren tonight.

She whisked her evening bag off the dresser and sashayed past him, unzipped. It was good for a man to work up an appetite, she decided. Let him drool. When she got to the bedroom door, she turned back with a sexy splash of a smile. "Did I thank you for the belated birthday gift? I love it."

"I love it, too, but I can't take credit."

For the dress? she thought, wondering if that was what he meant. She gazed at him, perplexed, until it gradually dawned on her that perhaps he hadn't sent it. He was actually quite sexy and adorable in his confusion. And clearly as perplexed as she was.

But that was impossible. He had to have sent it. Who else could have?

21

"Looks like Cupid's arrow struck true," El Martin whispered as Wallis turned to him.

They exchanged knowing glances and Wallis had to quell a triumphant smile. She took a sip of her chilled Sauterne to keep her excitement at bay. "I think we could safely say it's a bull's-eye," she agreed.

Wallis was secretly delighted that her little dinner party for Jay and Sophie was going so well. She had placed the couple across the table and up a few chairs, where she could keep an eye on them without being too obvious, and so far, they were exceeding all her expectations.

El had refused to discuss the details of his matchmaking scheme, but whatever he'd done, it seemed to have worked. They'd been officially dating for at least a week now, and tonight they couldn't take their eyes off each other. As clichéd as that old line was, it was undeniably true. Wallis could feel the potent energy of their attraction from where she sat. Romantic sparks were flying. She'd never seen Sophie look so beautiful—or so happy.

She could have been spun from gold. Her marigold-yellow sundress had a sheered bodice and fitted waist that was marvelously slenderizing, and her hair sparkled with blond highlights. It couldn't just be the aura of chandelier light that made her appear so fair and delicate tonight. She was luminous, especially in contrast to the darkly handsome man seated next to her. They looked as if they'd walked off the pages of the fairy tales Wallis had read as a child.

As for Jay himself, Wallis studied the way he watched Sophie and experienced an unwanted pang of envy. There should only be joy tonight, she told herself, but she was unable to dismiss the feeling. Jay had been distant lately. Wallis understood the exclusiveness of any budding romance, but she couldn't help feeling a little shut out. She hadn't expected that he would be the Jay she'd lost, everything considered, but she had hoped for a warm, gratifying relationship, some sort of bond between them. El had promised that the treatment would make a difference, but she was beginning to wonder when and how, even if.

The charm bracelet jingled on her wrist as she set down her wine. She touched the circle and arrow, Jay's symbol, but got no response. Fear crept up behind her heart, chilling her. She hoped it hadn't been a mistake orchestrating this romantic scenario between them. She didn't see how anything could go wrong now unless Sophie began asking too many questions as things progressed, or delving too deeply into what didn't concern her. That could make her an obstacle to several people, including Jay himself. No, she hoped her daughter-in-law would go right on cooperating. She really wanted that, for everyone's sake.

"When's the big announcement?" El asked, sotto voce. He spooned a bit of crème brûlée into his mouth, made a face, and laid the silverware across the plate.

Dinner had been marvelous, roasted tenderloin of pork with wild mushrooms and garlic potatoes. But Wallis hadn't enjoyed her dessert either. She would have to tell Mildred to be a little more liberal with the carmelized sugar.

"I would think very soon," she said. "The coffee is about

to be served." Jay had asked her to give a small party for the immediate family, but all she'd been able to get out of him was that he had something to tell them. Men were so secretive, she thought with an exasperated sigh. She assumed, and hoped, it had something to do with him and Sophie. Once they were together again, she was confident the strain with Jay would disappear, and that would go a long way to restoring her spirits.

To round out the table, she'd invited El and a couple of the Babcock cousins and their spouses from her husband's side of the family. Both of Noah's deceased sister's children held voting stock and sat on the Babcock board and she wanted to ensure their support in Jay's bid for power.

"Yes, Mildred, we'll have the coffee now." Wallis saw the housekeeper hovering near the doorway with the silver pot and signaled her with a nod.

"None for me." Muffin turned her bone-china cup upside down, as if she were in some cheap diner.

Wallis shuddered at the loud clink.

"Is she getting sloshed?" El murmured. "Or am I?"

He meant Muffin, and Wallis had to concede that she probably was. Her first daughter-in-law had insisted on coming tonight, even though she normally avoided Wallis's dinner parties like the plague. Worse, she'd brought a friend with her, a mysterious creature named Delilah, with jade-green eyes, whose sleek black one-shoulder jumpsuit was set by only one piece of jewelry, a delicate white-gold hoop that pierced her nostril.

Not exactly a fairy-tale couple, but Wallis had her eye on them, too. Muffin hadn't eaten a bite since the first course, a lovely salad of roasted peppers and creamy goat cheese. She'd moved her food around the plate, yet drained every glass of wine Mildred had poured.

Her friend, Delilah, was drinking heavily as well, and the two of them had been going on all evening about their revolutionary cosmetics line, either to impress Jay or the Babcock cousins. It hardly mattered which. Pitching business deals at the dinner table was appalling taste in Wallis's opinion. Even worse was Muffin's pointed interest in Jay. At least she'd had the foresight to seat Muffin on the same side as Jay and Sophie, which made it difficult for her to watch their every move.

Jay rose as the housekeeper scurried in. "Mildred, could we have a round of champagne before you pour that coffee?" he asked.

"Champagne! That's more like it." Muffin began to applaud, and Delilah tapped her empty wineglass with the spoon.

They were acting like a couple of incorrigible children, and Wallis could only imagine that flaunting bad manners brought them some kind of perverse enjoyment. She was determined to ignore them, but Jay sent Muffin a quelling look as he sat down.

The brazen smile she flashed back at him gave Wallis a bad moment. Muffin loved being provocative, and Wallis was afraid she might take Jay's disapproval as an invitation to bait him further.

Mildred saved the day with a tray of flutes and an open magnum of Dom Pérignon, steaming in a crystal ice bucket. At least Muffin would have to wait for Jay's announcement before she could drink any more, Wallis thought, pleased.

Jay was on his feet by the time the glasses were foaming. "Sophie and I have something to tell all of you," he said. He slipped an arm around Sophie's waist as she rose to join him, and Wallis noticed that she had something clasped tightly in her fingers. It looked like a wishbone that had been snapped in two.

"My lovely wife has made me the happiest man in the world," Jay said, his voice husky and ardent at he gazed at Sophie. "She's agreed to move back into the Big House as soon as that can be arranged. We're going to be together again."

"Jay! Oh, Jay, that's wonderful!" Wallis sprang to her feet, her eyes sparkling with tears. "Sophie, I'm so pleased, so very happy for both of you."

The guests rose as one. Even Delilah lifted her glass. The

only holdout was Muffin. With a defiant smile, she drained her flute and thrust it out, demanding a refill. Mildred, who was hovering at Wallis's end of the table with the tray, didn't budge.

"El?" Wallis prompted, anxious to get the good wishes started and draw attention away from Muffin. "Why don't you do the honors."

El saluted the couple with his raised flute. "Love isn't about gazing at each other," he announced in his sonorous elder statesman's voice. "It's about gazing outward in the same direction. But whichever way you gaze, children, may you grow old on one pillow."

Laughter eased the tension, but Muffin was still stubbornly sitting when the congratulations had gone around the table, and it came time for her to make a toast.

Wallis swiftly took her seat and signaled the others to do the same. "Let's have our coffee now," she suggested.

But as the guests sat Muffin stood. Wallis could have killed her. Wallis was going to kill her.

"Now that everyone's done gushing, I'd like to make a little toasty-woasty." Muffin raised her empty glass. "To Sophie and the snake charmer—"

Wallis clutched her hands.

There was a faint gasp from down the table.

"Oh? Did I shock?" Muffin asked sweetly. "Did I offend? But I meant that in the nicest possible way. Snake charmers must be among the most gifted of men. Think of the skill it takes to charm a deadly viper into doing your bidding."

"Muffin," Wallis said sternly, "Mildred's trying to serve the coffee."

With a flip of her hand, Muffin blew off both Wallis *and* her housekeeper. "Of course, our Sophie's not a snake," she allowed. "She's not nearly lean or mean enough, so I guess it's not a very good analogy, is it?"

Delilah gave Muffin's hip a jab with her elbow, her tone urgently low. "Cool it."

But Muffin was on a roll. She pushed up the sleeves of her powder-pink sweater dress as if she were preparing to give one of the massages that had undoubtedly pommeled Colby into submission. "Some of us are plenty lean and mean enough to qualify, though. Don't you think, Jay? Hmmmm? Want to take me on for size?"

Wallis nudged El, but Jay rose first.

"Muffin, could we have a word?" Jay asked.

It was not a request. It was a demand, and there was enough steel in his voice to back it up. Jay pushed back from the table, and for the first time Muffin looked startled. When he got to her chair, he pulled it back, politely but icily took her elbow, and brought her to her feet.

"Where are we going?" she asked.

"To wash your mouth out," he warned under his breath.

"That could work." A dazed smile appeared. "Only I don't swallow," she retorted, tossing her elegant silvery blond tresses.

Wallis watched him hustle her from the room and knew she'd been right. Muffin had designs that went beyond business. If she couldn't have the kingdom, then why not the man next in line for the throne.

Wallis mouthed a word against the knuckles of her hand that she hadn't meant anyone to hear, not even El, but his low response filtered back.

"Not dangerous, desperate," he said. "And desperate people make mistakes."

Muffin's feet barely touched the ground. Jay made sure of that. He didn't stop in the marbled hallway outside the formal dining room or the Blue Salon where Wallis had once served "musical" teas for the ladies in her book club. He didn't even stop in the obelisk entrance hall with its dramatic tower and windowed staircase. He marched Muffin straight out of the two-story doors and into the chilly night air.

"What are you doing?" Dwarfed by moonlit Corinthian columns, she hissed at him like an indignant feline. "It's f-f-freezing out here."

The hiccup that racked her body made him fight a smile.

He allowed her to shake him off. He didn't care where she went at that point, but he wasn't letting her in the house. "Take a walk," he told her. "Down to the carriage house and back."

She grabbed her arms and rubbed them fiercely. "I won't do any such thing. Th-that must be half a mile."

"At least. Get going." The carriage house was a storage area with living quarters built into the brick wall that bordered the estate. During Noah's reign, he'd had a groundskeeper in residence full-time. Now security guards were stationed in the quaint cottage, and if there was any justice, they would fail to recognize Muffin and clamp her in irons. Jay could hope.

She stared down the dark road, seething. Another spasm racked her.

"You have two choices, Muffin. Sober up or spend the night outside."

She whirled on him, but whatever she was going to say got cut off as the doors swung open and Delilah joined them. Her lush, flame-colored hair was wrapped tight against her skull in a granny knot alongside her ear. Even so, she was beautiful, Jay admitted. The woman would be beautiful with a sack over her head. Too bad she was from another planet.

"Okay, whatever you guys are doing—" She gave out a strange little snort. "Keep doing it. I like to watch."

"Stick around," Jay said sardonically. "You can watch Muffin walk off her snootful."

"I'm not walking anywhere, unless it's to your public execution," Muffin snapped. "Let's go, Delilah. I'm bored with the company."

"No way, I love family fights."

"You'd be right at home here," Jay muttered.

"Mm-mm-mmm." Delilah arched an eyebrow. "Was that an invitation?"

Muffin gave out a little moan of exasperation. "Delilah! Are you flirting with that asshole? You saw what he did to me."

"Beast!" Delilah shot Jay a wink and rushed to Muffin,

scooping her up protectively. "Don't worry, pet, I know just what you need. How about a session with Roto, the wonder trainer?" She gave Jay a glance over her shoulder. "Join us?"

Jay just smiled.

"Sure?" Delilah persisted. "Roto does groups. Ouch!"

Apparently Muffin had kicked her.

Jay watched the two women make their way down the steps to a glow-in-the-dark yellow Maserati. Delilah looked woman enough to handle the powerful car and just about anything else that came her way. Muffin didn't fare so well by comparison. She looked like a fuse about to short out, and Jay didn't have to ponder long to figure out why. It was because of him.

When the women reached the car, Muffin turned back to Jay and got out two whole sentences without a hitch. "Something terrible is going to happen to that sweet little wife of yours. Something un*speak*able."

Jay glared at her. He shook his head. "Don't be stupid. You're not going to hurt Sophie. You're not going to hurt anyone. You don't have the nerve."

"I'm not talking about me. It's *you* she should be afraid of."

Car doors slammed forcefully. An engine revved and roared.

As the Maserati sped away, its tail lights formed orange streamers that were still visible against the darkness long after the car had disappeared. Jay listened to the drone of the engine receding into the distance, and by the time it was gone, whatever amusement he might have felt at Muffin's antics was gone, too, cold.

He might have shrugged off her tough talk if she hadn't dragged Sophie into it—and then turned it into an accusation. Now he had to take her seriously. She had forced his hand. But if anyone should be afraid, he thought darkly, it was Muffin.

A tap at the bathroom door startled Sophie.

"Are you in there? Can I come in, dear?"

It was her mother-in-law. Sophie had been holed up in the guest bath for the last ten minutes and shouldn't have been surprised that Wallis had come like a hostage negotiator to cajole her out. It would have been more surprising if she hadn't.

Sophie had excused herself from the table after Muffin left because the embarrassed silence and furtive glances were becoming harder to endure than what Muffin had done. Jay might have been able to smooth things over with a joke or a witty comment, and have the entire table laughing, but Jay wasn't there, and Sophie's social skills had been honed on toddlers.

"Sure, come on in," she told Wallis.

The door opened a crack, and Wallis slipped inside like a wraith moving through a secret passageway. "I hope I'm not intruding."

"No, of course not." Sophie attempted a smile, but Wallis saw through it. She immediately grasped Sophie's hands and held them tightly in her slightly chilly ones.

"She's jealous, Sophie. You know that, don't you? You're about to get everything she wants."

"I suppose that's it, but it still came as a shock. I thought of Muffin as a friend."

Wallis shook her hands. "I hate to be the one to disillusion you, darling, but nothing is sacred when wealth and power are up for grabs. Even the closest relationships are vulnerable. Families can be shattered. Muffin's been after the business since Colby died. She always felt it should have gone to her, and maybe it would have if the attorneys and the board hadn't intervened."

Sophie had just realized how strong Wallis's perfume was. Overpowering floral notes fought with the bathroom's fragranced candles. "I've never wanted the business. She knows that."

"But you're going to have it, you and Jay, and that's all that matters to her. The empire is rightfully yours, but never forget that jealousy poisons people's minds. It twists their thinking in dangerous ways."

Wallis emitted a sound of exasperation at the look on Sophie's face. "What's wrong with me? I shouldn't have said
that. Now I've frightened you."

It hadn't frightened Sophie as much as it had given her
pause. She found it impossible not to wonder who else might
be poisoned by jealousy besides Muffin. How many other
people wanted what she was getting? Wallis herself might
even be on that list, except that her mother-in-law seemed to
see it as a family-versus-the-attorneys situation. They were
the enemy, and Sophie was one of the family. Muffin's position wasn't nearly as clear-cut.

Wallis's charm bracelet jingled and clinked. "I'll never
forgive myself if I've made everything worse. Tell me I
haven't."

"No, of course not."

"Good." She beamed an approving smile and released Sophie's hands with a little squeeze. "Now let's get these tears
blotted," she said, whisking a tissue from a gilded box on
the inlaid marble countertop.

For once Sophie hadn't been crying, but that didn't seem
to matter. Wallis was determined to clean her up anyway.
She dabbed at Sophie's lower lashes, then stood back to in-
spect her handiwork. Apparently satisfied, she gave a brisk
little nod and turned to the mirror to work on her own image.

Sophie watched her freshen up with a certain reverence.
Even in direct lighting, Wallis's makeup was immaculate.
She'd always had a presence about her that Sophie admired,
but tonight there was something slightly off, a forced quality
in her manner. Normally that would have made her seem
fragile, Sophie realized. Tonight it made her seem brittle, as
if she might shatter from too much pressure. Sophie found
herself wondering if Wallis had recovered enough to deal
with Jay's return. She could barely deal with it herself.

Wallis glanced up from her fine-tuning and saw Sophie
watching her. The two observed each other for a naked moment, and Sophie picked up a frightening premonition of an-
imosity. No, that couldn't be. She'd always been close to her
mother-in-law. She must be rattled or still reacting to Muffin.

Magically, Wallis's expression turned warm, reassuring. "What is it, darling? You are upset, aren't you?"

"To be honest, I'm not sure I can go through with my promise to Jay. I agreed to move back because he seemed to want that so much. But I don't see how we can all be under the same roof together. Not after what Muffin did tonight."

"Ah, Sophie, you'll break his heart. I've never seen him happier." Wallis brought her hands to her throat pleadingly. "You must trust Jay to take care of it. He will. Muffin is no match for him. You saw that tonight."

Sophie was touched by the emotion in Wallis's voice. She was just beginning to fathom how important all this was to her mother-in-law. "It doesn't have to be decided tonight," she said. "Jay will be away most of next week anyway, and it makes no sense for me to move back until he returns."

"Do you know I'd forgotten," Wallis exclaimed. "Jay's scheduled to be at the clinic for several days, isn't he. El said it's an important phase of the treatment. Well—" She tossed up her hands, seeming delighted with the solution. "We'll just have to work around it."

Apparently content with that, Wallis rushed to smooth her hair so that she could get back to her guests, and Sophie promised she would join them as soon as she'd put on some lipstick. She pretended to be searching through her makeup case as Wallis left. But moments later, lipstick tube in hand, she was still standing at the counter.

Muffin's outburst had upset her far more than she'd let on. Sophie'd had no idea Muffin harbored such bitterness. She really had thought they were friends, and despite Muffin's warning about Jay, Sophie had believed her sister-in-law wished her well. Now she didn't know what to think. It sounded like Muffin was saying Sophie had been duped by Jay into reconciling, that he'd "snake-charmed" her into coming back for his own ulterior motives.

The doubts were spiraling back, and God, Sophie didn't want to go there again, not to that awful place. She reminded herself that Muffin had been drinking and people did stupid things when they drank. It would be foolish to take her comments to heart. But even as Sophie vowed not to overreact she remembered the appointment at Delilah's salon that Muffin had set up. It was the following week, during the time Jay would be gone. Sophie would have preferred not to go, but she'd promised. To cancel now would only strain things more between her and Muffin.

Sophie whisked on some lipstick and picked at her hair, feathering her bangs. What she spotted as she dropped the tube into her makeup case was Jay's half of the wishbone. She'd tucked it in her evening bag for safekeeping.

He'd given her the piece to keep when she admitted to losing hers. Afterward, driven by guilt as much as a desire to know if the two pieces would fit, she'd searched the rambler again. She'd even put Blaze back on the scent, hoping his tracking instincts would be triggered. The setter had brought back bones all right, a half dozen of them he dug up from the backyard.

Now Sophie took the delicate thing in her fingers and willed it to tell her where its other half was. The wishbone had come to symbolize her relationship with Jay in all its phases, she realized: joined as one, then broken apart, and now there was the possibility of being brought back together again, a perfect fit.

A sense of wonder filled her as she came to another realization. She was about to have everything she'd ever wanted, the man of her dreams and the stability she'd always longed for. Even her dream day-care program!

Where was Wallis now? she thought, laughing as she fished a tissue from her bag. Her eyes were actually misting, but as she blotted her lashes she wondered if perhaps it really was her turn. Was she to have what her heart had always longed for? Did the heavens allow that much happiness?

22

Muffin was reasonably sure of a couple of things. One, she was not in her own bed, and two, the naked thigh she'd just glimpsed was not her own. She buried her face in a puff cloud of white feather bedding, hoping to block out the vision. Praying it *was* a vision and not a real body part.

"Where am I?" she mumbled.

"You're at my house, hon." Husky laughter squeaked with the bedsprings. "Mixing business with pleasure. Ain't it fun?"

The moan Muffin let out had nothing to do with pleasure. That was Delilah's voice, which could only mean it was Delilah's thigh. Which could only mean—

Muffin's breathing slowed, but her thoughts took off like a shot. Lying very still, she strained to remember what had happened the night before, but nothing stood out beyond calling Jay Babcock a snake charmer and bringing Wallis's dinner party to a crashing halt. Everything that happened afterward was hidden away somewhere, as if a black curtain had dropped to conceal it.

" 'Scuse me," she said, increasingly aware that Delilah was not the only one *au naturel*. She herself was sans clothing. And worse, much worse, she couldn't move. She squirmed a little, struggling to get up, and sank down in defeat. The bedding had her in bondage, and there was a leaf blower roaring inside her head. Her stomach was churning, too, like a Cuisinart on puree. She must have been god-awful drunk last night.

"Quit struggling. You'll sprain yourself." Delilah gave Muffin's backside a pat and sprang out of bed.

Muffin closed her eyes, wishing the bed would quit moving. She was afraid to look as her business partner flitted around to Muffin's side of the room. And she knew Delilah was flitting because that was what Delilah did. Flit. Whoever's listening, please take notes, she thought. If I ever wanted to know what she looked like naked, I don't anymore!

"Have a hangover, do we? Want some O_2? I've got a tank here at the house. Cappuccino-flavored."

"I'll pass."

"Sure? Low-lead? High-test?"

"Thank you, no. I can still breathe on my own. I would like to know what happened here last night, though."

Muffin took a peek, relieved to see evidence of clothing on Delilah's lithe body. Not much. It resembled one of the rompers Sophie's two-year-olds wore, but at least Muffin wasn't dealing with unfettered breasts and the like.

From what she could see of the bedroom, it was an odd combination of dotted Swiss flounces and black panne velvet. Just behind Delilah there was a chaise heaped with plush pillows. And hanging in the corner from silver chains was a canvas swing with a bucket seat and leg holes that made Muffin tilt her head at an awkward angle, trying to imagine how they worked.

"Delilah, what is that?"

"An Adam and Eve Intimacy Enhancer, otherwise known as a sex swing."

Why wasn't she surprised? A nineties woman's bedroom wasn't complete without one. "Did you . . . ? Did we . . . ?"

Delilah crouched down and cocked her head. An innocent smile appeared. "Did we what?"

"Did anybody go for a . . . swing last night?"

"You don't remember?" She cracked up. "In that case, of course we did, *Muff*."

"I was drunk! You took advantage."

Muffin was truly outraged, but Delilah just peered down her nose, through a gorgeous fan of lashes. "You got that right. You *were* drunk, which is why I didn't take advantage. Sex with the semiconscious goes against my moral code."

Muffin turned her head the other way and mouthed the B-word, but there was no satisfaction in it. It was herself she was furious at. First the fiasco with Jay in his room, then the dinner party, and now this? Fortunately, life wasn't a baseball game, or she'd be out.

Smart was the one thing Muffin knew she was good at. The only thing. She had brains. Her IQ tested in the genius range, but even that seemed to have deserted her. Delilah was probably questioning the wisdom of their business deal right now. "I have news of Sophie," Delilah offered enticingly.

"And which Sophie would that be?" Muffin muttered. "The one who's about to prance off with *my* inheritance? If it isn't news of her demise, I don't want to hear it."

"She's coming to the salon later this week. She called for an appointment this morning."

"Poison her oxygen," Muffin said, burying her face in a suffocating cloud of feathers and very afraid she was going to be sick right there in Delilah's bed. "Better yet, make her ugly."

"Just look at you, girl! You're so gorgeous I could eat you."

Sophie blushed at the bold compliment, not at all sure how to take the impetuous gleam in Delilah's eye. The cosmetician looked as if she had little girls like Sophie for breakfast every morning.

"Well? Do you like what we did with your hair?" Delilah positioned herself in front of Sophie and combed her hands into Sophie's windswept hairstyle, letting the shining tresses flare out and magically fall back against her face. It was all very dramatic and dazzling.

"I love it," Sophie assured her.

"As well you should," Delilah said without a hint of false modesty. "This is more than just a pretty do. It's a low-maintenance, shower-and-shake Wonder Cut. Plus, we wove in some red and blond highlights. Sexy, yes?"

There was applause from the gallery, where the other stylists were working, some of whom had been involved with Sophie's makeover. She'd had nearly every treatment the salon offered, including being doused with a vial of fruit oil, which was supposed to kill her appetite. It seemed to be working. She hadn't felt hungry, but she was a little spacy and light-headed, perhaps because she hadn't eaten since that morning, and it was now late afternoon.

Or maybe it was the milk-chocolate oxygen. . . .

"Time for some wine and cheese?" Delilah asked, waving her hand toward the lounge, a spacious octagon with leopard-spotted upholstery and the air of a modern conversation pit. "We have a yummy Meursault Rougeot-Latour today and some mouthwatering Gruyère."

Sophie wasn't sure which was wine and which cheese, and she was already too uneasy about the L.A. commuter traffic to risk the former. It got deadly out there this time of day. "I'll take a little cheese for the road, but not because I'm hungry," she was quick to add. "Just to keep my strength up."

As the spa assistant made up a CARE package for the trip back, Sophie asked Delilah about Muffin, whom she hadn't seen since the dinner at Wallis's.

"She's been hanging out at my place the last couple of days," Delilah explained, "recovering from her toot. Riot, wasn't she?"

"Nothing but," Sophie agreed dryly. "Let her know I love my makeover, would you? It was her idea."

"Trust me, she knows. There's nothing you do that she doesn't know about. You, child, are the Jodie Foster to her John Hinckley."

Delilah's tone brought Sophie an uneasy moment. There might have been a warning involved, but Sophie couldn't be sure. She'd been wondering what to expect from Muffin when they met next and hoping they could talk about what happened. It hadn't occurred to Sophie until this moment that she could make things worse with her sister-in-law.

She was saved from having to respond. Teri appeared with the provisions for Sophie's trip, and Sophie exclaimed all the way out the door over the cleverness of the foil swan stuffed with crackers and cheese.

The dilemma with Muffin was still very much on Sophie's mind as she drove away from the salon. But not fifteen minutes later, she was stranded in bumper-to-bumper traffic on the 405 south, and it was all she could do to concentrate on making the right freeway connections. The light-headedness was back and she was grateful for the cheese and crackers Teri had packed. Her stomach had been funny all day, too, but she didn't know whether to blame it on the fruit oil or simple starvation.

She hadn't been feeling herself the last few days, she realized as she thought about it, especially since Jay left, but even before that. It seemed to have started the night she'd had the dream at the beach. For several nights afterward she'd sunk into an exhausted image-filled sleep, and though she hadn't had that dream again, she'd had others that were disturbingly real, all of them to do with Jay in one way or another. What concerned her most was the possibility that the lucid dreaming might be recurring. She couldn't go through that hell again.

You've created your own escape hatch, Sophie. It's Alice's looking glass, but remember that each time you use it, it will be more difficult to get back.

Claude's words. But Sophie didn't feel as if she'd escaped into these recent dreams with their mazelike darkness and hauntingly familiar voices. It was like being swallowed up. She stepped too close to the whirlpool and was swept down the drain with the bathwater. There hadn't been a choice.

The low whine of the Jeep's engine drew her attention.

Stop-and-go traffic was putting a heavy strain on the air-conditioning system, so Sophie turned it off and rolled down the windows. The fresh air might be good for her anyway. Not that the air on a crowded California freeway could ever be considered fresh.

The traffic picked up a little, and as she negotiated her way into a faster lane, she thought back on her lifestyle recently, her eating and sleeping habits, anything that might have contributed to the fog she was in. Of course there was Jay. Until recently she'd been doggedly resisting his seductive magnetism, resisting as if to give in would destroy her.

The wishbone had been the final assault on her defenses. Their keepsake had opened the floodgates, and since that night they'd grown breathtakingly close, sharing memories, some too sensitive to dredge up except with the utmost care, making urgent love, and opening their hearts to each other in ways Sophie wouldn't have thought possible. The old Jay would not have been capable of that kind of intimacy. Sophie wasn't sure she would have been either. This was as vulnerable as she could ever remember being. And as happy. She was desperately happy.

But her fears had skyrocketed since that night, too. Especially the fear that she might be giving up too much. Love put you at risk, she'd discovered. The more you needed someone, the more powerful they became—and the more dangerous. It felt that way with Jay at times—risky—but she didn't seem to have any choice anymore. She'd lost the ability to back away.

The stress of their relationship probably had a great deal to do with the strange symptoms that had assailed her. But, wishful thinker that she was, she kept hoping it was something else, something simple, like the Rosy Posy tea Wallis had given her. She'd been drinking several cups a day, and caffeine could be the reason she hadn't been sleeping well.

The hour-and-a-half drive home and bumper-to-bumper traffic explained the fatigue she felt by the time she reached the rambler, but Sophie still had lots to accomplish that evening. There was a note from Ellen about what chores needed to be done and directing her to a plate of vegetable lasagna in the refrigerator that was left over from the kids' lunch. Other than that, and Blaze's eager welcome home, the house was quiet.

Too quiet, Sophie thought as she fixed the setter his dinner. Jay had told her he wouldn't be able to call during this phase, because, as with any experiment, the conditions had to be carefully controlled. But she'd been disappointed to find no message from him on the machine. She must have been hoping he'd find a way to beat the system and reach her. Dejected, she warmed the lasagna up for herself, even though she still had no appetite.

It came to her as she sat heavily in the chair, picking at her food, that the lack of sleep, the stress, all of it must have caught up with her at once. She wasn't half done with the lasagna before she'd decided to quit fighting the exhaustion and go to bed early. The chores could wait until tomorrow.

Her fork clinked against the dinner plate, and she leaned in to her hand for a moment, cradling her forehead with her palm. She didn't seem to have a temperature, though she was feeling a little flushed. Maybe she was coming down with something.

Lie down, she thought. I need to lie down.

Her white wicker bed was the most deliciously inviting thing Sophie could remember seeing. She gave out a sigh of relief, flopped down, and rolled to her side without even bothering to undress. All she needed was a little nap to catch up on some of the lost sleep. A couple of hours. When she woke, she would do the dishes and get ready for bed.

The air smelled faintly of tangerines, and she was aware of a noise as she drifted off to sleep, a scratching sound that she knew must be Blaze, trying to get back in the house, only she couldn't remember letting the dog out. She hoped he wasn't tearing holes in the screen.

"Blaze," she mumbled, "stop that."

Why was the dog still scratching at the door?

Sophie came awake to a noise so gratingly low she knew

it must be what had roused her. Broken pieces of Styrofoam scraping against each other, that was what it sounded like. She managed to get off the bed, but wandered in a daze for a moment before she found her way to the bedroom door. The drugged, dreamlike feeling clung to her like netting. She couldn't shake it off. Worse, she'd fallen asleep without turning on the night-lights, and now the house was dark.

She found the switch at last. The bedroom overhead came on with an audible snap and gave her enough visibility to find the hallway dimmer. Ancient linoleum tile was cold and clammy against her bare feet as she made her way to the back of the house. She must have taken off her shoes at some point, but she was fuzzy on when.

"Blaze?" Her voice boomed in the silence. It made her hesitate. A hard metal edge dug in as her fingers curled over the patio slider handle. She couldn't hear the dog now, but she knew it must have been him. The scratching had stopped, and he didn't seem to be anywhere in the house.

A quick check of the patio confirmed that he wasn't out there either, not within eyeshot. She opened the door wider, poked her head out, and called him again. Something was wrong. Blaze would have been right there, quivering with impatience. Obedience school or not, he would have knocked her over in his eagerness to get inside.

Not even a breeze blew as she stepped onto the cool concrete patio. The night was so quiet she could hear the sounds of her own uneasiness, the thump of her heart, the gurgle of her empty stomach. The light from the house threw her shadow across the patio, and with every step she took, it flickered wildly.

"Blaze?" The backyard was walled in by a sturdy cedar fence, but to her right there was a small arbor with flowering vines and thatches of leggy bougainvillea. The sounds had come from there, she thought. "Is that you?"

Something lurked in the bushes. She could see movement, shadows. A wild animal could have wandered down from the hills and dug its way in under the fence. She approached cautiously, hesitating every few steps to look behind her.

Inching closer, she saw something hidden in the gloom.

"Who is it?" she whispered. "Is someone there?"

A scream surged into her throat, but she couldn't release it. There was a man in the shadows, and from what she could see of him, he could have been her husband. Jay. It looked like Jay. She stumbled closer blindly. It was Jay. But there was no eye patch, and his shirt was ripped and bloodstained. This wasn't the man who'd come back to her. This was the man who left.

No, it couldn't be.

Sophie felt as if she were collapsing from the inside. She would have staggered, she might even have fallen, except that her legs were frozen. Indecision stopped her as much as fear. She didn't know whether to go to him or run. And in the split second it took her to decide, he was gone, vanished like a mirage.

She stepped backward and spun toward the house. A dog was barking frantically, and the noise was coming from somewhere inside. Panic sent her running in that direction. As she entered through the patio she saw Blaze at the front door, barking and clawing at the wood. The slider slammed behind her. She forced the lever lock up, then ran to the front door and bolted it.

Trembling, she sank to the floor and clutched Blaze to her. "Shhh," she pleaded, completely forgetting whatever the right command might be. The dog's barking drowned out what she needed to hear, but hoped to God she wouldn't hear, the sounds of someone trying to break in.

That could not have been Jay, she told herself. He couldn't be outside her house. He was at the clinic. And if it wasn't him, maybe it wasn't anyone, just shadows. It was nighttime, and the darkness created ghosts and bogeymen out of nothing. Fear made you see things.

"This is Mrs. Jay Babcock," she whispered into the kitchen phone a moment later. "My husband was scheduled to be at your clinic for treatment this week. Could I speak with him?"

"Mrs. Babcock, is something wrong? It's after midnight.

Your husband's asleep and has been for some time. I'd have to get the doctor's permission to wake him."

It wasn't Jay, then. He was at the clinic. Sophie's hand began to shake as she eased her grip on the receiver. Still, she was relieved more than anything else.

"Midnight?" She pretended surprise. "I'm sorry. I didn't realize it was so late." She could hear concern in the woman's voice and knew there was no point in telling her what had happened. She was probably talking to a receptionist or an intern, someone who had no authority beyond relaying messages, and now that Sophie knew Jay was there, that it couldn't have been him, she didn't want to alarm anyone or interfere with his treatment. She would call the police instead, report a prowler.

"Shall I page the doctor?"

"No, there's nothing wrong," she assured the woman. "Don't even bother to tell Jay I called. I just woke up and was confused. I didn't realize how late it was. Thank you anyway."

"No problem," the woman said.

The line went dead, but Sophie didn't hang up the phone. She was fixated on the way it trembled in her fingers. She couldn't believe she hadn't dropped it, *couldn't believe what happened next*. A hand struck out of nowhere. It flashed from the darkness and cuffed her wrist like iron. There wasn't time to react. She was caught mid-turn and shoved up against the wall by a massive force. Another hand muffled her gasp of terror and jerked her head back. The receiver was pried from her fist and jammed back into the cradle.

It was futile to struggle. Her assailant had superhuman strength. Sophie was completely overpowered in seconds. She couldn't even get a blow in before he'd forced a gag in her mouth and tied her hands behind her back. His body weight kept her locked to the wall.

"Don't fuck with me and you won't be hurt," he told her. "Do you understand? Nod if you do."

She nodded frantically. Where was Blaze? Why hadn't Blaze attacked him? The answer came to her with a force that made her moan. Sophie felt as if someone had struck her in the stomach, though the assailant hadn't touched her beyond the hold he had her in. The dog was across the room, watching them as if this were some kind of game.

Blaze knew who this man was, just as she did.

"Who's Jay?" the intruder asked. "Who is he? What is he to you?"

He *was* the man she'd seen outside. Either he'd come in the front door, or she hadn't shut the slider tight enough for the locking mechanism to engage.

"You're going to answer," he told her, his voice a low snarl in her ear. "You're going to tell me what I want to know, or I *will* hurt you."

Sophie nodded her head. She had already decided not to fight him. He was too strong and the risk of retaliation too great. The weight of his body had shifted, but he still had her pinned to the wall. She was grateful now that she hadn't had the energy to undress.

His hands were everywhere, bars holding her prisoner. Steel. One of them locked her hands behind her back while the other gripped her hair and forced her head around. "Who is this kid?" he asked, holding a snapshot in front of her.

It was a picture of Albert. He must have taken it from the refrigerator. Sophie went still. She wasn't going to tell him anything about Albert, no matter what he did to her. The child was in her care. She had to protect him.

Suddenly the intruder yanked the gag from her mouth and left it hanging around her neck. It looked like a strip of material torn from a white sheet. He walked away from her, seeming confident that she wasn't going to try to escape. The picture of Albert landed on the kitchen table, apparently forgotten as he began to rifle questions at her. He'd meant it when he said he wanted to know everything about her. He wanted to know how long she'd lived there, what kind of work she did. He even asked her age and birth date.

She was aware of him pacing the small room, and she strained to get glimpses of him without being noticed. The way he moved and the way he sounded brought a premonition that nearly made her ill. In some bizarre way this was the Jay she remembered. This man had the exploding passion, the wildness she'd always associated with her first love. Tears sprang to her eyes. It couldn't be Jay. Was she going crazy again?

Her mouth filled with a horrible taste, fear mixed with the acid of regurgitated food. She was going to be sick. Dizziness washed over her and left her slumped against the wall, barely able to hold herself up.

She did her best to answer his questions. When he demanded to know who Jay was and why she'd called him by that name, she tried to explain. "Jay is my husband. He disappeared five years ago, and you look like him. You could *be* him."

The abrupt silence told her that he was staring at her, probably as if she'd gone mad.

"I'm not your husband," he said in a low voice, brutal with unwanted emotion. Jay's voice. "I don't even know you, except for the dreams. The woman who *fucking* torments me. The woman's whose name is Sophie. She's you."

He knew her name?

"And here's another name for you. Noah. Why does it keep going through my head? Who the fuck is Noah?"

"You are! You're Jay—" That was all she could get out. Confusion made her shake her head wildly. She had no idea what he meant by dreams, except that this must be one. He couldn't be real. It couldn't be happening.

Exhaustion quickly depleted her. Silent, barely breathing, she realized the house was quiet, too. Her first thought was that he had gone. Her second was that he had never been there. The stretch of silence that passed was endless, but finally she took the risk of looking over her shoulder.

She braced herself for a reaction, but there was none. She couldn't see him anywhere. Still expecting threats or physical force, she eased away from the wall and managed a jerky turn. She was alone in the room. Horror gripped her mind so tightly she could hardly think. No, she could not have imagined this. Or him. It could not have been another nightmare.

Because that would mean she *was* going crazy. A man had forced his way into her house, a man who looked and sounded like Jay.

But that wasn't possible either. Jay was at the clinic, being monitored around the clock. Jay wore an eye patch. He wouldn't have asked all those questions. He knew who she was. He loved her. He was her husband.

She closed her eyes and swam in the black ocean there, glad for the darkness. Let the waves wash up and engulf her. She wanted that, wanted oblivion. The void. Peace. She willed that to happen as she felt herself sliding down the wall.

Stop, she thought. Please make it stop. The noise was going to drive her mad, that same horrible scraping. It was like something trying to get inside her mind, clawing endlessly to get into her thoughts and rake them apart.

She opened her eyes to an ocean as black as the one that had engulfed her. It was several moments before she could see well enough to be sure that she was in her own bedroom. The thin stream of yellow seeping from the hallway lit the lace hem of her nightgown and her sprawled legs.

Foreboding stirred inside her. She didn't remember putting on a nightgown. Or how she got to bed. And the way her legs were spread, it looked as if—

She sat up too quickly and the room began to spin. Gripped by a wave of nausea, she caught hold of the night table and convulsed over the side of the bed. After several dry, racking heaves, she fell back, exhausted. There was nothing in her stomach.

The scratching sound grew more frantic.

It wasn't a dream. It was real. She was awake, and she could hear it. All night long that god-awful noise had been grinding in her mind, driving her insane. She had to stop it. She would do anything to stop it.

It took her several minutes to get to the patio door.

The dog was there when the slider rolled open. Blaze was there. He darted inside, yipping and dancing, crying for Sophie's attention. She wanted to hug him. She needed the comfort herself, but she didn't have the strength.

There were claw marks on the aluminum frame. She crouched down to touch them, felt the sharp edges, and wanted to cry. The dog had been making the noise. He was trying to get in the house. At least she hadn't been imagining that.

She rose and turned to the kitchen table with one question on her mind. "Oh, my God," she whispered into her hand. The picture was gone. The man who'd broken in had dropped the snapshot of Albert on the table. Sophie had seen him do it. And yet now it was back on the refrigerator, stuck to the door in exactly the place she left it.

She could hardly breathe. A man that desperate wouldn't have bothered to put the picture back.

Her nightgown felt like ice against her skin as she rushed across the room to the telephone. Shuddering with cold, she tapped out the numbers. She didn't know where else to turn for help. It startled her that she got an answering machine, and then she remembered it was the middle of the night.

"Claude," she said, "it's Sophie. I know it's late, but when you get this message, could you come over to the rambler. Please, I need you."

23

"I'm going to give you a sedative, Sophie. It will calm you and help you sleep."

"I'll be fine, Claude, really. I don't need anything."

Sophie was lying on the couch in her living room and Claude had pulled a hassock next to her. He had a glass of water and a large dark green capsule that Sophie didn't like the looks of. She'd felt drugged for days without taking anything.

"You're distraught," he insisted firmly. "Either you take the pill, or I'll call Wallis to come stay with you. I can't leave you alone like this."

"All right, then." She didn't have the energy to go into it with Claude, but he could hardly have picked a more effective threat. She didn't want her mother-in-law to know anything about what had happened. Wallis already thought Sophie was cracking under the stress. This story would convince her.

She took the glass from him first, aware of the familiar warmth of his hand. Everything about Claude was familiar and comforting, including the cardigan sweater and the sweet redolence of pipe tobacco. He hadn't smoked in years, but he packed his briar Prince full of rich Bombay Court every morning anyway, just because he loved the aroma and the "doing," as he called it. Even his voice soothed her, deep and sonorous.

"Give me the silly pill," she said, unable to find the words to tell him how good it was to see him again. She hadn't realized how much she missed his calming presence until now.

The capsule was difficult to swallow. It took all the water to get it down, and even then, she struggled against choking. She was distraught, still. She sank back into the pillow when she was done, but wouldn't let go of his hand.

"I didn't get a good look at the man who broke in, but he sounded exactly like Jay, the old Jay, the one who vanished. He did, Claude. You believe me, don't you?"

"Yes, Sophie . . . I do."

She'd already told him what happened, but she found herself repeating the details. "He asked me questions, questions about him and me." She so wanted him to believe her. "And you don't think I was dreaming?"

He grew quiet. If she hadn't been holding on, she had the feeling he would have drawn his hand away.

"I'm sorry, Sophie, but there is a very real possibility that this was another of your lucid dreams. You might even have been sleepwalking. People have been known to do all kinds of things while they're asleep, including commit murder. It's not impossible that you went to the kitchen to let the dog in, changed into your nightgown, any of those things."

"Wait, Blaze knew him," she exclaimed as if that were certain proof. "Blaze didn't bark!"

"Blaze didn't bark because he wasn't there. It was a dream."

"No!"

"I'm only saying it's not impossible. It could have been brought on by the shock of having Jay come back unexpectedly. You did have another life, a whole new future planned.

You and I were happy, or I thought we were. Perhaps the dream is trying to tell you something.''

He still loves me, Sophie thought. It felt like the pill he'd given her was caught in her throat, a stricture that couldn't be swallowed away. It hurt her to think that he still hurt, but she was too fuzzy-headed to know how to respond. Anything she said could be misconstrued as encouragement, and that would be cruel. She loved him, too, but it was different now, that awful cliché. She loved him like a dear and trusted friend, but she couldn't tell him that.

''Claude, what if it wasn't a dream? What if it really was Jay?''

His walnut-brown mustache had gone nearly stone gray, like his temples. She noticed the change as he began to stroke the bristles. ''If that was Jay, then who's the man about to take over Babcock Pharmaceuticals? Are you suggesting he's an impostor? That's a little fantastical.''

''But not impossible? It could be happening? I'm not the only one who thinks so. From the beginning, Muffin—''

He patted her hand to quiet her, and Sophie felt a dull throb of pain. There were black-and-blue marks on the inside of her wrist. ''Rope burns,'' she whispered. ''Look, Claude. That proves he was here. He tied my hands!''

She ran her fingers over the small dark welts and held her arm up for him to see. She wasn't imagining the bruises. They were real. She winced at their tenderness as he examined them. But he was shaking his head.

''What's wrong? He tied my hands. I told you that.''

''Yes, but these aren't rope burns, Sophie. You've done this before, remember? Pinched yourself when you were trying to wake up. Maybe that's what you were doing tonight while you were dreaming.''

She sank back, not wanting to accept his explanation, struggling to think clearly. She could see in her mind what he was describing. Her wrist had looked like this while she was in therapy with him, honeycombed with pinch marks, and she hadn't even known she'd done it. But that was years ago, not tonight. She couldn't have pinched herself with her hands tied. Surely he understood that.

Claude's voice came to her soothingly. "Come on now," he coaxed, cradling her arm in her lap. "You're supposed to be relaxing, letting the pill work. Try to remember that Muffin has her own reasons for not wanting him to be Jay Babcock."

"Muffin?" He'd gone back to their prior conversation. He didn't want to talk about the bruises and was trying to distract her. She turned her head into the pillow, aware that the pill was working. She felt heavy and sad. Obviously she was hoping that Claude, of all people, would take her seriously. He was the doctor who had led her through a chamber of horrors and it was only natural he would think she was slipping back now, regressing at the first signs of stress.

He might even want to think she was doing badly without him.

"I am getting sleepy," she said.

He settled her hand by her side, and she knew he would be leaving shortly. He'd been right to give her the pill. The sadness had already slipped away. All of her feelings were slipping away, good and bad. She was oddly detached from the panic rising inside her at the thought of being alone. The hollow sensation was there, but it didn't seem to matter somehow.

"Thank you for coming over," she said, heaving a sigh that turned into a huge yawn. "I'll be all right now. It probably wasn't anything . . . just a dream. . . ."

She closed her eyes and felt something warm stroke her face, the back of his hand with its swirl of dark hair. She wondered if that was going gray, too.

"A dream, Sophie, yes," he said. "But this is the last one. I promise there won't be any more dreams."

Bad dreams, she thought as she drifted toward some place as warm and gentle as his hand. No more bad dreams. That was what he meant.

•   •   •

Sophie awoke to the muted ring of the telephone. She was vaguely aware that it was morning and she was still on the couch, curled up under the coverlet that Claude must have put over her. Drifting in a cozy fog, she couldn't imagine who was calling, and didn't want to be bothered anyway. Claude's green pill had worked a miracle. She hadn't felt warm and safe like this in ages.

The bell sounded three more times, and then the answering machine clicked on to take a message. Sophie could hear Blaze stirring in the kitchen. He'd probably been asleep in front of the refrigerator.

Suddenly a man's voice cut through the background noise. "Where are you? *Sophie, where are you?*"

Sophie went still with disbelief. That was Jay's voice, exactly as it had come to her in the dream. He was even asking the same question. Where are you? She sat up and hugged the coverlet around her, fighting a wave of desolation. Someone was playing sick games with her, trying to make her doubt her sanity. She could hardly allow herself to believe it might be him.

Pain constricted her throat. *Ah, Jay, how could you? How could anyone be this cruel. All I ever did was love you. All I ever wanted was to be loved back.*

She sank against the couch, weighed down by disbelief. Of all of the things that had seemed impossible in the last twenty-four hours, this was the greatest, that he would intentionally hurt her.

A nudging pressure against her leg lifted her out of the quandary for a moment. It was cool and wet. Blaze was trying to nose his muzzle under the coverlet. With a despairing laugh, she reached over to scratch the dog's head. We all need it, she thought. Love is a requirement, like air. But why was it such a tormenting struggle to meet that need?

"Sophie? Are you there? Pick up if you're there—"

Blaze's head jerked up. Sophie froze again, listening. It really was Jay. He was trying to get her to come to the phone. The urgency in his voice dragged at her, but she couldn't do it. She still had the image of the other man in her head. Dream or not, the horror and confusion were too fresh.

"Sophie?" He called out her name several more times and then a heavy click told her he'd hung up. She felt sick inside, but she couldn't have talked to him and made any sense about what happened. At least this would give her some time to calm herself and decide how to tell him about the intruder. Claude hadn't convinced her it was a dream, but she couldn't be sure it wasn't either. As much as she needed to talk, she didn't know what that would accomplish, except to upset Jay.

The phone rang again just as she'd untangled herself and the dog from the comforter.

"Sophie, are you there? Goddammit, I've called every-one—" His voice cracked, harsh with concern.

Sophie didn't hear anything else he said. She sprang from the couch and rushed to the kitchen, suddenly compelled to get to the phone before he hung up. It sounded as if he were about to drive over and break down her door.

Breathless, she grabbed the receiver. "Jay?"

"Sophie, is that you?"

"Yes, I'm sorry—"

"God, you had me worried. I knew you must be there, and I couldn't figure out why you weren't answering the phone. The kids are coming this morning, aren't they?"

Kids? What day was it? She glanced around at the calendar hanging next to the wall clock. There was a field trip planned today, but she didn't have a van for transportation, so the mothers were dropping the kids off at the aquarium. She was supposed to meet Ellen there in fifteen minutes.

"I overslept," she said.

"I won't keep you, then. I just walked in the door from La Jolla. I haven't even unpacked yet, but I had to hear the sound of your voice. And speaking of packing, I'm ready to move you in today. Right now. What do you say?"

He sounded so strong, so sure. Sophie wished she could respond. She would have given anything not to be filled with doubts. Again she debated whether to tell him about the intruder, but decided against it. She'd listened carefully to every word and inflection of his voice, but hadn't heard anything that made her think it could have been him. Quite the opposite, he was a shaft of sunshine penetrating a dark cloud.

The sad truth was she didn't trust herself or her perceptions anymore. She simply didn't. In some ways it would be so much easier to believe that stress had thrown her out of sync again. At least she'd been through it before and knew what to do. Claude could recommend a therapist.

Yes, maybe it was a dream. Otherwise, well . . . She anchored the phone with her shoulder and touched the bruises on her wrist. The implications were too frightening.

"Tell me no," he said. "Or I'll be in front of your door with a U-Haul in fifteen minutes."

"I can't, Jay, not today. Ellen can't handle ten kids on a field trip all by herself."

"Will you come over this evening, then? Spend the night? I should warn you that Wallis is entertaining again—a barbecue out by the pool. I'm starting to feel like a political candidate. There are some board members invited, and I've been ordered to charm them, but I'm hoping Muffin will get drunk and throw somebody in the pool."

"Maybe herself?" Sophie suggested, perhaps unkindly. She wasn't up for another party, but she did want to see Jay. She needed to see him. It seemed the only way to quiet the turmoil inside her. "I'll be there," she promised.

And she would tell him what happened, she promised herself. As soon as things settled down and they could get some time together alone.

He sighed as if a great pressure had been taken off him. "Did I tell you how much I missed you?" he asked, his voice softening with throaty sensuality. "At one point they had me hooked up to an EEG, and my alpha waves were spelling your name. I'm going to have trouble keeping my hands off you tonight, I can tell."

She was beginning to think the sound of his voice was as seductive as his touch. When it took on that low, breathing, hungry quality, she was lost. "How long is this party?"

"They're out the door as soon as they finish their ribs."

She fought a smile and was glad he couldn't see her. "Is there a dress code?"

"The usual."

"And that would be?"

"Where you're concerned, as little as possible."

"Sorry, this is a family affair. I have to wear something."

"A dress, but nothing else?"

She laughed. "Nothing but a smile."

His tone turned even huskier. "You keep that up, and they'll have to put me back in restraints."

A call beeped in on his line and he was gone for a moment. "We're starting early, around six," he told her when he returned. "Can you make that?"

She knew it would be tight but promised to try.

"Great. Don't be late, I've got a little surprise planned that you're not going to want to miss. I've got to take this call. Have I ever told you I *love* the way you smile?"

She shot a question right back at him. "Little surprise?" But he was gone before she could get a response. She glanced at the receiver as she hung it up and wondered how he had done that. How had he made her smile?

Muffin's plan was to slip into the kitchen while no one was around and quickly steal back to her room with some provisions: a package of caramel rice cakes and a thermal carafe of coffee would hold her for several hours, maybe all day. She'd been skulking around the house unnoticed since returning from Delilah's last night, and so far there'd been zero confrontations with the family. She wanted to keep it that way for a while. In particular she wanted to avoid Jay, who was supposed to have returned from the clinic earlier that morning.

The coast looked clear as she left her room, but when she came within earshot of the entry hall, Mildred's apologetic contralto caught her attention.

"I'm sorry, Dr. Laurent," the housekeeper was saying, "but Mrs. Babcock's already gone out, and I don't expect her back until after lunch. Shall I have her call you when she gets in?''

''Please. I'd like to talk with her as soon as possible.''

Muffin was immediately intrigued. Unless she was mistaken, this Dr. Laurent was Claude, Sophie's ex-fiancé. She tucked her voluminous poet's shirt more snugly into her jeans, glad she hadn't come down in her robe.

''Wait, Mildred!'' Muffin called to the housekeeper as she was about to shut the door on their visitor. ''Maybe I can help Dr. Laurent. Hello, Claude, how are you?''

Towering in the doorway, the psychiatrist seemed startled, but smiled as Muffin walked over to him and extended her hand.

''I'm fine, thanks.''

His deep voice lumbered like a truck in low gear. Not unpleasantly, Muffin thought, though he always sounded a little creaky, as if springs were in need of oil. The same unsteadiness seemed to permeate his entire being, which prompted her to hold on to his hand that much more firmly. She had no intention of letting go until she was done with him.

''Thank you, Mildred. I'll take care of Dr. Laurent.'' She dismissed the hovering housekeeper with a nod and turned back to Claude. ''Wallis may not be back for some time. Is there anything I can do?''

He assured her that there wasn't, but Muffin insisted on walking outside with him. ''It's such a lovely day,'' she said, guiding him down the steps and toward the front courtyard with its classical fountain centerpiece. ''Why don't we take a moment and enjoy it.''

One moment stretched into several, and as they walked among the ornamental hedges Muffin deftly ferreted out the reason for Claude's visit.

''I'm concerned about Sophie,'' he told her. ''I spoke with her recently, and she seemed unusually fearful. I thought I might enlist Wallis to keep an eye on her and make sure she's all right.''

''Fearful?'' Muffin struggled to keep pace with his long-legged gait. "What do you mean?" He truly was a giant. Gentle, she imagined, though there was something faintly malevolent about him. But maybe that was true of all big men.

He seemed reluctant to say anything more, but Muffin had always had a gift for honing in on people's strings and how to pull them. Claude had been Sophie's therapist, and apparently he still harbored an exaggerated sense of responsibility for her, which told Muffin to try the universal motivator. Guilt.

"I can't imagine what you were going to tell Wallis that you couldn't tell me," she said in a hurt tone. "Sophie and I have been friends for years, even when the Babcocks wouldn't speak to her. You can't have forgotten that I was the only member of the family who came to your engagement party."

His nod said that was true. "It's Sophie's privacy I'm concerned about," he admitted.

"It's her welfare I'm concerned about."

They walked in silence for a few more moments, Muffin intentionally letting the awkwardness build. One of them would have to speak first and it wasn't going to be her. She, after all, was the one who had been deemed unworthy—and intended to play the "hurt" card for all it was worth.

"It *is* her welfare that's important," Claude admitted.

That was all the opening Muffin needed. It took very little more coaxing before he cracked like a piñata and spilled the whole story. Muffin honestly didn't know what to make of it. Sophie was attacked, or thought she was, by someone who looked and sounded exactly like Jay Babcock. Either her sister-in-law was going off the deep end, or she really had something to fear.

"I warned her he could be dangerous," Muffin said.

Claude hesitated and came around, staring at her. "What do you mean?"

"She doesn't believe he's really Jay. She never has. That makes her a threat to him."

"You think he's capable of hurting her?"

"He may already have tried." Muffin wasn't sure if she

believed that or if she was just determined to find some way
to even the score with Jay Babcock. After a moment she
decided it didn't matter what her motives were. She finally
had a weapon she could use against him, the bastard.

Jay lifted his fist, staring blankly at the remains of the antique
crystal picture frame. Someone had smashed it to pieces. The
frame, the glass, the photograph of his father, all of it had
been shattered with one blow. Blood dripped from the side
of his own hand and splashed onto the leather desk blotter.
It splattered the cracked picture glass with crimson flecks,
making it look as if the hunter himself were the casualty.

Noah's countenance was as forbidding as the rifle wedged
under his arm. The quintessential gamesman, he had bagged
several quail that day, and everyone, the entire household,
had been summoned to witness the occasion. Jay couldn't
have been more than ten at the time. He hadn't understood
his father's predatory instincts in those days. He did now.
They were second nature.

But if that disturbed him, this disturbed him more.

Someone had shattered the picture.

He hardly needed more evidence that he'd done it himself,
but he didn't remember. He didn't remember anything except
the jagged pain that struck his eye. It must have been so great
that he blacked out for a moment. So great he needed to
destroy something.

A box of tissues sat on the antique secretary he'd converted
to a bedroom desk. He grabbed a handful and held them to
the oozing cuts. The heirloom chair creaked as he dropped
back and closed his eyes. When had it started, these blank
spots, this white-hot agony?

The drug regimen hadn't touched his headaches. The pain
had grown worse, not better, and there were other symptoms,
too, episodes like the one today. Violent thoughts and impulses. The picture wasn't the first thing he'd destroyed. One
day he'd found the medicine cabinet mirror smashed to
pieces, and all he could remember was that he'd been staring
at himself one moment and the thing had exploded the next.

Blood on your hands. You're as guilty as the rest of us!

He'd heard Noah's accusations as he stared at the splinters of glass in his flesh. Today it was the same. But he wasn't any closer to knowing what it meant. Or what the hell was happening to him.

A grimace of recognition twisted his mouth as he applied pressure to the soaked tissues and the bleeding ebbed. He'd stanched the flow, and someone was out to do the same thing to him. Stop him. His symptoms weren't being helped by the treatment, they were being caused by it. There was a plan to stop him—to incapacitate him if possible—and the list of suspects was vast.

Even she was in on it. Even Sophie.

He'd told himself that wasn't possible. She couldn't be the enemy. She wasn't grasping or ambitious for herself. And yet it made all the sense in the world. She'd been acting strangely, secretive. She changed her mind about who he was on a daily basis. But neither reason was the real one, he admitted. She was dangerous because he was vulnerable to her in ways that he wasn't to anyone else.

She triggered impulses that were dark and brutal and beautiful. Impulses that burned in his soul. She was the torch, he realized, the blue-white flame that flickered inside him. Without her, there was nothing but night, the void he'd come from.

Vulnerable, yes. Emotional. Not quite sane. He was all that and more because of a sweet little thing called Sophie. He said her name now, said it softly, whispered it, and felt the staggering impact of his own desire. A body slam that could have knocked the wind out of him if he'd let it.

What was this hold she had over him?

The question obsessed him as he stared at the blood and glass all around him. His head had begun to throb again, but as he surveyed the mess he noticed something that brought him up in the chair. There was writing on the desk blotter, words slashed across the calendar.

String Me Along. Someone had written the phrase repeatedly, and it had to be him. The handwriting was his, and as he studied the familiar scrawl he realized that he had written it not only on this blotter but on the tabletop at Dirty Dan's, too. He just didn't know why or when.

He rose out of the chair, propelled by the force of his own confusion and frustration. There were too many questions crowding his aching brain, too many unknowns. Someone was fucking with him, and he was going to fuck back. Tonight he would lay out the bait and see who took it.

24

Her smile and nothing but. Sophie had been preoccupied with that image all evening, but it was nearly nine before Jay brought the subject up again.

"I need to be with you," he whispered. "God, I need that so bad."

He had come up behind her, and she quickened pleasurably as his fingers slid down her bare arm and closed over her hand. The party had been winding down for the last hour or so, and Sophie had wandered away from Wallis's "backyard barbecue" and come over to the far side of the pool, enjoying the soft play of lantern light over the water and the muted buzz of conversation. The effects were dreamily hypnotic, and though she'd been thinking about Jay, she hadn't heard him approach.

"Did you charm the pants off the board members?" she asked, her tone as piquant as her lurking smile.

"Sure did." He drew her hand behind her back and held it there possessively. "And now I'm after yours."

"Mine? Didn't you tell me there was a dress code?"

"What are you saying? That you're not wearing—"

She laughed, pleased that her black-and-white-print sundress would keep him guessing all evening. "You know I always follow the rules."

It was a reckless thing to bait Jay Babcock. She, of all people, should know that, but she couldn't seem to help herself. He brought something out in her, a desire to risk that she might never have known existed if he hadn't come into her life.

A soft growl reverberated in his throat. "If you're trying to drive me crazy, it's working."

He brushed up against her with the evidence. He was already aroused and the hardness that jutted hotly into her flank told her if the circumstances were different, he would be engaging in a dress-code inspection right there at poolside. She doubted they would even make it to a cabana.

"Time for the surprise," he said.

"Will I like it?"

"Satisfaction guaranteed," he whispered. "But yours comes later. Right now I need to make an announcement."

"Something to do with the business?"

"You'll see."

He was being incredibly mysterious, which made her all the more curious about what he had in store. "Is there something wrong?" she asked after a moment, wondering why he hadn't moved.

"An anatomical problem. Do you want the world to see what you do to me?"

"I suppose you could walk behind me all evening."

"You don't think the grin on my face would give me away?"

"No more than my breathy little moans."

Fortunately, he made a quick recovery, and nobody had to resort to grins or moans. "I think I'm presentable now," he said, sotto voce. "Coming with me? I'd like you there when I give my Henry the Fifth imitation."

She would have preferred to stay in her own little world on the far side of the pool and daydream about him, but she had the feeling he really did want her with him, and she was curious about what he was going to spring on the well-heeled crowd that his mother had gathered together.

As they returned to the party, hand in hand, Sophie found herself marveling at the effect he had on her. What amazed her, truly amazed her, was how quickly he'd distracted her from the fears that had assailed her while he was gone. It seemed that he could seduce her into a receptive mood with nothing more than a look or a word or a touch. Sometimes the sound of his voice on the phone was all it took. This morning was proof.

She still intended to tell him about the intruder, but the situation no longer seemed life-threatening, or even pressing. She would love to have known how he did that, how he managed to seduce her away from all other concerns and make her feel as if no one else existed but the two of them. Perhaps calling him a snake charmer was not too far off. It felt like sorcery, what he did. It felt like some kind of a spell.

His unscheduled announcement caught everyone by surprise, including Wallis. Sophie could see the look of confusion on her face when Jay clanged a soda can against the side of a huge iced tub to get the crowd's attention.

"Are you all enjoying yourself?" he called out from the gazebo they'd used as a bandstand and stage for parties when they were kids.

All eyes turned to the two of them, including Jerry White's, Muffin's, and the various Babcock cousins. Sophie was uneasy, but she was held captive by the firm grip Jay had on her hand.

"Since we have so many of the Babcock 'family' assembled here tonight," he said, "I thought it might be a good time for a progress report. There's been a lot of speculation about my taking over the company, and I know many of you must be wondering when and if I'm going to do that."

He laughed disarmingly. "The short answer is yes. I not only plan to run Babcock, but I'm ready to start now, tonight."

The ripple that went through the small crowd did not have

the ring of enthusiastic support. There were guarded expressions everywhere Sophie looked, and Jerry White's piercing stare could have cut through steel girders.

Wallis had gone pale with shock. She was grasping one of the charms on her bracelet, and El was already by her side. It was his reaction that concerned Sophie. He was dark with anger. His eyes were hot, burning.

If Jay had noticed any of this, he didn't let on.

"I don't expect you to take that on faith," he said. "Let me tell you why I'm ready and how I plan to make Babcock more powerful and profitable than it's ever been, including bringing the value of your shares to an all-time high. And then there's something you can do for me."

They went quiet, all of them, even Jerry White.

It was just that quick, Sophie realized. A few words, the right words, and he had them in the palm of his hand. Whatever he'd done to her, he was doing it to them, too. They were riveted, but he paused anyway, as if testing the sincerity of their gazes.

Are you listening to me? he seemed to be saying. *Are you paying careful heed? Because I'm only going to say this once, and if you don't get it, I'll take my Midas touch somewhere else. I'll make someone else a fortune.*

"I had several hurdles to get over before I could run this company," he told them. "Nobody said as much, but you all knew it. And I knew it, too. First, I had to prove that I *was* Jay Babcock, and then I had to successfully complete treatment for the post-traumatic stress disorder I was suffering as a result of my 'involuntary' confinement, shall we call it."

With a quick glance at Sophie, he pressed her hand and released it. "I have some good news on that score. Not only did I clear that hurdle with flying colors, but so did *we,* Babcock. The trials aren't over yet, but it's clear that our experimental drug treatment for PTSD works. Neuropro does work. Used in combination with our beta-blocker, Endol, it accomplishes what no other tricyclic antidepressant in the history of pharmacology has been able to do. It not only blocks the kindling effect associated with flashbacks, but it can be used to inoculate against PTSD in advance.''

The murmurs rose again, but the crowd was clearly more receptive now. They were riveted, just like Sophie. Who wouldn't be? she thought. He was making some extraordinary claims.

"Think of the impact," he told them. "I foresee a time when our military can be immunized against war shock before they set foot on the battlefield. Anxiety and panic attacks will be a thing of the past, too. Our French and German research facilities are doing those studies now. Picture an entire population unafraid to fly. The airlines should be paying *us* to do this research.''

He popped the top on the soda can and held it up, toasting Neuropro's success—and the crowd's burst of laughter. They were excited. Just what he intended, Sophie realized. She couldn't help wondering if it was all true, this fantastic news of his, and hoping that it was. She wanted it as much as everyone else did.

"Yes, we could dilute our efforts by moving into other areas," he told them, "but we shouldn't. We shouldn't. That's not what Babcock does. We're a research-intensive company, and there are still fortunes to be made by focusing on important therapeutic advances. Neuropro alone stands to generate revenue in the eight-figure range.''

He gave them a moment to digest that news while he took a swig of the soft drink. "That brings me to the last hurdle, and the toughest one. I made it my personal goal to refamiliarize myself with every aspect of the business, from research to marketing to corporate management. I wanted to know Babcock from the inside out—especially why profits are down, consumer confidence is ebbing, and the stock has dropped. I'm prepared to say that I've done all that now—''

The soda can ended up on the railing in front of him, a visual aid. "And I'm prepared to say even more. Babcock was once a world leader in research and innovation, but I don't want to restore this company to its former glory. I want to surpass the golden days. I want Babcock to mean pharmacology the way Coca-Cola means soft drinks.''

He was stumping like an old-time politician, Sophie realized. He could have been in the back room wheeling and dealing with the good ol' boys, but he was going for popular support, instead. It was an appeal to the Babcock cousins, that faction who knew nothing about the company beyond the value of their dividend checks.

''Did everyone hear that?'' He raised his hands, a preacher asking the crowd to be quiet and listen to the words that would be their ticket to heaven. ''Was I talking loud enough? I said research. Babcock is not a cosmetics company—and never will be as long as I'm running things. We don't make lipstick. We save lives. We save minds and bodies from the ravages of disease.''

Muffin's reaction was audible. She swore under her breath and stepped back as if someone had struck her, then pushed her way through the startled throng and disappeared into the house. Sophie was as shocked as the rest of them. After her trip to the spa, she'd been prepared to recommend that Babcock check out Delilah's cosmetics and especially the appetite suppressant. But Jay had just jettisoned any possibility of that.

It was a bold move. He was stepping up and taking over, making his acceptance speech before he'd been elected. Jerry White was clearly unhappy, too. Sophie saw the acting CEO signal his wife, who'd gone to the bar for another drink, and now both of them were making their separate ways to the door.

But the cousins were still hanging on Jay's every word, and as he elaborated on his vision for Babcock, one of the women began to clap. Soon there was a smattering of applause and the milling crowd had begun to move closer to the portico, as if drawn by some invisible force.

Wallis noticed it, too. She looked around her with a desperate hope in her expression.

El was the holdout, to Sophie's surprise. The scientist was still peering at Jay like he was some kind of monster, even though Jay's commitment to research would almost certainly give him back his power. El had the most to gain, but you'd never know it by his reaction. Still, Sophie doubted if he could resist the others' building excitement, or Wallis's trembling relief, for very long.

"You're all family," Jay was telling them. "Please make yourselves at home. There's plenty of food and we have bathing suits in the cabanas if you want to swim. You're always welcome here, just as you are at my office. As of next week, you can reach me at the Babcock corporate offices in Newport Center. I think we can find a cubbyhole for me somewhere in that vast executive suite."

The "vast" suite he was referring to was Jerry White and Phil Wexler's domain. Wexler hadn't come to the party. He was out of town on personal business, but Jerry White and his wife had apparently heard all they wanted to hear, based on their very noisy exit. Jerry slam-dunked his beer bottle into a trash can, and his wife made almost as much racket with the iron gate on their way out. If Jay noticed, he didn't let on.

"And now, if you'll excuse my wife and me," Jay said. He draped an arm around Sophie's shoulder and pulled her close. "We've been trying to celebrate our second honeymoon ever since I came home. I'm sure you understand."

There was another wave of applause and this time even Sophie could feel the energy swell up and roll toward them. She snuggled into the warmth of Jay's shoulder and pressed a hand to his chest, the very picture of a devoted spouse. It felt like a game of let's pretend, and Sophie rather enjoyed playing it.

"My God, Jay," she whispered, "you have them in your pocket. They're yours."

"It's not them I want," he whispered back. "It's you."

The raw, male grip of his voice thrilled her. But even he couldn't have denied that there was something magnetic going on with the crowd. Their excitement seemed to feed him, and he in turn fed them. Heat and energy radiated from him, creating an aura that was as physical as a flame's. Sophie felt as if she could actually see the vortex for the first time—and they were all being drawn into it, maybe even Jay himself.

"Let's go," he said. "Before they decide to come with us on our honeymoon."

"What honeymoon?"

Jay grinned. "Didn't I tell you? We're going on a little trip tonight. I booked the best room in the house, all soft lights and flowers. You'll love it."

He pulled her with him, and Sophie thought they were going into the mansion. Instead he headed for a gateway that led to the gardens, but it wasn't until they reached the vine-covered arbor to the rose beds that she realized what he meant. He was taking her to the hothouse.

There were candles glowing everywhere when he opened the door for her and lifted her into his arms. As he carried her over the threshold and down an aisle bowered with wisteria and climbing roses, she saw the champagne chilling in a crystal bucket and a small, exquisitely set table for two. Its white lace cloth fell to the floor and its round surface was laden with silver pots of foie gras and caviar, fresh strawberries and soft mounds of whipped cream.

"Hungry?" he asked, setting her down.

"I'm sure I could manage something." It wasn't true. Her stomach wasn't calm enough to deal with food, but she had a feeling that wasn't what he meant anyway.

"Can it wait until I finish this?" He turned her toward him and pressed her up against a potting table. She'd braided her hair tonight because she knew he loved it that way, and he was already examining one of the red-gold wisps that haloed her face as he posed the question.

"Finish *this*?" she asked.

The sunny strand tickled pleasurably as he drew it across her lips. "This . . . looking at my wife, drinking her in, eating her up with my eyes . . ."

My wife. Two words that could send her soaring. Or crashing. "Tasting, nibbling, sipping?" she said, bantering in self-defense. "All those sexy food metaphors?"

"Mmmm, sampling, savoring . . ."

He let the words trail off as he continued to caress her mouth. Sophie caught back a sigh at the sparkling intensity of the sensations he created with a feather of her own hair.

He was the one who was supposed to be ticklish, not her. Maybe this was karmic payback for all those times she'd tormented him. It felt as if she'd been invaded by fireflies. Hot little things, they flashed and shivered with unbearable brightness. Everywhere.

"Do more," she whispered. It was an invitation to take her all the way to ecstasy. He must have known that, and yet he pulled back, wringing a gasp out of her. The sparks burned higher, hotter. It was frenzy. And when he finally brought his mouth down on hers, she shook under his soul-deep kiss.

"Jay, I love you."

The endearment whispered from somewhere inside her as he relinquished her mouth. And she was silent witness to his reaction. His head jerked back with a concussive sigh. It came out of him like a gunshot. But the moment he recovered, he caught hold of her arms and made her his prisoner. He searched her face for the truth, searched the lips that had spoken. A devouring impulse growled in his throat.

"Wait," she whispered. But it was far to late to stop him. She'd lost control of the situation the moment she admitted vulnerability. Ignoring her feeble protest, he picked her up and settled her on a table covered with red-checkered vinyl.

With an appreciative sound, he slipped his hands beneath the black-and-white print of her dress and slid them up the outside of her flanks, taking her skirt with him. The sudden ache of desire startled Sophie, tightening her muscles as his hands crept upward. She felt a sinking warmth between her legs.

"Oh, my God . . ." It was the best she could manage as he dropped to his knees in front of her. Her weighted lids made him look like a dark angel between her legs, and the touch of his tongue destroyed her. One slow, sliding caress and Sophie was lost. She began to scream . . . and never stopped.

Wallis walked among the weeping willows that formed a crescent around her budding summer garden. The graceful trees had always soothed her, and she needed their special balm tonight. The leaves were slender black lancets, their brilliant green muted by the lack of light. But Wallis was glad for the cloak of darkness. She hadn't been able to slow her racing thoughts, or her heart, all evening, and down here, away from the glaring lights of the house, the deep shadow would conceal what she couldn't.

She caught her hands together and brought them to her chest. Would she never get control of the shaking? Was she always to be a dottering old loony who couldn't even speak without sounding tremulous and overwrought? That was what had happened tonight. She hadn't been able to eat she was so agitated.

"Hiding down here won't solve anything, Wallis."

She turned to his breathing fury and knew that this was what she'd been avoiding, a confrontation with El. He was enraged. Noah used to leave her in ashes with his anger, and for all her tenacity and drive, Wallis still wilted like the flowers in this garden under the blaze of male wrath.

She was from an old Southern family who'd lost their wealth in the Depression. "Genteel poverty," her mother had proudly called their situation, instilling in her only daughter a strong sense of heritage and place. But Wallis wasn't content to live in noble deprivation. She wanted the grandeur that had once been theirs, and Noah was a man so like her austere father it was awe at first sight on Wallis's part. She never entirely recovered from her hero worship, but it wouldn't have been a love match or a true partnership regardless. Noah didn't share power. Wallis had been forced to wield her influence quietly and behind the scenes through the years of their marriage. Still, she'd become quite good at getting her way.

Tonight El Martin reminded her of the two forbidding men in her life. Normally she would have been soothing, cajoling and apologizing by now, whether she meant it or not. Instead she could feel her chin lifting and her backbone stiffening.

"He has to be stopped, Wallis," El stated. "You know it as well as I do."

"What do you mean?" The silvery swish of willow branches nearly concealed her whispered question.

He'd hesitated by the circular bed of flowers as though he was waiting for her to come out of the shadows. Now he broke from his stance and walked toward her. Wallis could feel the heat and frustration that propelled him, but she didn't cower. She stood her ground.

"It means *I'm* going to stop him," he said. "Our plan has backfired. He's out of control."

"I thought it was thrilling what he did," she said, passion in her voice. "My God, El, did you see the way he took charge? He actually sounded like Noah, only even more powerful."

El stared at her, incredulous. Clearly he'd expected resistance, but not this, not that she would heap praise on the infidel.

"He's not stable enough to take control, and you know it. He was never supposed to take control. Not this way, for Christ's sake!"

"Maybe he's ready, El. Maybe we underestimated him."

"Shit, you're as crazy as he is." He struck softly at his palm and made a fist. "I'll do this without you if I have to, but I'm not letting some hotshot punk kid walk in and take over this company."

"He's approaching forty. That's hardly a kid." The comparison to Noah was apt, she realized. These were her husband's bullying tactics. El could taste power, and it had made him aggressive. Win through intimidation. Strike out and scare them into "believing." Wallis had had plenty of experience with the way power-driven men behaved when they were threatened.

"Where are you going?" she asked.

He had turned away from her, apparently to clear his head. But suddenly he started walking toward the Big House.

"To have a talk with Jerry White and Phil Wexler. Maybe the only thing that will stop Jay is a show of force."

"No, you wouldn't!" Nothing else could have galvanized

Wallis but that one threat. He was going over to the enemy camp. "You can't!"

He did not look back, and his stony mien made her feel like a frantic child. She set out after him but couldn't catch up. Her heels sank into the grass and she stumbled.

"El, wait! Don't do anything rash. I have an idea."

"What? A motherly talk with your *son*?"

The disdain in his voice was withering. It filled her with a sickening awareness. He'd never spoken to her in that tone, never done anything but revere her, even when she was at her worst. Something had changed. He wasn't bluffing, and she couldn't lose him to Jerry White, not to that bloated opportunist. She couldn't lose El.

"Please," she whispered. He had won, she realized. She would cajole and coax. She would do anything.

He came around, arms folded, seemingly unmoved by her pleading.

She hated him for that. And for this, what she was about to do. "I've been thinking. There may be a way to get to Jay through Sophie."

She worked at the top button of her batik cotton shift, hardly able to believe what she was doing. "She's his Achilles' heel, El. At least hear me out on this."

"What do you mean, Achilles' heel?"

"He's not vulnerable in any other way." She was stalling for time. She did have an idea, but it was a risk, exactly what she'd begged him not to try. She needed time to think it through. Breathless, she realized the bodice of her dress was undone and lying open. She was wearing nothing underneath but a sheer nylon camisole and panties. El could see right through the material in the moonlight, and perhaps, if he looked, right through her.

"Wallis—"

His confusion gave her pleasure, especially since hers had vanished at the first sign of his interest. Unless she was mistaken, the glint in his eyes was pure male lust.

Nothing more was said, but in the quiet space some understanding was formed between them. The balance of power had shifted. She was in control now.

She shrugged out of her dress and let it drop to the ground. Shivering in the breezes and aware of how lovely she looked in the moonlight, she said, "If you leave this way, you may get the company, but it will be over between us. Make your choice."

25

With a pillow folded under her arm, Sophie studied her husband's sleeping form and realized why she was having a difficult time, beyond the fact that he was forbiddingly beautiful lying naked in the moonlight. She'd never been able to sleep anywhere but in her white wicker cocoon, so it was no wonder that she couldn't manage it here in his bed. But that wasn't the problem either.

The problem was with what they'd done tonight. As impassioned as their lovemaking had been, it hadn't brought them closer. When she'd collapsed in his arms afterward, it was with the sense that she had been possessed rather than loved.

She still had that feeling now. Something had changed since he'd come home from the clinic. She'd been swept up in the sweet urgency of his emotion, but at some point she'd realized there was something darker feeding it. After the hothouse, he'd gathered her up and carried her here, to his bedroom, where he'd taken her again, and that was the only word to describe it. Taken. Possessed.

His kisses had been dark and consuming, as if he could inhale her like the sweet night air he breathed. His touch released a gasp that only the heavens could hear. Sophie could easily imagine him taking control of her senses with his fingertips. And she'd had to stop him. Otherwise he would have made love to her all night, ravished her until there was nothing left of her.

It had always felt as if she lost a little bit of herself when she was with him, but this time he wanted it all, things she could never give him. Yes, he had frightened her, but she had frightened herself even more, because for a moment she had wanted that, too—to be completely possessed by him, to cease to exist except through him. Just for an instant she'd wanted to be swept into the vortex again, and the impulse had terrified her. It was like standing on the edge of a cliff, overwhelmed with the urge to jump.

With a sharp sigh, she sat up and slipped from the bed. It was beginning to feel as if she were dealing with two men, and one of them frightened her. The perfection of their time together at the beach house seemed like an aberration now, and she was tired of being confused and not knowing who he would be from one meeting to the next, even when they made love. Life was imitating her dreams, where the hauntingly romantic ghost could as easily have been a faceless dream monster—and sometimes was.

She'd been dazzled by the way he moved so powerfully to assume the Babcock throne. His commitment to the company promised a security she could never have known with the old Jay. But even that had a reckless first-strike quality to it.

Gooseflesh rippled her bare shins. The house was chilly, and since she hadn't planned to stay the night, she had nothing to wear but a large white dress shirt of Jay's. Arms clutched around her, she walked to the far window. She could see the hills in the near distance, the cliffs where Jay used to climb long before she knew him . . . and where Noah Babcock had nearly shot her when she was fourteen years old.

Sophie's heart began to thud as she stared at the hills.

She was catapulted back by the crack of a rifle. She would

never forget that earsplitting sound, or the terrifying encounter with the man who was to become her surrogate father. She'd been hiding out in the woods for weeks when she came upon a towering figure, a hunter in a khaki vest and red hat. He had an injured doe lined up in his rifle sights and was about to destroy it. There was no way he could have known it was an animal that an emaciated runaway had been nursing back to health. Or that the fight to keep it alive had kept her alive.

Sophie was paralyzed with disbelief. She couldn't even shout at him to stop. But when she saw his finger squeeze the trigger, she burst from the shadows and flung herself in front of the trembling animal. The shot he fired went wild— and so did he. She scared him so badly he was shaking as he yanked her away from the deer and raged at her for her stupidity.

He threw her to the ground in his fury and stormed away. But moments later he was back, kneeling beside her, peering at her with a mix of suspicion and confusion. He had recognized a bravery that even he didn't possess, a willingness to sacrifice herself for a helpless creature. He had lived his life believing weakness was to be crushed, but she would have given her life to save it. He didn't understand the impulse, but he revered true courage.

When he found out her circumstances, that she'd run away from her negligent aunt to avoid being shipped off to a boarding school, he'd taken her home with him and let Mildred bathe and feed and fuss over her. Sophie hadn't experienced that kind of caring from blood relatives, much less strangers. Even Wallis had welcomed the bedraggled waif into the fold, though Sophie had sensed her reserve at the time, and wondered if it had more to do with Noah's open admiration than with her questionable background.

That was how she'd come to live at the Big House as the Babcocks' ward, and why later she'd chosen to work with underprivileged kids. She knew what it meant to be given a hand. Noah had turned out to be a good man, formidable but good. She missed him.

''Sophie?''

She swung around, thinking Jay was awake, but he was lying exactly as she'd left him. Suddenly he rolled to his back and flung his arm out as if reaching for something.

''Right here,'' she said. When he didn't answer, she knew he was asleep. The stark white sheets made him seem all the more dark and restless by contrast, but his tossing and murmuring had given her an idea. She didn't know if it was fact or fiction that people who talked in their sleep could sometimes be engaged in conversation, but she was tempted to try. Having no idea what she would do if he woke up, she made her way silently to the foot of the bed.

''Who are you?'' she asked.

He rolled his head and mumbled something unintelligible. It sounded as if he'd repeated her question.

She moved closer. She was opposite him now, by the window. Speaking slowly, she asked again who he was.

''Noah,'' he said. ''Ask Noah.''

''Noah? Your father?'' She couldn't imagine what he meant. Noah wouldn't be able to tell her anything. Tragically, it was a rare moment when he could remember what had happened five minutes earlier. Sophie had visited him regularly in the rest home until Wallis asked her to stop. Her mother-in-law hadn't thought it appropriate, especially after Sophie and Claude began to see each other. She'd essentially banished Sophie from the family, apparently for having the audacity to love someone other than Jay.

''String . . . string game . . . ask Noah.''

She bent over him, straining to hear, but nothing he said made sense. The patch covering his eye caught her attention as she realized she might be able to lift it without his ever knowing. Some voice had been whispering to her all along that her suspicions about him would either be confirmed or denied if she could see him without that obstacle. It was a compelling hunch, although it made no logical sense.

She was close enough to touch the black cup when she hesitated. No, she didn't dare. He would surely wake up and catch her.

Her shadow danced across him as she inched away. She could hear the hush of her own breathing, and it gave her the sense of having narrowly escaped. But the feeling had as much to do with what she might have seen if she'd looked as with waking him. Something frightening was being concealed by that eye patch. She could feel it.

Sleep was going to be impossible, she realized, looking about the bedroom. He'd thrown his jeans across the chair, and there was probably a wallet in the back pocket. But his ID wouldn't reveal any secrets. She was sure everything would be in order there. However, the mahogany armoire with its myriad drawers and compartments might house something interesting.

Jay teased her about following the rules, but it was true. She didn't go through other people's things without permission, and she was reluctant to do so now, even under the circumstances. Jay was the one who thumbed his nose at convention, which was undoubtedly part of the allure he held for her. There were times when she wished she'd been graced with his sense of daring, and perhaps that explained the nervous flutter in her stomach now as she approached the armoire.

She came across something odd in the very first drawer. Stashed in the pocket of a pair of cotton pajamas, which she couldn't remember him ever wearing, she found a treacherous-looking piece of equipment. It might have been part of his rock-climbing gear, an unusually sharp-edged piton, but she couldn't be sure. There was nothing in the four smaller jewel drawers, but in the second to the last, she found a ten-inch metal shaft with four holes that looked too big even for Jay's fingers. It had a sharp hook at the end and was tucked into a balled pair of sweat socks.

The bottom drawer held a truly frightening surprise. She gingerly pulled the axlike object out from under a layer of T-shirts, still not sure whether she was dealing with equipment or weapons. A beam of light glinted off the long curving blade, making it glow like the devil's scythe. At the opposite end of the wooden handle was a deadly sharp spike.

She could imagine it shattering a human skull with a single blow. The grisly thought flashed unbidden through her mind and made her want to shove it back where she'd found it. Instead she stepped away from the armoire, forcing herself to examine it. But as she did so the overhead fixture snapped on, washing the room in white. And her in dizziness.

"What are you doing?"

Jay had come up behind her. "I couldn't sleep." Her fingers curled around the wooden shaft as she fought to keep her balance. There was no way to pretend she hadn't been going through his things. She held the evidence in her hands.

"Did warm milk ever occur to you?"

He was angry, but it could be guilt as easily as betrayal, she told herself. Her own guilt had vanished when she found the first weapon. She had reason to question his identity after what had happened at the rambler. Someone had broken in and accosted her. And now look what she'd found.

She had already realized what the object was, but she asked him anyway, a wealth of accusation in her tone. "What is this thing?"

He took it from her, and with a faint grimace dropped it back in the drawer. "An ice ax," he said. "They come in handy in the Himalayas."

"Why was it hidden in your drawer?"

"I don't know."

She scrutinized him with a look that he returned, unflinching. "Someone else put it there?" she asked.

"I put it there. I stash things, anything that resembles a weapon. I do it without thinking, sometimes without even remembering. I assume it's a legacy of my prison experience."

Sophie bowed her head, still trying to ease the spinning. "A man broke into my house while you were in the clinic," she blurted.

"Broke in? What do you mean? Did he rob you?"

He gripped her shoulders and brought her up sharply.

"No, he tied my hands and asked me questions."

''For God's sake, Sophie, why didn't you tell me? Did you call the police?''

''No, I didn't tell anyone.''

''Why not?'' His fingers dug into the flesh of her arms. ''Did he hurt you? Did he rape you?''

She shook her head, unable to meet his gaze as he searched her face. If he didn't stop shaking her, she was going to be ill.

''A man broke in, but you didn't call the police. You didn't tell anyone, not even me?'' His hands dropped away in a gesture of confusion. ''Explain that to me, Sophie. I don't understand.''

''He looked like you,'' she said. ''He sounded like you. I thought he *was* you.''

She turned back to the armoire and shuddered as she saw the ice ax. She didn't doubt that the deadly thing was a climbing tool, but she still wished she'd never opened the drawer.

''Someone pretending to be me broke into your house?'' he pressed.

She didn't know whether to be relieved or disturbed that he was so aggressively questioning her. He didn't seem to know anything about what happened that night, although it wasn't clear what that meant either. It could be that he was lying, or didn't remember, which made no sense. She couldn't think of an explanation that did make sense, except that it hadn't been him who had broken in.

''He wasn't pretending, Jay. And I wasn't dreaming. It happened.''

His head lifted, froze. ''How could it have happened? I was in the clinic, hooked up to an EEG all night, a machine that was monitoring my brain waves.''

She nudged the dresser drawer shut with her foot, no longer able to stand the sight of the gleaming blade and spike. ''Then you have a doppelgänger. Because this man could have been you. Everything about him reminded me of you, except—''

A graphic image halted her. ''Except that he wasn't wearing an eye patch.''

His hand came up as if he were checking to make sure the patch was intact. Instead he made a dismissive sound. "That should have told you it wasn't me."

Perhaps it should have, but it hadn't. And there were too many glaring discrepancies for her to let it go. "I asked you once before to show me what happened to your eye, but you wouldn't. You have to now, Jay. Please, I want to see it."

"No, you don't," he said coldly. "Trust me, you don't. It isn't pretty."

He strode to the chair and she realized that he was naked. She didn't want to see that, didn't want to watch him as he yanked on his jeans. A moment later he was sitting on the bed, lacing up a pair of Nikes.

"Are you going out?" Please say no, she thought. Please stay and talk to me, clear things up.

"Yes, out. Out for some air. I'm assuming you don't want to venture out in the middle of the night with the man who broke into your house and bound and gagged you."

It was cold in Jay Babcock's bedroom, cold enough to make Sophie shudder. But she was barely aware of the chill as he pulled a hooded jacket over his head and disappeared through the door. Her thoughts were fixed at a point moments earlier, on something he'd said. She'd never mentioned being gagged. She didn't understand how he could have known about that unless it was a lucky guess. And why hadn't he wanted to know what questions the man had asked her?

Nothing helped, including groping his way off the bed and staggering to his feet. He was trying to find the bathroom when he tripped on something that felt like clothing and nearly fell. He couldn't see shit, but it was probably the blue jeans he'd left on the floor when he came in last night, half in the bag.

Sophie was gone by that time, which was probably just as well. She wouldn't have liked the condition he was in. And he couldn't have blamed her. Fuck, if he'd known he was going to have the mother of all hangovers this morning, he would have put a bullet through his head last night and saved time.

The agony was centered in his bad eye as always, and the pain radiated out in wiry spikes. It made an odd crackling sound, like electricity. It was almost as if he could hear his own nerve endings frying. There was color, too, bright red bolts of lightning and blue tongues of fire.

When he finally found the bathroom, he felt his way to the sink and cranked on the cold water as high as it would go. With a savage growl, he ripped off the eye patch and tossed it aside. The pain exploded like a bomb, nearly cracking his skull with the violence of it. He would have dropped to his knees if he hadn't had the sink to hold on to.

The terry washcloth he'd thrown in the bowl was soaked with icy water. He rung out the dripping thing and held it up to his face, to the gory mess of flesh that had once been an eye. But he felt no more than an instant of relief before the pain surged again. His vision was still badly blurred, though he could focus enough to be repulsed by what he saw.

Why would anyone want to look at this ugliness? Why did she? An image flashed into his mind, as stark as it was disturbing. It was Sophie, whirling on him in anger and suspicion. He was angry, too, enraged, but he didn't understand why until he saw her lunge at him and rip the eye patch from his face. He could hear her gasp in revulsion, but it was his own reaction that shocked and sickened him. He struck her. With one blow she was on the floor.

Jesus, no, that couldn't have been him. He shook his head to block the image and felt pain roar through his skull like a firestorm. Someone was screaming. A woman.

He bent over the sink, covering both eyes with his hand, and in the darkened theater of his mind, he saw the reason for her terror. She was submerged in a bathtub of steaming water, writhing, fighting for her life. Someone was holding her under and trying to drown her.

Jay couldn't see the faces of the woman or her deadly assailant, but he knew who they were. With a guttural moan, he dropped to his knees and forced out the only prayer he could ever remember saying in his life.

Please God, don't let me hurt her.

"I don't know about you, Delilah"—Muffin hoisted a magnum of "supermarket special" pink champagne in the air—"but I plan to get smashed out of my mind, and do something I'll regret for the rest of my life."

Delilah loudly snapped the leg of her dripping bathing suit, releasing rivulets of pool water. "You need cheap booze for that?"

Muffin had already begun to wrestle with the wires that held the cork fast. "Keep swimming," she said as she flopped into a pool chair. "I know it's not polite to pop in on friends when you're having a nervous breakdown, but don't let me disturb your workout."

With a sardonic "Thanks," Delilah dove into the no-nonsense Olympic-size pool and resumed her laps.

When the cork finally blew, Muffin's linen trousers and crepe de chine shell were soaked with foaming champagne. The swig she took surged into her nose and left her gurgling bubbly laughter. She really did have plans that could involve lifelong regrets and she really did intend to get drunk. There was no other way to face what had to be done. The only decision that remained was whether or not to share her rather desperate scheme with Delilah, who admittedly had a stake in things.

"I take it the barbecue didn't go well," Delilah said when she finished moments later. In one fluid movement, she pulled herself from the pool and rose to her full five feet nine inches, as gleamingly fit as a competitive athlete.

She couldn't just be skinny? Muffin thought bitterly. She has to be lithe, supple, and strong, too? Bitch.

Muffin had come straight over to Delilah's Beverly Hills rooftop condo from Wallis's fiasco of a party, stopping only long enough to buy the champagne. She hadn't even bothered to call and was probably lucky that she hadn't found her friend "entertaining."

"Jay Babcock shoved a pie in our faces tonight." Muffin was seething. "All of us, everyone who thought they had a shot at Babock Pharmaceuticals, we got meringue instead."

"Wish I could have been there."

"It was quite a show. He was good," Muffin admitted. "But it was his last performance. He's too fucking cocky to live."

"And you're going to bump him off? That's why you're getting drunk?"

Muffin set the magnum on the table next to her chaise. "No, ducks, I'm not going to kill Jay. That would be much too obvious. I'm going to let him finish what he's already started."

She related Claude's story for Delilah's benefit, emphasizing Sophie's belief that the intruder was Jay. "Sophie could still blow the lid off if she gets a notion in that sweet little head of hers, and he knows it. It's only a matter of time the way I see it. He's psycho."

"Sorry to burden you with mundane logic at a time like this, but have you considered filing an injunction against him to stop him from taking over the company?"

Muffin knew nothing about filing injunctions, nor did she have any interest in such things. She only knew about finding the weak link and stressing it until the chain snapped. Hell, that seemed perfectly logical to her.

Delilah was still drip-drying at the pool's edge. Quelle exhibitionist, Muffin thought dryly. But the truth was that the other woman had intimidated her from the first, as much by her calm acceptance of who she was and what she wanted as by her cool beauty. Delilah was bold and unapologetic. She was real, a prospect that terrified Muffin.

"Don't you want a towel?" Muffin asked.

Delilah just grinned and shook her shoulders, which managed to create a very impressive ripple effect. "So then why are you getting drunk? What are the regrets all about?"

Ah, yes, the regrets. Muffin grabbed the booze and sprang from the chair. She hadn't eaten all day and the champagne was already going to her head. With a reverberant sigh, she walked to the open terrace doors and absently considered the room Delilah called a conversational salon. It looked like an Art Deco living room to Muffin, but then what did she know? She came from the working classes. If water sought its own level, she was a mud puddle.

"Muffin, I think I know what this is about, and you're going at it the wrong way. You're not a bad person for wanting what's in your heart. You deserve to have everything you want."

Delilah's voice was odd, breathless. Muffin was confused by the sudden concern. She had never thought of Delilah as especially sensitive, but she was touched, too. Deeply. Tears struck at her eyes and fire burned her throat. "I'm about to do something so crazy even I can't believe it," she said. "God help me, I am."

"Hey, it's okay," Delilah assured her. "I know what you need, I really do."

"You know *what*?" Muffin swung around, wondering what she was talking about, and stopped in teetering surprise. Delilah was totally nude. She had stripped off her bathing suit and it was lying on the tiles at her feet.

"What are you doing?" Muffin gasped.

"This isn't about us? About—"

Muffin was startled into a fit of hiccups as she realized what her friend was going to say. "About *sex*? I don't sob about that, although maybe I should. It's never been that good." She took another gulp from the bottle and choked again, only on tears this time.

Delilah didn't seem to know whether to laugh at her friend or to cry with her. Finally she marched across the terrace and thrust out her hand. "Give me that bottle, Muff, you've had enough."

Muffin lurched away and sank to her knees in a huddle, hugging the bubbly to her chest. Slightly drunk and slightly horrified, she realized she'd come to a crossroads, but not with Delilah. Neither of the paths stretched out before Muffin led to an erotic fling with her business partner. But one of them could take her straight to hell, nonetheless.

"Put on your clothes, ducks," she told Delilah. "This isn't about us. It's about a woman on the brink of suicide . . . or salvation. Right now I don't know which."

26

"Sophie? Are you in there?" Ellen rapped sharply on the front door of the rambler. She could hear a child crying inside, but she couldn't get anyone to come to the door.

It was early, just six-thirty in the morning, but Sophie was always up by that time, getting things organized for the kids' arrival. It was probably Albert whom Ellen could hear inside. His mother usually dropped him off early, which meant Sophie had been up and around to let him in.

"Sophie!" The door buckled under Ellen's heavy thud. It was a rickety old thing, and if there hadn't been a dead bolt, she probably could have forced it open. But she was reluctant to do anything that would frighten the child. Calling the police seemed extreme, too.

She was about to go around the back when she heard a familiar click. The door had creaked open, but only a few inches.

"Albert?" she said, addressing the pair of moist brown eyes that peered at her through the crack.

"I think Soapy's got a tummy ache," he said in a voice so low she could hardly hear it.

"Albert, step back and let me in, sweetheart." She pushed on the door, praying it wasn't chain-locked. To her relief, it swung open, and she saw immediately where the little boy was pointing. Sophie's feet and ankles were visible down the hallway, poking out from the kitchen area. It looked like she'd fallen.

Ellen asked Albert what had happened as she hurriedly shut the door. She could hear the dog barking out back, which meant he'd already been fed and let out.

"She didn't eat her fruit pop," Albert announced gravely. "Is she sick? Or jus' resting?"

"Probably resting." Ellen didn't want the little boy to see how alarmed she was, but when she reached the kitchen and saw Sophie sprawled facedown, she knew her friend was unconscious.

Ellen knelt to check her pulse and found it faint but steady. In a calm voice, she asked Albert if Sophie had fallen. "Did she trip over something? Or choke on food?"

"Yeah, maybe." He hunched his shoulders and his eyes began to fill up again. "She fell asleep while I was going potty. Will she be 'kay?"

The child clearly hadn't witnessed what happened, and Ellen didn't want him to feel as if it might have been his fault.

"Come on," she said, forcing some brightness into her voice. "Let's get you going on that jigsaw puzzle we started yesterday."

She got Albert settled at the kitchen table with the puzzle and returned to check Sophie for signs of air blockage or contusions. She found nothing, but was reluctant to roll her over and check further, for fear of broken bones or internal bleeding. As much as she hoped it was a simple fainting spell, she couldn't take a chance. She had to call for help.

Moments later as she sat on the kitchen floor next to Sophie's body, waiting for the paramedics to arrive, she realized that she hadn't asked Albert if there'd been anyone else in the house that morning. Sophie had told her there'd been a break-in, and to be particularly careful about locking up. It frightened her to think that the intruder might have returned.

Sophie awoke in a hospital bed that was walled off by dark green curtains. She guessed it for an emergency room by the plastic tag on her wrist and the hustle and bustle that could be heard outside the cubicle.

She couldn't think what she was doing there, except that there was a dull throbbing at the base of her neck, and she vaguely remembered the tiny kitchen in her rambler spinning around like the Raptor. Everything else was a blank.

"Oh, you're awake." A nurse had poked her head through the curtains and was smiling at Sophie. "How are you feeling?"

"Woozy . . . what happened?"

"Apparently you fainted." She whisked the curtain back and entered, a pleasant-looking brunette with an official-looking thermometer in her hand. "Other than a couple of bruises, you seem to be fine, but the doctor would like to talk to you about having some tests."

"Sure—" Sophie's other questions were silenced by the thermometer.

"Your friend, Ellen, called," the nurse said. "She asked if there was anyone you wanted her to notify, and she said to tell you the kids are fine. I'll send the doctor in, okay?"

Sophie nodded. There was little else she could do.

"Where to, ma'am?" the taxi driver asked as he opened the back door of a war-torn Lincoln Town Car and waved Sophie inside.

"The Babcock estate near Silverado Canyon. Do you know where it is?" Please say you do, Sophie implored silently. I don't think I can give directions. I can't even remember where I live.

"I'll take you right there." Once she was settled, he gave her a friendly nod and shut the door.

Sophie was grateful for the courtesy and the sure way he took over his mission. Fortunately, the traffic was light and

the trip back to the estate a short one, because she was bat-
tling motion sickness from the moment he pulled out of the
hospital driveway.

She wouldn't have believed one more thing could go
wrong in her life. If anyone had tried to tell her what was
going to happen to her that very morning, how it would rock
her world like an earthquake, she would have called them
crazy. Utterly crazy.

She'd read an article on stress once that assigned values to
the traumatic events in your life: birth, deaths, weddings,
even job promotions. The more stressful, the more points,
and the more points, the shorter your life span. This last week
alone she'd accumulated enough points to put her in her
grave.

Her stomach did an aerial roll as the driver swung into
another lane. She dug in the cargo pocket of her overalls,
searching for the antacid mints the doctor had given her.
What she found was a clown dispenser of Pez candies and a
Tootsie Pop wrapper, but no mints.

"No mints," she whispered. Her voice caught poignantly.
She sounded like one of her kids when they broke a special
toy.

No matter how old you were, there were times in life when
you needed to talk to your mother. If any proof of that were
required, it could be found in the enormous amounts of
money therapists like Claude were paid to be absentee par-
ents. Sophie didn't have a mother or a psychiatrist, so she
was doing the only thing she could do. She was going home.

Mildred opened the door of the Big House when Sophie
rang. Sophie still didn't feel comfortable using the key Jay
had given her, although she knew Wallis and all of them
expected her to. She was supposed to be living there, one of
the family again.

"If you're looking for Jay, he left around noon," Mildred
said. "I don't know where. He didn't say, but he was wearing
a jacket and tie."

The housekeeper relayed the information nervously, but
then Mildred did everything nervously. She seemed to expect

Sophie to be disappointed, but Sophie was relieved. Enormously relieved.

"Is Wallis in?" she asked.

"In the library, working on her correspondence. Shall I tell her you're here?"

"That's all right, Mildred." Sophie moved quickly past the housekeeper. "I have news that can't wait."

The library was on the ground floor, the last room on the northeast hallway before the main quarters branched into the honeymoon wing. Sophie had always found the atmosphere a little dark and dreary, with its heavy cut-velvet draperies and English oak shelves and moldings. But today Wallis had the curtains drawn and tied back, and she was sitting at the beautiful old inlaid leather desk, curled up like a sleek gray cat on a cushion as she gazed out at the willow trees.

"Wallis?" Sophie spoke softly, not sure if the older woman was daydreaming or dozing.

The chair creaked as her mother-in-law turned. "Darling, come in! Just the person I wanted to see today."

Sophie had to fight tears as Wallis rose and held out her arms. The older woman met her halfway and Sophie embraced her almost fiercely. "Thank you," she whispered.

"Thank me for what?" Wallis pulled back and smiled at her. "Oh, dear, something's wrong, isn't it? Jay said you went back to the rambler last night after the barbecue. I was afraid you might have had an argument. Here, come with me."

Wallis led her to a sofa in front of the fireplace and they sat down, Sophie on the edge of the cushion. Normally the room was redolent of lavender and old ashes, a musty blend that wasn't unpleasant, but today Sophie picked up another scent. Spirits. Unless she was mistaken, her mother-in-law had been drinking.

"Now, what is it?" Wallis pressed. "Nothing could be as bad as you're thinking it is. Share the burden—isn't that what they say?—and lighten the load. There's no need to carry it all by yourself."

Sophie brought her hands to her mouth. "I don't know how to tell you this. I can't believe it myself." She went silent, shaking her head, until Wallis's question interrupted her.

"Should I get you something to drink? Sherry? A brandy? That would calm you."

"No, I can't—"

Wallis tilted forward, studying her. "Why ever not? Sophie, what is it?" She emitted a gasp. "You're not pregnant?"

Sophie was too startled to do anything but stare dumbly at her mother-in-law. "How could you possibly know that? I just came from the doctor."

"I'm right, then? You're pregnant?"

Sophie nodded, and Wallis clasped her hands together. They were shaking so hard she could hardly manage them, nor could she seem to speak. It was some time before she could gather the steadiness to explain herself.

"I suppose it was when you refused the drink," Wallis said, her voice still light with shock. "Although I did have some help. Jay told me you hadn't been feeling well."

Sophie couldn't remember telling Jay she wasn't feeling well. She couldn't remember telling anybody but Claude. But even if she had, how could Wallis have guessed her condition when she knew Jay couldn't have children?

"Oh, Sophie!" The older woman fell back against the pillows, shaking her head, but clearly pleased. "You have that same look about you that I did when I was pregnant. Noah used to call it 'peaked.'"

Sophie didn't understand her mother-in-law's reaction at all. This wasn't cause for celebration. It was a nightmare. "Wallis, I'm frightened. I don't know what to do."

"Well, of course you are. The first time is quite terrifying, but you'll be fine. Morning sickness doesn't last forever, and there's a point in the middle where you really do glow the way everyone claims, though it doesn't last very long."

Sophie rose from the couch too quickly and nearly toppled from the dizziness. Wallis had completely missed the point.

It hardly seemed possible that her mother-in-law didn't understand what this pregnancy meant.

The willows were swimming in golden waves as Sophie walked to the window. She was afraid she was going to faint, afraid she would never make Wallis understand, *never make anyone understand.*

"Jay is—was—infertile," she said, not even sure who she was talking to anymore. "He couldn't have children."

"What, Sophie?"

She swung on her mother-in-law, incredulous now. "You knew that," she said. "We all knew it. Jay couldn't have children."

"Well, yes, I remember something like that, but it wasn't conclusive. He was never tested."

"But he was! Jay was tested first. They checked a sperm sample." Sophie couldn't remember the name of Jay's condition, but the doctor had told her there was no known way to treat it. He'd also assured her she was fine. She had to make Wallis understand that and acknowledge the truth. Someone, somewhere, had to understand what was happening.

"It *was* Jay," she insisted. "And you knew, dammit!"

Wallis sprang up, shushing Sophie frantically. "Stop now, please! You have to stop upsetting yourself this way."

But Sophie was on the brink of hysteria. It was tearing her apart, never knowing what to believe, whom to believe. Even her own body had lied to her. It had told her he was Jay when he couldn't be.

"Why won't you admit it?" she pleaded with her mother-in-law. "What's wrong with you? What's wrong with everyone? Have you all gone crazy? He's *not* Jay!"

"Sophie, don't!" Wallis pointed toward the hall. "Look behind you."

Sophie caught her breath. Jay was standing in the doorway, taking in the ghastly little drama between his mother and his wife, and Sophie had no idea how long he'd been there. He might have heard everything.

Wallis hurried to him, a pleading quality in her voice. "Let me have a little more time with her, won't you? She's over-wrought.''

She grasped the lapel of his single-breasted suit as if to detain him, but he barely seemed aware of what she was doing. He was looking past her at Sophie.

Sophie was in a state of shock that had nothing to do with her physical body. It was beyond her understanding how any-one could do what he'd done. Let her believe. Let it come to this. A pregnancy. Her mind was numbed by grief. But she lifted her head and returned his probing stare, defying him. She was glad he heard what she said, all of it. It was time he knew he hadn't deceived everyone, not her.

''It's all right, Mother,'' he assured Wallis. ''Sophie and I can discuss this like two adults. Can't we, Sophie?''

''What is there to discuss? You heard what I had to say.''

''I heard that you're pregnant with my child. I think we have plenty to discuss.''

Wallis turned to Sophie, clearly concerned. ''Are you go-ing to be all right?'' she asked. ''I'll stay if you want.''

The gesture surprised Sophie. Her mother-in-law seemed to be siding with her over the man she believed was her son. Of course, Sophie was pregnant with what could be the only Babcock heir, and that obviously played into things in some as yet undefined way.

''I'll be fine,'' she told Wallis. ''Perhaps he and I do need to talk.'' She wouldn't call him Jay.

Wallis seemed reluctant, and turned to Sophie again as she left. ''You will let me know if you need anything? Have Mildred come get me.''

''Of course,'' Sophie agreed. She'd moved close to the desk for support. She was unsteady, and the cushioned chair looked irresistible, but to sink into it, as Sophie wanted and needed to, could signal weakness.

A tray of brandies and cordials sat on an antique table behind the sofa. Jay walked to it and poured himself a gen-erous splash of cognac.

''A drink?'' he asked, glancing over his shoulder. ''No, I guess not. You shouldn't have one, should you?''

Sophie didn't answer. She was hardly feeling like conversation at the moment. She'd just realized how rarely she'd ever seen him in a suit, and how unlike "Jay" he looked. It was expensive, no doubt, European-cut and hand-tailored. But the effect of the pinstripes, coupled with a black eye patch, was sinister. Elegant, but sinister. She could only wonder about the reaction at Babcock corporate headquarters.

He took a sip of the cognac, clenched his jaw, and drank down the rest. The snifter landed on the table. But it could as easily have been on the floor in pieces. He was looking at her, walking toward her.

Sophie braced herself.

"I am your husband," he said, his voice low but powerful. He confronted her head-on, as if he could make her believe him by the sheer force of his will. There was heat now, fire. He was breathing fire. The brandy seemed to have ignited it.

"What's it going to take to make you believe me?"

Her head filled with swirling lights as she looked away. Something about him tugged at her, despite everything. It was hard to believe anyone could have that kind of power. She didn't understand how he exerted such control over people, over her.

"What is it going to take, Sophie?"

His voice had the low hiss of flames. It burned like the torch he'd described that day at the stream. She remembered the ice and heat, the pain of experiencing both at once. It had stunned her then. Now it alerted her senses, a warning. She sensed the threat and knew instinctively that she might be in danger. She had just openly accused him of not being Jay.

"A miracle?" She was as cold as he was hot. "Like this pregnancy?"

She might be light-headed and queasy, she might be frightened, but she wasn't going to let him intimidate her, something he was so good at. The pungent smell of ashes penetrated her nostrils, and the room took on a sharp hush as she faced him, telling him with the arch of her neck that she wouldn't be silenced like some trembling teenager, not anymore.

"I need to get back," she said. "I've been gone all day, and Ellen's expecting me." She moved around him, hitting his hand away as he reached out.

"What are you afraid of, Sophie? When are you going to stop avoiding me and deal with this?"

He caught her and pulled her around to face him, and though she fought to keep her balance, even that much motion was more than she could handle. Her knees buckled, and if he hadn't been holding her, she would have fallen.

"What's wrong? Is it the baby?" He lifted her, braced her shaking body with his hands as he searched her pallid features. "Jesus, you're sick."

"You knew that. You told Wallis I was sick."

"I didn't tell Wallis anything. Come here, sit down."
He urged her toward the couch, but she wouldn't go with him.

"Sophie, for Christ's sake, stop fighting me." There was rage in his voice as he swept her off her feet and bodily carried her to the couch. Black rage. He settled her in the cushions, then caught her arms and gave her a shake.

"You have to stop fighting me, or—"

It was a threat, and as weak as she was, she flared. "Or what, *Jay*? What will you do to me?"

"You're hurting the baby. Can't you see that?" His voice hung up on some emotion, and he released her.

Tears sprang to Sophie's eyes. He was so obviously enraged with her, but she didn't know why. Was he trying to protect her because of her condition? Or was he threatening to hurt her if she exposed him, just as Muffin had warned he would?

My God, she thought, I'm carrying this man's baby, and I don't know who he is. *I don't know if I'm safe in the same room with him.*

27

*W*here'd you get to? Sophie Sue! You hiding again? *Those welfare people better damn show up today. They promised to take you off my hands!*

Sophie's aunt had tied her up once. Tied her with laundry-line rope to a kitchen chair so she couldn't hide. Hours dragged by and Sophie's hands and feet went numb while her aunt mumbled and smoked cigarettes and restacked the dirty dishes in the sink. Trudy was her name. Aunt Trudy. Tallish and wiry thin, she sipped on iced tea all day and Sophie often wondered if the long, sweaty glass was spiked, because by dinnertime, her aunt was stumbling and repeating herself. But Sophie never saw the booze. Her aunt was good at hiding. Everyone was.

Beautiful hair, though. Aunty Tru, as she insisted on being called, had beautiful hair. Golden, with streaks as red as a copper kettle. Just like Sophie's hair. Sophie prayed all the time not to be like Aunt Tru. *Please don't let me be like her.* Instead, she prayed to be like her mother, the dead girl on the bathroom floor, whom Sophie had turned into a heroine.

Her aunt never talked about Sophie's mother, never even mentioned her name, though Sophie knew it was Priscilla. Bits and pieces slipped out in her aunt's mumbling conversations with herself. But Sophie had blocked most of it out. She didn't want to hear about her mother from Tru. She didn't want anything to interfere with the fairy-tale heroine she'd created in her mind all those years ago.

Pris was strong and fierce and capable. Pris would have been a doctor or a firefighter if she'd lived. Someone who saved lives.

What would you do now, Pris? Sophie asked as she sat at the kitchen table in her rambler, feeling as bound and helpless as the restrained child had been. How would you get out of this? Maybe you were smart, checking out at fourteen. Maybe life is pain, like Wallis says.

Sophie had been doing battle with fear and paranoia since she left the Big House that afternoon. The image in her mind was of Jay and the menace he had seemed to exude. Even his mother had been frightened of him. Sophie had left the mansion over Jay's protests, but her flight had only seemed to escalate the fear.

She was home now, safe. Just like a game of hide-and-seek, she'd reached the base without being tagged. She'd tried to tell herself that all evening. She'd already been through the rambler twice, checking the doors and windows to be sure they were locked and bolted. Blaze had trotted along beside her as she made her rounds. But when she was done and everything secure, curtains drawn and blinds shuttered, the emotion that washed over her was loneliness.

She couldn't remember feeling more isolated or alone as she sat stiffly in her shoebox kitchen. Even after Jay vanished and Noah was put away, she had people she loved and trusted to turn to. Family, because she had always thought of the Babcocks as that, and for the most part, they were—the only family she had.

Now she trusted no one. God, that was sad.

"No one but you, Blaze." She knelt to hug the dog, and the emptiness that welled up inside her made her pull him close. She buried her face in his warm russet coat.

"I'm going to have a baby," she whispered, and somehow, saying it aloud, to this gentle, quivering animal, who had been Jay's beloved pet, made it real for the first time. "Can you believe it, Blaze?"

The actuality of it overwhelmed her, and she sank to her haunches. After a moment she released the dog and pressed the flat of her hand to her stomach. The sound that whistled out of her was one of shaking disbelief. How long had she been waiting for this, a child of her own? And especially one conceived of her love for Jay. It should have been a joyous occasion, but instead it brought despair. She needed a friend, and the only one she could think of was Claude.

He'd left a message on her machine after the break-in, assuring her that he would always be there, that she could call him anytime. He'd been a source of solace and strength through a difficult part of her life, but he'd also been much more than that, and it seemed cruel to drag him into this. Despite her fears about the father of this baby, it was obvious that she still had unresolved feelings about Jay Babcock and would never be going back to Claude. No, she couldn't involve him.

The dog bumped her leg and whined softly, claiming her attention. "It's you and me, Blaze," she murmured.

She knelt to give him what he loved most, a power-scratch. But as she worked down from his ears, she glanced at the glass oven door. It was a reflex action by now. There seemed to be no avoiding that particular window on her soul. The kitchen was so small she could see herself from almost anywhere she happened to be, but the picture was not a pretty one. Her nose was red and her eyes swollen and slitty. She made a face and a sucky noise, which Blaze seemed to find enchanting. He cranked his tail and gave her an adoring swipe with his tongue.

"Gee, thanks for the bath," she said, wanting to cry, to sob the way she had at the beach house after making love. She was that desolate. Stoically she endured the dog's moist, eager licking, squeezing her eyes closed as he began to drench her in earnest. "Keep this up and I'm going to *need* a bath."

Later that evening, reeking of Blaze's affection and knowing she would never get to sleep, Sophie took her bath. She would have killed for Calgon, scented candles, and a romantic saga to get lost in, but all she could find was a box of Mr. Bubble and a couple of Wonder Woman comic books. In place of candles, she had her choice of a Pocahontas nightlight or a Benji Bear flashlight, and for soothing background music, there was PlaySkool Teach-A-Tune with its piano rendition of "Mary Had a Little Lamb."

Settling on her knees in front of the filling tub, she wondered if there were self-help groups for beleaguered thirty-year-old pregnant runaway wives. The sigh she emitted wasn't quite laughter, but at least it kept her from crying.

She poured a steady stream of bubble bath into the rising water, and magically, mounds of white foam rose from the steam. The smell was surprisingly fragrant. It might not be Calgon, but it looked heavenly to this beleagured, pregnant thirty-year-old. She couldn't wait to close her eyes, have a good soak, and pretend the world was a safe place for a while.

By the time she was back on her feet, she'd kicked off her terry skuffs and shrugged out of her robe, but she was still feeling a little shaky. Jay had not wanted her to come back to the rambler alone. He'd been so adamant she'd had to insist that it was the only way she would be able to calm down and rest. He'd wanted her to stay so they could resolve things, but when she reminded him that emotional turmoil was bad for the child she was carrying, he relented and let her go.

The look on his face as she left had struck at her heart. He was enraged that she was leaving, going against his wishes, but the darkness hadn't hidden another emotion, anguish. The pain in him had pulled at her, but the anger had sent her running. If it had been about the baby, she could have understood. But she deeply feared it was something else.

He couldn't possibly have known what it cost her to do

that. Or how urgently she'd wanted him to be her husband. How many times in the aching recesses of her heart had she wished that he would make her believe? If only he could have.

With a start she realized the tub was about to overflow. Optimistic fool that she was, she wrenched the tap hard, hoping to stop the steady drip, and then she rose on wobbly knees and took hold of the safety bar. She had one foot in the hot, billowing suds when the front doorbell rang. Sophie knew from experience that only someone selling magazine subscriptions had that kind of timing. But Blaze was already up and barking.

"Just a minute!"

Metal brackets creaked as she leaned on the safety bar. The bar was attached to a console shelf, and she used it to avoid slipping in the deep tub. But something—that horrible ripping sound—told her it was about to give way. She reared back as it tore loose from the wall and plunged toward the water. An instant before it hit she jerked her foot out.

Horrified, she watched the tub water begin to crackle and spit like a cauldron. There was a curling iron and some other paraphernalia on the shelf, and as Sophie backed away from the roiling water she realized the curling iron must have been turned on. She didn't know how that could be. She hadn't used it in ages, months.

The bell was still ringing, but Sophie didn't move. She was caught up in a ghoulish vision of a woman thrashing helplessly in the charged water. It wasn't until Blaze bumped open the bathroom door that she was jarred loose from her horror and revulsion. Any contact with the water, and the dog would be electrocuted, she realized. In her haste, she cracked her elbow on the porcelain toilet bowl as she dropped to her knees. The pain made her want to vomit, but she fought it back, yanking plugs until the tub stopped seething like a pit of snakes.

Jay filled the front doorway as she opened it a moment later. "Jesus, what happened?"

His voice was harsh with concern. It caught her like a

blow, and Sophie began to tremble. Her bathrobe was on wrong, and she was only wearing one skuff.

"Did he come back? The intruder?"

"No—it's the tub, the water, I—"

He wanted to know what had frightened her, but she couldn't get it out coherently. Finally, rather than struggle to explain, she took him to the bathroom and showed him the curling iron floating in the water.

"An accident?" he asked, and by the grave tone of his voice, she knew he didn't believe it was, especially when she admitted that she couldn't remember when she'd last used the iron.

Moments later, as they sat at the kitchen table, Sophie sipping the herb tea Jay had made, and Jay watching her quietly with his hands steepled, he began to ask her more questions, including some pointed ones about the break-in while he was gone. This time he wanted to know what the intruder had said and done. He even questioned her about Claude.

It didn't occur to Sophie not to tell him everything he wanted to know. What did bother her was the direction his questions were taking. "Why would someone want to hurt me?" she asked, because that was clearly what he was getting at.

He pushed up the raglan sleeves of his sweater and settled back in the chair, though his manner was anything but casual. It was focused, diamondlike. "It's not you they're after," he said, "it's me. I'm the target because of what I've done with the company, but they're trying to get to me through you. It's clever, actually."

Sophie wanted to know details. How were they trying to get to him through her? And who were *they*? But he answered her questions with another question.

"How many people know about the man who broke in, the one you thought was me?"

Fragrant steam wafted from the hot tea. "Only Claude, but he doesn't believe it actually happened. He tried to convince me it was another dream."

"Could it have been?"

Her sigh held genuine despair. "This all feels like a dream, to be honest. One big ghastly nightmare."

She linked her fingers around the heavy stoneware mug, absorbing the warmth of the drink. The amber brew left a honied, walnutty taste in her mouth that was delicious. Jay had picked it from her selection and either he knew something about herbs or it was a good guess. Dandelion tea was known for its calming properties, and Sophie was actually beginning to feel drowsy, something she couldn't have imagined even moments earlier.

"What did you mean they were trying to get to me through you?" she asked. He hadn't answered the question before.

"If they hurt you, and they can make it look like I did it, they get to me. First, someone who looks like me breaks in, and then there's an accident that may not have been an accident. If you hadn't stepped out of that tub, it would have been fatal."

That was true. And the rest of what he was saying did reveal some kind of macabre logic, but it seemed farfetched to Sophie. If someone wanted Jay out of the way, why wouldn't they go after him directly? And of all the people who might want her out of the way, the only one she could think of with an obvious motive was him. Jay, himself.

She untwined her fingers and missed the warmth of the cup immediately. When they sat down at the table, she'd buttoned every button of her robe with great care, but somehow she'd skipped one, the second to the last. As she did it up now she thought about the timing of magazine-subscription salesmen—and Jay Babcock. What were the odds, she wondered, of his showing up at her door when he did? He'd saved her life by ringing the doorbell at that moment. But she would never know if that was his intention. *Perhaps he'd arrived too soon.*

On the same night as Sophie's disastrous attempt to bathe with Mr. Bubble, someone else was taking the bath she dreamed of, but in a vastly different atmosphere. Wallis's favorite color was mauve, and she'd had her luxurious indoor spa done in shades of the deep smoky pink, with accents of gold foil and black marble.

Tonight the room was aglow with scented candles and festooned with baskets of white lilacs. There were even white petals floating in the bubbling Jacuzzi bath, where Wallis lolled in perfumed water. A pearl-black ice bucket held a bottle of French champagne and one hoarfrosted flute. The other flute, filled to the gold rim with the sparkling wine, sat on the marble countertop next to Wallis's draped hand.

She hadn't done anything this decadent in years. The water was so relaxing she probably could have fallen asleep, especially after all the champagne she'd had . . . except that the squeak of crepe soles on marble told her she was no longer alone. She opened her eyes to see El standing in the doorway.

"You summoned?" he said.

She lifted her glass. "Not a summons, an invitation."

El took in the candles and wine with an air that was mildly sardonic. "This can't be a celebration," he said, "so it must be a wake. Who died? Anyone I know?"

"Someone you know intimately." She laughed richly. "Of pleasure."

They both knew what she was referring to. "Splendor in the grass," she had facetiously called it afterward, but mostly to relieve the tension. Their rendezvous among the willows had begun as a power struggle and ended as one of the most explosive experiences of her life. She still hadn't caught her breath, or been able to think of El in the same way since. She'd had no idea her lifelong friend harbored such animal passions. He had honestly frightened her a little, and more than once since, she'd wondered what else she might not know about him.

But Wallis had had a great deal to drink tonight, and she was feeling rather bold. Beneath her deceptively cool exterior, she was as frantic and fizzy as the champagne, and she had reason to be optimistic. They were going to win this battle with the attorneys, and they were going to win big. She knew that now. She had only to convince El, and that shouldn't be too difficult once he heard her "news."

"Don't be a party poop," she said liltingly. She patted the pearly bucket with its second glass. "Come join me."

He relented with a stern look that she found quite adorable, and poured himself some champagne. As he sat on the marble ledge next to her, they touched glasses in a toast. "To willows," he said. "Long may they weep."

Wallis moved within the bubbling froth of the water to take a sip of her wine. It was delicious, icy crisp and tasting faintly of pears. Damnably expensive, but worth it. She would have to remember to stock up. But it wasn't the taste of the champagne on her mind as she drank again. As the sparkling liquid ran down her throat she glanced up at El, wondering if he could see her body moving beneath the warm rush of the water.

She'd emptied a capsule of bath oil into the tub, and the slippery caress of the water as it slid over her breasts and legs put her in mind of other physical sensations. She was imagining intimate things, his touch, his kiss. But he seemed preoccupied, and the possibility that his interest might have waned after their night together sent a wave of insecurity through her.

She couldn't remember a time when El hadn't wanted her. She'd been aware of his desire for her throughout the long marriage with Noah, and had secretly savored it. Knowing had empowered her in private ways that she had always believed were exclusively female. But the delicate balance had changed between them recently. El had subtly upped the ante, and she intended to find out whether or not he was bluffing.

"Is everything all right?" she asked. He'd already drained his flute and poured himself another glass, which wasn't like him.

The question seemed to bring him back to the place, the ambience, her. His gaze warmed a little. "How could it not be all right? Champagne, flowers, and thou, a beautiful woman, naked *and* wet."

"Cad," she said, flicking water at him. Secretly she found this new earthy side of him quite exciting. She was a mess of flutters inside. Lovely flutters. And as much as she wanted the upper hand, she also craved the sensations his boldness evoked. Given the men in her life, she would have found it difficult to respect one who wasn't her match.

She drank deeply of her champagne, then decided it was time to tell him why he'd been summoned. "I have news," she said, feeling as giddy and breathless as a girl.

"Good, I hope."

"Sophie's pregnant."

He nearly spilled his drink, and Wallis erupted in laughter, a raspy squeak that was decidedly unladylike.

"That *is* news," he said. "Maybe we need to rethink our strategy."

"No! That's exactly what we shouldn't do. It's perfect, El. Don't you see how this puts her at a disadvantage? She's even more vulnerable now. It shouldn't take much more to crack her. No, not much at all."

He went silent, but it was impossible to read his expression in the flickering light. She couldn't tell if he was studying her or deep in reflection. "Perhaps you're right," he said at last. "Perhaps this does work to our advantage."

Wallis watched him closely as he finished his champagne and stood. He pulled off his sport jacket and tossed it on the vanity chair. When he turned back to her, he was unbuttoning the collar of his shirt, and his eyes were hot.

"Getting comfortable?"

"Getting naked." He yanked his shirttails from his pants. "This is my kind of wake."

"El, what are you doing?"

"Joining you," he said, his hands on his belt. "After more than twenty years of fantasizing about making love to you in this very bathroom, I'm joining you in every sense of the word." The gleam in his eye sharpened. "And you had better be as wet as you look."

28

Routine is good, Sophie told herself. Routine is comforting. Mixing a great tub of rat chow was the first thing she did most mornings, and the last thing she wanted to do today, but she badly needed to restore some sense of normalcy to her life, for herself and for the kids. And nothing brought you back to earth quite like hoisting a twenty-pound bag of rat chow.

The turd-brown plugs recalled bite-size shredded wheat, only made of wood shavings. Sophie had been assured by the local pet-store mavens that their chow was the delicacy of choice among rodents, but she couldn't bring herself to serve wood in any form to her finicky gerbils, so every weekend she cooked up a little sauce made from vegetable stock, and froze enough for the coming week.

She often had a "funny tummy" these days, so she was being ably assisted in the kitchen this morning by Albert, who was the early bird as usual. She'd just poured the warm sauce over the chow and Albert was diligently tossing it in a large stainless-steel salad bowl.

"It's all in the presentation," she told him, sprinkling some parsley over the lumpy stew. "See."

"Mmmm . . . looks good." He nodded in agreement and gave the mixing spoon a big lick.

Helplessly, Sophie watched his cherubic features take on the contortions of a medieval gargoyle. His nose scrinched and his mouth stretched like rubber. Choking sounds heralded a tiny pink tongue that wagged like a bug-eyed toad's.

"Euuuuu," he said as Sophie scooped him up into her arms and hugged him. "Yeiiick."

"Oh, Albert, what would I do without you?" He was not only her little shield against the world, but the kid cracked her up. She rocked him back and forth, hugging him fiercely and laughing as tears rolled down her face.

"Glad I'm not a gerbil," he said as they trudged outside a short time later to feed the unwitting "aminals."

"Me, too."

Sophie noticed that Blaze's breakfast had gone untouched as she and Albert crossed the patio to the petting zoo, and by the time they were done with the feeding, she'd begun to wonder where the dog was. Please don't let him have gone back to the beach house, she thought. Jay isn't even there.

Blaze's master had returned to the Big House, as far as she knew. She'd finally had to ask Jay about his "timing" last night. She couldn't believe it was coincidence that he'd shown up at the exact moment she was stepping into the tub, but all he would say was that he'd had a "bad" feeling and come to check on her. She must have wanted to believe him, but when he'd refused to explain what he meant, she hadn't been able to hold back the fears, or the suspicions. She was beginning to think he enjoyed letting her twist in the wind, and she didn't understand that at all. She had asked him to leave.

"What's that noise?" Albert asked. He stepped around in a circle like a tipsy weather vane, then stopped, facing the gate.

"Noise?" Sophie listened, too, and picked up a low, snarling sound coming from beyond the gate. It was probably

Blaze, playing with some poor hapless lizard he'd found in the field. The setter was always bringing back "gifts" of lizards and snakes and dropping them at Sophie's feet. But that didn't explain how he'd gotten out. She locked the gate at night, and she hadn't opened it yet this morning. She didn't want the kids wandering in the field.

A crow flew by, scolding loudly. The small flock that followed squawked like dozens of fingernails on blackboards.

She shook her head, confused. Unless . . . she *had* opened the gate. She'd been so forgetful lately, but that wasn't too surprising considering her other distractions. Well, no matter, she told herself. Whatever the dog was playing with, she hoped it wasn't something tiny and cute, a petrified field mouse. "Albert, would you be an angel and take the bowl back to the house? I'm going to let Blaze in."

The snarling grew louder as Sophie approached the gate. For some reason the dog was scratching at the fence and seemed desperate to get inside. Sophie was reminded of the clawing sounds in her dream and felt an unpleasant shiver of recognition. It had been frantic, someone determined to get to her, and then she'd been assaulted by—

She shook off the thought. This was clearly an animal.

"Blaze?" If it wasn't the dog, it could be a coyote or some other wild creature. But the noise stopped and the setter's familiar bark greeted her as she depressed the gate's lever lock.

The door creaked open slowly, then banged explosively. Sophie leaped back as a dark, snarling form lunged at her and caught the sleeve of her blouse, tearing a strip from the cotton. Blood spurted and Sophie screamed at Albert to get in the house.

She grabbed a broken branch to ward off the animal and inched toward the door, hardly able to believe what was happening. The dog stalking her like a menacing beast was Blaze. His teeth were bared in a snarl and foam dripped from his mouth. Despairing, she realized that he must have been bitten by a rabid animal.

"Soapy?" Albert whispered. "What's wrong with Blaze?"

Sophie glanced over her shoulder and saw that the little boy was still on the patio. Clutching the bowl in his hands, he stared with huge round eyes at the dog he played with every day. They were pals, the two of them. Not enemies. He didn't understand what was happening.

"Albert," she pleaded, "go inside. Please!"

Her heart wrenched as she foresaw the agonizing choice that faced her. In order to protect the child she loved, she might be forced to hurt, even kill, the dog they both loved. Oh, no. Please, no—

Blaze coiled to leap again, and this time Sophie didn't move fast enough. A stunning force hit her shoulder, and she was knocked backward. But the dog had been stunned, too. He staggered and shook his head. Sophie scrambled to get away, but she couldn't get her footing. The grass was slick with dew.

She fell forward on her hands, screaming as the dog hurled himself at her again. She flailed with bleeding fingers, trying to get away, but he lunged for her throat, and as she struck out, his flashing teeth made contact. They ripped her arm and this time there was pain. Searing pain.

Dizziness brought her down. She was crushed under a weight so heavy she could hardly think or breathe. But even as she slumped to the ground she understood one thing. She would pass out if she didn't get help soon. She and Albert would be at the dog's mercy. The world was going chalk white, spinning off in a spiral. Blaze's snarling fury roared in her ears, and as she struggled one last time to push him away, she felt a gush of icy water hit her.

Blaze was hit with the blast, too. He yelped and darted away as the spray struck him full force. The jet of water kept him at a distance while Sophie fought to gather herself together. As she staggered to her feet she saw that it was Albert who'd scared the dog off. It was all the slight four-year-old could do to control the spewing hose, but he was down on his knees and hanging on with gritty determination.

Along with teaching the kids how to care for the animals in the petting zoo, Sophie had shown them how to separate fighting animals with water. Albert had remembered what he'd been taught. He'd turned the water on full force and was holding the dog off with it.

"You saved my life," she gasped as she fell to her knees beside him and took the spigot from him. "You did, Albert."

His dark eyes welled with tears. "Are you going to die, Soapy?"

"No, honey, of course not. Why—"

"You got blood everywhere."

Sophie hadn't realized until then that she was bleeding profusely from several wounds, especially her arm. It was a deep gash, and she'd undoubtedly lost a lot of blood, though she could feel nothing but a strange exhilaration.

Shock. She'd already gone into shock. They weren't out of danger yet, she realized. She could still lose consciousness, and Albert would be left to fend off the dog. Blaze was lunging at the water, attacking it with frenzied fury. The dog had gone completely mad. Struggling to hold him at bay, Sophie sent the little boy in to call 911.

Time raced before her eyes like a red blur. It felt as if she were going to pass out, and she lost track of everything but the effort to stay awake and hold on to the hose. Her eyelids twitched uncontrollably, and she swayed from side to side. Her head jerked back as she heard someone shout her name.

Astonished, she saw Jay burst through the patio door. When he saw what was happening, he ducked back in the house and returned with a blanket that he threw over the dog to subdue him.

Sophie must have looked even worse than she thought. Like death. Once Jay had bundled the thrashing dog into one of the large animal cages and called the local pet hospital to send someone out, he rushed back to her and lifted her into his arms.

He was clearly too stricken to speak, and Sophie was growing woozier by the moment. Her eyelids drooped and her tongue was thick. "What are you doing?" she managed as he turned toward the house.

"Taking you to the hospital, of course."

"You can't leave Albert."

Jay looked at her blankly. "Who?"

"The child," she said, pointing to the little boy who was standing right next to them.

The world had begun to spin again, whirling on its axis like a top gone berserk. Sophie couldn't fight it anymore. The spiraling whiteness had turned dark and enveloping. She couldn't feel her wounds anymore, but there was a deep, cramping ache in the pit of her belly and she wondered dazedly if that meant she was going to lose the baby. All of those things swirled through her drunken mind, but the last thing she remembered before she blacked out was the expression on Jay's face. He stared right through the terrified four-year-old as if he couldn't see him.

Sophie felt as if she'd fallen asleep in the middle of a spring shower. The warm and gentle downpour felt lovely on her skin, like a mountain mist, but when she opened her eyes to a mint-green sky and saw Jay gazing down at her, she realized that she must be in another hospital room, and that he had been bathing her face with a rag.

"Welcome back." His voice was warm and strong, but his features were wreathed in one of the saddest smiles she'd ever seen.

"Blaze," she said softly, remembering, and certain that they must have had to destroy the dog. That was why Jay was so sad.

"It's okay, Sophie. Everything's fine."

"Fine?"

He brought her hand to his lips and kissed it with such reassuring tenderness that her throat tightened. Everything was not fine. Something terrible had happened.

"Blaze is at the vet's, recovering," he explained. "They pumped his stomach and found some tainted meat. He's going to be fine and so are you. No rabies shots."

She still didn't believe him. She couldn't. There was something wrong. He was holding her hand too firmly, like a father consoling a child. He was touching her too tenderly. "What about the bab—"

"The baby's fine, too. Shhhh." He tapped his fingers lightly against her lips, trying to quiet her. "You lost some blood, and you're supposed to rest."

She couldn't. "Where's Albert?"

"I'm right here." Albert's little brown face was beaming at her from the end of the bed. "Jus' waiting for my mom to come get me."

"Oh, thank God." A sob broke inside her as Sophie realized that everything might really be fine, just as Jay had promised. Tears flooded up and spilled over, driven by the wave of relief she felt.

"Is he all right?" she asked Jay.

"He's fine, Sophie."

"I'm fine, Soapy," Albert piped up. "We had burgers and fries in the hospital caf-cafa—that place downstairs, right, Jay? Jay says he remembers me, but I don't remember him."

Sophie looked at Jay in confusion. It wasn't possible that he could remember Albert, although she sensed that this was not the time to say anything. Albert was born after Jay disappeared. Jay must be remembering Donald, Albert's older brother, she realized. He was one of her original six kids when she opened the day-care center, and Jay had often helped her by taking them on field trips into the woods. He'd even tried to teach them to climb on the rocks.

"Albert and I have been catching up," Jay said. "Right, Albert?"

The little boy grinned and scampered to Jay's side. But even as Jay tousled the child's dark hair and looked down at him, Sophie saw something in his expression change. Very much as before, he seemed to be looking right through the child, as though he didn't see Albert at all, but a haunting memory that was in some way associated with him.

Suddenly chilled, she remembered the man who broke in that night. He'd shoved the snapshot of Albert in her face and demanded to know who the child was. Something about Albert had compelled him, but he hadn't given her any clues as to what it was. Or what his reaction might mean.

What *did* it mean? she wondered. Some bizarre and frightening thing was happening to her world and everyone in it, and Sophie didn't know how to account for any of it. At times she even wondered if it was real. She hardly knew where to turn anymore. Or who to love. Would her darling Albert turn on her next?

All Sophie's fears were confirmed that night at the rambler. Jay had some terrible dark secret, and she had to know what it was. Despite the fact that he was unfailingly concerned and caring, the suspicion that he wasn't telling her everything had been building all evening. He buttoned her up in flannel jammies, kept track of her medicine, and made sure she took everything she was supposed to. He fixed her chicken soup and sat beside her at the table as she ate it. He did everything but spoon-feed her, but she still sensed that something was dreadfully wrong.

"Jay, please tell me what's going on with you," she pleaded. "You keep urging me to rest, but I won't be able to rest until we've talked."

He sighed heavily. "You've been through enough, Sophie. I don't want to worry you any more."

She'd refused to stay in bed and was sitting cross-legged at the kitchen table, her anklebones burning against the wooden seat. "I'm already worried, and nothing you could tell me could possibly be worse than my imagination."

But she was wrong. When she finally persuaded him to open up, what he revealed terrified and astounded her. He told her that he was haunted with doubts and suspicions about the break-in and the "accidents" Sophie had been having. And he didn't believe that any of those things were coincidental.

"The meat was tainted with a compound that mimics the symptoms of rabies," he told her. "It was no accident, Sophie, and whoever's doing it isn't trying very hard to cover their tracks. They wanted it to look like a botched murder attempt.''

''Another attempt by you?'' she asked.

''Possibly . . . although there is another explanation.''

The silence stretched so long that Sophie jumped when he finally spoke. ''There were problems with the treatment,'' he told her. ''I started having headaches, severe ones, and there have been other symptoms—''

Sophie shook her head. She didn't want to hear that. She wanted to hold out hope that something in their relationship was stable, and the success of his treatment had given her that. Now he was going to take away that tiny shred, too.

''But that night at the barbecue—'' She would argue if she had to. ''You said you'd come through with flying colors. You made it sound as if the doctors would back you up.''

''I didn't tell anyone the headaches were getting worse. I didn't want to compromise the clinical trials.''

''Maybe they should have been compromised if something was wrong with the drug.''

''It wasn't Neuropro, not in my case. I'm virtually certain I was never getting the drug. There's something else going on.''

She grew quiet, aware by the jutting blue veins in his forehead that this was becoming difficult for him, and it wouldn't help if she prodded.

''It's more than headaches, Sophie. I don't want to frighten you, but lately I've been plagued with obsessive thoughts and impulses, sometimes violent. I've been able to keep them under control, but they're worsening.''

She was silent, frightened. When she found her voice, it rose with urgency. ''Jay, you have to tell someone. Why not El? He would keep it confidential. He has Babcock's best interests in mind, too. You must, Jay—''

''I can't. Not yet, and even if I were going to take someone into my confidence, someone besides you, El would be the last person I'd pick.''

She waited for him to explain what he meant, but he passed over the comment. ''I'm concerned for your safety, Sophie.

More than concerned, obsessed with it. Whether they're trying to get at me or not, someone wants you out of the way,
and I think they're desperate enough to try anything at this
point.''

He rose from the table and turned to the patio. Reflected
in the black mirror of the glass, he looked like a figure out
of time, a medieval sorceror with a cutaway eye. ''Christ,
look at what they've done so far.''

She had the most uncanny feeling that he knew. ''Who are
they, Jay?''

''It could be anybody. They all want the company: Jerry
White, Wexler, Muffin. Wallis sees you as a threat because
you won't accept me as the rightful heir. And El has his own
motives. He isn't happy with the way I've taken over.''

''I can't believe that any one of them would do something
so extreme. We're not talking about criminals, Jay.''

''I've seen people pushed to the wall, Sophie. I've seen
what they'll do. Most of them are capable of violence, bar-
baric violence. That's what worries me. I haven't told you
the worst of it.''

He returned to the table and pulled out the chair, but didn't
sit. Instead he studied her for a moment with the same sad
expression she'd awakened to in the hospital.

''My worst fear is that it wasn't any of them who did those
things.''

''Then who?'' Her anklebones burned against the wooden
seat as she sat forward.

''I knew what was going to happen, Sophie. I had flashes
of the attacks before they took place.''

''Flashes? Like a psychic?''

''Yes, of the break-in, too. I saw the man who attacked
you. I saw what happened.''

''Dear God.'' What was he saying? That he knew who it
was? Why hadn't he told her?

She untangled her legs and stood, dizzy as she backed
away from him. It felt as if all of her fears had crystallized
into one realization. ''You're not Jay. That man who broke
in was Jay, wasn't he? Wasn't he!''

"Sophie, don't—"

"No," she cried. "He'd lost his memory. He didn't even know his own name!"

The chair crashed to the floor as he came around the table toward her. Sophie screamed and bolted for the patio door. But he got there first.

29

"What are you doing?" Jay caught her in his arms and whirled her away from the door.

"Who are you?" Sophie cried.

She wrenched back and forth, but couldn't get free. He'd come up on her from behind and gripped her wrists. Now he locked them at her waist, apparently determined to subdue her without hurting her.

"You're pregnant, Sophie. If you don't care about yourself, then think about the *baby*."

She slumped against him in defeat. The warning had been far more effective than any physical force he could have used. In the depths of her belly, a network of muscular bands had pulled tight, and she could feel an echo of the cramping sensation she'd had before she blacked out. Until this moment she hadn't realized that she'd given up all hope of ever having her own child. She had surrounded herself with kids because she loved them and never expected to have any.

No, she didn't want to lose this baby. She didn't.

She drew herself up and felt his grip tighten. "I'm all

right,'' she said. ''Please let me go. I'm not going to do anything crazy. Please.''

He did then, and she walked unsteadily to the table. The refrigerator was making rattling, shuddering noises, as if it were about to expire. The possibility rocked Sophie. In some way the old appliance had become her symbol of survival. If it could hang on, so could she.

''Tell me who you are,'' she said, taking hold of the chair. ''I'll keep your secret, just please tell me who you are.''

''Keep my secret? What are you talking about?''

She shook her head, not knowing how to answer him. ''I feel like I'm going crazy, Ja—'' She stopped short of saying his name and turned to him. ''I won't tell anyone, I promise. Nothing will change, but I have to know.''

''I wish I could tell you,'' he said. ''I wish I knew.''

She must have been staring at him in shock, because she wasn't able to believe what she was thinking, the questions that bombarded her.

''You're not him,'' she said with all the finality of a death sentence. ''But then how could you know so much about me? The private details? No one else could have known about the guess-who game. Pilson's Creek. The *wishbone*. No one.''

Her mind went off on a tangent, remembering all the other precious things that were woven into the time they shared, the threads of their life together. Maybe she hadn't been telling the truth. Maybe it did matter who he was because it felt as if her heart was tearing like fabric, as if he were ripping it apart with his bare hands—her heart, their relationship, the past. It was all she had.

Abruptly she left the kitchen and went to her bedroom. When she returned, she had the Dirty Dan's hat crushed against her chest. Her voice was strident. ''How did you know about this? And why did you buy it for me? How dare you do that!''

He started to speak, but she wouldn't allow it. Nothing he could say would satisfy her outrage. He'd trampled on the only things she had left of that time. She remembered a movie where two men shared a cell in a third-world prison. They didn't expect to live and confessed secrets and precious memories. One of them died, and the other escaped. He took the dead man's identity.

Peering at him now, she wondered how he could look so much like Jay. It was uncanny. "You knew Jay in prison, didn't you? He told you about me."

His sigh was audible. "I can remember only brief flashes of that time. The doctors said I blocked it. But I suppose it could have happened the way you say. Maybe I knew Jay Babcock and assumed his identity, but I didn't do it knowingly."

Sophie curled her fingers into the warmth of the felt hat and closed her eyes briefly, wishing that everything could be as simple as the sweetness she'd felt the day he gave it to her.

Watching her, he tried to smile but couldn't. Normally that wouldn't have surprised her. Jay had never really smiled. But this wasn't the faintly ironic curve she'd always associated with his mouth. This was taut, sad, almost wistful in a man so inaccessible.

He really didn't have the answers, she realized. "How do you explain it, then?" she asked. "If you're not Jay, how can you have his memories?" *How did you know that I melted when he touched me, that I screamed when he made love to me. How did you know those things?*

He came around and pulled out the chair for her, obviously intending that she sit down. He wanted her to rest and take care of herself—and perhaps he wasn't going to go on if she didn't. None of that was said. All of it was understood.

"There are ways to alter memory," he told her once they were both seated at the table again, "all of them experimental. There are even ways to surgically transfer memory from one brain to another, a transplant, so to speak, although it's never been done in humans."

"You were *given* Jay's memories?"

"I woke up in a Swiss clinic with images running through my head like newsreels, intricate pictures, full of details and voices. I could *hear* the voices, yours, mine. I could see it all, but there was no emotion attached. It was like watching a black-and-white videotape of my life—or someone's life.''

''They did this to you in Switzerland? Who? Why?''

''I don't know who did it, or if anything was done. But I do know that El is one of the few men in the world with the expertise. He's devoted his life to the neurophysiology of memory. He knows everything there is to know.''

The refrigerator was racked by a shudder. Sophie heard it and brought her hands together. It was ridiculous that she should care what happened to an ancient appliance. She was clinging to things, silly things. Anything.

''Years ago he and his research people were working on an experimental memory drug. It was supposed to create instant learning, and it was used in conjunction with a highly controversial process called RNA memory transfer, that surgical procedure I just mentioned. It was a pet project of El's, despite the fact that the early studies had been repudiated. Everyone thought he persisted because of Noah's condition, but now I'm beginning to wonder.''

''So you think that it's . . . El?''

If he could hear the disbelief in her voice he didn't acknowledge it. He touched behind his ear, shook his head. ''There aren't any scars, nothing to indicate that surgery was performed, though with today's microtechnology that doesn't mean much. But yes, to answer you, I do think it's El. I just don't know what he's done.''

She didn't have to ask why. She knew. El and Wallis wanted to regain control of the company through Jay—or through this man, whoever he was.

''Could it have anything to do with the La Jolla clinic?''

He nodded slowly, as if surprised she'd made that connection so quickly. ''I was supposed to undergo the same treatment regimen as the subjects in the formal trials. They said it was the same combination of drugs and therapy—but I got suspicious one night and convinced the nurse I'd already had my injection. The notations on my chart checked out, but later on, when they assumed I was asleep, someone slipped into my room and gave me another injection. Before I lost consciousness, I heard a man saying that I would remember nothing when I woke up.''

''A man? El?''

He shook his head. ''Possibly. The voice was familiar, but I couldn't place it. When I woke up I was told they'd been doing sleep studies, and I vaguely remembered being hooked up to an EEG. But it felt like a dream, all of it, a surreal dream.''

Sophie knew that feeling. Her dreamlike states had not been drug-induced, although Claude had hypnotized her several times, and he'd always used something to relax her.

Jay was gazing at her, studying her. ''Or maybe there's a much simpler answer to all of this,'' he said. ''Maybe I *am* Jay Babcock.''

''Then who was the man who broke into this house?''

He clasped his hands and brought them to his mouth. ''What if I said it was me.''

She gaped at him. ''What are you talking about?''

''I've had flashes of the entire incident, in much more detail than you described it. I can see it as if I were here, as if I were him. I think I am him.''

She stared at him in bewilderment. ''But how could it have been you? You were at the clinic. I called. They said you were asleep.''

He didn't seem to hear her. His focus had changed. It had shortened, as if he were looking inward. ''Is there a picture of Albert on your refrigerator?'' At her nod he said, ''And the man who broke in asked you about it, didn't he?''

''Yes . . . why?''

''Because that's one of the flashbacks I've had, of him— of me—and that picture. And there's another image that runs through my head. It's of a man catching a little boy who looks like he's falling out of the sky. That man is me, too.''

''You did.'' She tried to stand, but her legs weren't steady enough. ''Only it wasn't Albert you caught. It was Donald, his older brother, and it was the year I started doing day care. He fell from the bluffs where you were teaching the kids to climb. Don't you remember? You probably saved his life.''

"The bluffs?''

"I tried to talk you out of it, but you were convinced that the four-year-olds could learn the basics safely. You said Noah had taught you and Colby at that age. You'd played some kind of game in the bluffs.''

"String Me Along, a hide-and-seek game with a ball of twine. That was what we played.'' He murmured the words, then even softer, *"Christ—"*

"Jay, what is it?''

"The bluffs. That's where it's hidden, the chimney fissure where we used to play String Me Along.''

He was talking to himself. It was some kind of insight, and she couldn't get him to say anything more than that. It was as if he were in a trance. But a moment later, as he looked up and saw the concern on her face, he came to the table and knelt beside her.

"I think there's something hidden in the bluffs that may be the key to all of this. I can't tell you what because I don't know.''

He took her hand and she knew he was leaving.

"You're not safe here alone,'' he said. "I'm going to bring in a private security guard to protect you until this is resolved.''

"No—"

"Yes, Sophie, it's the only way. Someone's trying to kill you. And if you don't remember anything else, remember this. They not only want you dead. They want *me* to do it, so don't let anyone near you,'' he warned. "Not even me.''

His jaw caught with emotion, then flexed savagely. "Do you hear me? If you want to stay alive, don't let me near you.''

Sophie had the horrible premonition that she would never see him again. As he stood to leave she struggled to get up, too.

"Jay, wait, please. There's something I need you to do before you go. Take off the patch, please. Let me see you without it.''

He drew away as she reached out. "Please,'' she said. "It

will haunt me otherwise. It will always haunt me.''

His hands dropped to his sides as she came around the table, and she knew this would be her only opportunity. If he wouldn't remove the patch, at least he might not stop her from doing it. He towered in front of her, and it seemed a terribly risky thing to do. But she had no choice.

She took his statuelike stance as permission. Dizzily, she raised on tiptoes and worked the black triangle from his dark head, exposing the powerful lines and angles of a face that his own mother had once described as classically male more than classically handsome.

Expecting to be horrified at what she saw, she staggered backward in shock. ''My God, Jay—''

He quickly covered it with his hand. ''I told you.''

''No . . . there's nothing wrong with your eye. Nothing at all. Look!''

''What do you mean?''

There were mirrors lining the back of the china cabinet that sat against the wall. He turned to them and touched his face.

''Nothing wrong with it?'' He moved in closer, peering at his reflection. ''My eye is gone. They cut it out of my head. It's scarred and multilated, hideous.''

Sophie didn't know what to say. She was almost afraid to tell him that his eye was perfect. There were no scars. No sign of mutilation whatsoever. As he turned away from the mirror in disgust and reached for the patch, she realized that she had to let him go—and not just for her own safety. Something terrible had been done to him.

You've created another life for yourself, Sophie, a dream life where Jay still exists.

Claude had said that to her years ago, in one of their first sessions, and she had agreed. ''It's true,'' she'd admitted, ''and if I could, I would live there all the time, with him. I would be the woman in the dream instead of me.''

Now Sophie paced her living room in a state of rising agitation, oblivious to the young, ruddy-faced security guard who sat at her kitchen table, playing solitaire with a pack of huge Dr. Seuss cards. The adrenaline that rushed through her veins seemed to rinse away everything in its path, including the dizziness that had plagued her.

She was trying to remember that session, and Claude's explanation of her condition. He'd described how the personality could fragment into different parts to avoid pain, and he'd called it dissociation. In its extreme form, the subject disintegrated into multiple personalities. Her condition had been milder, but he'd been concerned about that possibility. She'd slept and dreamed constantly, sometimes even through sessions, to avoid the pain of reality.

With his help, she'd begun to work through her loss and face the world again, instead of trying to escape. Claude had thought her recent episodes of "seeing" Jay were a regression into that dream state, but she was almost certain now that they weren't. It was something else entirely, something that had to do with Jay, not her. It even seemed possible she hadn't been dreaming of him at all, that he was really there.

She glanced down at her hands and realized they were soaked with perspiration. She'd crushed the Dirty Dan's cap into a damp black ball. Soon there would be nothing left of it. She had to see Claude, talk to him, and find out if she was right.

"Are you okay, ma'am?"

The guard looked up as Sophie walked past him to the phone. It was closer to morning than night, nearly four A.M., and she'd tried earlier to reach Claude at home. He was either away or asleep, because he wasn't picking up.

"Shit," she whispered as the message machine came on. She clunked down the receiver.

"Ma'am?"

"Oh!" She whirled to face the guard, who'd come up behind her. A buzzing dial tone told her she'd knocked the phone off the hook.

"Do you know what time it is?"

"I know," she said placatingly. "But there's someone I have to talk to, my psychiatrist. Please, it's so important. He works out of his home. Maybe you could take me there?"

He reached around her and hung up the phone. "Sorry, ma'am, I really am, but my orders are to provide security for you here, in this house. I was told not to take you anywhere. You heard Mr. Babcock."

"Yes, but I'm feeling strange, panicky, and I desperately need to see my doctor. I don't know what will happen if I can't see him. You wouldn't want to be responsible, would you?"

If anything she was downplaying it. Strange and panicky didn't begin to describe how she felt.

"Responsible, ma'am? For what? Are you really sick?"

He read his own answer into her silence. And as she gave in to her despair and leaned heavily against the wall, he said, "Where is this doctor of yours?"

"He's in Newport Beach, on the peninsula down by the wedge. It'll only take a few minutes."

He hung back, but Sophie caught hold of his hand and pleaded, sensing that he was about to relent. "Please help me, please! I'm afraid of what will happen if you don't."

She gripped him so hard her fingers left a bloodless impression on his hand. "I'm pregnant," she whispered.

With those words, he finally seemed to understand her desperation.

"All right," he said, checking his watch, "but you're not going to be alone with this guy at any time. Doctor or not, I'm staying in the room while you talk to him."

"But he's my therapist. The things I need to say are personal and private."

"I don't care about his credentials or your privacy. My job is to protect you, and that's the condition. If you don't agree to it, we don't go."

Sophie agreed, hurriedly, but as she led him to the garage where the Jeep was parked, she realized she couldn't do what he wanted. The information she had to discuss with Claude was potentially so explosive, it could not be revealed to anyone, certainly not a total stranger. He could blackmail the family with it or sell it to the tabloid press. No, she could not let this man in the room with her and Claude.

The guard was trained in security work, but she had one advantage. She was the expert on how to disappear. She knew every nook and cranny in the garage. She knew where the light switch was, where the tools hung over the workbench, and the cubbyhole where a person could hide in the dark. Fortunately, they were all on the same side of the room and easily within reach of each other.

"Wait a minute." He waved her behind him as he pushed open the garage door with his foot and entered the dark room to check things out. When the light came on and he moved away from the switch, Sophie sneaked in behind him and brushed up against it.

Concealed by darkness, she made a lunge for the crowbar and got it on the first try. The cubbyhole was a narrow space about four feet high where Jay had stashed his duffel bags and climbing gear. She ducked inside, crouched, and thrust out the crowbar.

As the guard groped his way toward her the metal tool caught him in the shins and pitched him forward. Knowing she had only seconds, Sophie sprang out of her hiding place and flicked on the light. He was already up on his hands when she got to him. It was only a glancing blow, but she didn't flinch. She swung hard and true, and the force of the crowbar against his temple sent him back to the floor.

She prayed he would stay unconscious long enough to let her get away. But it wasn't until she had the Jeep out of the garage and was heading down the highway toward Newport that she allowed herself to take a deep breath. That was when the violence hit her—the cringing horror at what she'd done, the fear and trembling.

30

The car barreling down the highway toward Jay at break-neck speed looked exactly like Sophie's old Jeep. He knew it couldn't be. She was interned at the rambler with a Neanderthal ex-marine who'd been told to watch her every move. Still, Jay was curious when it roared by going nearly as fast as he was, the beams so high and bright they forced him to avert his gaze.

He glanced in the rearview mirror, but it was too dark to read the plates. Any car wailing by in the dead of night would have caught his attention, but this one had a crazed momentum. He might have checked it out if it hadn't been for the object lying in the passenger bucket seat.

The steel combination-lock briefcase gleamed in the moonlight like something left by an alien spaceship. The dark vault haunting Jay's thoughts had been a natural crevice in the stony heart of the bluffs and the metal object it contained was this briefcase. Rust and corrosion had eaten the lock away. He'd easily forced it open, but what he found inside was a mind-numbing revelation. It was a detonator that had been ticking for five years, waiting for Jay Babcock to remember its existence and return to set off the blast.

It didn't reveal Sophie's attacker, nor did it convince him that he was Jay Babcock, but it did tell him unequivocally who the Babcocks were, and what they'd done. The documentation inside could end an era. It could bring down not only the family as it now existed, but the entire pharmaceutical empire that had been conceived and built over generations. It also revealed the truth about what had happened to Jay.

He hit the brakes and felt the car shimmy beneath him as the entrance to the family estate suddenly came into sight. The security gate opened so slowly it brought him to a full stop, which allowed him to look up the long driveway to the Big House and think about what his next move would be.

Even though it was not yet dawn and the mansion was still dark, the Babcock family was in for a rude awakening. He knew a great deal more than he had before, but there were important questions left to be answered, including why a briefcase full of damning documents had been stashed in a rock—and why he himself had put them there—*if* he was Jay Babcock.

Among other things, the briefcase contained a massive trial transcript and a personal journal written by Noah. There was also a letter from Noah stating that the documents had been entrusted to his son, Jay, for safekeeping, and that Jay would make them public knowledge should anything happen to Noah.

The sky was already fading from blue black to lavender by the time Jay began his journey through the halls of the silent house. The briefcase swinging in his hand, he took the backstairs with the natural grace and speed of a big mountain cat. And when he reached the south hall, he could see pale light seeping under the door of Wallis's bedroom. He didn't know if someone was up and around or if it was the rising sun, but it hardly mattered. His concern was not with courtesy.

El answered, opening the door just enough to peer out.

"Jay?" He was obviously startled. "Wallis said you were staying with Sophie tonight."

Jay was only momentarily surprised to see the lean, handsome scientist in his mother's room. He'd always suspected the relationship went deeper than friendship, and might even have been glad that they were finding happiness with each other if it had not been for his awareness of the bloodletting that was to come.

Jay's sense of distaste at what he had to do was so great he would have preferred to walk away from it and forget what he'd found. But there were innocent victims involved. And he himself had a vital need to know who he was and what had been done to him. And then there was Noah. It was possible his father was a victim in this monstrous cover-up, too, if that's what it was.

"Is Sophie all right?" El asked.

"Sophie's fine." Jay was determined not to be sidetracked. He'd called Wallis from the hospital and given her a full report on Sophie's condition. "Is my mother up?"

"No, but I'll wake her if it's important."

"It is, but you and I need to talk first."

The spacious French country kitchen glowed with dawn-pink radiance as they entered, El barefoot and wearing a robe that might have belonged to Noah. Jay had some vague recollection that the crest on the pocket was the Babcock-family insignia, but he felt no jealous stirrings for the man who had apparently taken his father's place. He felt nothing but a desire to understand how decent, humane people could do the unthinkable in the name of . . . what? Corporate profits?

El went immediately to make some coffee, insisting he couldn't get his pulse going without it. Jay observed the older man's forced joviality without responding to it. El clearly knew his way around the kitchen, but he showed no signs of recognition as Jay settled the rusty briefcase on the large butcher block island that dominated the center of the room.

The perking coffee wafted pleasurable sounds and smells, all familiar, and all militating against the silent tick of the bomb. El turned with a steaming mug for both of them, but

Jay shook his head. Let the man have his coffee, he told himself. Even traitors got one last request before the firing squad. But he couldn't postpone it any longer. He opened the case and beckoned the other man over.

"You're going to want to read these transcripts," he said. "The dog-eared pages are your testimony. The notes in the margin are Noah's."

You remember Noah, he thought, unable to quell the biting sarcasm that welled up.

El set the mugs down and picked up the pages. "The Trizene-B trial? That was years ago. Turned out to be little more than a nuisance suit."

Jay nodded. "I guess you could call irreversible brain damage a nuisance. What was the plaintiff's diagnosis? Paralytic dementia? But who cares as long as Babcock won, right, El? It was a major victory, thanks to your testimony."

El flashed him a look that was cold, murderous. The trapdoor had already closed, but he didn't know it. "The court found in our favor," he said stiffly. "The plaintiff was suffering dementia before he took the Trizene B. Our antidepressant wasn't held responsible and we weren't deemed negligent." He slapped the papers down. "That's what these transcripts say."

"That's not what Noah says. Read his notes."

"Noah? What the fuck does it matter what Noah said? He was failing, man. His own mind was going. He was senile and paranoid. He saw conspiracies everywhere."

Jay felt a dull throb of pain and knew it was one of the cluster headaches. "You lied under oath, El. You lied. You altered statistics and gave false testimony, committed perjury to get the company out of a suit that would have bankrupted it and, worse, destroyed its reputation. Trizene B damaged people—their brains, their bodies, their lives—and we got off scot-free."

El grabbed up the papers, crushing them in his hand. "Do you have any idea what this information could do to the company, to your mother? To you, Jay?"

"I know what it could do to you, and if I don't get some

answers, I'll use it." He pulled Noah's handwritten letter out from beneath the transcripts. "Sound like a threat? It is. I'll go public, El, just like Jay Babcock apparently promised his father he would."

"Just *like* Jay—what are you saying?"

"I want to know who I am."

"You are Jay Babcock."

The throbbing increased. A hot wire was being driven through Jay's eye. He touched the patch and knew that nothing would relieve it. "Then who is the man who broke into Sophie's house? The man she keeps 'seeing'?"

"I have no idea."

"You're lying! It's a fucking lie, El."

"No!" El shouted back, just as adamantly. "I'll tell you anything you want to know, but ask me a question I can answer."

"Why do you want me to kill Sophie?" Jay tore the patch from his eye and nearly doubled over with pain. He couldn't yell anymore. He could barely talk. "Why am I wearing this eye patch when there's nothing wrong with my eye? What have you done?"

There were no comforting kitchen sounds now, no brewing coffee and rich aromas. Everything was preternaturally silent.

Battered by pain and rage, Jay wondered if El were controlling the agony with a remote device. Was he some kind of mad scientist who could raise the voltage of Jay's punishment with the same impunity he would a lab rat's?

El picked up the transcripts and dropped them as if they were a bomb. "We had to do it, Jay. We had to do it because of these. There was no choice."

"Had to *what*?"

"Alter your memories."

"Jesus!" Jay clutched his head.

"What is it? Pain?" El asked, inching closer. The patch had fallen to the floor at Jay's feet. El swept it up. "Put this back on. Do it now!"

"Why?"

"It's hypnotic suggestion, drug-enhanced. The pain is programmed to start once the patch is removed.''

Jay snarled at him like an animal, keeping him at bay. ''Programmed? What the fuck did you do?''

''We modified certain memories and implanted new ones with electronic stimulation and psychosuggestive drugs. The eye patch was a backup, in case we missed anything. The brain is a very adaptable organ. It abhors a vacuum, and when crucial neural networks are blocked, it tries to create new ones. We couldn't let that happen.''

Jay could hear the note of pride in El's voice. He was pleased at what he'd managed to do, at the monster he'd created.

''The patch functions like an antenna and feedback loop,'' he went on. ''A photoelectric cell beams light onto the retina, which relays it to VI, the brain's clearinghouse for visual input. The frequency of the light determines where it goes and the brain's reaction determines the strength and duration of the bombardment.''

''You did all that so I'd forget what happened at the trial?''

''Not exactly. We had to help you forget what did happen and remember what *didn't*. The mutilation of your eye in prison, for example. It never happened.''

The soft kitchen light blinded Jay as he looked up at the man who'd gone to lengths that were almost unimaginable. He'd violated the sanctity of another man's mind, his thoughts and memories, for his own purposes.

''It's not what you're thinking,'' El said. ''It's not mind control or science fiction. In the most simple terms, we took out some bad memories and put in some good ones.''

''Jay Babcock doesn't need simple terms. He went to pharmacology school, remember? You're talking about some form of RNA memory transfer, right?''

El almost smiled. ''You still don't believe me, do you? We didn't need to give you Jay's memories. You *are* him. But you had to be stopped. You were going to blow the whistle, you and Noah.''

Jay tried to think over the pounding in his skull. Noah had ended up in a convalescent home, robbed of both reason and sanity, and Jay had ended up in a prison cell, robbed of his freedom and his past. Neither was coincidence, he was sure.

"So you eliminated us," he said.

"No one eliminated anyone, not in the way you're thinking. Noah had been showing progressive signs of Alzheimer's for years. His decision not to defend Babcock's position in court was unconscionable. He was raving about his responsibility to the public, but you don't throw your own to the wolves. I believed that then, and I believe it now. He *was* incompetent, Jay. He had to be removed from leadership, or he would have destroyed the company."

For a moment El was the statesman again, his voice full of conviction and oddly persuasive. He sounded like he really believed what he was saying, and probably he did by now. Over the years he must have convinced himself of Babcock's rightness in order to live with what he'd done.

"So you institutionalized Noah?" Jay asked.

"It wasn't me who made the executive decisions. I didn't have the authority. It was your brother, Colby. He got power of attorney over Noah's affairs after he had him hospitalized."

"And for me you conveniently arranged an accident?"

"I didn't arrange anything. I didn't even know you had a climbing expedition planned. Colby told me after you were reported lost. He also told me you'd insisted on taking the trip so you could clear your head and come to a decision about the trial. He gave the impression that you were coming to your senses and were ready to give up the fight. At the time I believed him, and to be honest, I was relieved."

Jay made no attempt to hide his bitterness. "Blame it on the dead man? How convenient."

"It *was* Colby, Jay."

The speaker of these words, Wallis, entered the room in a perfumed cloud of mauve silk, the robe of her peignoir set flowing from her shoulders. There was pain glittering in her eyes, but somehow she managed to look strong and proud, stronger than Jay had seen her in years.

"Colby's death doesn't absolve him of what he did," she

said. "It doesn't absolve us either, for our part in it. But the master plan was Colby's, and he carried it out privately—and ruthlessly."

She walked to El and stood beside him, clear in her allegiance. "Your brother had been under Noah's thumb and in your shadow for years. This was his chance to take over and do things his way. It's true that El and I took his side, but that was before we knew what he was capable of."

Wallis had slipped her hands in the pockets of her robe and curled them into fists, the only visible sign of her inner conflict. "Colby told no one what he'd done to you. I found out only after going through his things after his death. He'd taken over Noah's office without bothering to change the combination of the safe, and Muffin was in Europe, so I had some time. When El and I found out where you were, we began making plans immediately to get you out."

"And to have me lobotomized?"

"Jay, please, don't. It was for your own safety, for everyone's safety. We thought it would be easier if you didn't remember the details of the trial—and Noah's collapse." Her chin began to tremble before she got control of it. "You wouldn't have wanted to remember that. It was horrible."

She clutched her hands without taking them out of the pockets, and her voice turned pleading. "Please understand my decision. I didn't know how else to bring you back and give you everything that should have been yours: the company, your wife. It was the future Noah wanted for you. It was his legacy, Jay. I would have done anything to see Babcock safely in your hands."

Even sacrifice lives, he thought.

But suddenly there was a proud tilt to her head again, and she linked her arm in El's. "It's not what you think, Jay. El would never call himself a hero, but I can. Colby knew Trizene B was dangerous long before the lawsuit, but he refused to take it off the market, even after what happened to Noah. It was El who forced him to recall the drug."

"What *happened* to Noah. What do you mean?"

"Your father took Trizene B."

El spoke up then. "Noah came up with the original formula for Trizene B over twenty years ago. Later he swore it was the magic bullet for depression, better than Prozac or Zoloft or any of the drugs his competitors had developed. His chief researcher warned him the compound was dangerous, particularly when prescribed to people with certain preexisting conditions, but Noah felt so strongly he eventually decided to experiment on himself."

"No one but Colby knew what he'd done," Wallis said. "And by the time I found out, it was too late. We learned later that Noah had incipient Alzheimer's, and the drug had virtually turned the condition into a virulent disease. He deteriorated into a mental skeleton right before our eyes, and finally there was nothing to do but put him away. He was still lucid enough to insist on testifying when the Trizene-B trial came up, but of course, Colby wouldn't allow that."

"Your brother discounted the danger," El explained. "He wanted to relabel the drug with nothing more than a warning to those at risk for Alzheimer's. The only way I could get him to take it off the market was by agreeing to testify, and altering the test data seemed a small sin compared to the alternative—destroying more lives and probably the company."

"What about the woman you defeated in court? Doesn't her life count?"

Wallis answered Jay's question. "El and I made private restitution to the plaintiff's family, hundreds of thousands of our own money, and if that isn't enough, we'll give them more."

Jay's smile was grim, unforgiving. "How much money is a life worth?" he asked her. Odd that he could not bring himself to call her mother. He didn't know who she was to him anymore, or how he felt about her. But he had decided that he was going to claim his father's legacy. Whether it bankrupted Babcock or not, he was going to take over the company and dedicate it to the realization of Noah's vision. That much he could do.

"Help!"

The rending scream blared through Jay's head. Confused, he turned to the doorway, but no one was there. Another scream nearly deafened him, and he clapped his hands over his ears. El and Wallis were staring at him like he'd gone mad. That was when he realized the sound of the woman screaming was in his mind.

It was Sophie!

Someone was trying to kill her. He could see flashes of her desperate attempt to fend off her attacker. She was struggling and shrieking his name. "Jay, no!" He could hear the sound of a blade whistling through the air and see the deadly glint of its metal edge. His ice ax. Her beautiful face contorted with terror as the scythelike blade came down on her. Blood spewed like a fountain, and Jay let out an agonized groan as the blunt end of the ax shattered her skull. "Sophie!"

"What is it, Jay? What's wrong with Sophie?"

"You want her dead," he raged at El. "You set me up to kill her—programmed me—why?"

"No, I didn't. I swear I didn't! I don't know how that happened. Your last EEG showed some abnormalities and there were behavioral changes while you were under hypnosis. There is evidence that a trance state alone can create multiples, but that's assuming one believes in such things. God knows I never have, but I don't know how else to explain this. Another personality may have emerged under stress, a violent alter ego—"

Violent alter ego? He barely knew what El was saying.

"Jay, it could be dangerous. You could revert."

Wallis and El shouted at him as he turned and sprinted from the room, but he didn't stop until he got to his own bedroom. He ripped open the doors of the armoire and jerked out the bottom drawer. Clothing flew everywhere until he got to what he was looking for. The ice ax was still there, exactly where Sophie had found it.

31

Jay didn't know where to find her. There was nowhere else to start besides the rambler, but his skull was splitting apart by the time he got there—and turned himself into a human battering ram. The blows that racked his body as he slammed it against the bolted door were a pleasure compared with the blinding agony in his head.

Jesus, why wouldn't she stop screaming! He had to find her, stop her! His head was going to explode.

At last the door buckled and gave, shrieking in protest. Jay burst into the living room, not knowing what he would find. The guard wasn't stationed at the kitchen table. That told him instantly that something was wrong. The house had an eerie, empty feel. A quick check of the bedrooms turned up nothing. There was no sign of either Sophie or the guard, but Jay spotted the blinking red light on the phone machine as he entered the kitchen.

''Sophie, I know it's the middle of the night, but I have to talk to you. It's urgent—''

The message Jay played back was from Muffin, asking

Sophie to meet her at the beach house. Her voice had a sharp, shrill edge, as if she were close to the breaking point, too. It hurt Jay's head and made him snarl in agony.

Sophie was at the beach house. It was an emergency and the guard had taken her. Pain nearly drove Jay to his knees as he fought to make sense of those rudimentary facts.

Jay, no! Don't hurt me—

"Fuck!" The machine clicked and snapped and whirred. It was all he could do not to rip the thing out of the wall and destroy it. He stabbed a button to shut it off. But it began to rewind, and he nearly went insane. *Why would he hurt her? Why did she keep saying that? Who wanted him to kill his own wife?*

He ripped the machine loose and flung it across the room. As it crashed against the patio slider the messages began to play at a slowed, thick speed. Blaze was barking outside, but Jay couldn't let the dog in. The noise—the pain—had sent him over the edge. He didn't know what he might be capable of.

Get out of here before you do some real damage, he told himself. Find her!

He got no farther than the front door. Another message halted him. Another voice. The smashed machine was still playing, but like sludge, its quality distorted the sound. Jay couldn't make out what was being said. He couldn't even tell if it was a man or a woman. But there was something about the voice he recognized. The softness.

This was the killer. He knew it. Pain struck as he searched his blaring hell of a mind. So many people had reason to hurt Sophie. Faces scrolled through his head: Muffin and her pierced friend, Wallis and El, despite their denials, Jerry White and his business cohorts. The images kept flooding. Jay couldn't stop them. The security guard. Christ, even the biker who'd accosted him at Dirty Dan's.

Who wanted her out of the way? His own voice was on that tape, too, message after message. But it wasn't him. *Not him! No matter what she kept screaming.*

The pain spiked through his temples from both sides and

exploded inside his eye. He staggered and caught hold of the door frame to steady himself, wondering if he could drive. He could barely stand.

His Jeep was parked out front, halfway up on the lawn. But by the time he got to it, the screams had stopped. Everything had stopped—the whirring tape, the barking dog, the muted voice. It was so quiet inside his mind he could have heard the second hand of a clock ticking. He didn't know what that meant.

He didn't know who he was.

Sometime later he opened the hatchback and began to rummage through a duffel bag full of climbing equipment. "Yeah," he said, his voice soft and whispery as he found what he was looking for and pulled it out. The solid wood grip was familiar in his hand, reassuring. That other one in his drawer was a spare. This was the ice ax he climbed with.

Sophie hadn't expected that Claude would be in session at six in the morning, but as she entered the foyer she saw that the door to his office was slightly ajar. He always left the front door open when he was expecting a client so they could come in and wait for him in the outer office, where it was comfortable.

This morning she could actually hear him speaking to the person. She moved closer, listening and wondering if she dared interrupt.

"You take great strength from our sessions and find that they're helping you open up and be more loving and trusting. Is that right? Answer me now."

"Yes," came the soft reply.

"Say 'yes, Claude.' "

"Yes, Doctor—uh, *Claude*."

The woman's voice was almost too soft to hear, but it sounded disturbingly familiar. The doorknob creaked under Sophie's grip, and she froze, hoping they hadn't noticed. She didn't want to interrupt now. She needed some time to try to make sense of what she'd just heard. It had the sound of a hypnosis session, but his client couldn't be who she thought it was.

Sophie had undergone several such sessions, although she couldn't remember anything about them. Claude had always given her something that he said would open the locked doors of her psyche and reveal the secrets that were hidden away there, even from her.

Now his voice droned softly. "When you go to bed tonight and every night, you will sleep soundly and wake up refreshed. If you dream, you will dream of these sessions, where you are happier than you've ever been and deeply fulfilled by our work together. Can you feel that happiness now?"

Sophie couldn't hear the woman's answer.

"Who saved you, Sophie?" he asked her. "Who walked with you through the wilderness? Who held your hand?"

"You . . . you did."

"And who do you trust implicitly?"

"You . . . implicitly."

Sophie released the doorknob with an aching gasp. The client *was* her. She was listening to Claude and herself in session. How could that be?

"Say my name," he coaxed. "Say it again and again. With love."

"Claude—" The woman whispered his name until her voice broke and she couldn't go on.

A chair scraped the floor as if Claude had risen. "The bond we share is sacred, Sophie. I will never violate it or betray your trust. What I feel for you is pure, like a father's love for his child, like a god's for his creation. Say that you believe me."

"I believe you."

But Sophie was engulfed by *dis*belief. It wasn't just that she was listening to herself, it was the tone of Claude's hypnotic suggestions. They sounded like brainwashing. Her fingers throbbed as the blood returned. She'd made a mistake in coming here now. She needed some time to get her bearings. But while she was struggling with what to do next, the door swung open and a man's towering form filled the space.

Sophie stepped back in alarm. For a moment she wasn't sure it was Claude. Everything about him was familiar—the uncombed mop of dark hair, the old sweater and slacks—everything except the suspicion in his expression. It was enough to make him seem malevolent.

"I'm sorry," she said. "I heard voices. I thought you were with someone."

"How long have you been out here?" he asked.

"Not long. I just came in."

He didn't believe her. His gaze flickered over her with a coldness she'd never seen before. But then, she'd never lied to him either. She'd forgotten there was a chime in his office that sounded when someone came through the front door.

"Are you shaking? I frightened you."

"No . . . I'm fine." This wasn't Claude, she thought. She didn't know who this man was, but it wasn't her soft-spoken friend and former fiancé. He stood aside as if to let her enter, but she was reluctant to go in.

"Is something wrong?" he asked.

"I thought there was someone with you."

A semblance of his gentle sadness returned. "There's no one here, Sophie. I'm quite alone."

Still she hesitated, but a grave, reassuring note slipped into his tone as he added, "Please . . . come in."

Finally Sophie walked past him, praying she was wrong about the premonition that had stirred a chill in her very marrow. This felt dangerous in some way she couldn't gauge, and yet she must have been wrong, must have misunderstood the situation. She'd never associated Claude with any kind of risk. Quite the opposite; he was her friend and protector.

Each tap of her heart felt like an unexpected reminder of some detail forgotten as she looked around the room, searching for something that could explain what she'd overheard. But there was nothing. This was Claude's office, exactly as she remembered it, lined with musty bookshelves and glass-paneled cabinets, cluttered with old editions and nautical paraphernalia. There was no evidence of a client, or a session in progress.

Claude was sitting on the edge of his desk, his arms crossed, his body bowed in the slight hunch so common to very tall men. There was something odd about the alignment of his head as he looked up, a faint tremor, and she wondered if he'd always seemed so unsteady. Sympathy for him overwhelmed her. She did hope this new frailty had nothing to do with her.

"I tried to call you," she said. "I left messages."

"Yes, you said it was about him, Jay."

"No, not really. It was—" She made a dismissive sound. "Actually, it was nothing. Me again, overreacting. It was nothing." *He knew that she'd called, and he hadn't responded?*

"Then what brings you here?" he asked.

"I was worried. You didn't answer the phone, so I came over to see if you were all right." She was a bad liar, but he'd already figured that out.

He rose slowly, laboriously, yet he was an imposing figure without the stooped gentleness to soften him. There was an antique curio cabinet near his desk. He walked over to it as if he might be looking for a particular object, but Sophie had the feeling he was staring at his own rather frightening reflection in the leaded-glass doors.

"You needn't worry about me," he said in a monotone. "I'm fine now."

"Claude," she implored, "what's wrong?"

He turned on her, and Sophie caught her breath. His huge brown eyes glittered with pain. Unshed tears welled in their depths. But beneath the sadness there burned a frightening light.

"There's nothing's wrong with me," he said. "I'm not the one who's repulsed and trying to deny it. Look at your wrist, Sophie. You've pinched it black-and-blue. What could that mean except that being here, with me, is a nightmare for you."

Sophie glanced down in bewilderment. Her wrist wasn't

bruised. She hadn't touched it. Her hands were pressed to her sides and had been since she entered his office. "A nightmare? Why would I think that? Why would I ever think that, Claude?"

His voice was slowed, thickened by his effort to express himself. "Why won't you admit it? I know what's in your heart, Sophie. I can see it in your eyes when you look at me. Pity. You pity me. Women do, they all do. Claude, the freak. Claude, the monster. But it's not me who's the monster. It's him."

"Him? Jay?" She could see the tremor now as he tried to nod. It was far more pronounced than she'd thought. He was ill, she realized. Something frightening had happened to him.

"You don't b-believe he's your husband," he went on, faltering on the words. "You've even had nightmares of him breaking into your house and attacking you."

Sophie wasn't afraid of him anymore. She was afraid *for* him. "I had no idea you were so upset about this. You yourself said it was all a dream."

"I just wanted to be loved," he whispered. He rocked away, rocked back, agony in his voice, wounded rage soaring out of control. "My God, Sophie, how could you do that? I saved you from him. How could you go back to him? How could you love him after what he's done to you?"

"What . . . do you mean?"

"He wants you out of the way. He's tried to kill you twice, and he'll do it again."

"No!"

He couldn't seem to stop rocking, shaking his head. "He's the monster, not me. What more evidence do you need? He rigged the accident that nearly electrocuted you and gave his own dog tainted meat."

"Claude, please, stop. I don't know why you're saying these things."

Her breath caught hard as he suddenly came out of it. He looked up and saw her moving toward the door. She froze mid-step, not sure what to do. She had to get out of his office. She had to find Jay. There was no way Claude could have known about the accident with the curling iron. She hadn't told him. She hadn't told anyone but Jay.

"Sophie," he said imploringly, "you're frightened. Look at you. There's terror in your eyes. Let me help you. You know I can. I made the nightmares go away before. I can do it again."

"There are no nightmares, Claude. Not anymore."

Her voice was firm now, though she was shaking inside. She couldn't tell if he was delusional or just distraught, but she had to get through to him somehow. The premonition she'd felt earlier had been true. She was at risk.

"I can help you—" He started toward her, and suddenly she was screaming.

"Claude, be careful!" She pointed toward something on the floor, a framed picture that must have fallen off his desk. She hadn't seen it before, but there was shattered glass everywhere. "There! By your feet!"

He looked down and came to an awkward halt.

Sophie froze for an instant, unable to move as she realized it was a picture of her. It could have fallen, but she knew that it hadn't. He'd smashed it, destroyed it.

He was going to do the same thing to her.

She turned and ran for the door. If she could get outside, scream, make it as far as the street. There might even be someone on the jetty—

She burst into the entry, but he caught her as she flung open the front door. There was nothing frail about him as he slammed an arm around her stomach and lifted her off the floor. His huge hand muzzled her mouth and nose, cutting off her air. She couldn't scream—and fighting him might endanger the baby.

He carried her back into the office that way, her feet dangling well above the floor. His arms nearly crushed the air out of her. She could have kicked him, but caution wouldn't let her. A blow to his shins would surely enrage him, and if the struggle turned violent, she would lose.

But more than anything else, it was what he said that stopped her from fighting. His voice was soft, broken with emotion. He pleaded with her to understand that he didn't want to hurt her. "I can help you. I can save you, Sophie, but only if you let me."

He had said this over and over again in their early therapy sessions. "It's important that you feel safe with me, that you trust me. Think of me as a lifeguard. I can only save you if you let me."

But moments later Sophie stood in stunned silence while he straitjacketed her hands and arms in a heavy white canvas restraining halter. She would have told him about her condition, begged him not to hurt her for the baby's sake, but he hadn't given her the chance. He'd forced a gag into her mouth, a thick strip of toweling that he knotted tightly behind her head.

When he finished and she was bound like a mental patient in restraints, he picked her up and very gently, very carefully, settled her in his treatment chair. "Don't be afraid," he whispered. "I can help you."

He caught hold of her face with his hands and pressed a kiss to her hair. "I can make you love me again." As he stepped back from her she saw the tears in his eyes, the sorrow that weighed down his head and bent his body at the shoulders.

Was that what he wanted, to make her love him again? He wasn't going to kill her? Hope surged as she realized she might be able to reason with him. She strained against the bonds and twisted her head back and forth, trying to talk through the gag.

"I know," he said, watching her. "I know you're frightened. I'm going to give you something that will calm you."

No! The baby—

As he turned to the stainless-steel sink where he kept his medical supplies, she saw the wastebasket beneath the counter. It was full of broken glass and smashed pictures. She'd sensed something missing when she entered his office, but she hadn't realized what it was. All of the photographs of her had disappeared from his desk and bookshelves. Now she knew why.

He was obviously in terrible conflict, some war raging within him. Love and loss had mutated into something dark, but he hadn't completely given up on getting her back. As long as he wanted that, she might have a chance.

We're not the evil creatures pain twists and shapes us into. Pain makes us cruel.

But when he turned to her with the syringe, she knew she couldn't let him inject her. He wasn't rational. There was no telling what drug he might give her, or what he might do while she was unconscious. She moaned and thrashed as he came toward her, pleading with him, hoping he could see the message in her eyes.

"Sophie, don't—" He hesitated, tears welling again, as if her very struggle was breaking his heart. "Don't you understand. It's not me you should fear. It's him. He's dangerous. Something went wrong during the treatment. Another personality emerged, a violent alter ego. That's who made the attempts on you."

"No!" she screamed through the wadded material. She wanted to call him a liar, but Jay had sounded as if he feared exactly what Claude was describing.

"I did everything I could," he insisted. "I've been watching out for you all this time, trying to protect you."

As he held the syringe up to the light and tapped the air bubbles from the clear fluid, she realized that he must have been the one following her, the unseen presence, perhaps even the one who sent the belated birthday gift.

"This will help," he said. "It will make all the monsters go away. No more bad dreams."

Sophie bucked upward and nearly rocked herself out of the chair before Claude caught her and pushed her back. She thrashed wildly, forcing him to hold her still. Exasperated, he yanked the gag from her mouth. "What are you doing?"

"You can't give me that shot," she gasped. "I'm pregnant. Please, Claude—"

"Pregnant?"

He stared at her until the terrible light came back into his eyes and Sophie knew she'd done the wrong thing. Telling him had not convinced him to save her, it had convinced him he could never have her. She'd been intimate with another man, impregnated by another man. There was a child growing inside her that belonged to someone else.

"Claude, please understand. I didn't want to hurt you. Or to fall in love with Jay again. I didn't think he was ever coming back. It was over."

"I do understand," he said, hushing her. "I do." He continued to search her features, studying her as if he were trying to decide who she was now, this woman who had rejected his devotion and committed sins against his lonely heart. This woman who had treated him as cruelly as all the others.

He set the syringe on a wheeled tray by the chair. A thoughtful expression tempered his hollowed-out face. "You should have been the one, Sophie. You could have redeemed all those laughing, shrieking little girls. Your love could have made up for their wrongs. You were different, not cruel. You could have restored my faith. If only you had, because now someone is going to have to pay for their unkindness."

"No, Claude—"

His hand covered her face and turned it away from him. She felt the gag slip between her teeth and cinch tight. And then he lifted her head and fumbled to fasten something around her neck. It was a Saint Jude's medal, the symbolic gift he gave all his patients when they left therapy. She had thought the tremor might be an act, but he couldn't control the shaking in his hands as he laid the medal against her throat.

"My last 'lost cause,'" he said. "That's what you are, Sophie. This is my own medal. I have no need for it any longer."

Sophie went still inside as he began to talk haltingly about himself, going back to a time before they'd met, before he went into private practice. She knew a great deal about his background, the important milestones, but she hadn't realized he was one of Noah Babcock's senior research fellows, that he had headed up the Trizene-B study.

"I'm dying," he told her. "And the hell of it is, my mind

will go long before my body. I'll be a zombie, my brain eaten out of my skull by Trizene B. I tried the drug secretly, hoping it would ease my depression. It appeared to be a panacea, but the side effects forced me to admit what I'd done to Noah. He refused to believe the antidepressant was dangerous, and to prove it, he took it himself. He was gone in a few months. My deterioration has been much slower . . . until recently.''

Sophie was familiar with the symptoms of paralytic dementia. She'd witnessed them in Noah—ataxia, spasticity, paranoia, delusions.

"I want you with me," he said suddenly. "I don't want to go this way, eaten away, wasting away. Death should be quick and painless—a release of all suffering—and I must have you with me. Please understand that, Sophie."

His eyes burned hotly, bright with tears as he stood above her. Sophie's neck snapped back as he pressed the heel of his hand to her forehead. He'd exposed her neck, and he had the syringe in his hand. She could feel the needle. She could feel the searing pressure as it pierced her vein and the drug spurted into her system.

"Laurent!"

Someone had shouted Claude's name. Sophie opened her eyes to see Jay crash into the room. He wasn't wearing the eye patch, and he looked like a wild man, the wild man who broke into her house. She was hallucinating. The drug had already reached her brain. He had the ice ax in his hand and he was rearing back to throw the deadly thing.

"Laurent, get away from her!"

The ax whipped through the air like a tomahawk, spinning end over end. It screamed like the whirlwind that had threatened to engulf Sophie Weston from the moment she met Jay Babcock. Sophie screamed, too, but no one could hear her.

She felt the impact when it hit her. She was struck with a dull thud of pain and toppled into a black whirlpool that swept her toward oblivion. Swirling oblivion. The weight that enveloped her sucked the oxygen from her lungs. The choked gasp that rippled through her was a death whimper.

"Sophie!" she heard Jay shouting. "Sophie . . . where are you?"

32

Jay never saw the ice ax strike home, but he heard the dry
crack of splintering bone. It was the awful thunder of a
skull being split open, of human devastation. And his entire
body convulsed with the sound.

The instant the weapon left his hand, he sagged to his
knees. He'd barely caught a glimpse of its path before he'd
been jarred senseless by the crack of his own bones as he
pitched forward onto his elbows. He hit the floor hard,
stunned by the impact. Pain speared him. Piercing wires of
it. Paralysis. The agony struck his eye and he was blind.

*Nothing can hurt us, Sophie. The gods watch over child-
hood sweethearts. We have special dispensation . . .*

But he couldn't get to her. Surely this pain would kill him
and he would never get to her. Even the gods couldn't protect
humans from themselves, he realized as he writhed in his own
torment. Nothing could protect them from their own destruc-
tiveness. Nothing could protect her from him.

The thought roared through his brain, a gun blast. It left a
terrible calm in its wake. The woman in his head had stopped

screaming, he realized. She had finally been silenced. The room was preternaturally still. No one was screaming anymore, no one except him. He was shouting at the top of his lungs, bargaining with the heavens, and it was the same horrible prayer he'd dropped to his knees with, the only prayer he'd ever said.

Please God, don't let me hurt her. I made her a promise and nothing else matters, least of all what happens to me. *I made her a promise.*

33

"Such beautiful brain waves," Sophie murmured, gazing with rapt appreciation at the slow, graceful joggles the electroencephalograph recorded. "They look a little like my noodle jewelry, don't you think?"

Jay was stretched out in the hospital bed next to her, the electrodes hidden in his thick dark hair as the EEG monitored his brain's electrical activity.

"Want to see them do back flips?" He crooked a finger and gave her a wink that was as wicked as his intentions. "Come here, you."

Sophie had no problem with that. She would have flung herself on him if she hadn't been afraid of short-circuiting something and bringing a nurse on the fly to his room.

Instead she sidled over to his bedside and smiled at him, knowing her heart was in her eyes. "If we send that EEG needle into orbit," she told him, "they may not let me take you home. And I do want to take you home."

The horror of the ordeal with Claude seemed like years ago to Sophie, though it had only been a little over a week, and she and Jay had come frighteningly close to losing each other. Sophie had been struck by a blow that knocked her unconscious, but she hadn't realized until she came to, covered in blood, that it was Claude. He'd toppled on her when the ax hit him.

But it was Jay who'd terrified her. He'd been sprawled on the floor, convulsing, and Sophie had been afraid he would die if she couldn't get to him. She'd heaved herself free of the chair and dropped to the floor. Fear had made her capable of things that no ordinary woman of her stature could have done. Praying she wouldn't harm the baby, she dragged herself across the room and kicked the phone down from Claude's desk. Fortunately it was pre-programmed with numbers, including 911.

El and Wallis had been at Sophie's bedside when she regained consciousness in the hospital. They'd assured her that the injection Claude had given her was nothing more than a mild muscle relaxant. Both she and the baby were fine. Jay had stabilized with medication, and there was every indication that he would recover completely, but El had conferred with the hospital head of staff, who was an old friend of his, and made arrangements for Jay to stay on a few more days for observation, just to be sure.

"Not as much as I want to be taken. Home," Jay said as an afterthought. But it was that word that brought Sophie's gaze up to meet his—and pierced her with sudden longing.

He emitted one of those sighs that sounded like mood music to her. It filled her so full she was tempted to sigh too, to ease the pressure. And finally Sophie couldn't bear it anymore. The emotion was too strong. She had to do something else. Talk.

"El swears you're going to be fine," she said conversationally. "One hundred percent."

"Would you settle for ninety-nine?" Her husband's gaze was watchful and protective, even though he was the one in the hospital bed. "El probably didn't want to alarm you, but he admitted to me that there could be some residual memory loss. Parts of the past may never come back, but that should

be the only permanent effect. There won't be any more cluster headaches or violent episodes. The personality fragmen-
tation is gone.''

Actually, El had given Sophie much the same news, to her
great relief. ''He tried to explain how it happened,'' she said,
''but I'm afraid he lost me when he got to the part about the
mind trying to protect itself against retinal bombardment and
chemical lesions and all of that. To be honest, Jay, I don't
think even he knows for sure what triggered the personality
split. He suggested that it could have been something as simple as hypnotic suggestion. Apparently a trance state alone
can trigger multiples in a psyche under great stress. But he
also admitted that there's still controversy about the very existence of multiple personalities, and you know El, a scientist
to the end. He begged me to believe that he never intended
for any of that to happen, especially the violence. That was
Claude.''

Sophie was still unable to imagine her trusted friend being
driven to such extremes. He could easily have killed her with
his plan to implicate Jay. He'd even jeopardized Albert and
Blaze. She hadn't yet told Jay that Claude had died of his
head injury. Jay had enough to deal with now in terms of his
own recovery, and although it had been terribly hard for Sophie to lose Claude in such an unthinkable way, over the past
few days she'd finally come to terms with the realization that
it would have been a greater tragedy if he'd lived. Claude
was where he wanted to be, at rest. None of them would have
had any peace of mind if he'd been forced to live out his
remaining days in some locked ward, slowly deteriorating,
least of all him.

''I still don't understand how he did it,'' she said, unable
to grasp how one man could have wreaked such havoc. ''I
didn't think people could be hypnotized to do something
against their will.''

''Claude's not a stage hypnotist. He uses powerful drugs
that make the psyche more vulnerable to suggestion. And
there's plenty of evidence in military intelligence data that
people can be programmed to go against their moral code,

even to kill, especially with today's advances. But I don't think that was Claude's plan. He wanted to turn us against each other, and he did it by making you think I was the one trying to kill you. The clever part was making me believe it, too.''

Clever perhaps, and yet Sophie wondered why it was that people so often put more effort into hurting others than into helping themselves. Maybe Claude was beyond anyone's help.

"His plan might have worked," Jay added, "if I hadn't connected the voice on your phone machine with the one I heard here at the clinic that night, before the drugs knocked me out.''

He had to mean the message Claude had left her, but he seemed perplexed about something. "What is it?" she asked.

"Muffin was on your machine that night, too, and it sounded urgent. Did you ever find out what she wanted?''

In fact, Muffin had called as soon as she heard what happened with Claude. Sophie'd been too preoccupied to pay much attention to her at the time, but what Muffin had had to say was fairly shocking now that Sophie thought about it. A baby bombshell, so to speak.

"Muffin isn't giving up," she told him. "She announced on the phone that she had an appointment to have her eggs fertilized with Colby's sperm so that she could produce the first-and-only Babcock heir. Poor kid.''

"Muffin or the baby?"

"Well, both, now that I think about it. She doesn't know I'm pregnant, and she sounded so distraught I didn't have the heart to tell her. Guess I'd better do that before she does something crazy.''

They were holding hands and Jay had begun making his signature circles. He seemed to do it unconsciously, and Sophie's reaction was equally automatic by now. She hoped their baby didn't mind that the bottom had just dropped out of her stomach.

"Jay," she said suddenly, "let's give Muffin the support she needs for the cosmetics line, at least through the R-and-

D stage. That's what she really wants, not to have a baby. And besides, she was married to Colby for a lot of years. She deserves something for that, don't you think?''

''You have a point.'' He stopped circling and glanced up at her. ''By the way . . . how is our little fertilized egg? And its mama?''

She brought his hand to her belly and covered it with hers, luxuriating in the kneading strength of his fingers, the heat flowing into her own body. She could imagine the baby feeling enveloped by warmth and affection. ''You do know how this happened, don't you?''

''The pregnancy? I think so.''

''No, not *that*. I mean what allowed it to happen. One of those pills they gave you at the clinic—the peacock-blue capsule, El said—is a brand-new male fertility drug Babcock just got FDA approval on.'' She laughed. ''Apparently it works.''

''And whose idea was this?''

He gazed up at her, and Sophie got the full impact of both beautiful dark eyes at once. He wasn't wearing the eye patch any longer, and she was still getting used to the effect, but it was his expression that gave her pause. She wouldn't have thought anything could faze him, certainly not this news— not if he was as happy about the pregnancy as she was.

''Wallis gets the credit,'' she hurried to explain. ''According to El, it was part of her grand plan to ensure the future of the 'empire.' But she also knew how much I wanted a baby, how much we both did . . . so . . . I think we should forgive her for that, don't you?''

His silence was beginning to frighten her. He'd been through a lot, the victim of more manipulation and abuse of power by his own family than anyone should ever have to suffer. She could understand that he wasn't yet in a place to deal with it. But now that he was primed to take over the company, and she was going to have a child, she'd hoped that he and Wallis could find some common ground and begin to live in harmony with each other, or at least, mutual respect.

''No Babcock wonder drug is going to fix what's wrong

with this family,'' he said at last. Another sigh welled, and
his voice took on a different quality, harsh and regretful.
''Maybe forgiveness can. Maybe it's the only thing that can,
but I don't seem to have much of that on hand these days.''

''Time,'' she said. ''Give yourself some time, and the forgiveness will take care of itself.''

The quiet that fell around them hung so oppressively it felt
like a curtain that would never rise. It seemed to Sophie as
if the mood might even jeopardize their relationship, but a
tug on her hand reassured her that their bond was safe, ex-
empt from the problems with his family. The tension flowed
out of her as he coaxed her closer. She dropped into his arms,
not caring if she short-circuited his equipment.

''I love you—'' Her voice broke with the soft passion of
the fifteen-year-old girl who kissed him in the meadow.

''God, I love you, too,'' he said, his fists crossed against
her back, his chest rising with a breath. ''I don't need memories as long as I've got you. We'll make our own.''

Sophie was flooded with sweet reveries of a sunlit beach
and a barking dog, of a death-defying amusement park ride
and a soaring monastery. She would never forget their trip to
the mountain and the ghostly monk who told her she already
was complete, but that only she could know what that meant.
Now she did. This was it, completion. Jay was her healing
spring, as she was his.

''And now that I've got *two* of you''—his breath feathered
the fine, golden hair that fringed her temple—''how am I
going to take you to Dirty Dan's on the bike?''

''It can be arranged,'' she assured him, nuzzling into the
curve of his neck and feeling his heart thud against her cool
cheek. When she had her equilibrium back and could speak
without rasping, she would suggest a motorcycle sidecar.
Meanwhile, with his talk of future trips to the biker hangout,
he'd touched a memory trace that took her back to the morning they had chili omelettes there—and the letters she'd discovered scratched in the table. She still didn't know what
they meant.

Enfolded in his arms, she was reluctant to move or do

anything that might break the mood. But curiosity denied was curiosity enflamed, and it wasn't long before she tilted back and asked him to explain.

He surprised her by admitting he didn't know himself. "It goes back to the drug trial," he said. "I'd been away through the whole thing, you remember, that trip to the Atlas Mountains. When I got back, it was all over, and Babcock had won. But no one would talk about the trial. No one but Noah."

She could feel him tapping her back with his knuckles as he hesitated, thought. "All I can remember now is Noah in the nursing home, railing at me to blow the whistle on Trizene B. He said I was as guilty as the rest of them if I kept quiet, that the blood was on my hands, too. He'd kept a journal, documenting Babcock's violations. He even had the trial transcript with the perjured testimony. But by then his mind had been devastated by the drug, and he couldn't remember where he'd hidden the journal. As I was getting up to leave he shouted, 'String Me Along,' but he wasn't able to explain what he meant. All he could do was repeat it.

"I went to Dirty Dan's that night, trying to make sense of what he'd said—trying to make sense of my entire life, to be honest—and I must have scratched those words into the table. The bouncer took exception, and a fight broke out, I can remember that much. It was probably the same guy who called me out in the alley the morning you and I were there, although I didn't have a clue who he was at the time. I just knew he was trouble."

He rolled his head back, as if straining to remember. "Noah was trying to tell me the journal was hidden in the bluffs where we used to play String Me Along. Or maybe he was telling me to hide it there, I don't know. I've had flashbacks, but until you mentioned Donald, the kid who fell, I didn't associate the game and the bluffs with the journal.

"It's sketchy." He gave up with a heavy shrug of his shoulders. "I may never know what really happened."

"It doesn't matter now." She smoothed his forehead, coaxing waves of lush dark hair away from his eyes. She didn't want him to tax himself. There was nothing he could do about any of it at this point. What he needed was some rest.

"If it's any consolation," she told him, "you're not the only one with memory problems. I've had my share and nobody's been tinkering with my neurons. But I did have a breakthrough this morning, and guess what I found?"

He watched with some interest as she gathered up her purse and produced the surprise she had stashed there.

The delicate toothpick-size object in her fingers brought him forward for a closer look. "The wishbone," he said. "Where did you find it?"

"In the hope chest, along with some other things I thought were lost. Your brush was there and my nightgown, of course. It's odd that in all my searches of the house for this I never once looked in the hope chest. I guess I wasn't ready to find it. But this morning when I woke up, I went straight there."

He was thoughtful, silent, intent upon her and the nearly invisible chicken bone she held as if it were as precious as gold.

"I could tell you what I wished for now," he ventured.

"No, don't! It won't come true."

She felt a rush of warmth and looked down. His hand was pressed to her belly, strong and tanned and sheltering against the faded denim of her cargo overalls.

"It already has," he said.

"The baby?" she whispered.

Tears welled as Sophie blindly dug through her bag and drew out the larger section of wishbone he'd given her to keep. She understood now why people feared love, feared it more than death. The pain was as piercing as the joy. Unbearable that pain, but probably as necessary to life as breathing. It was loss, she realized, all pain was loss, and without it you could never feel the joy of coming together again.

No more tears, Sophie, she told herself. *What was lost has been found.* But she couldn't manage the two fragile pieces of wishbone, couldn't manage them at all. She felt like that shy, awkward girl again, the one who used to tilt when he looked at her and run when he came close.

"Here," he said gently, taking the pieces from her. He joined them at the place where they'd been snapped and studied the result. The smile that shadowed his face was as sweet and sad as her own.

"What are you thinking?" she asked.

"How incredible it is that they fit. That we fit."

He raised his gaze to hers. Perhaps it was the light that poured through the window and dappled his hair, perhaps it was the trace of wonder in his smile, but Sophie was catapulted back more than a decade in time to the moment she first laid eyes on him. And knew.

His smile lit her heart. His love had coaxed it out of hiding and taught it how to trust. This was what she'd longed for all her life, the simple belief that others probably took for granted. To know that someone would be there when they reached out in the night, to calm their fears and dry their tears, to hold them until dawn came. She'd longed to know that someone would be there when she needed them, that anyone could possibly love her that much.

Did the heavens allow such happiness? Had Providence opened its arms to Sophie Weston at last?

Her answer was the wishbone Jay held in his hands, and the piercing tenderness she felt as she watched him press the pieces together. Her answer was hope—that fierce optimist who kept opening the heart again and again, allowing it to believe, despite the ravages of loss.

Her answer was him, beloved stranger. The man who taught her about love and loss, and how to cherish both. The man who came back.

He was here now. And he loved her that much.